big NATE
SILENT BUT DEADLY

Complete Your *Big Nate* Collection

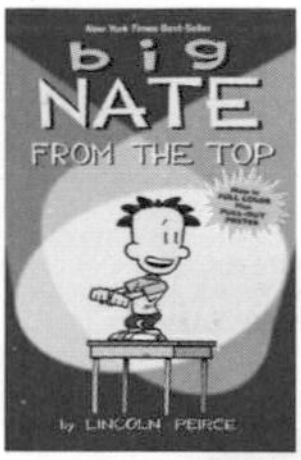
New York Times Best-Seller
big
NATE
FROM THE TOP
by LINCOLN PEIRCE

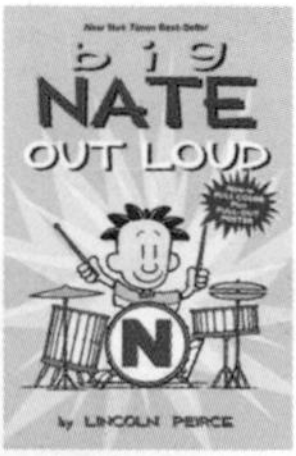
New York Times Best-Seller
big
NATE
OUT LOUD
N
by LINCOLN PEIRCE

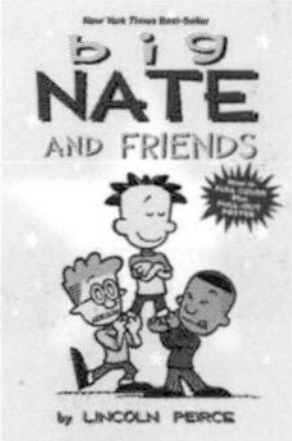
New York Times Best-Seller
big
NATE
AND FRIENDS
by LINCOLN PEIRCE

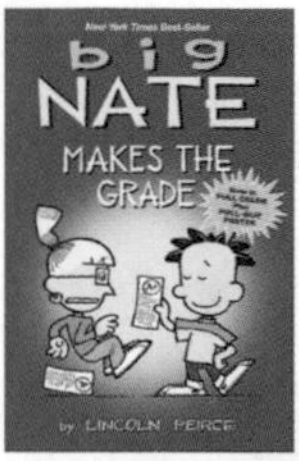
New York Times Best-Seller
big
NATE
MAKES THE GRADE
by LINCOLN PEIRCE

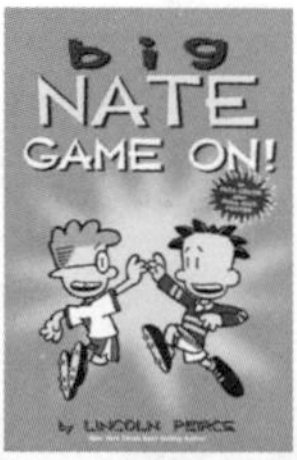
big
NATE
GAME ON!
by LINCOLN PEIRCE

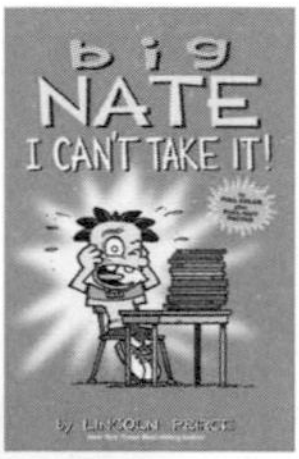
big
NATE
I CAN'T TAKE IT!
by LINCOLN PEIRCE

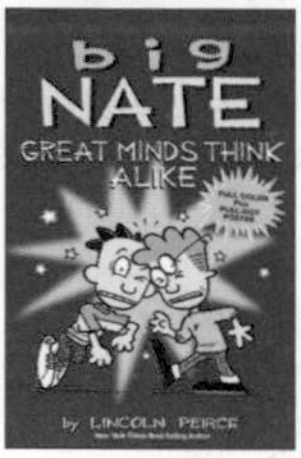
big
NATE
GREAT MINDS THINK ALIKE
by LINCOLN PEIRCE

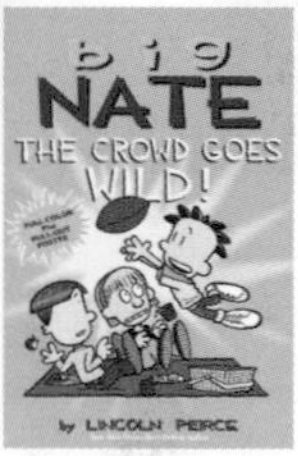
big
NATE
THE CROWD GOES WILD!
by LINCOLN PEIRCE

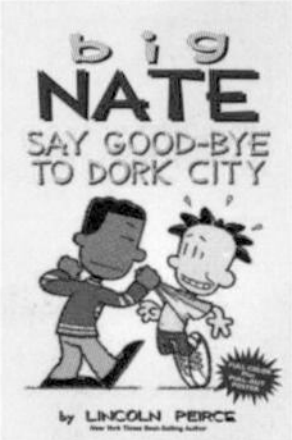
big
NATE
SAY GOOD-BYE TO DORK CITY
by LINCOLN PEIRCE

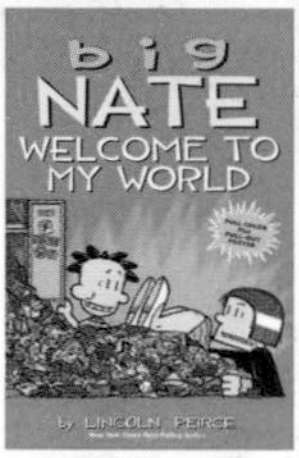
big
NATE
WELCOME TO MY WORLD
by LINCOLN PEIRCE

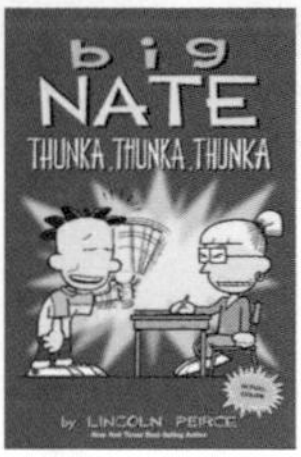
big
NATE
THUNKA, THUNKA, THUNKA
by LINCOLN PEIRCE

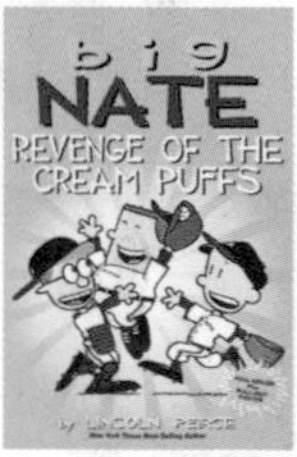
big
NATE
REVENGE OF THE CREAM PUFFS
by LINCOLN PEIRCE

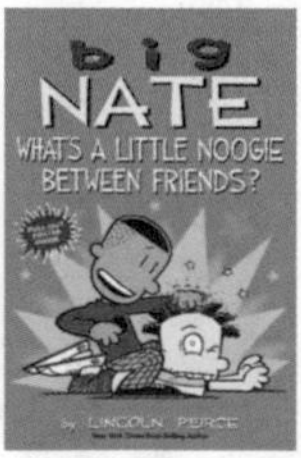
big
NATE
WHAT'S A LITTLE NOOGIE BETWEEN FRIENDS?
by LINCOLN PEIRCE

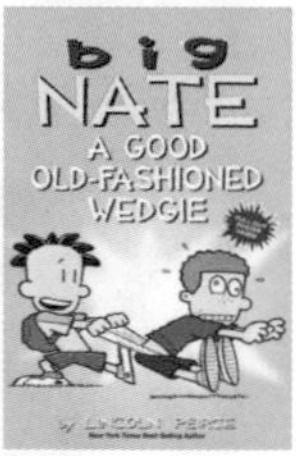
big
NATE
A GOOD OLD-FASHIONED WEDGIE
by LINCOLN PEIRCE

SPECIAL COLLECTIONS

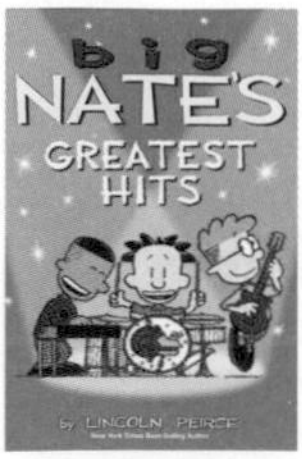
big
NATE'S
GREATEST HITS
by LINCOLN PEIRCE

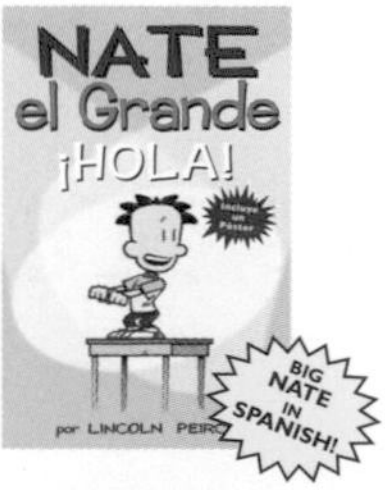
NATE
el Grande
¡HOLA!
por LINCOLN PEIRCE
BIG NATE IN SPANISH!

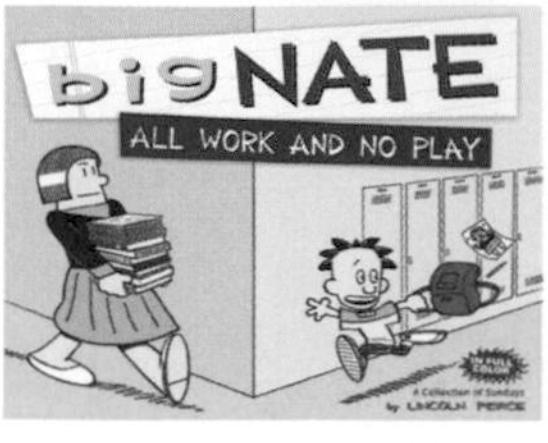
big NATE
ALL WORK AND NO PLAY
by LINCOLN PEIRCE

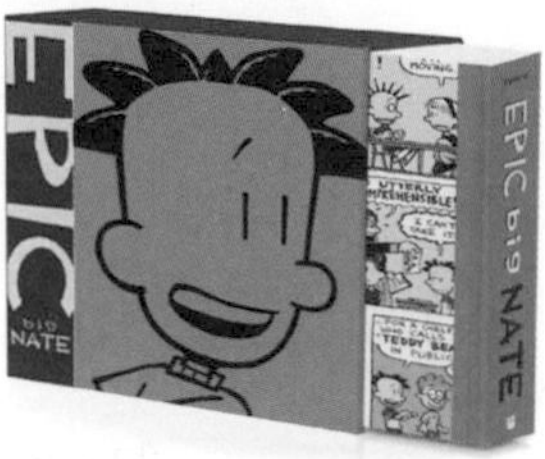
EPIC
big NATE
EPIC big NATE

big NATE
SILENT BUT DEADLY

by LINCOLN PEIRCE

Andrews McMeel
PUBLISHING®

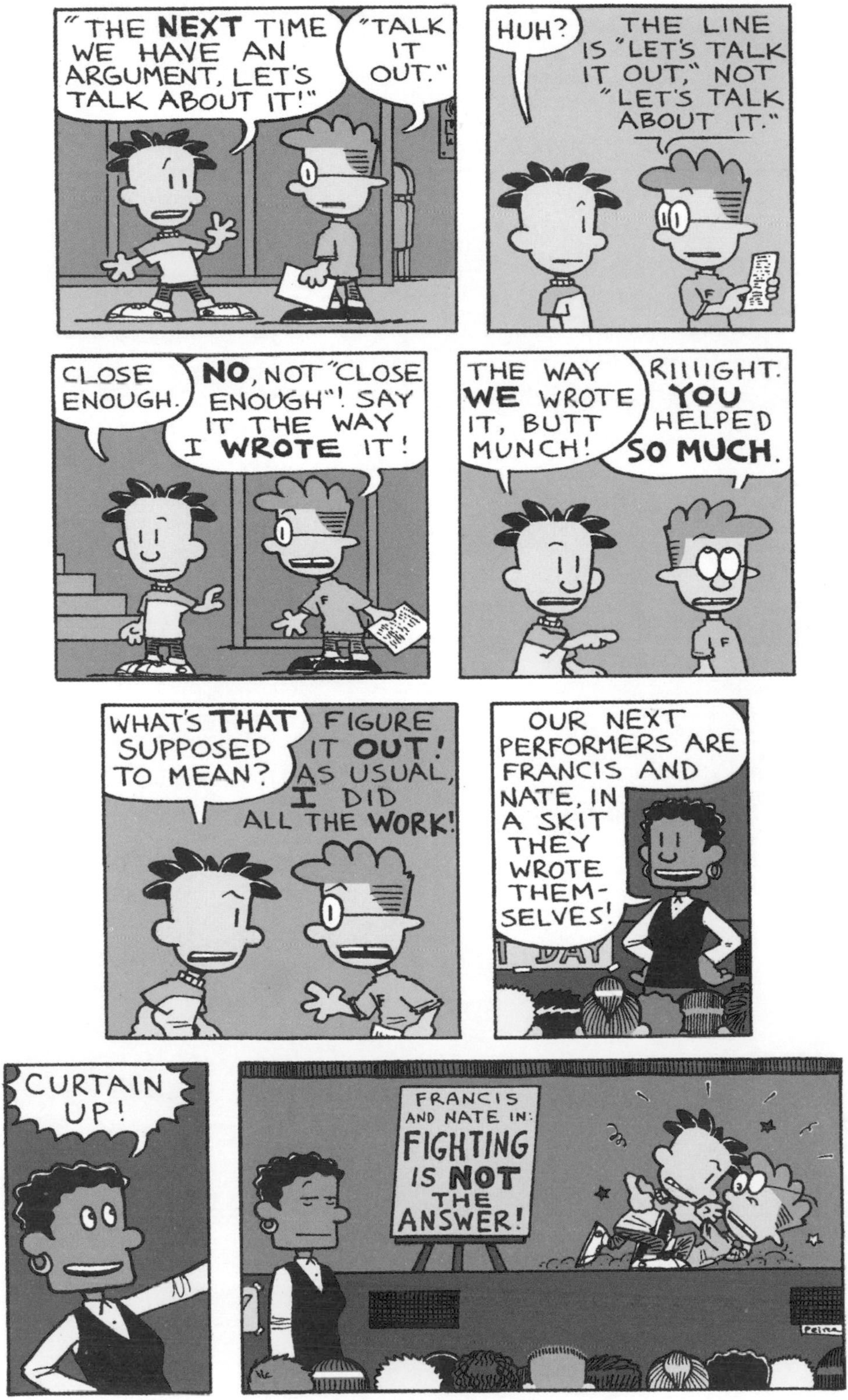
"THE NEXT TIME WE HAVE AN ARGUMENT, LET'S TALK ABOUT IT!"
"TALK IT OUT."
HUH?
THE LINE IS "LET'S TALK IT OUT," NOT "LET'S TALK ABOUT IT."
CLOSE ENOUGH.
NO, NOT "CLOSE ENOUGH"! SAY IT THE WAY I WROTE IT!
THE WAY WE WROTE IT, BUTT MUNCH!
RIIIIGHT. YOU HELPED SO MUCH.
WHAT'S THAT SUPPOSED TO MEAN?
FIGURE IT OUT! AS USUAL, I DID ALL THE WORK!
OUR NEXT PERFORMERS ARE FRANCIS AND NATE, IN A SKIT THEY WROTE THEMSELVES!
CURTAIN UP!
FRANCIS AND NATE IN: FIGHTING IS NOT THE ANSWER!
PEIRCE

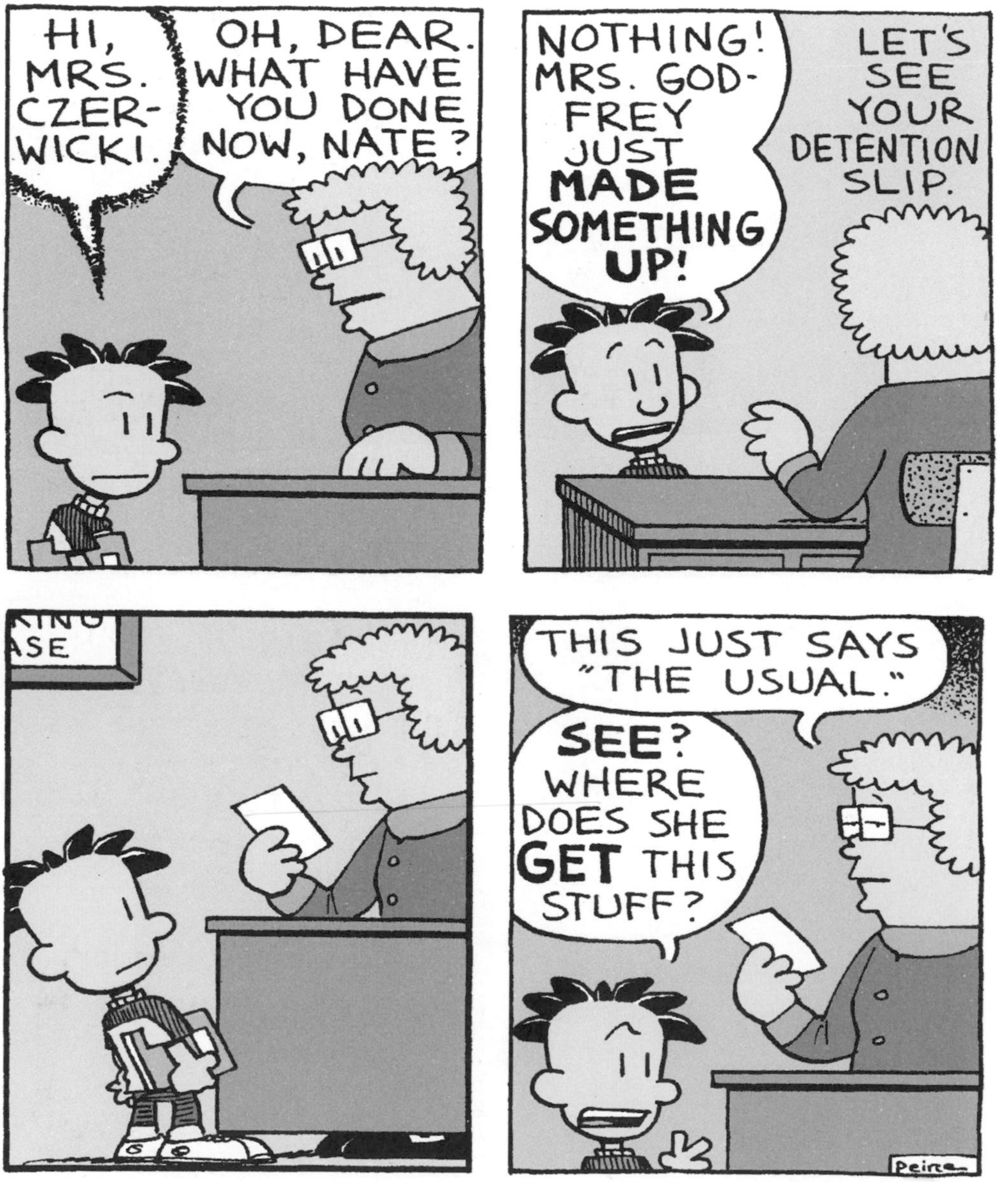
HI, MRS. CZER-WICKI.
OH, DEAR. WHAT HAVE YOU DONE NOW, NATE?
NOTHING! MRS. GOD-FREY JUST **MADE SOMETHING UP!**
LET'S SEE YOUR DETENTION SLIP.
THIS JUST SAYS "THE USUAL."
SEE? WHERE DOES SHE **GET** THIS STUFF?
Peirce

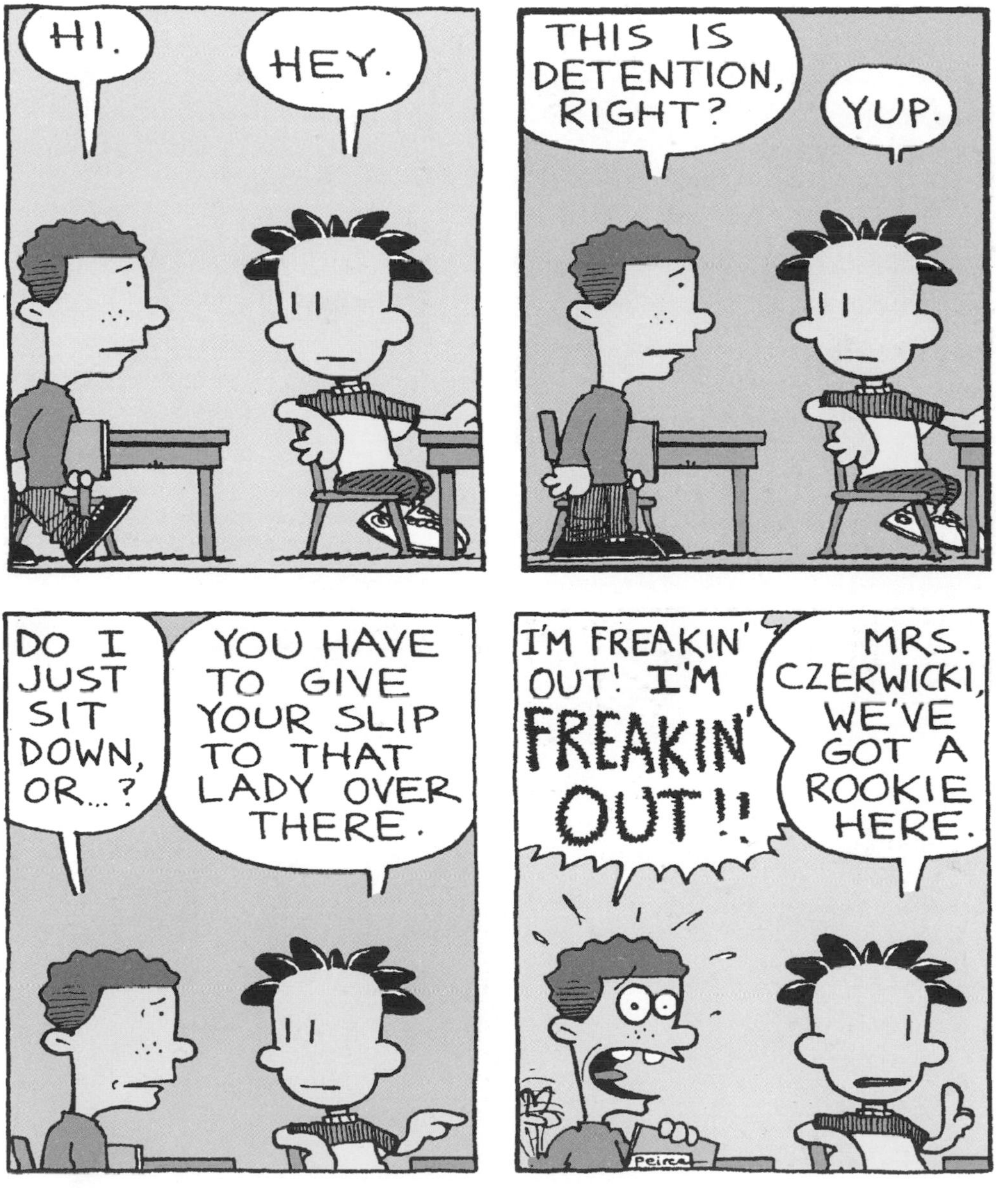
HI.
HEY.
THIS IS DETENTION, RIGHT?
YUP.
DO I JUST SIT DOWN, OR...?
YOU HAVE TO GIVE YOUR SLIP TO THAT LADY OVER THERE.
I'M FREAKIN' OUT! I'M FREAKIN' OUT!!
MRS. CZERWICKI, WE'VE GOT A ROOKIE HERE.
Peirce

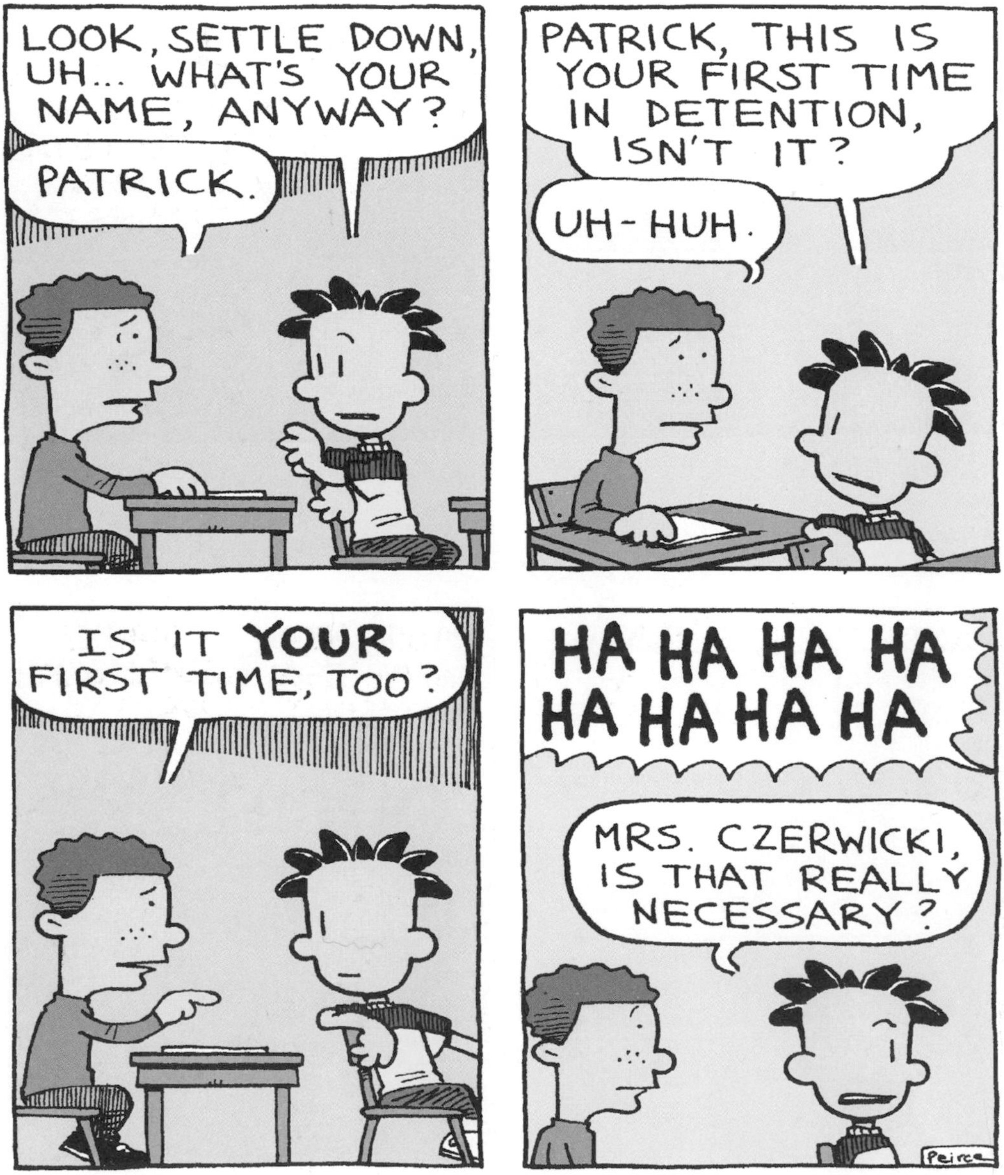
LOOK, SETTLE DOWN, UH... WHAT'S YOUR NAME, ANYWAY?
PATRICK.
PATRICK, THIS IS YOUR FIRST TIME IN DETENTION, ISN'T IT?
UH-HUH.
IS IT **YOUR** FIRST TIME, TOO?
HA HA HA HA HA HA HA HA
MRS. CZERWICKI, IS THAT REALLY NECESSARY?
Peirce

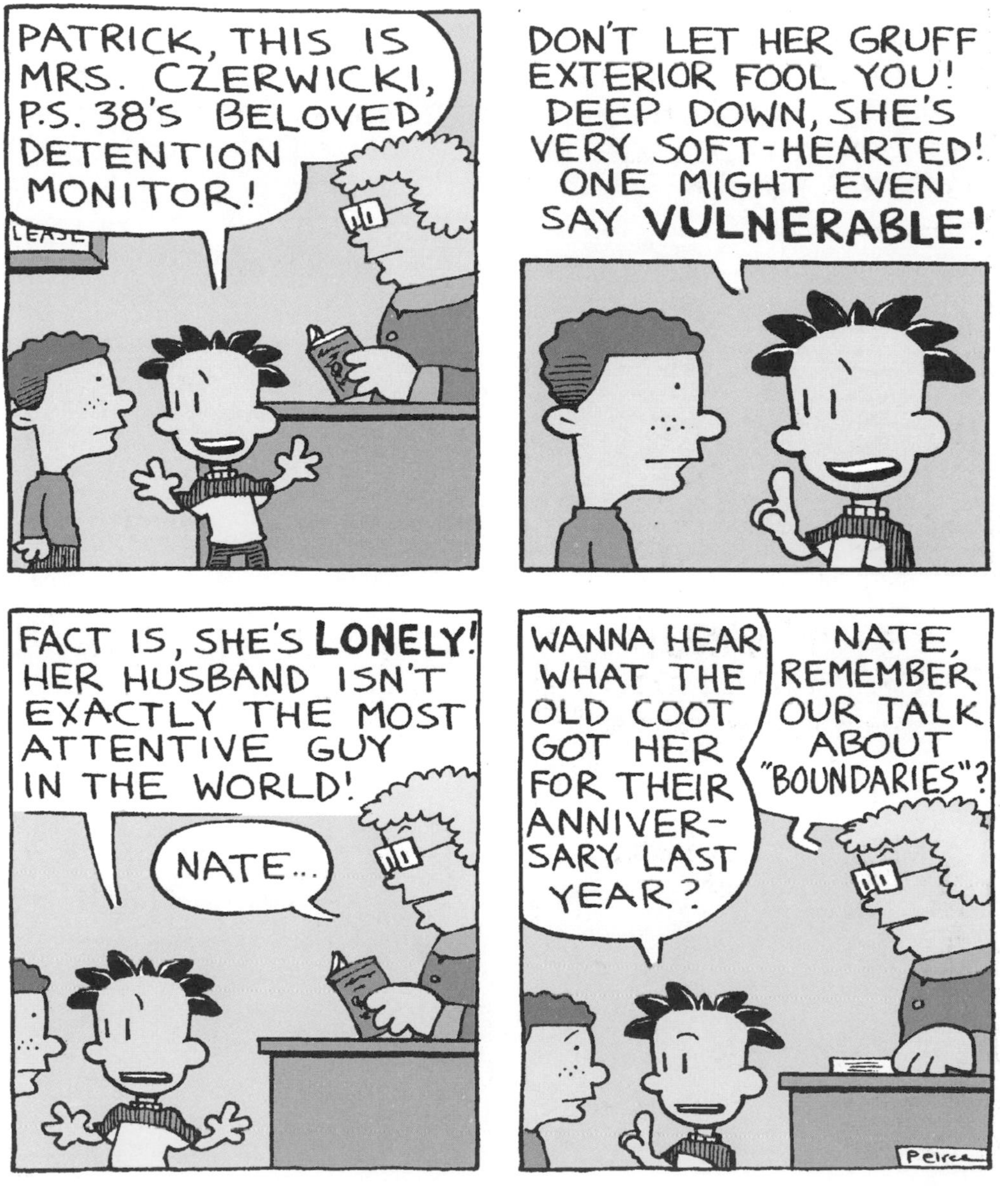
PATRICK, THIS IS MRS. CZERWICKI, P.S. 38'S BELOVED DETENTION MONITOR!
DON'T LET HER GRUFF EXTERIOR FOOL YOU! DEEP DOWN, SHE'S VERY SOFT-HEARTED! ONE MIGHT EVEN SAY **VULNERABLE!**
FACT IS, SHE'S **LONELY!** HER HUSBAND ISN'T EXACTLY THE MOST ATTENTIVE GUY IN THE WORLD!
NATE...
WANNA HEAR WHAT THE OLD COOT GOT HER FOR THEIR ANNIVERSARY LAST YEAR?
NATE, REMEMBER OUR TALK ABOUT "BOUNDARIES"?
Peirce

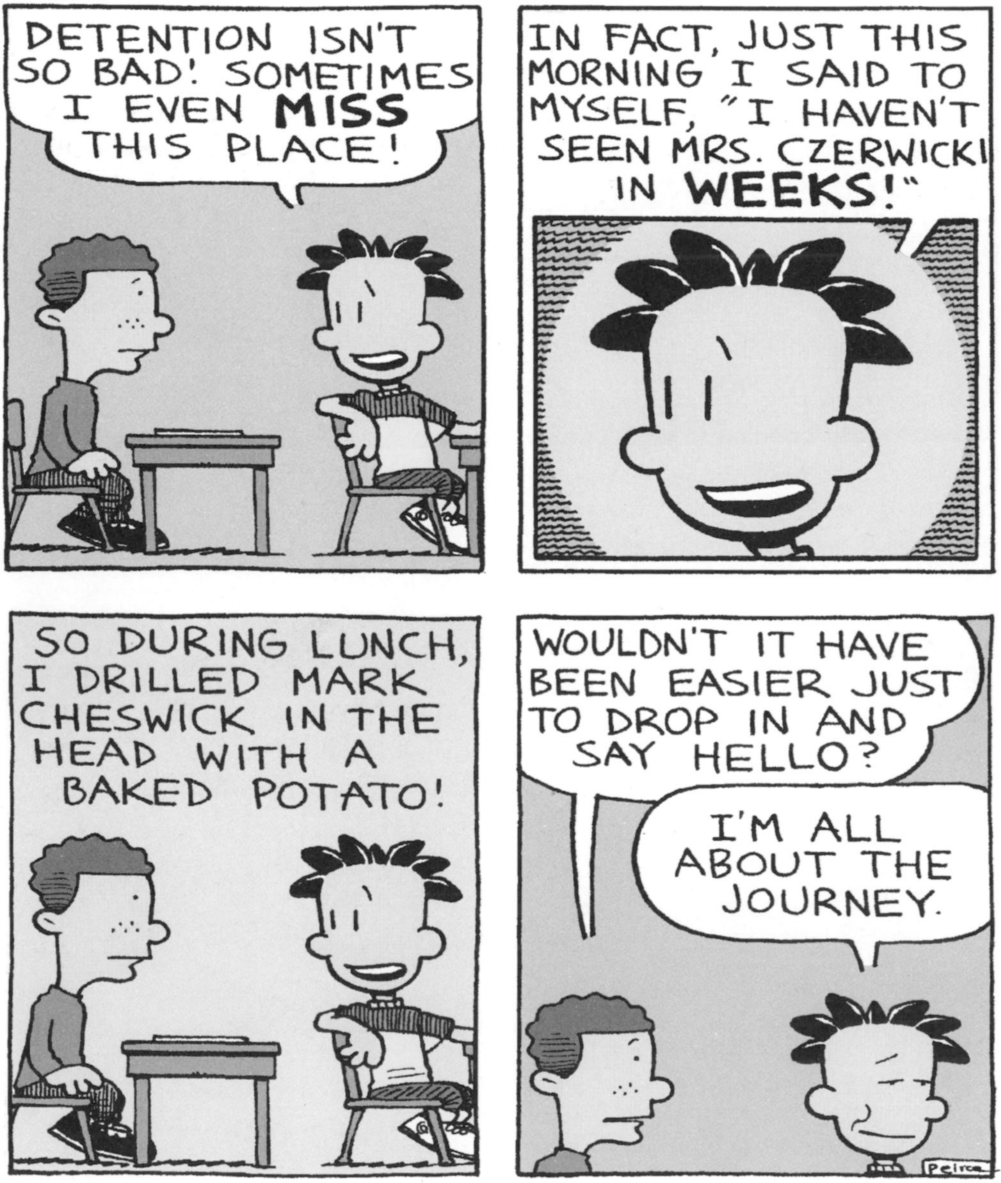
DETENTION ISN'T SO BAD! SOMETIMES I EVEN **MISS** THIS PLACE!
IN FACT, JUST THIS MORNING I SAID TO MYSELF, "I HAVEN'T SEEN MRS. CZERWICKI IN **WEEKS!**"
SO DURING LUNCH, I DRILLED MARK CHESWICK IN THE HEAD WITH A BAKED POTATO!
WOULDN'T IT HAVE BEEN EASIER JUST TO DROP IN AND SAY HELLO?
I'M ALL ABOUT THE JOURNEY.
Peirce

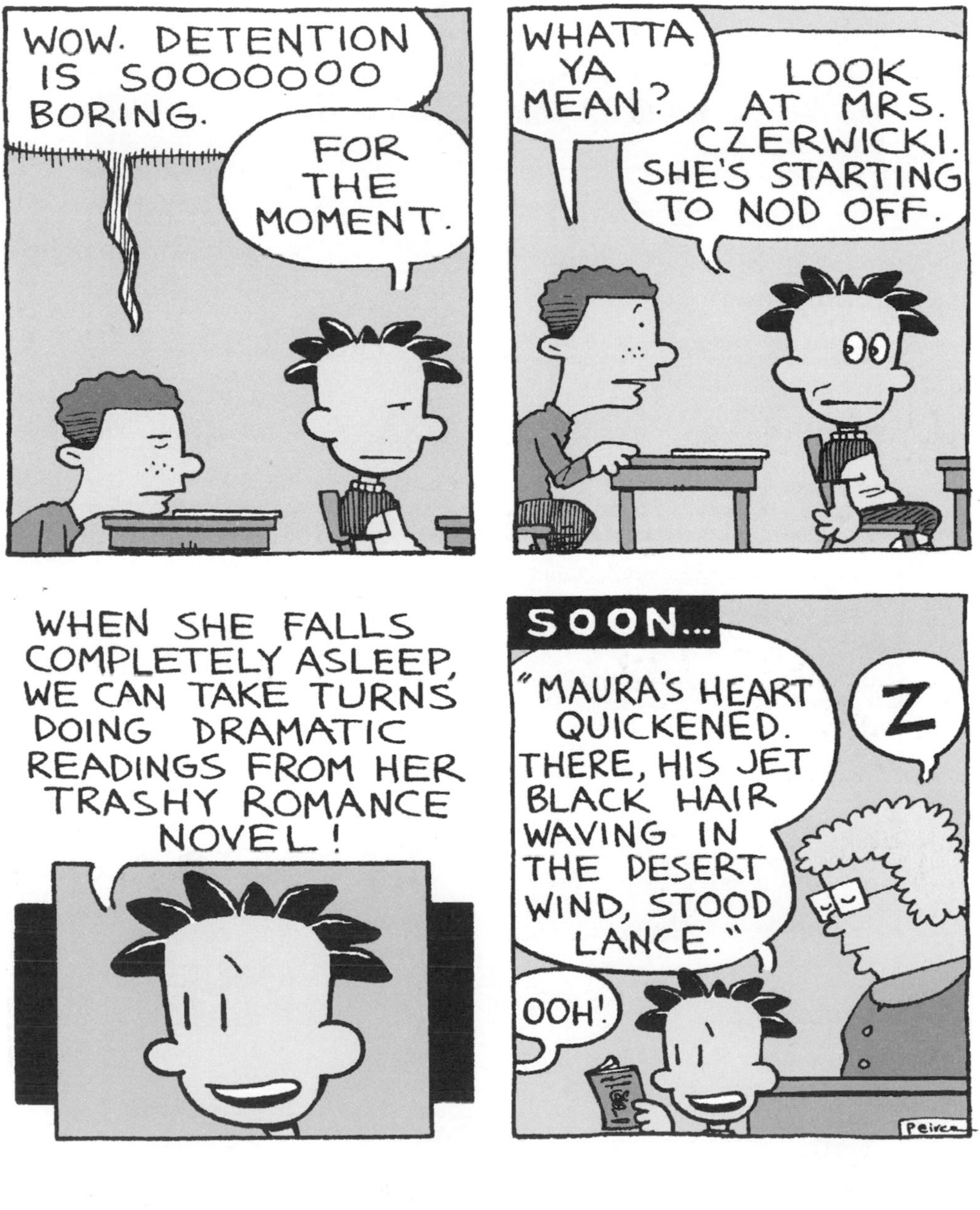
WOW. DETENTION IS SOOOOOOO BORING.
FOR THE MOMENT.
WHATTA YA MEAN?
LOOK AT MRS. CZERWICKI. SHE'S STARTING TO NOD OFF.
WHEN SHE FALLS COMPLETELY ASLEEP, WE CAN TAKE TURNS DOING DRAMATIC READINGS FROM HER TRASHY ROMANCE NOVEL!
SOON...
"MAURA'S HEART QUICKENED. THERE, HIS JET BLACK HAIR WAVING IN THE DESERT WIND, STOOD LANCE."
Z
OOH!
Peirce

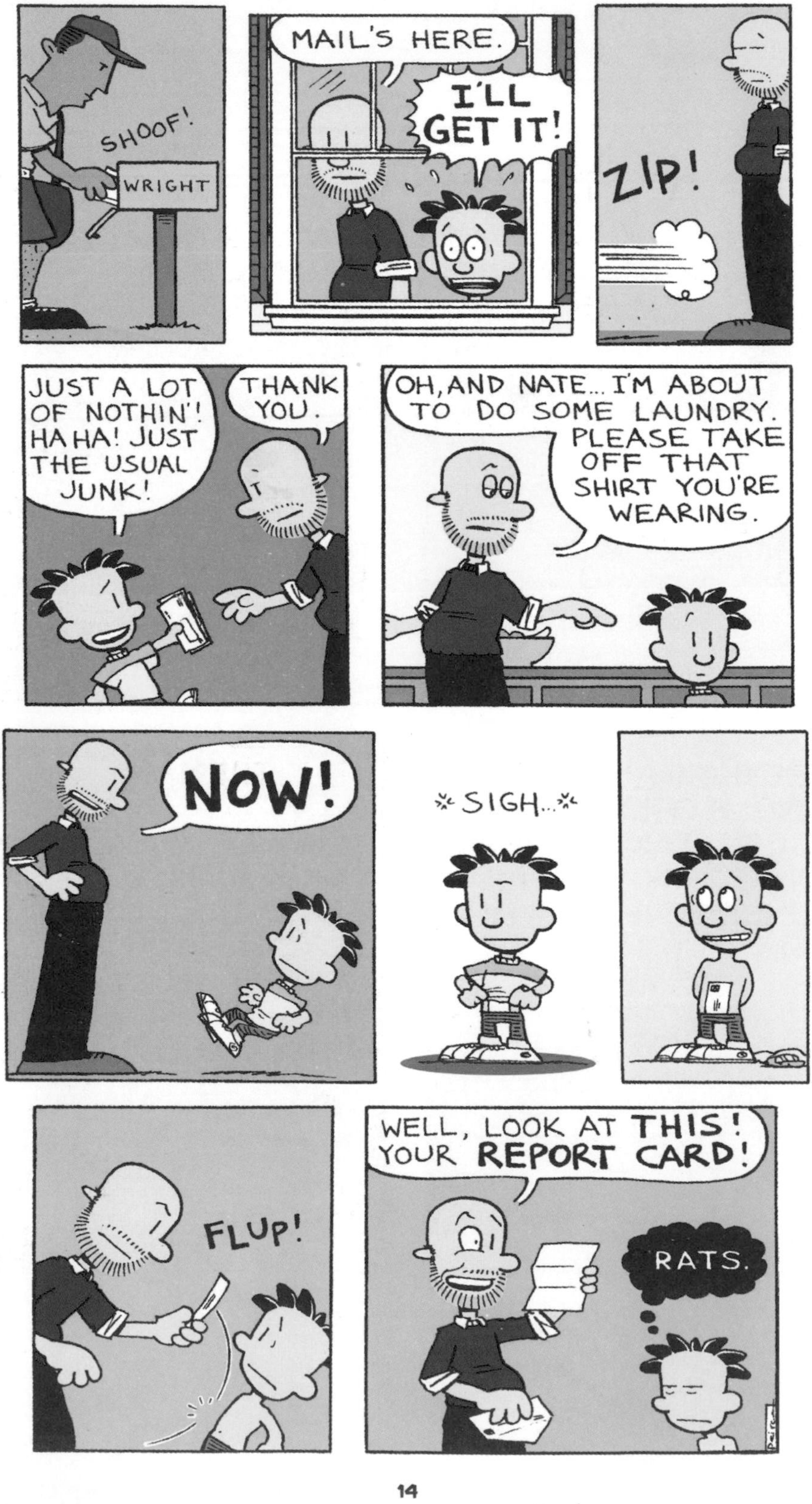
SHOOF!
WRIGHT
MAIL'S HERE.
I'LL GET IT!
ZIP!
JUST A LOT OF NOTHIN'! HA HA! JUST THE USUAL JUNK!
THANK YOU.
OH, AND NATE... I'M ABOUT TO DO SOME LAUNDRY. PLEASE TAKE OFF THAT SHIRT YOU'RE WEARING.
NOW!
SIGH...
FLUP!
WELL, LOOK AT THIS! YOUR REPORT CARD!
RATS.

SCHOOL PICTURE GUY!
AH, THE RETURN OF THE NATIVE! WHAT'S UP, KID?
CAN I BE YOUR HELPER AGAIN THIS YEAR?
NO NEED, AMIGO! NO NEED!
THE WHOLE OPERATION IS SO AUTOMATED AND STREAMLINED NOW, IT'S A ONE-MAN SHOW!
WELL, THEN, CAN I HANG OUT AND WATCH YOU MAKE PEOPLE LOOK BAD?
LET'S ROCK.
SMILE!

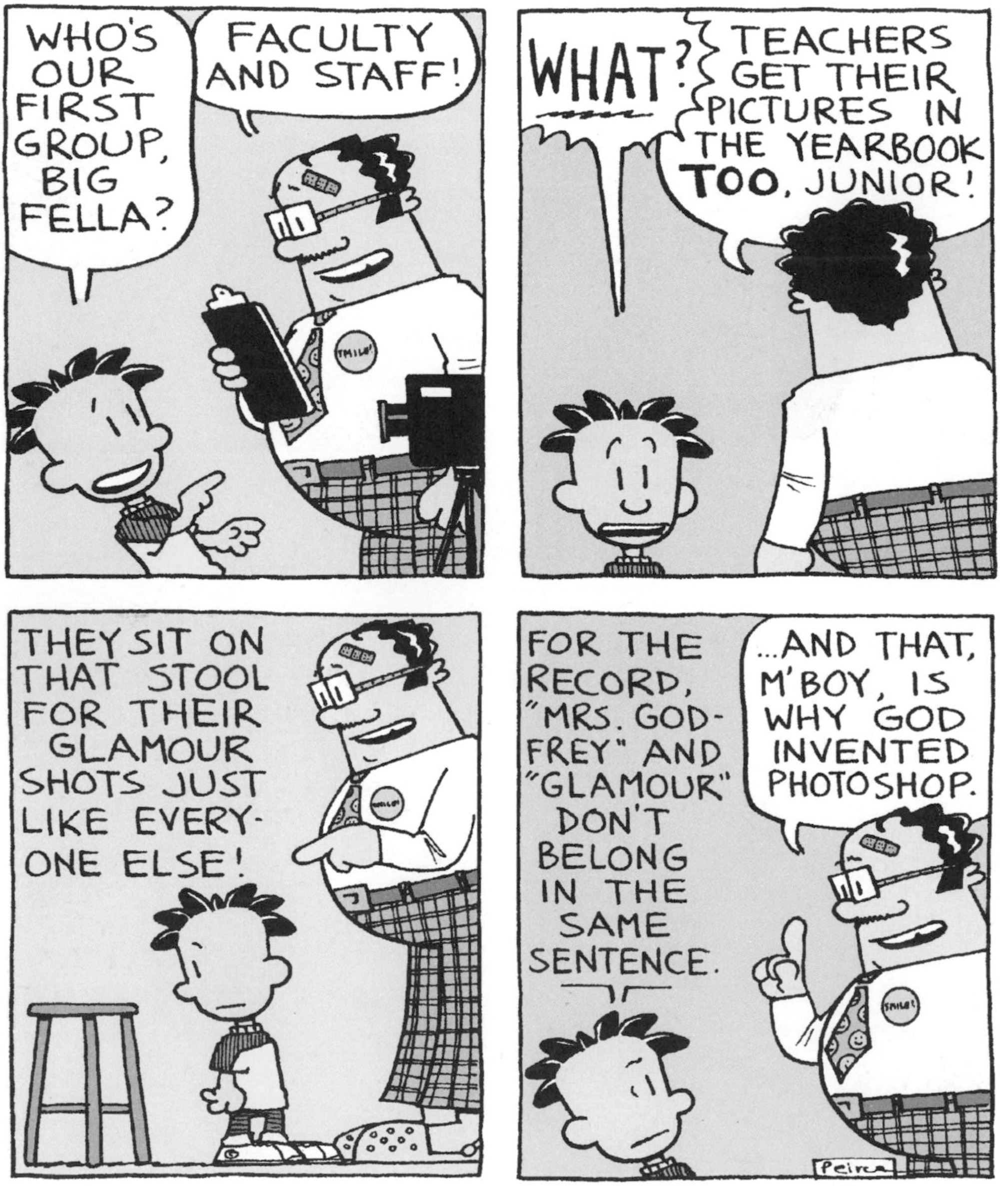
WHO'S OUR FIRST GROUP, BIG FELLA?
FACULTY AND STAFF!
WHAT?
TEACHERS GET THEIR PICTURES IN THE YEARBOOK TOO, JUNIOR!
THEY SIT ON THAT STOOL FOR THEIR GLAMOUR SHOTS JUST LIKE EVERY-ONE ELSE!
FOR THE RECORD, "MRS. GOD-FREY" AND "GLAMOUR" DON'T BELONG IN THE SAME SENTENCE.
...AND THAT, M'BOY, IS WHY GOD INVENTED PHOTOSHOP.
Peirce

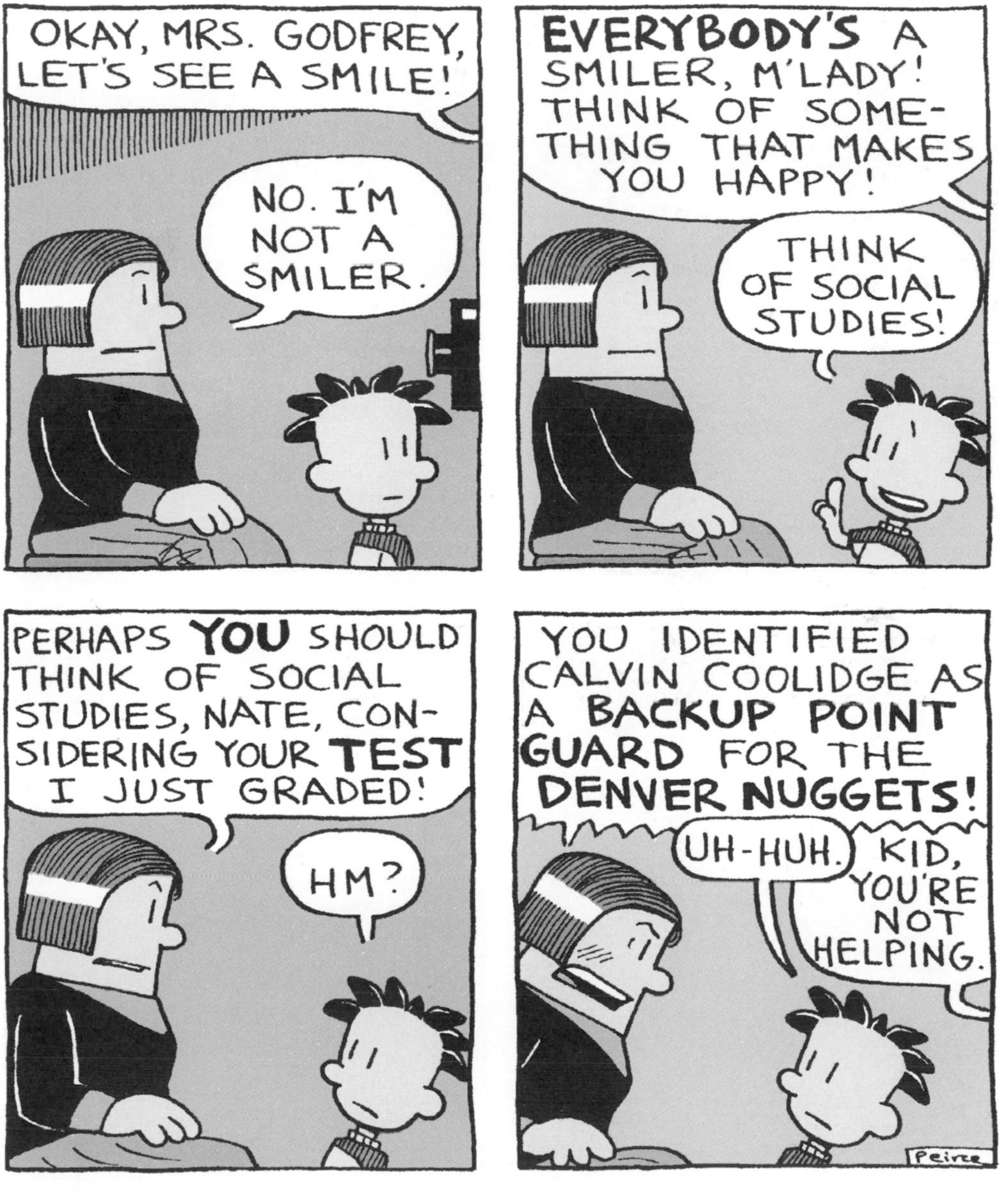
OKAY, MRS. GODFREY, LET'S SEE A SMILE!
NO. I'M NOT A SMILER.
EVERYBODY'S A SMILER, M'LADY! THINK OF SOMETHING THAT MAKES YOU HAPPY!
THINK OF SOCIAL STUDIES!
PERHAPS YOU SHOULD THINK OF SOCIAL STUDIES, NATE, CONSIDERING YOUR TEST I JUST GRADED!
HM?
YOU IDENTIFIED CALVIN COOLIDGE AS A BACKUP POINT GUARD FOR THE DENVER NUGGETS!
UH-HUH.
KID, YOU'RE NOT HELPING.
Peirce

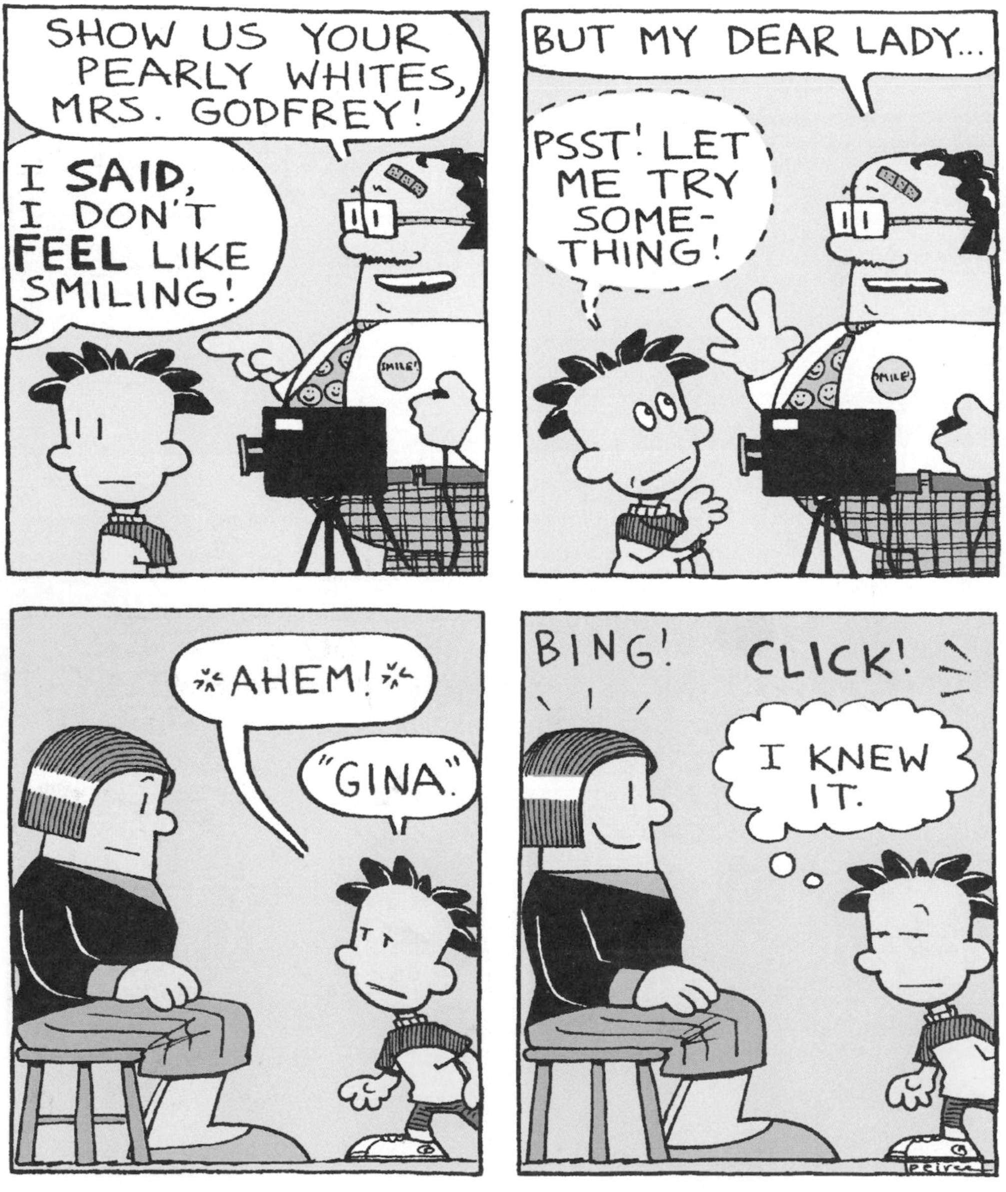
SHOW US YOUR PEARLY WHITES, MRS. GODFREY!
I **SAID**, I DON'T **FEEL** LIKE SMILING!
SMILE!
BUT MY DEAR LADY...
PSST! LET ME TRY SOME-THING!
SMILE!
AHEM!
"GINA".
BING!
CLICK!
I KNEW IT.
PEIRCE

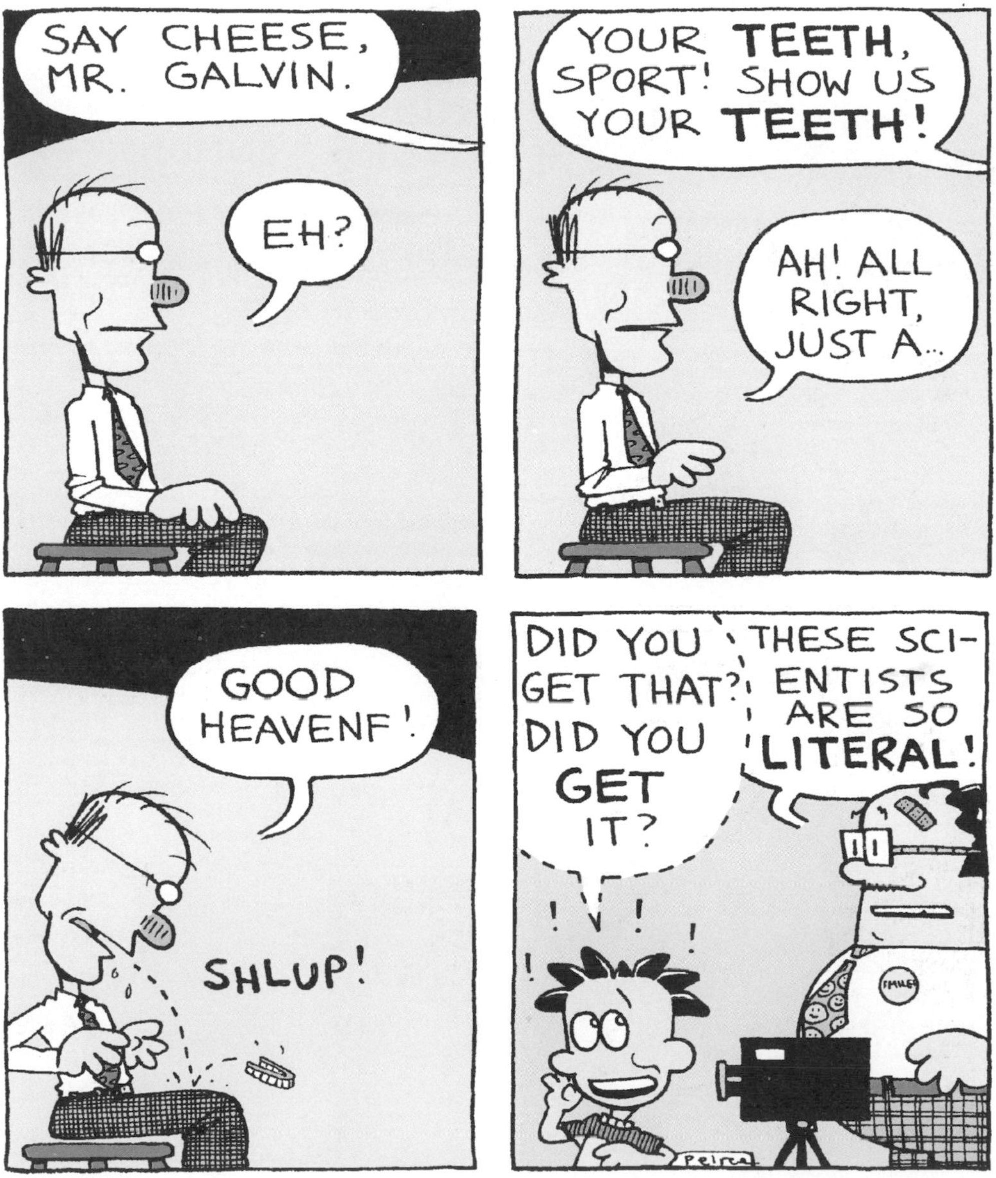
SAY CHEESE, MR. GALVIN.
EH?
YOUR TEETH, SPORT! SHOW US YOUR TEETH!
AH! ALL RIGHT, JUST A...
GOOD HEAVENF!
SHLUP!
DID YOU GET THAT? DID YOU GET IT?
THESE SCI-ENTISTS ARE SO LITERAL!
! ! ! !
SMILE!
Peirce

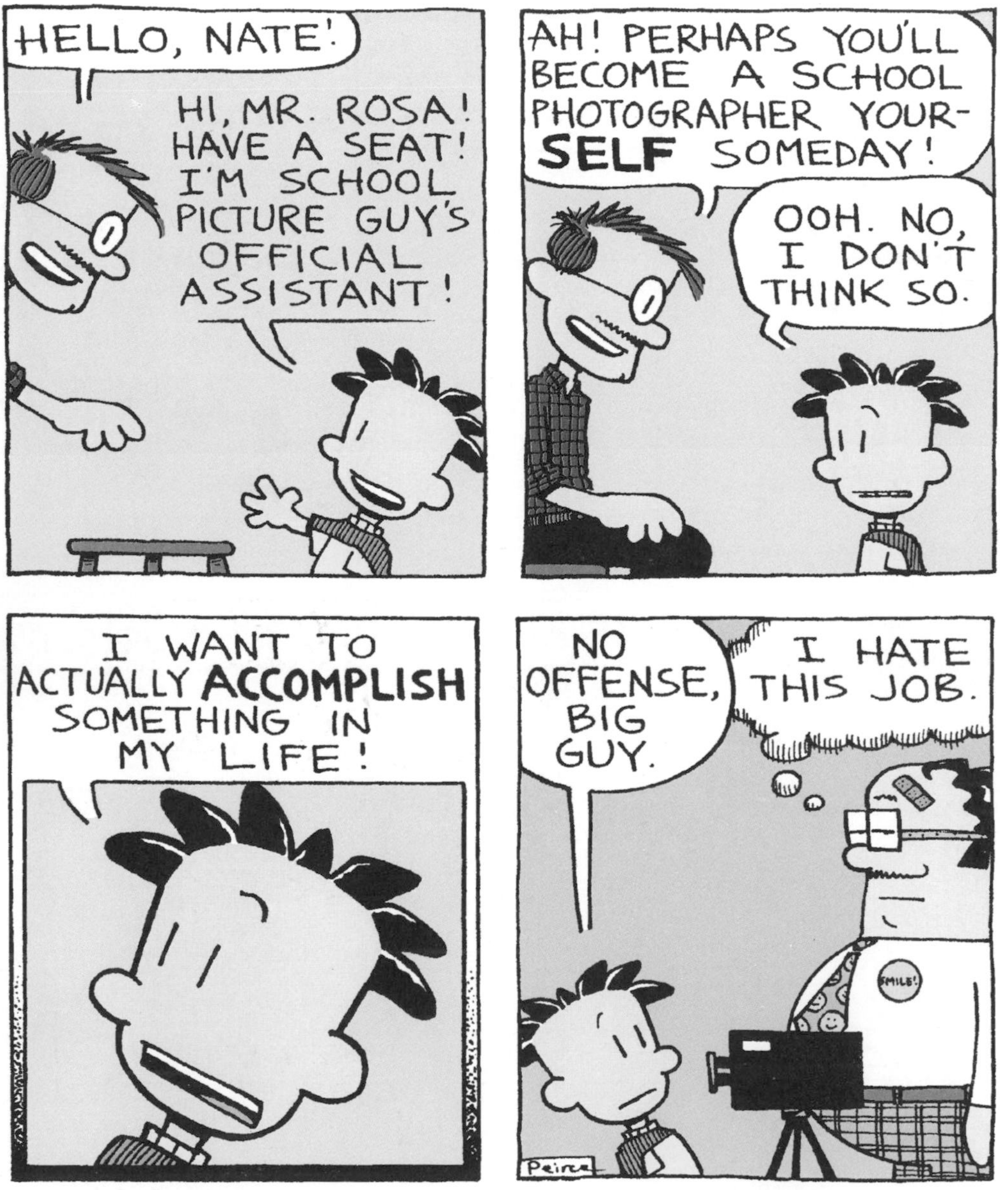
HELLO, NATE!
HI, MR. ROSA! HAVE A SEAT! I'M SCHOOL PICTURE GUY'S OFFICIAL ASSISTANT!
AH! PERHAPS YOU'LL BECOME A SCHOOL PHOTOGRAPHER YOUR-**SELF** SOMEDAY!
OOH. NO, I DON'T THINK SO.
I WANT TO ACTUALLY **ACCOMPLISH** SOMETHING IN MY LIFE!
NO OFFENSE, BIG GUY.
I HATE THIS JOB.
SMILE!
Peirce

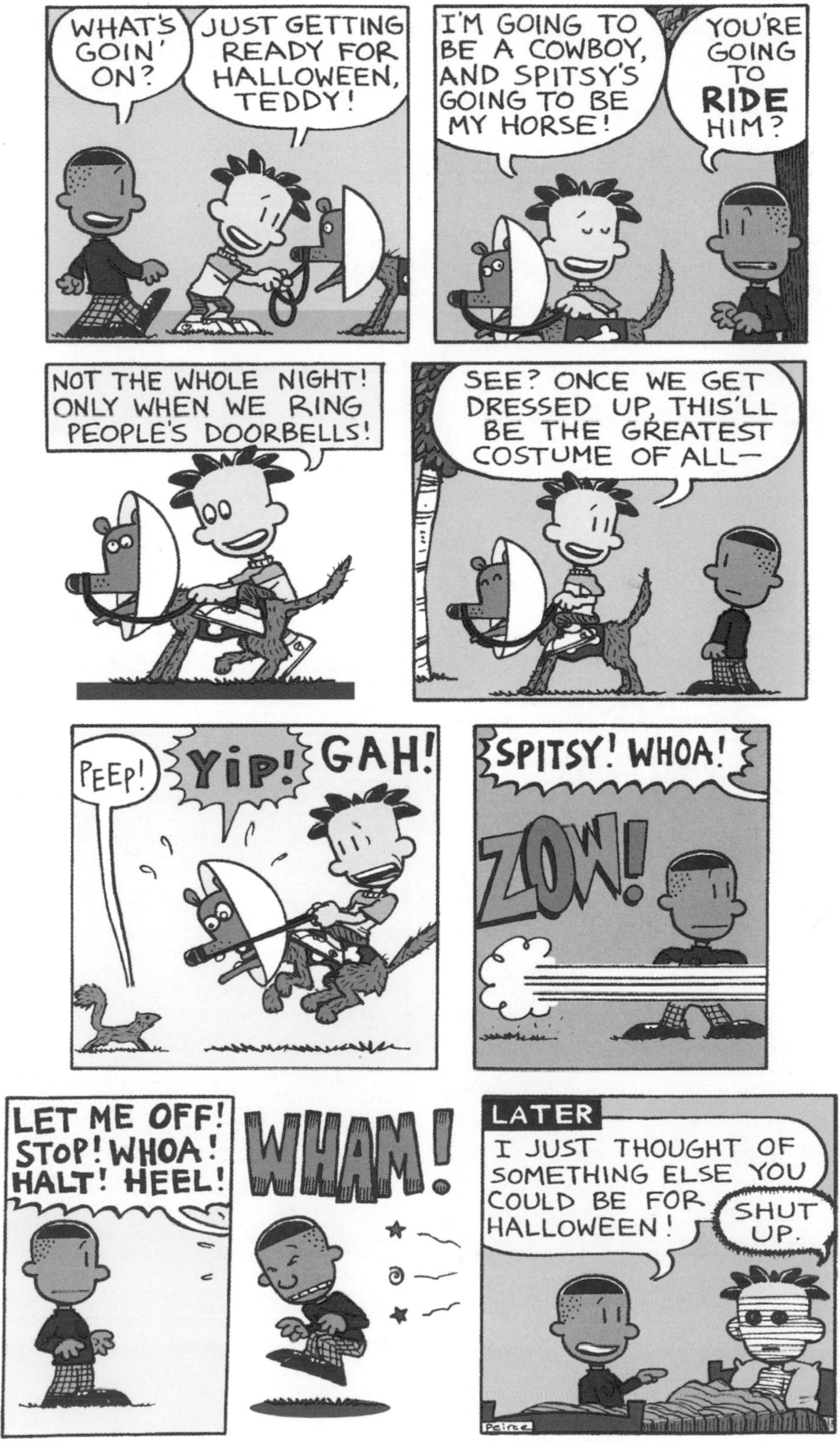

WHAT'S GOIN' ON?
JUST GETTING READY FOR HALLOWEEN, TEDDY!
I'M GOING TO BE A COWBOY, AND SPITSY'S GOING TO BE MY HORSE!
YOU'RE GOING TO RIDE HIM?
NOT THE WHOLE NIGHT! ONLY WHEN WE RING PEOPLE'S DOORBELLS!
SEE? ONCE WE GET DRESSED UP, THIS'LL BE THE GREATEST COSTUME OF ALL—
PEEP!
YIP!
GAH!
SPITSY! WHOA!
ZOW!
LET ME OFF! STOP! WHOA! HALT! HEEL!
WHAM!
LATER
I JUST THOUGHT OF SOMETHING ELSE YOU COULD BE FOR HALLOWEEN!
SHUT UP.
Peirce

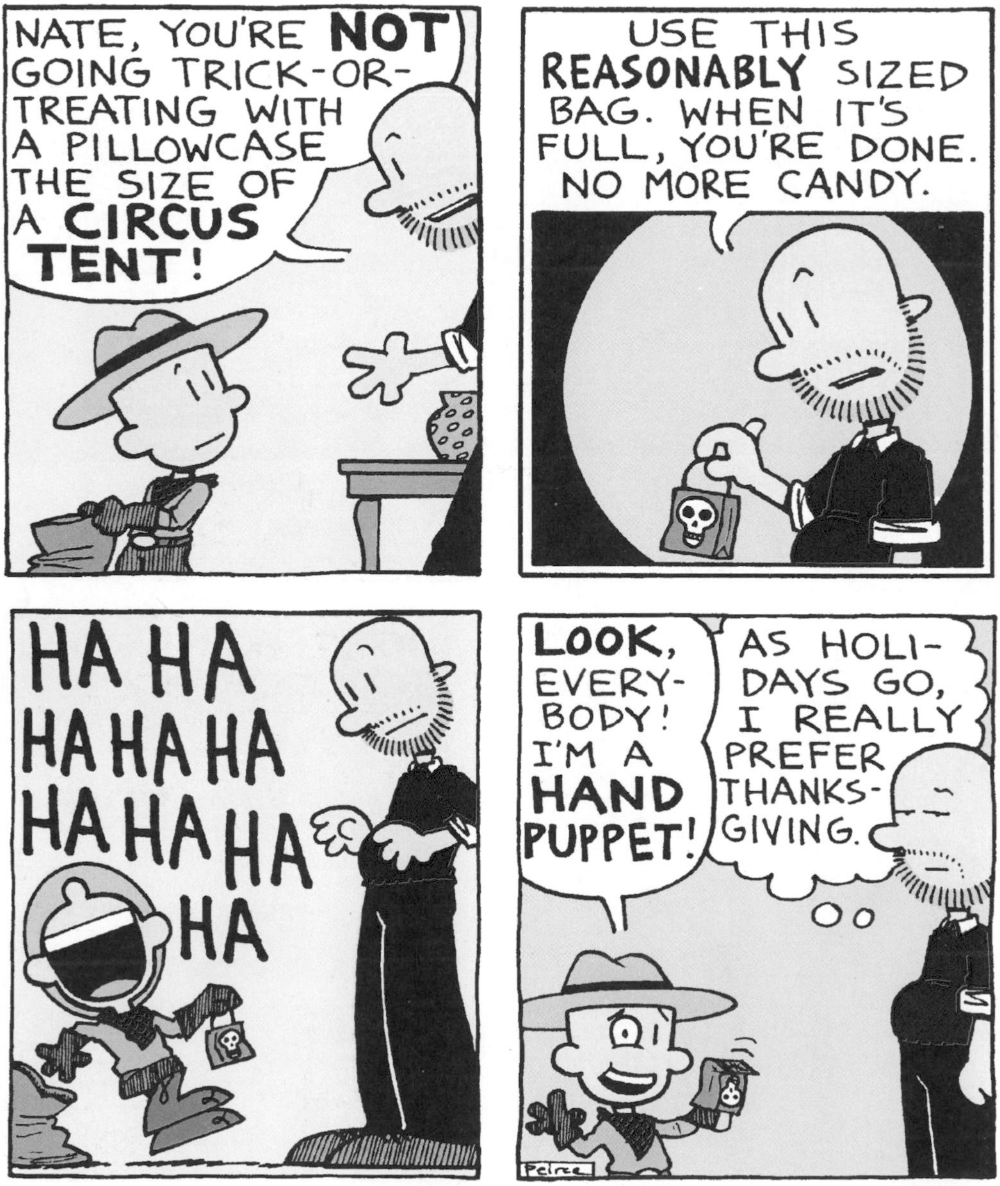
NATE, YOU'RE **NOT** GOING TRICK-OR-TREATING WITH A PILLOWCASE THE SIZE OF A **CIRCUS TENT**!
USE THIS **REASONABLY** SIZED BAG. WHEN IT'S FULL, YOU'RE DONE. NO MORE CANDY.
HA HA HA HA HA HA HA HA HA HA HA
LOOK, EVERYBODY! I'M A **HAND PUPPET**!
AS HOLIDAYS GO, I REALLY PREFER THANKSGIVING.
Peirce

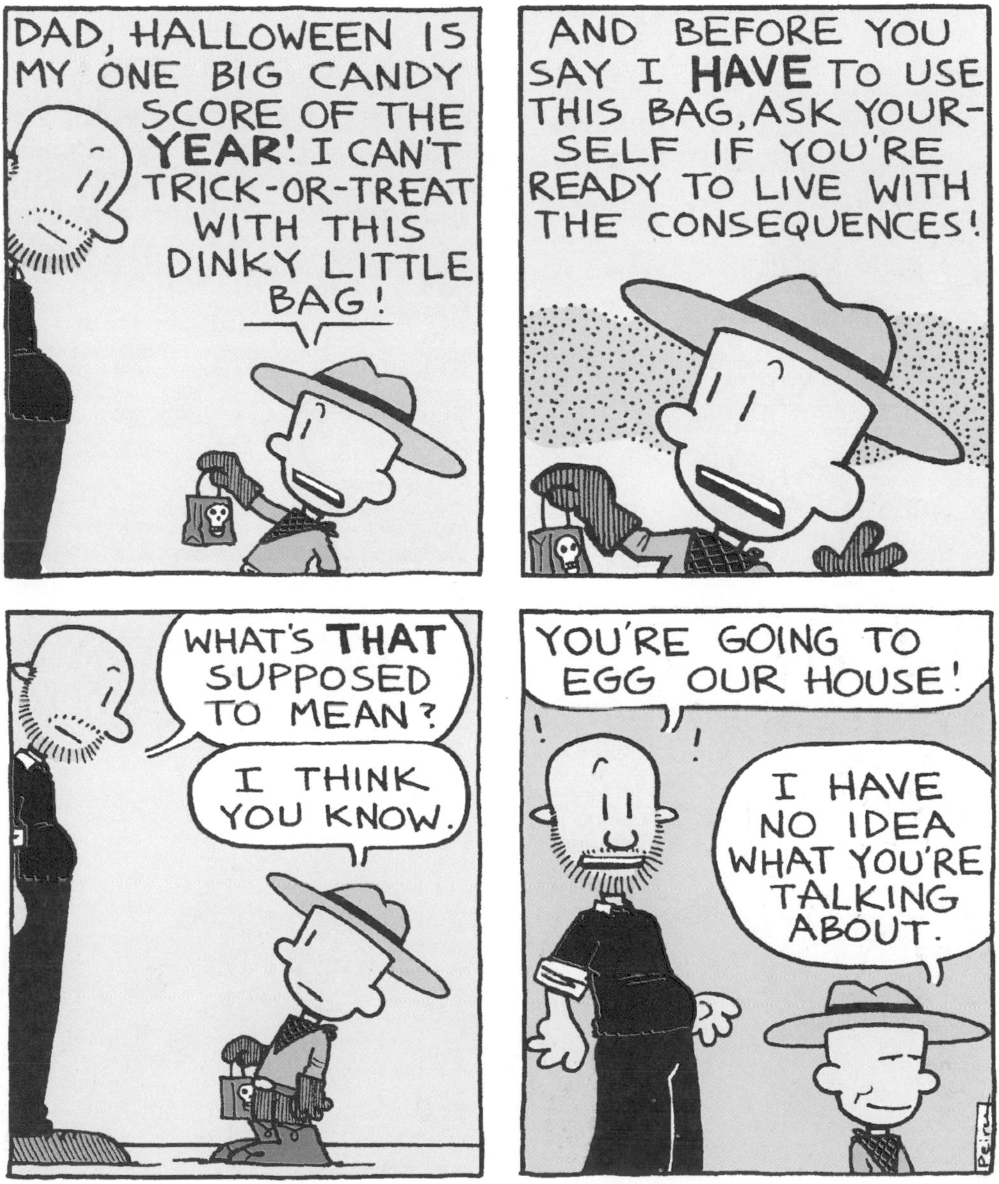
DAD, HALLOWEEN IS MY ONE BIG CANDY SCORE OF THE **YEAR**! I CAN'T TRICK-OR-TREAT WITH THIS DINKY LITTLE BAG!
AND BEFORE YOU SAY I **HAVE** TO USE THIS BAG, ASK YOURSELF IF YOU'RE READY TO LIVE WITH THE CONSEQUENCES!
WHAT'S **THAT** SUPPOSED TO MEAN?
I THINK YOU KNOW.
YOU'RE GOING TO EGG OUR HOUSE!
!!
I HAVE NO IDEA WHAT YOU'RE TALKING ABOUT.
PEIRCE

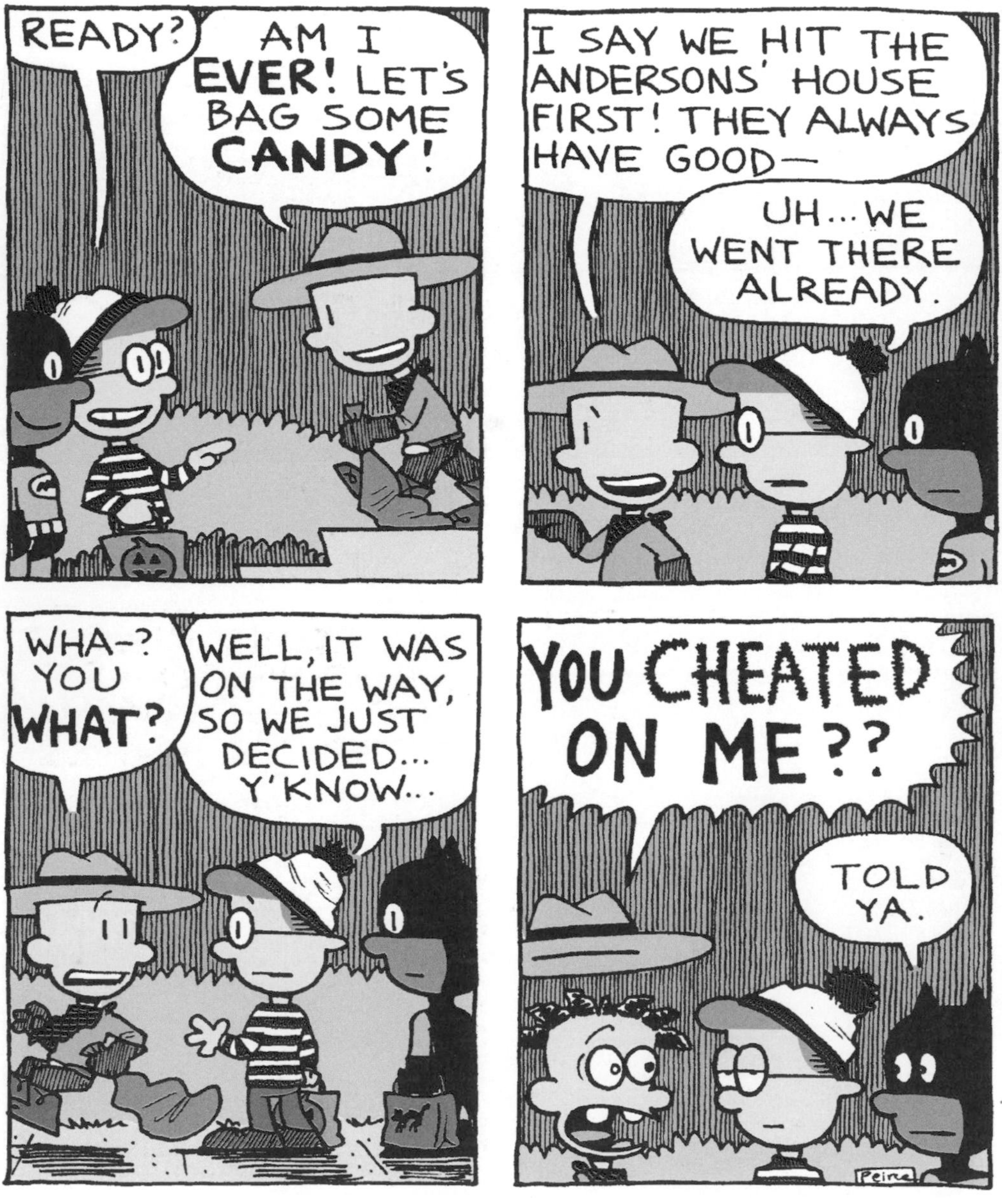
READY?
AM I EVER! LET'S BAG SOME CANDY!
I SAY WE HIT THE ANDERSONS' HOUSE FIRST! THEY ALWAYS HAVE GOOD—
UH... WE WENT THERE ALREADY.
WHA-? YOU WHAT?
WELL, IT WAS ON THE WAY, SO WE JUST DECIDED... Y'KNOW...
YOU CHEATED ON ME??
TOLD YA.
Peirce

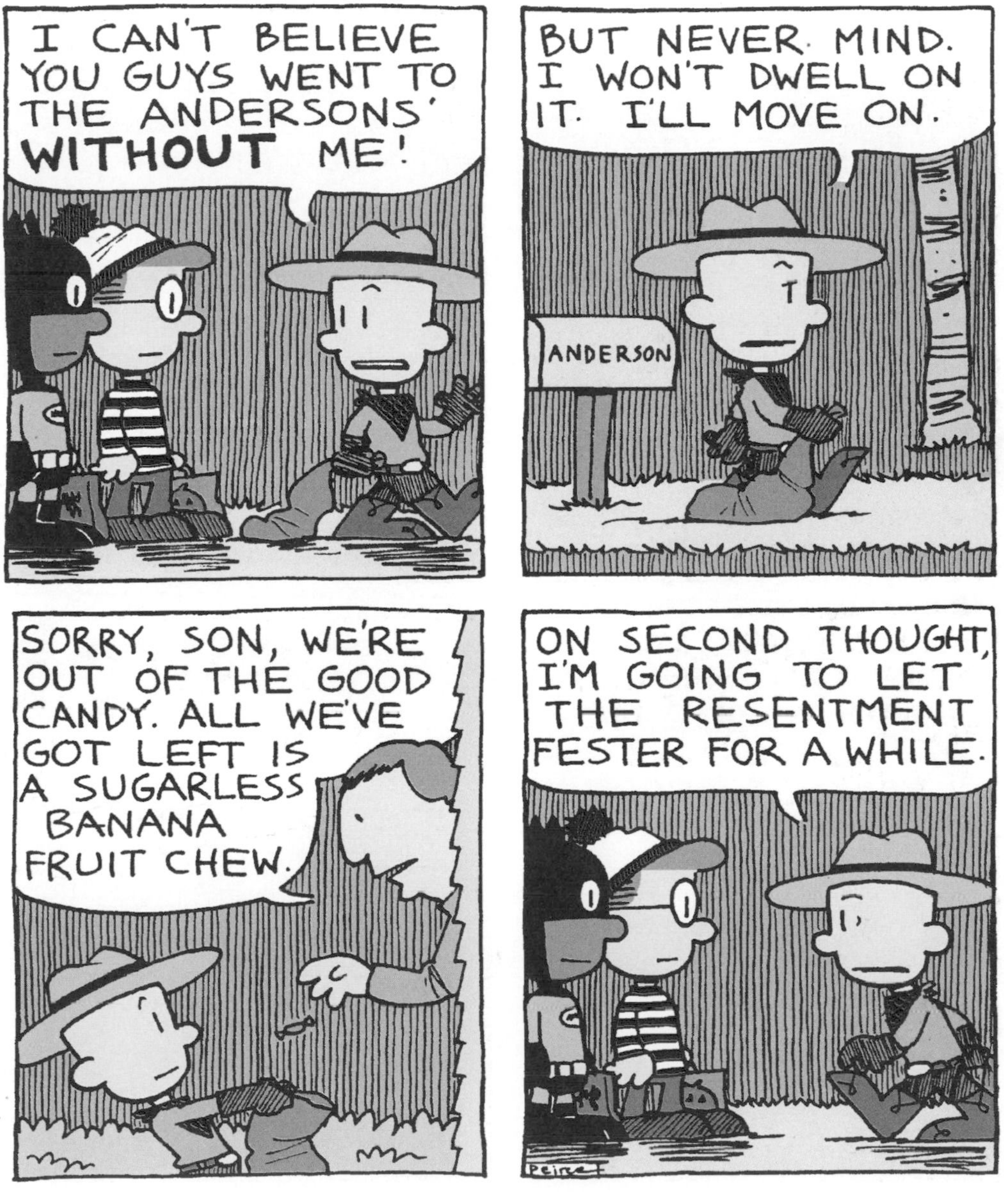
I CAN'T BELIEVE YOU GUYS WENT TO THE ANDERSONS' **WITHOUT** ME!
BUT NEVER MIND. I WON'T DWELL ON IT. I'LL MOVE ON.
ANDERSON
SORRY, SON, WE'RE OUT OF THE GOOD CANDY. ALL WE'VE GOT LEFT IS A SUGARLESS BANANA FRUIT CHEW.
ON SECOND THOUGHT, I'M GOING TO LET THE RESENTMENT FESTER FOR A WHILE.
Peirce

NATE, WE'RE SORRY WE WENT TO A FEW HOUSES WITHOUT YOU!
WE'LL GIVE YOU A SNICKERS TO MAKE IT UP TO YOU!
NOPE.
TWO SNICKERS!
AND A BAG OF SKITTLES!
EXCUSE ME, BUT MY FORGIVENESS IS TOO PRECIOUS TO BE PURCHASED WITH CANDY!
TWO SNICKERS, TWO SKITTLES. FINAL OFFER.
DEAL.

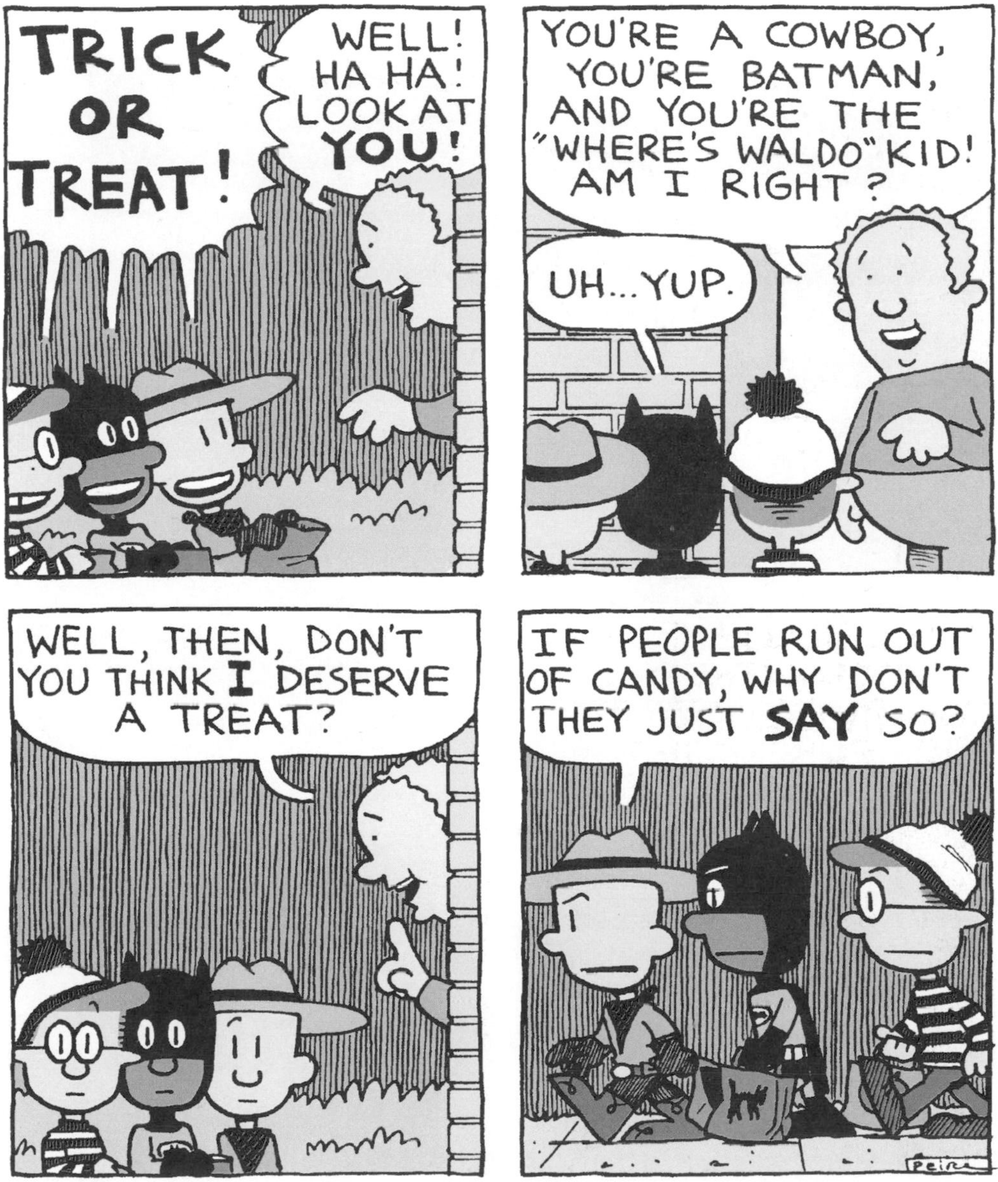
TRICK OR TREAT!
WELL! HA HA! LOOK AT YOU!
YOU'RE A COWBOY, YOU'RE BATMAN, AND YOU'RE THE "WHERE'S WALDO" KID! AM I RIGHT?
UH... YUP.
WELL, THEN, DON'T YOU THINK I DESERVE A TREAT?
IF PEOPLE RUN OUT OF CANDY, WHY DON'T THEY JUST SAY SO?
PEIRCE

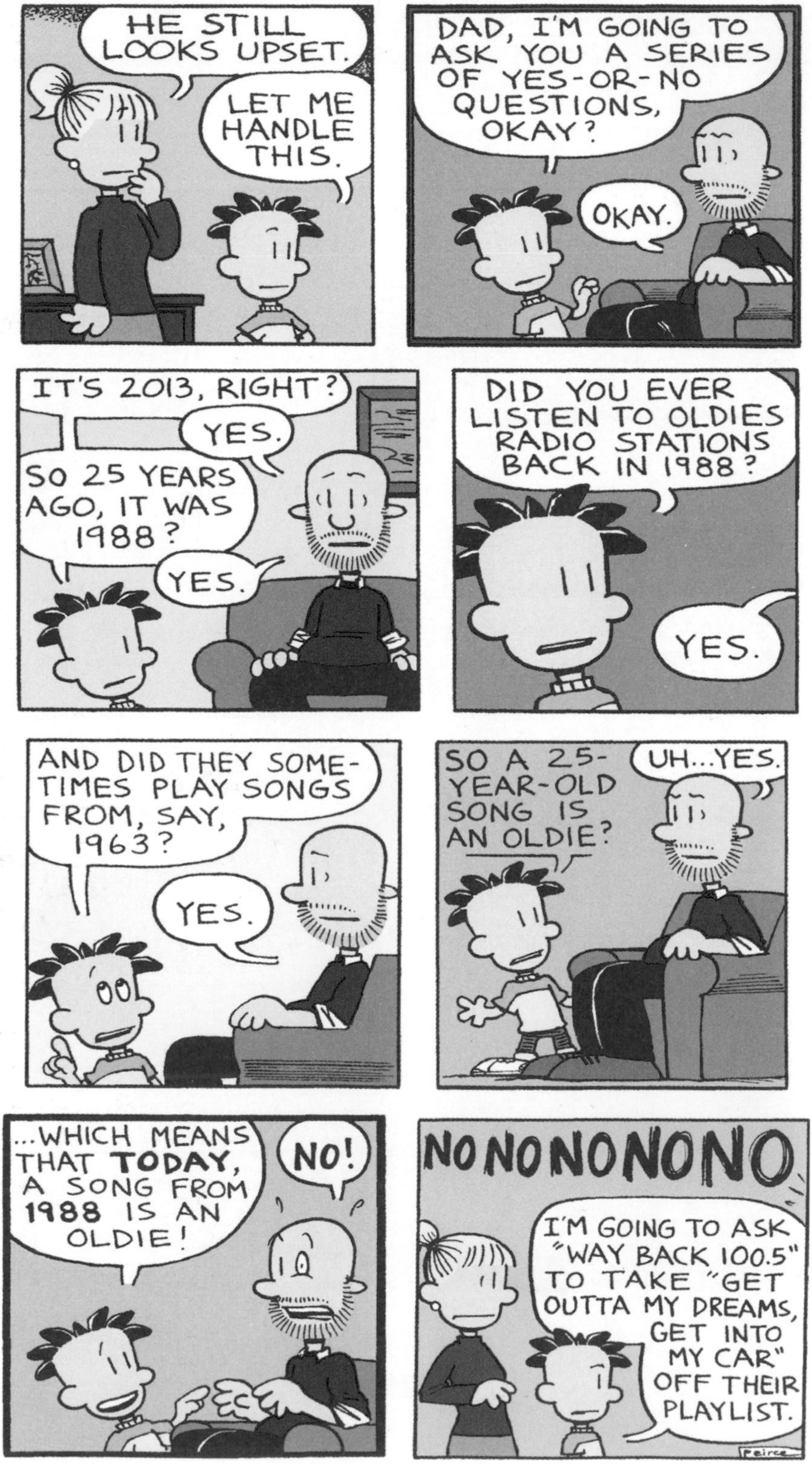
HE STILL LOOKS UPSET.
LET ME HANDLE THIS.
DAD, I'M GOING TO ASK YOU A SERIES OF YES-OR-NO QUESTIONS, OKAY?
OKAY.
IT'S 2013, RIGHT?
YES.
SO 25 YEARS AGO, IT WAS 1988?
YES.
DID YOU EVER LISTEN TO OLDIES RADIO STATIONS BACK IN 1988?
YES.
AND DID THEY SOME-TIMES PLAY SONGS FROM, SAY, 1963?
YES.
SO A 25-YEAR-OLD SONG IS AN OLDIE?
UH...YES.
...WHICH MEANS THAT TODAY, A SONG FROM 1988 IS AN OLDIE!
NO!
NONONONONONO
I'M GOING TO ASK "WAY BACK 100.5" TO TAKE "GET OUTTA MY DREAMS, GET INTO MY CAR" OFF THEIR PLAYLIST.
Peirce

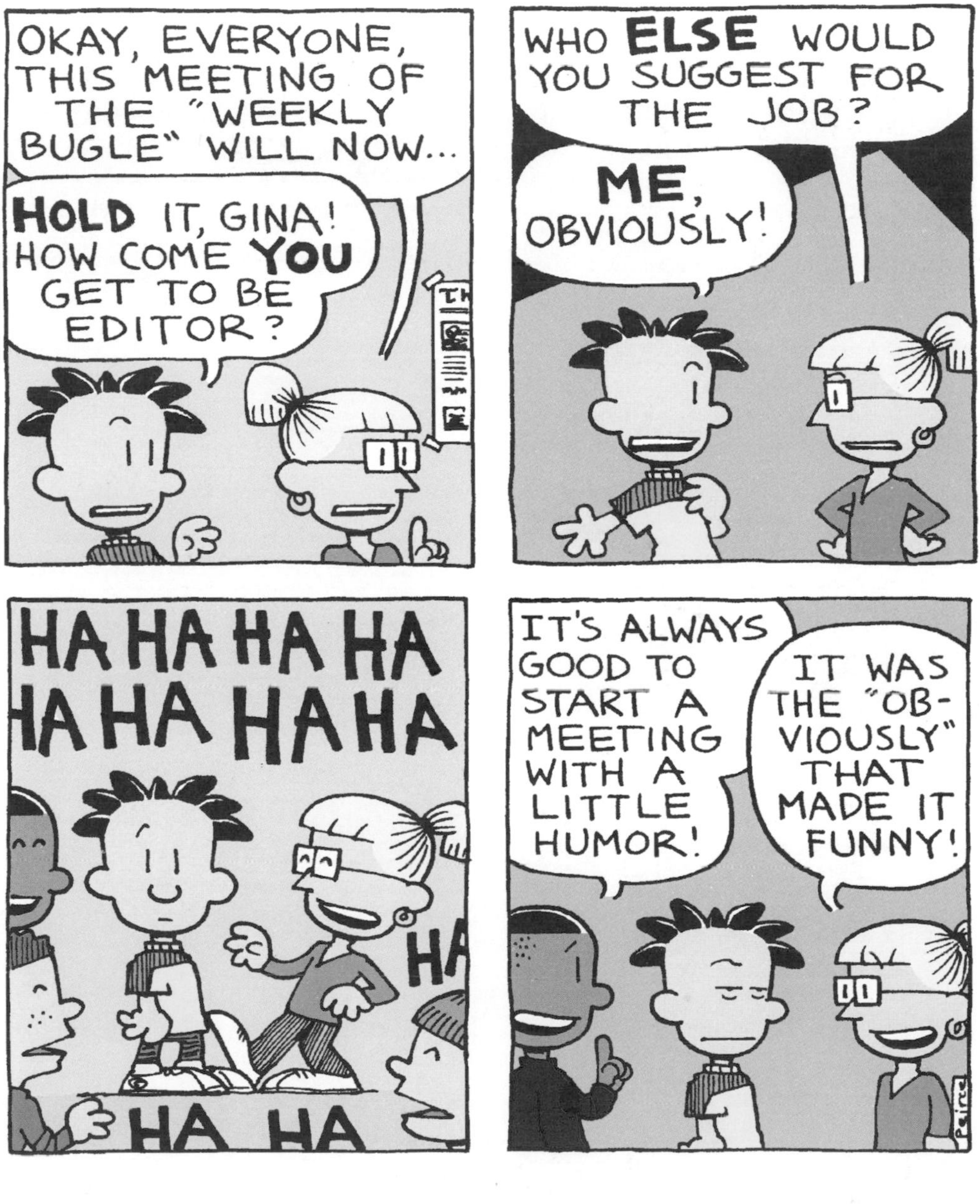
OKAY, EVERYONE, THIS MEETING OF THE "WEEKLY BUGLE" WILL NOW...
HOLD IT, GINA! HOW COME YOU GET TO BE EDITOR?
WHO ELSE WOULD YOU SUGGEST FOR THE JOB?
ME, OBVIOUSLY!
HA HA HA HA HA HA HA HA HA
HA
HA HA
IT'S ALWAYS GOOD TO START A MEETING WITH A LITTLE HUMOR!
IT WAS THE "OBVIOUSLY" THAT MADE IT FUNNY!
Peirce

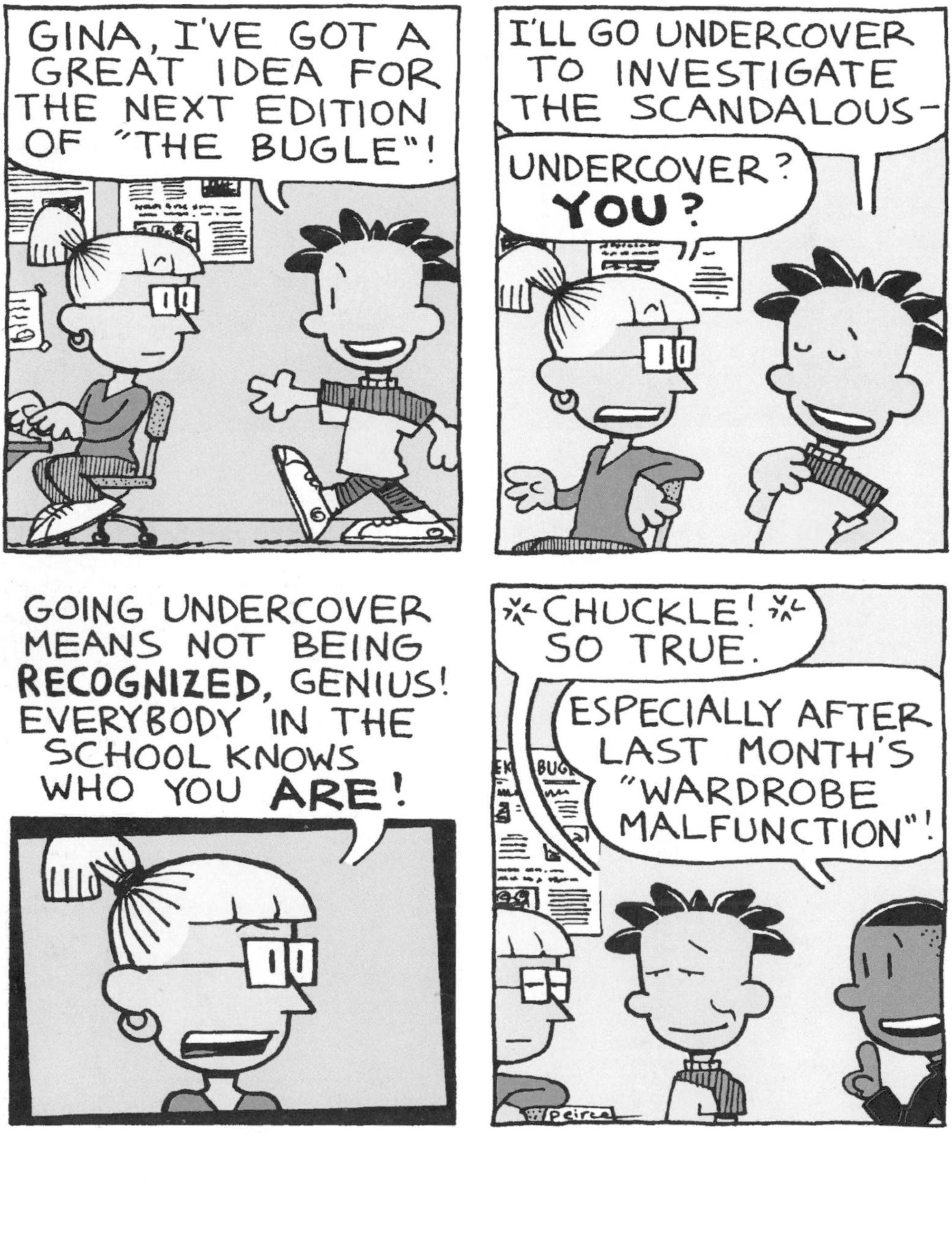
GINA, I'VE GOT A GREAT IDEA FOR THE NEXT EDITION OF "THE BUGLE"!
I'LL GO UNDERCOVER TO INVESTIGATE THE SCANDALOUS-
UNDERCOVER? YOU?
GOING UNDERCOVER MEANS NOT BEING RECOGNIZED, GENIUS! EVERYBODY IN THE SCHOOL KNOWS WHO YOU ARE!
CHUCKLE! SO TRUE.
ESPECIALLY AFTER LAST MONTH'S "WARDROBE MALFUNCTION"!
peirce

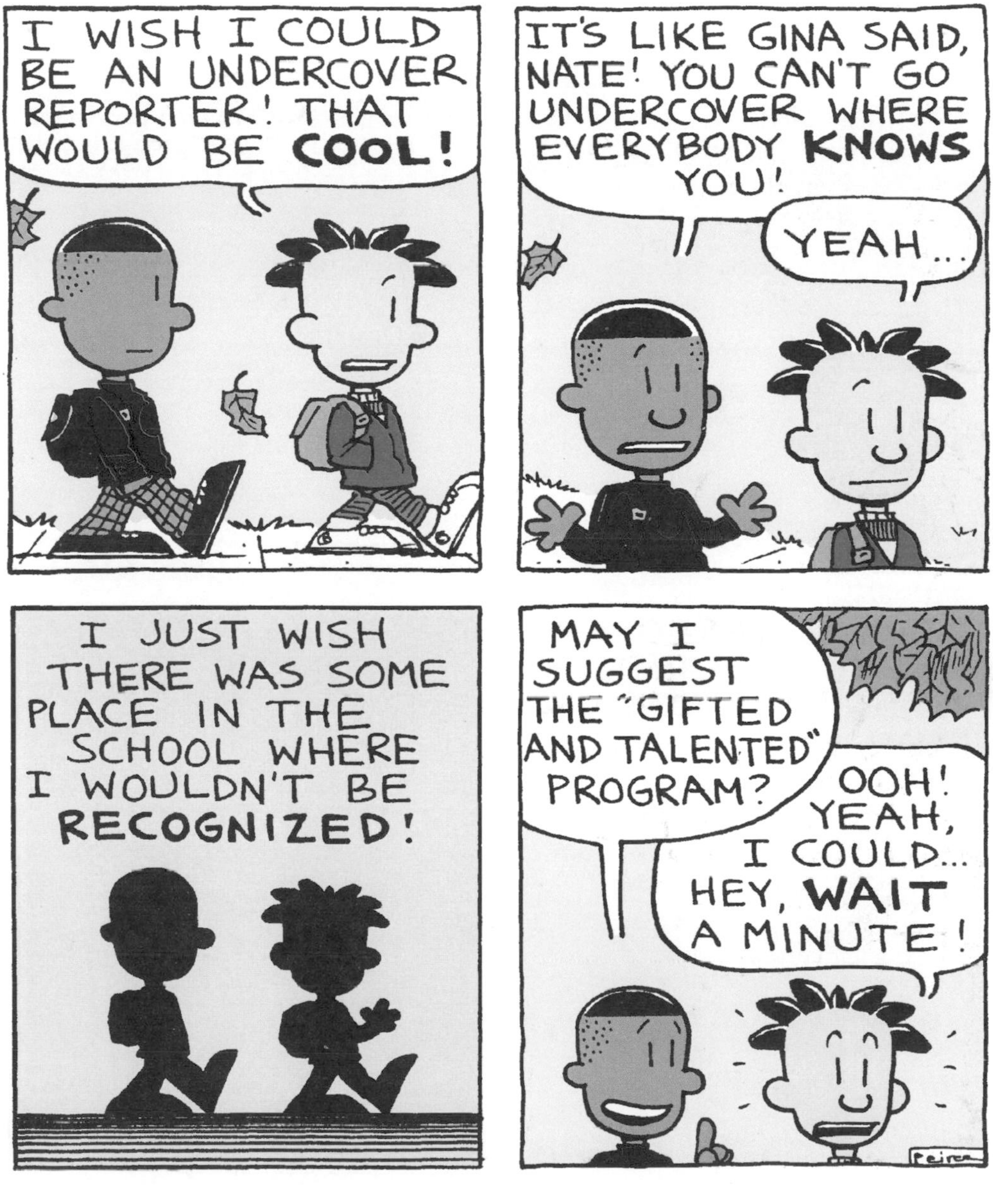
I WISH I COULD BE AN UNDERCOVER REPORTER! THAT WOULD BE **COOL**!
IT'S LIKE GINA SAID, NATE! YOU CAN'T GO UNDERCOVER WHERE EVERYBODY **KNOWS** YOU!
YEAH...
I JUST WISH THERE WAS SOME PLACE IN THE SCHOOL WHERE I WOULDN'T BE **RECOGNIZED**!
MAY I SUGGEST THE "GIFTED AND TALENTED" PROGRAM?
OOH! YEAH, I COULD... HEY, **WAIT** A MINUTE!
Peirce

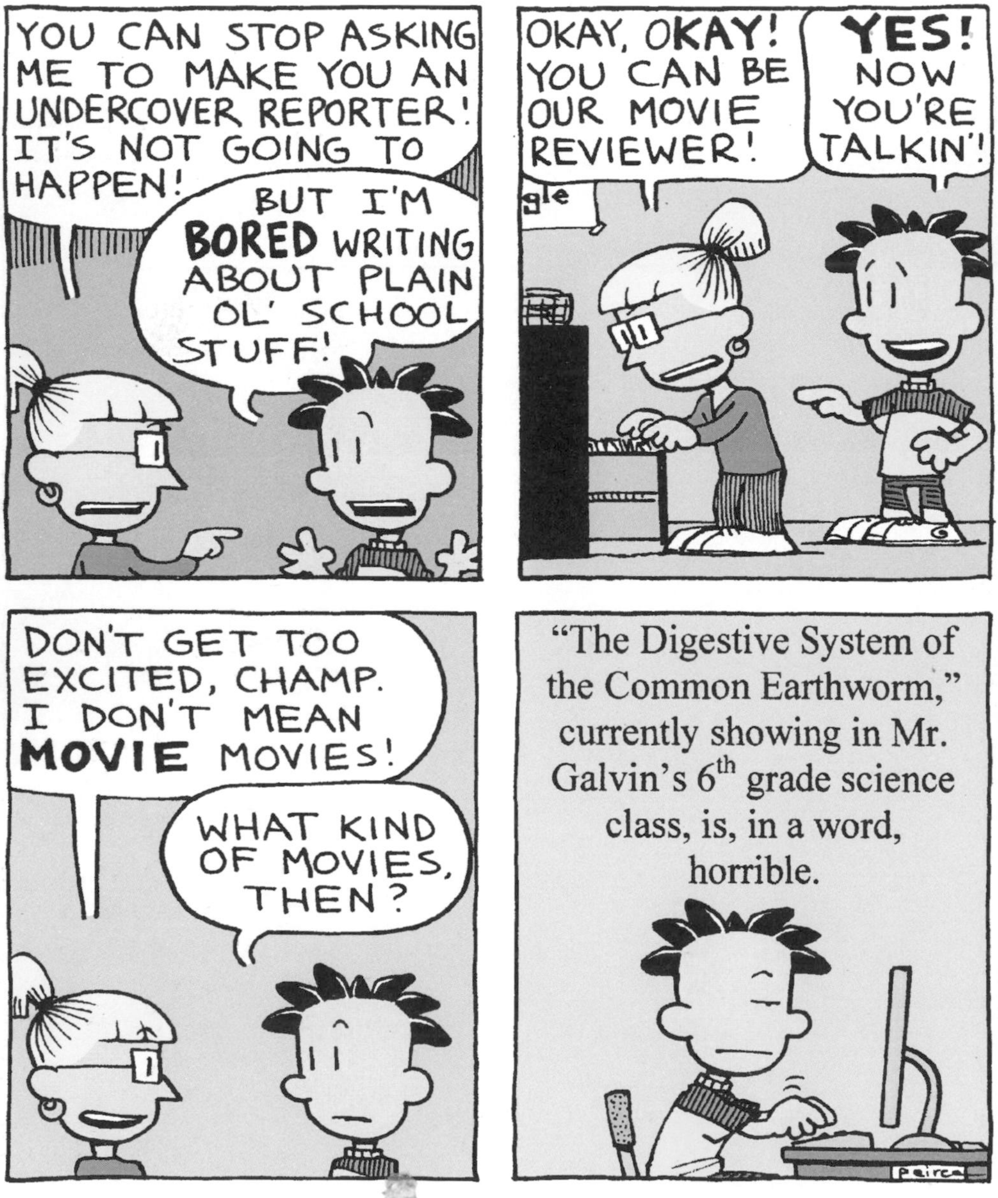
YOU CAN STOP ASKING ME TO MAKE YOU AN UNDERCOVER REPORTER! IT'S NOT GOING TO HAPPEN!
BUT I'M BORED WRITING ABOUT PLAIN OL' SCHOOL STUFF!
OKAY, OKAY! YOU CAN BE OUR MOVIE REVIEWER!
YES! NOW YOU'RE TALKIN'!
DON'T GET TOO EXCITED, CHAMP. I DON'T MEAN MOVIE MOVIES!
WHAT KIND OF MOVIES, THEN?
"The Digestive System of the Common Earthworm," currently showing in Mr. Galvin's 6th grade science class, is, in a word, horrible.
peirce

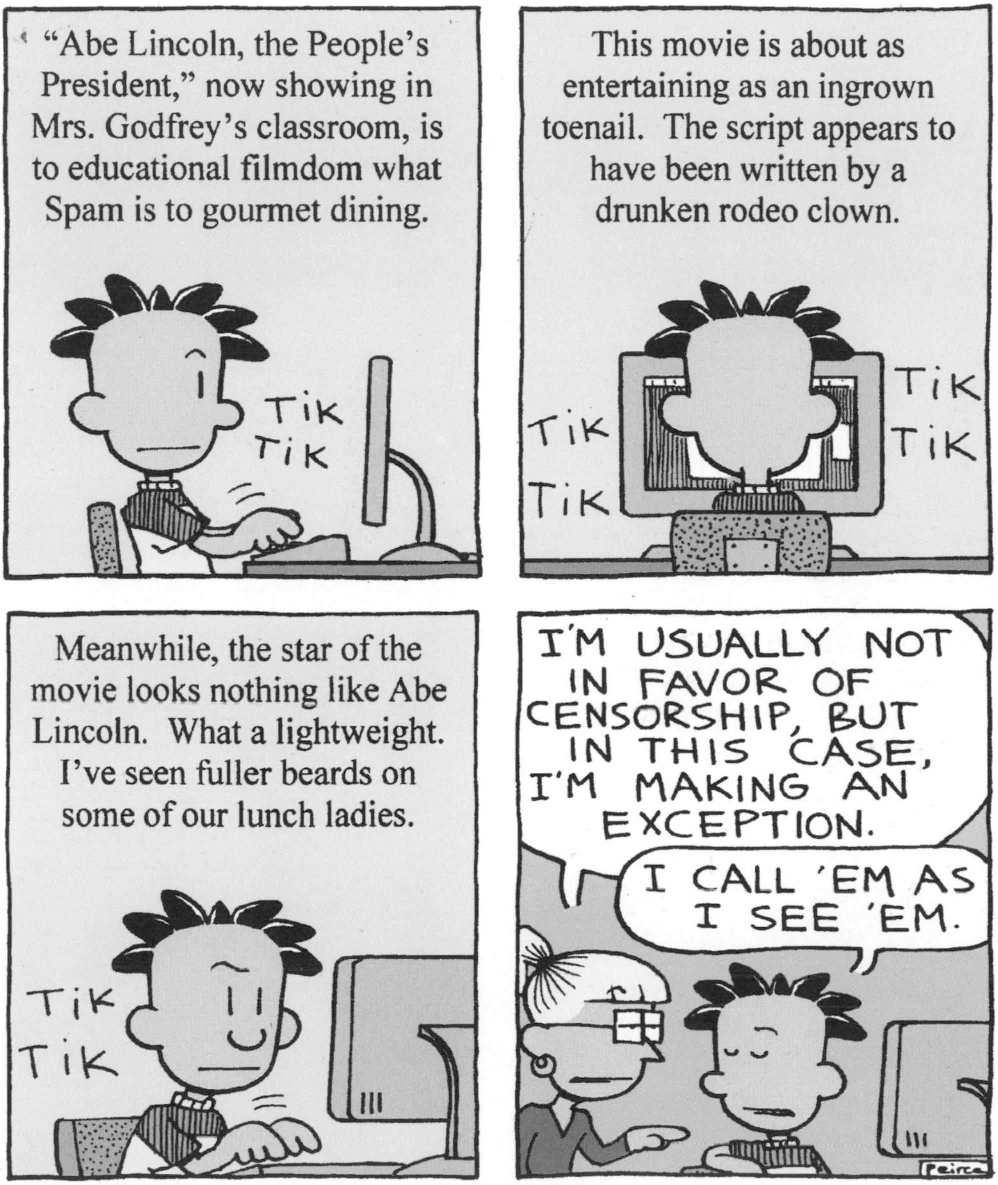
"Abe Lincoln, the People's President," now showing in Mrs. Godfrey's classroom, is to educational filmdom what Spam is to gourmet dining.
TIK TIK
This movie is about as entertaining as an ingrown toenail. The script appears to have been written by a drunken rodeo clown.
TIK TIK
TIK TIK
Meanwhile, the star of the movie looks nothing like Abe Lincoln. What a lightweight. I've seen fuller beards on some of our lunch ladies.
TIK TIK
I'M USUALLY NOT IN FAVOR OF CENSORSHIP, BUT IN THIS CASE, I'M MAKING AN EXCEPTION.
I CALL 'EM AS I SEE 'EM.
Peirce

"The Fascinating World of Fossils" may be the worst title for a movie of all time. The only thing fascinating about this turkey is why it got made in the first place.
TIK
TIK
TIK
The "plot": some annoying Cub Scouts go on a nature hike and discover a bunch of fossils. Just then some creepy guy comes along WHO JUST HAPPENS TO BE A FOSSIL EXPERT!
TIK
TIK
Then the Cub Scouts go and tell some random scientists about the fossils, and they end up saving the whole area from becoming a giant shopping mall.
TIK
TIK
TIK
SO IT'S A HAPPY ENDING!
EXCEPT FOR THE GUY WITH THE "ORANGE JULIUS" FRANCHISE.
F
Peirce

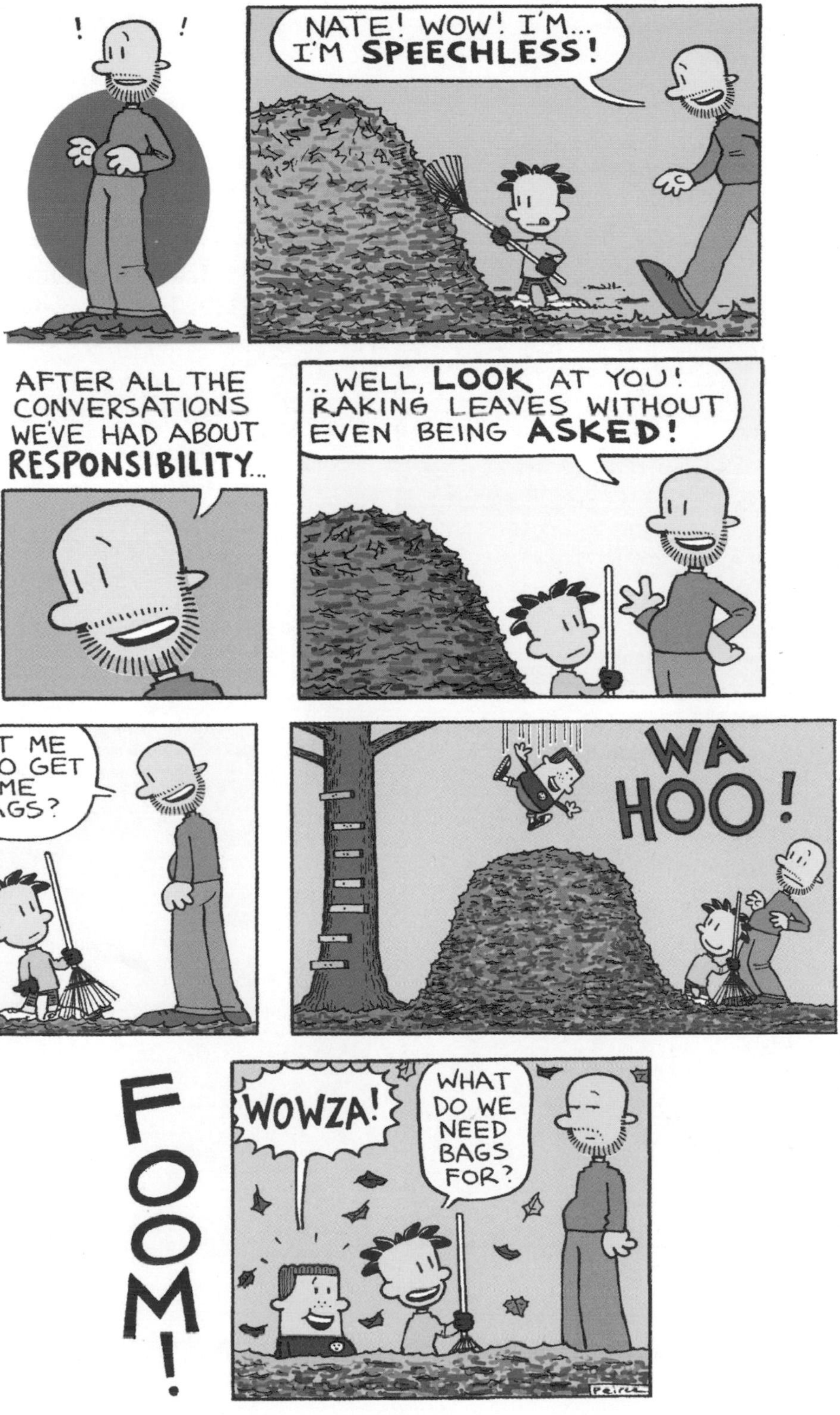

! !
NATE! WOW! I'M... I'M SPEECHLESS!
AFTER ALL THE CONVERSATIONS WE'VE HAD ABOUT RESPONSIBILITY...
...WELL, LOOK AT YOU! RAKING LEAVES WITHOUT EVEN BEING ASKED!
WANT ME TO GO GET SOME BAGS?
WA HOO!
FOOM!
WOWZA!
WHAT DO WE NEED BAGS FOR?
Peirce

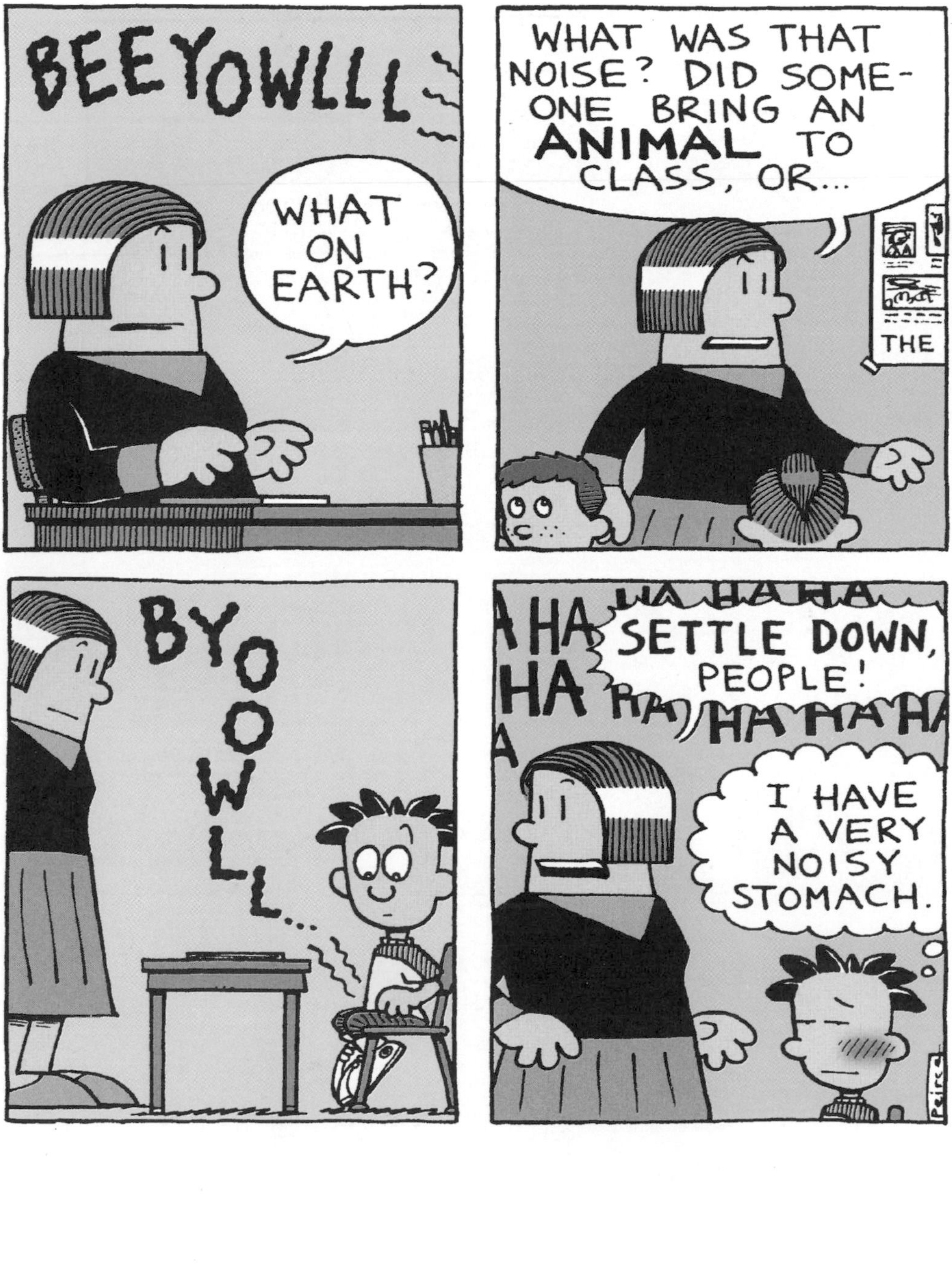
BEEYOWLLL
WHAT ON EARTH?
WHAT WAS THAT NOISE? DID SOME-ONE BRING AN ANIMAL TO CLASS, OR...
THE
BYOOWLL...
HA HA HA HA HA HA HA HA HA HA HA HA
SETTLE DOWN, PEOPLE!
I HAVE A VERY NOISY STOMACH.
Peirce

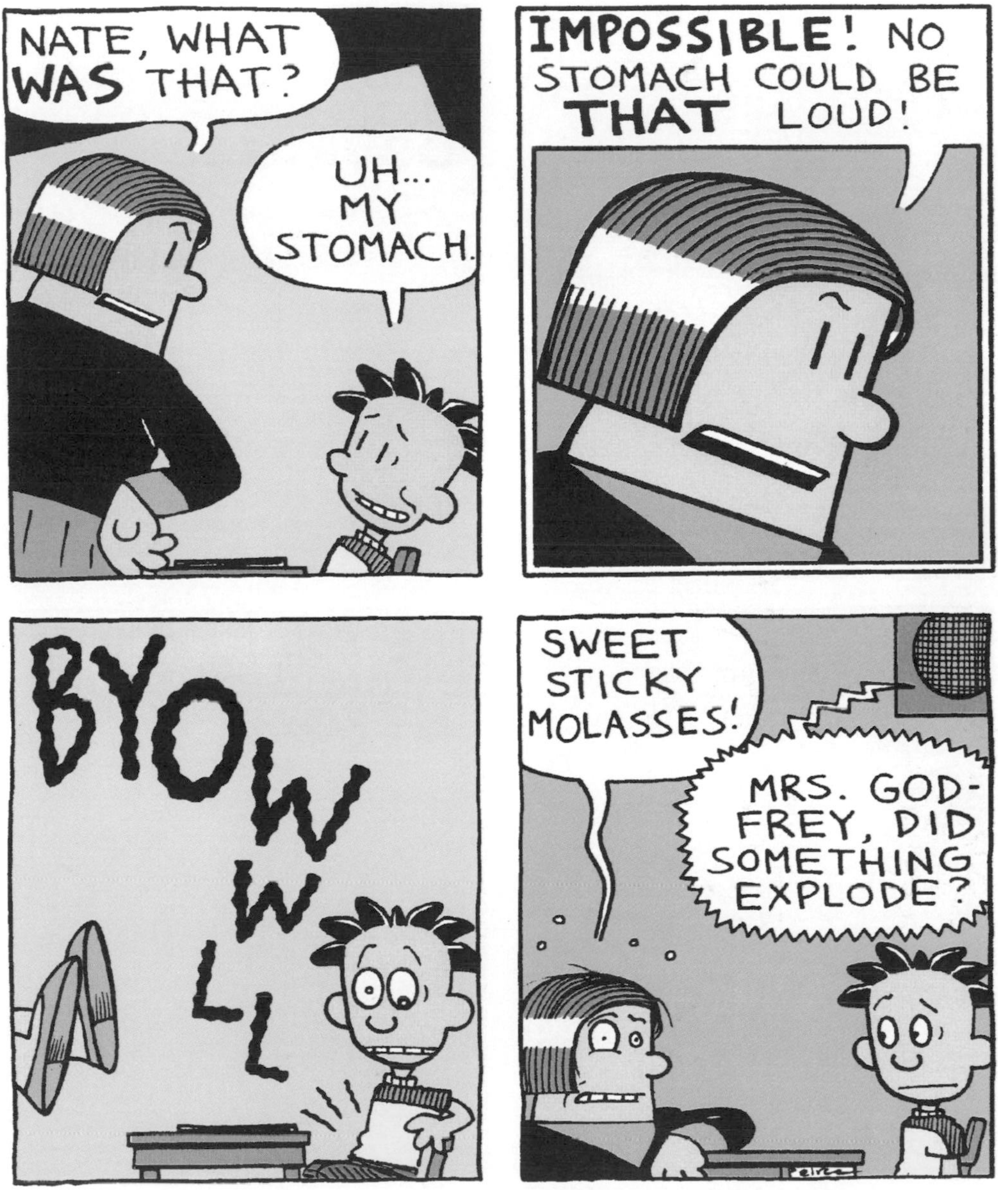
NATE, WHAT WAS THAT?
UH... MY STOMACH.
IMPOSSIBLE! NO STOMACH COULD BE THAT LOUD!
BYOWWLL
SWEET STICKY MOLASSES!
MRS. GOD-FREY, DID SOMETHING EXPLODE?

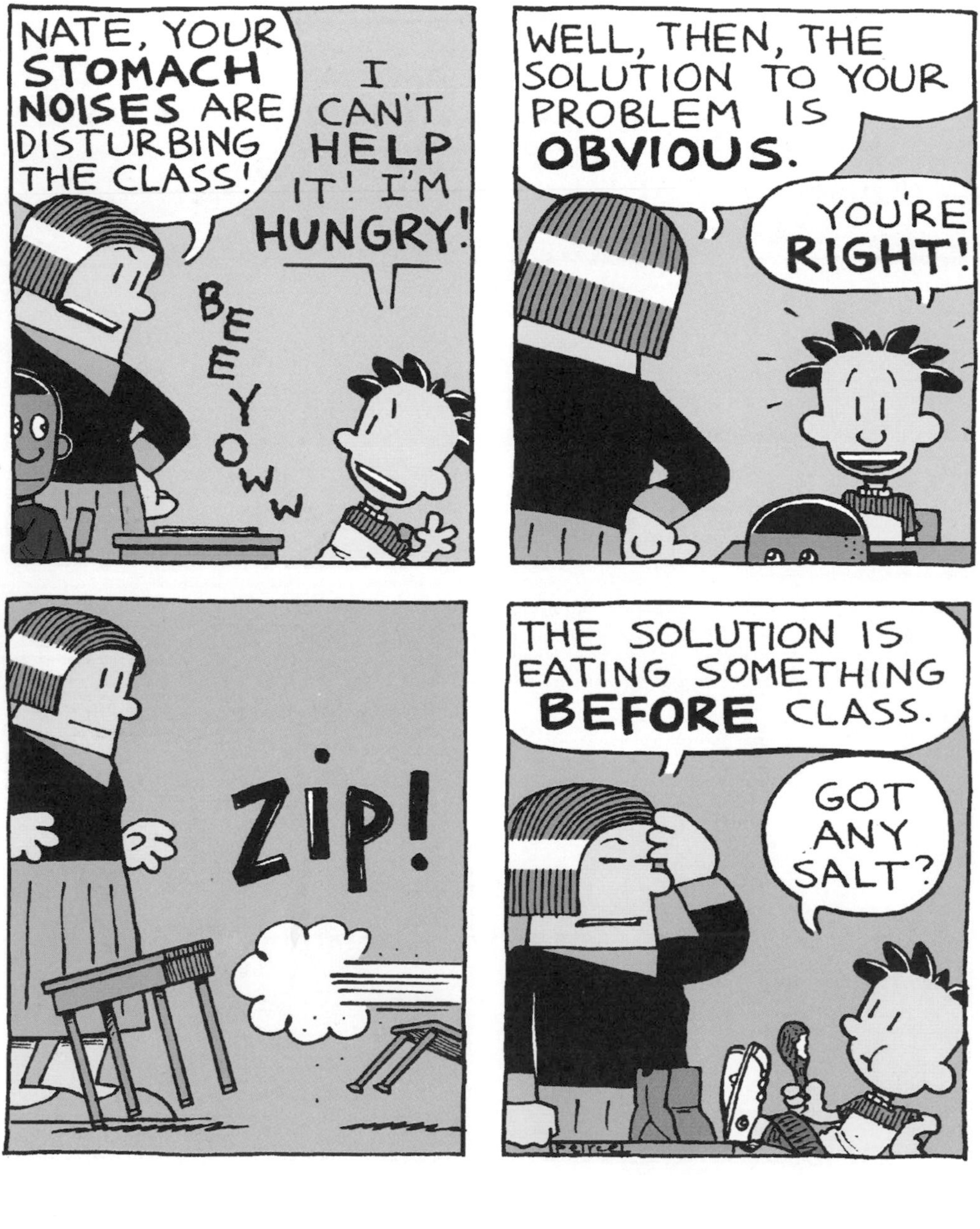
NATE, YOUR STOMACH NOISES ARE DISTURBING THE CLASS!
I CAN'T HELP IT! I'M HUNGRY!
BEEEYOWW
WELL, THEN, THE SOLUTION TO YOUR PROBLEM IS OBVIOUS.
YOU'RE RIGHT!
ZIP!
THE SOLUTION IS EATING SOMETHING BEFORE CLASS.
GOT ANY SALT?

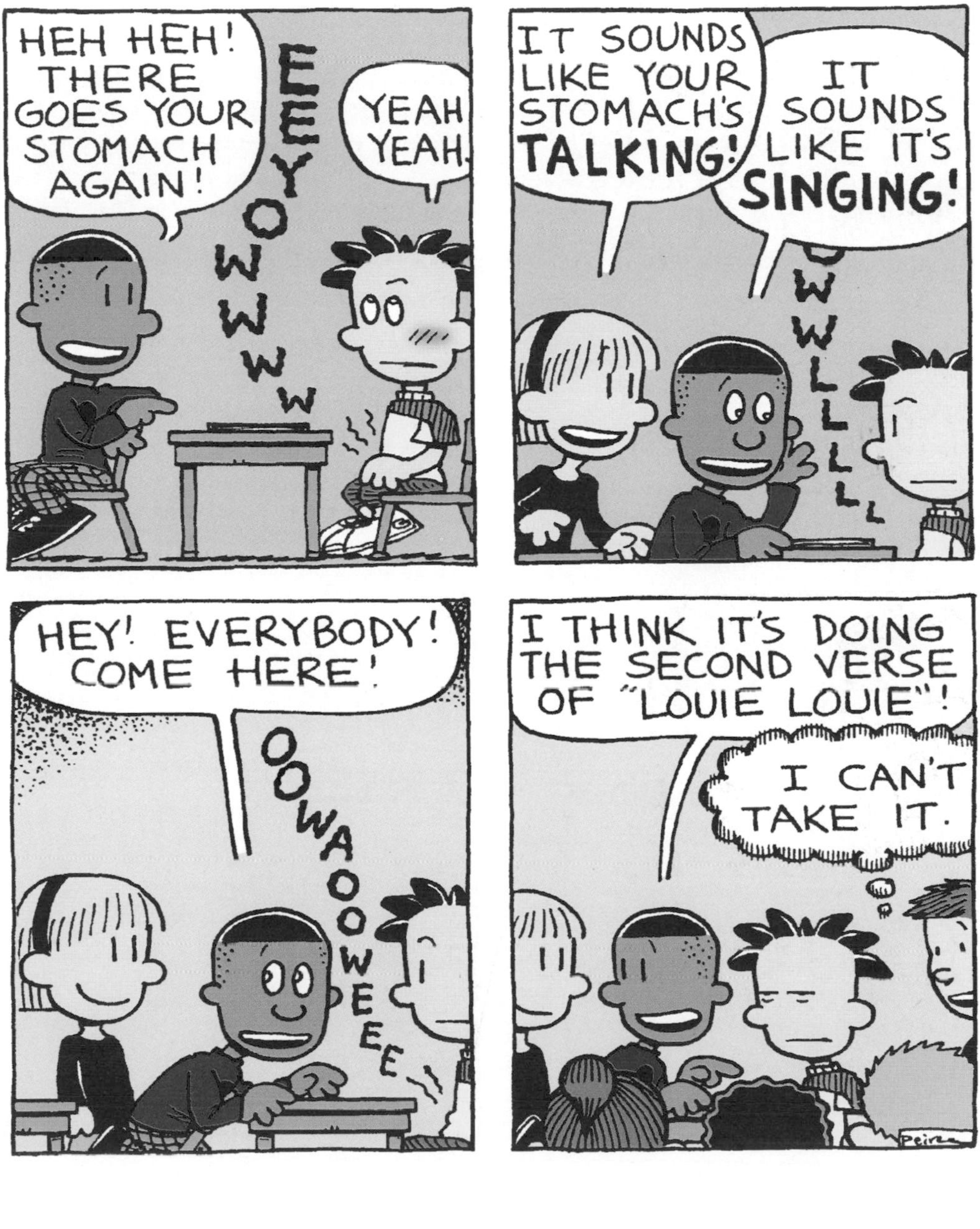
HEH HEH! THERE GOES YOUR STOMACH AGAIN!
EEYOOWWWWW
YEAH YEAH.
IT SOUNDS LIKE YOUR STOMACH'S **TALKING!**
IT SOUNDS LIKE IT'S **SINGING!**
WWLLLLL
HEY! EVERYBODY! COME HERE!
OOWAOOWEEE
I THINK IT'S DOING THE SECOND VERSE OF "LOUIE LOUIE"!
I CAN'T TAKE IT.
Peirce

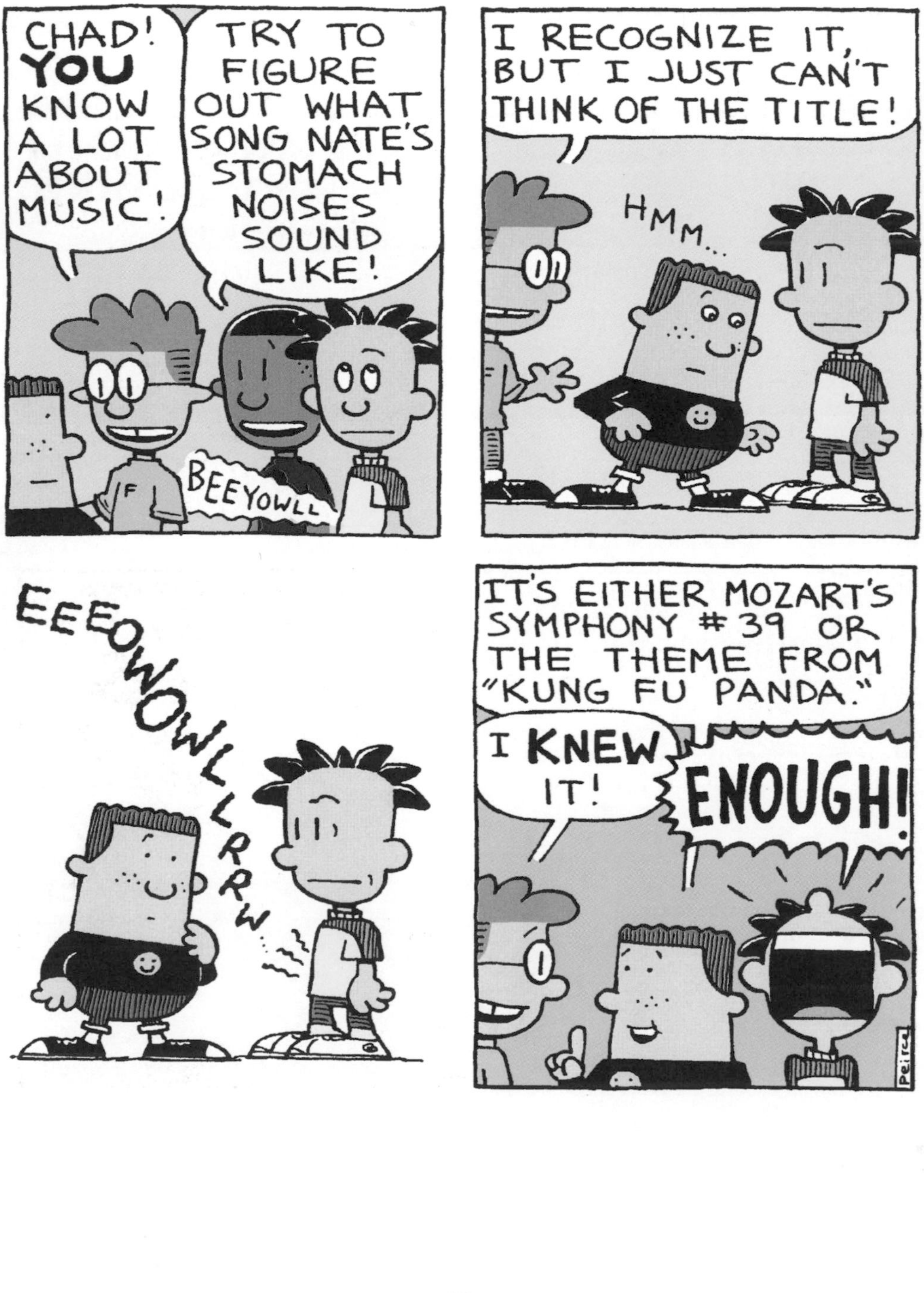
CHAD! **YOU** KNOW A LOT ABOUT MUSIC!
TRY TO FIGURE OUT WHAT SONG NATE'S STOMACH NOISES SOUND LIKE!
BEEYOWLL
I RECOGNIZE IT, BUT I JUST CAN'T THINK OF THE TITLE!
HMM...
EEEOWOWLLRRW...
IT'S EITHER MOZART'S SYMPHONY #39 OR THE THEME FROM "KUNG FU PANDA."
I **KNEW** IT!
ENOUGH!
Peirce

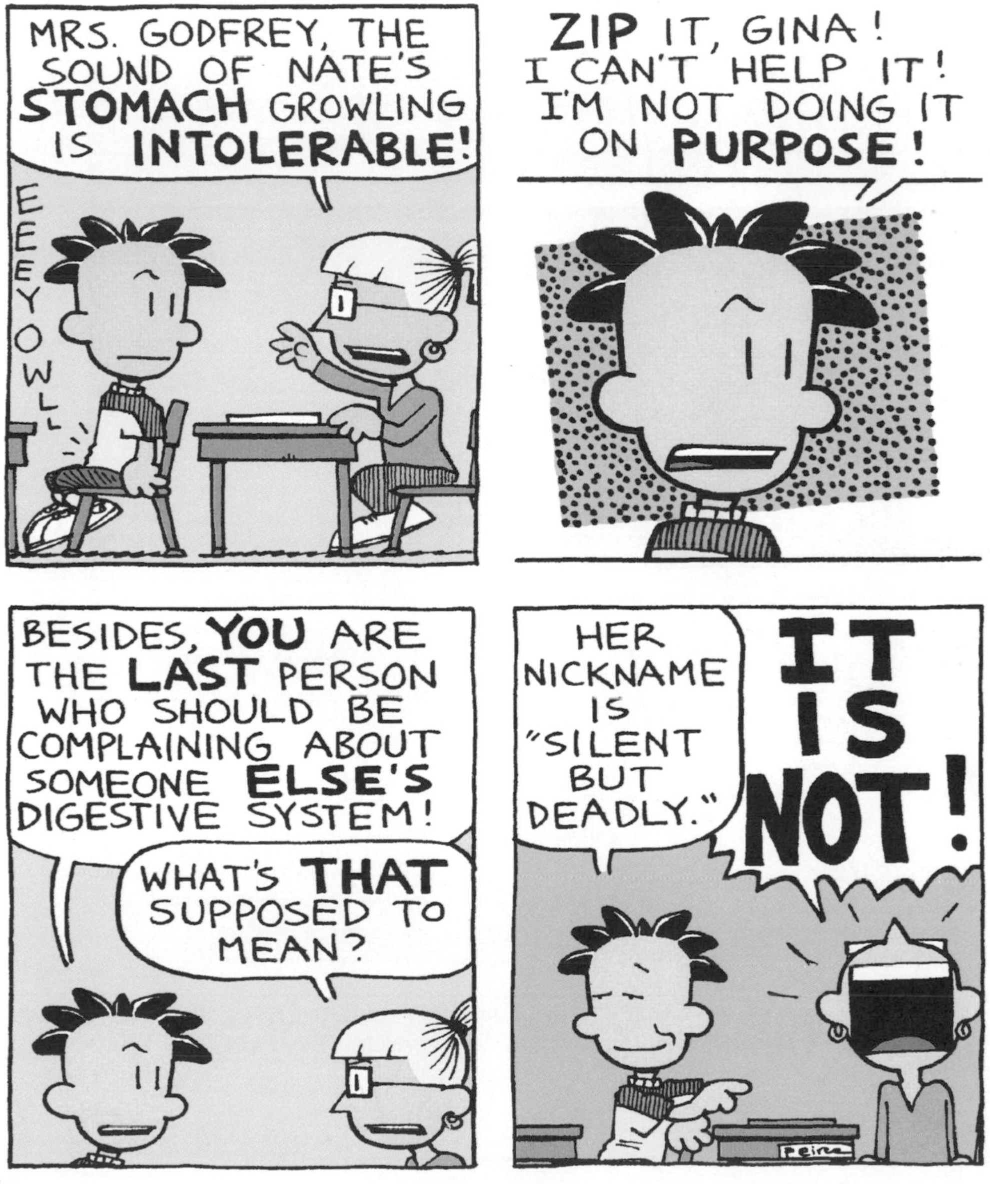
MRS. GODFREY, THE SOUND OF NATE'S **STOMACH** GROWLING IS **INTOLERABLE!**
EEEEYOWLLL
ZIP IT, GINA! I CAN'T HELP IT! I'M NOT DOING IT ON **PURPOSE!**
BESIDES, **YOU** ARE THE **LAST** PERSON WHO SHOULD BE COMPLAINING ABOUT SOMEONE **ELSE'S** DIGESTIVE SYSTEM!
WHAT'S **THAT** SUPPOSED TO MEAN?
HER NICKNAME IS "SILENT BUT DEADLY."
IT IS NOT!

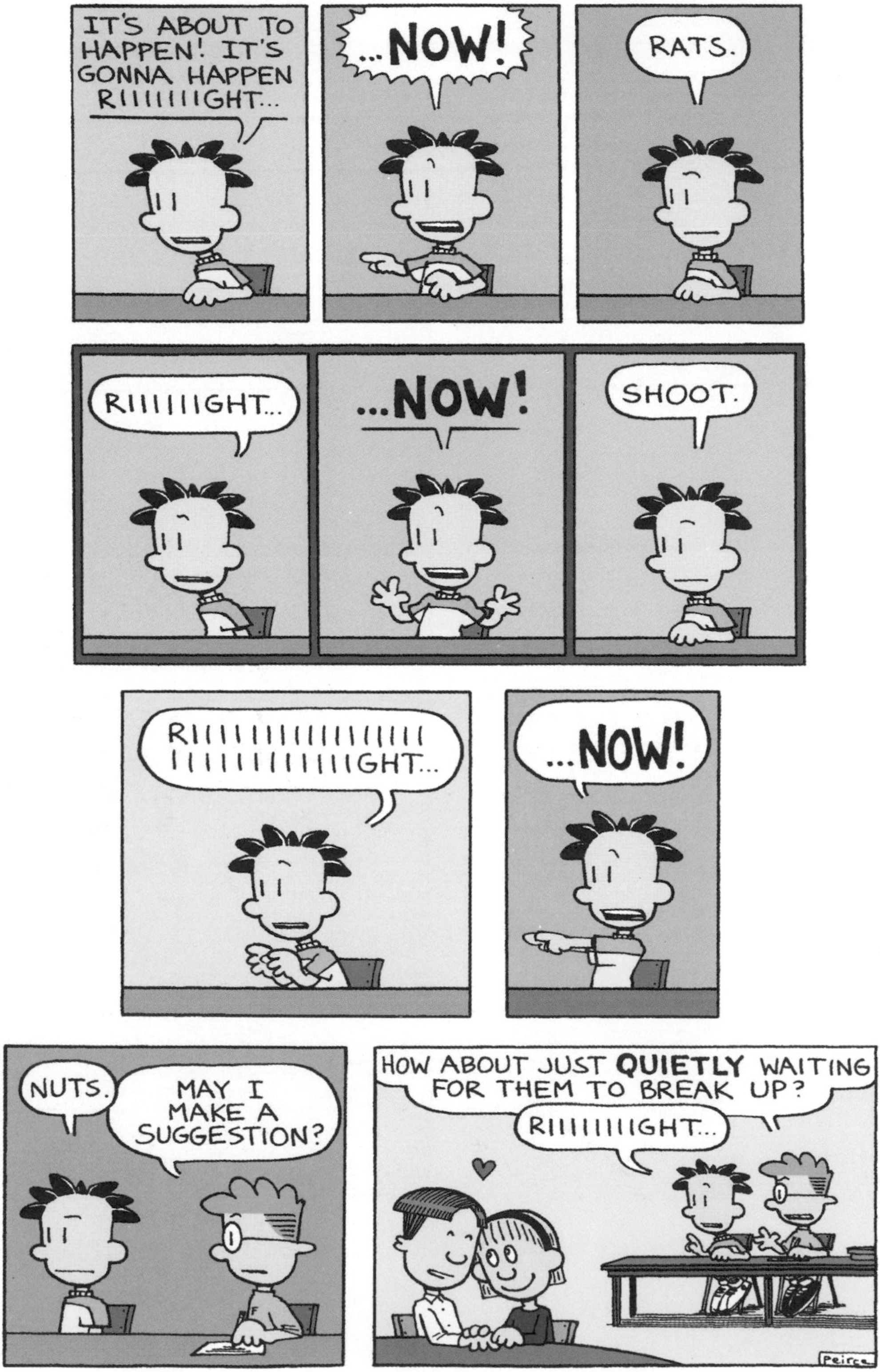
IT'S ABOUT TO HAPPEN! IT'S GONNA HAPPEN RIIIIIIIGHT...
...NOW!
RATS.
RIIIIIIGHT...
...NOW!
SHOOT.
RIIIIIIIIIIIIIIII IIIIIIIIIIIIIGHT...
...NOW!
NUTS.
MAY I MAKE A SUGGESTION?
HOW ABOUT JUST QUIETLY WAITING FOR THEM TO BREAK UP?
RIIIIIIIIGHT...
Peirce

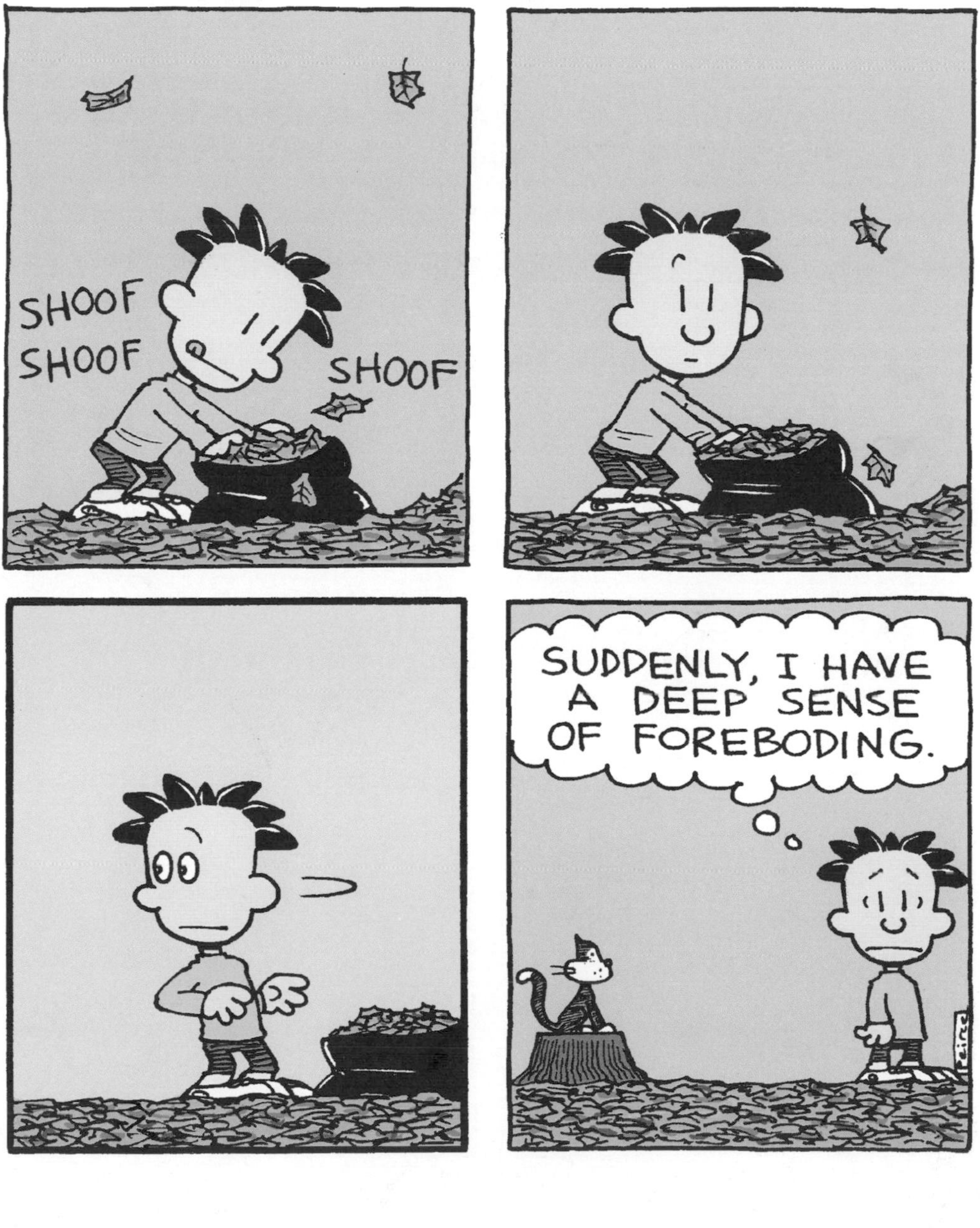
SHOOF
SHOOF
SHOOF
SUDDENLY, I HAVE A DEEP SENSE OF FOREBODING.

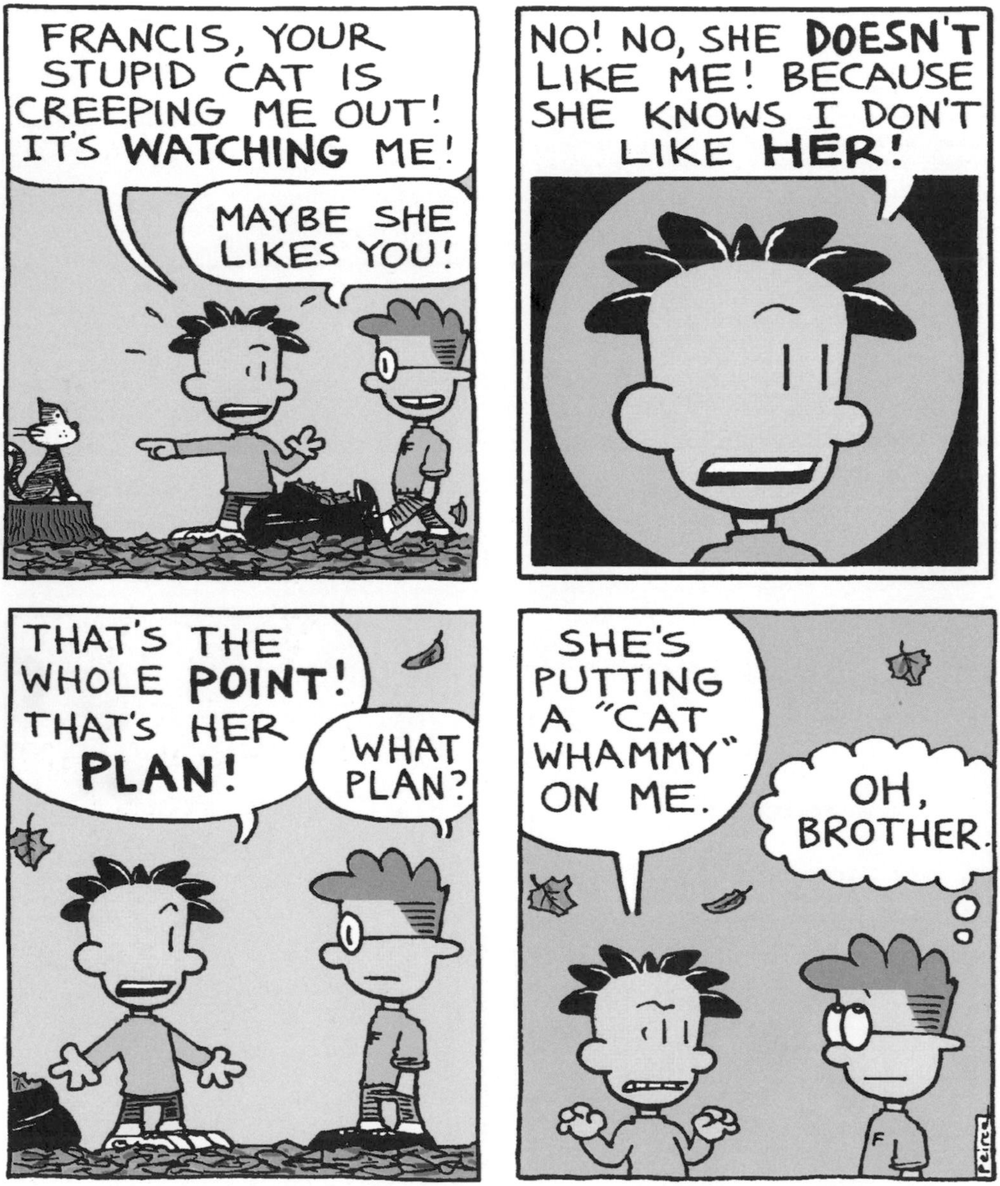
FRANCIS, YOUR STUPID CAT IS CREEPING ME OUT! IT'S **WATCHING** ME!
MAYBE SHE LIKES YOU!
NO! NO, SHE **DOESN'T** LIKE ME! BECAUSE SHE KNOWS I DON'T LIKE **HER**!
THAT'S THE WHOLE **POINT**! THAT'S HER **PLAN**!
WHAT PLAN?
SHE'S PUTTING A "CAT WHAMMY" ON ME.
OH, BROTHER.
PEIRCE

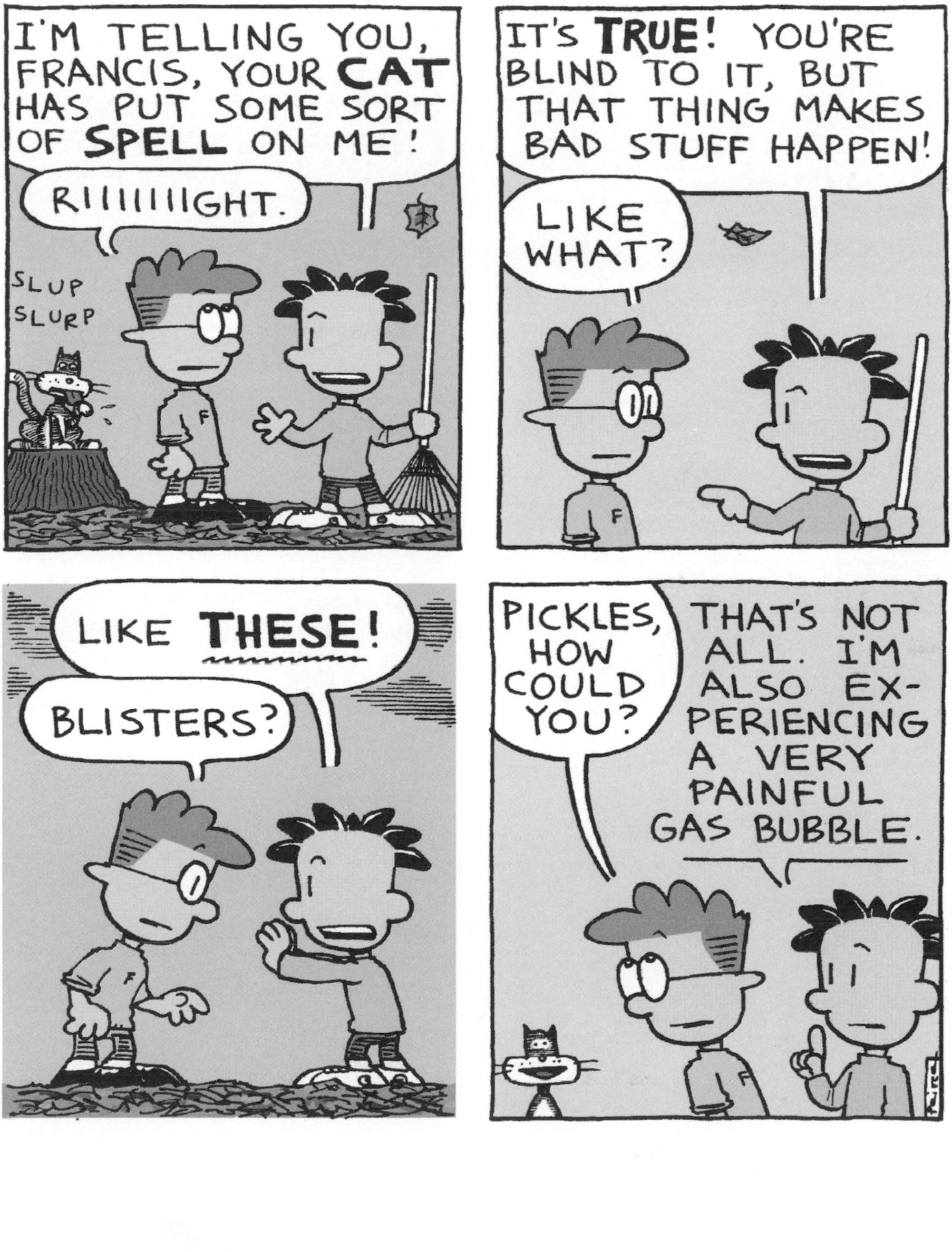
I'M TELLING YOU, FRANCIS, YOUR CAT HAS PUT SOME SORT OF SPELL ON ME!
RIIIIIIIGHT.
SLUP SLURP
IT'S TRUE! YOU'RE BLIND TO IT, BUT THAT THING MAKES BAD STUFF HAPPEN!
LIKE WHAT?
LIKE THESE!
BLISTERS?
THAT'S NOT ALL. I'M ALSO EXPERIENCING A VERY PAINFUL GAS BUBBLE.
PICKLES, HOW COULD YOU?

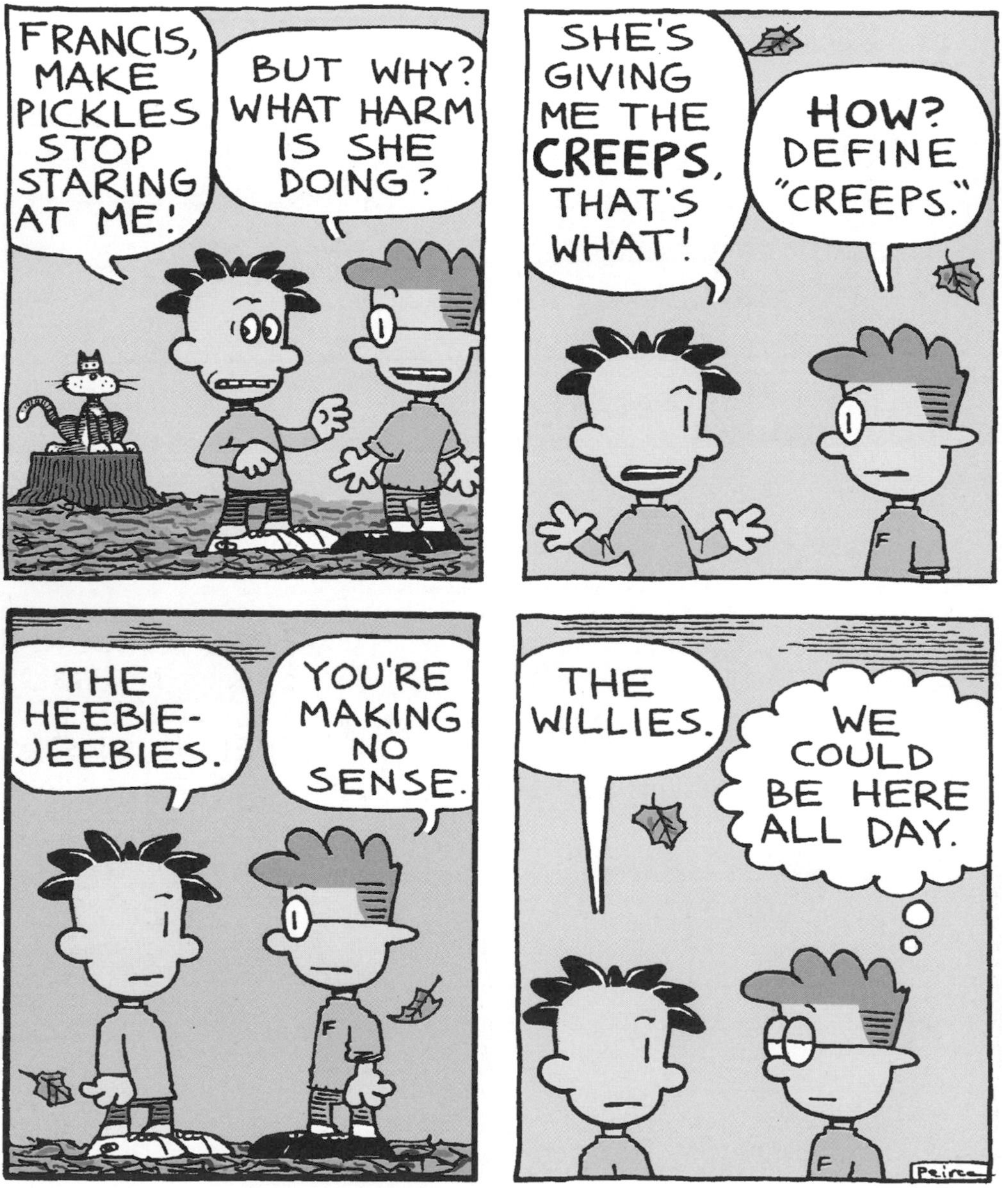
FRANCIS, MAKE PICKLES STOP STARING AT ME!
BUT WHY? WHAT HARM IS SHE DOING?
SHE'S GIVING ME THE CREEPS, THAT'S WHAT!
HOW? DEFINE "CREEPS."
THE HEEBIE-JEEBIES.
YOU'RE MAKING NO SENSE.
THE WILLIES.
WE COULD BE HERE ALL DAY.
Peirce

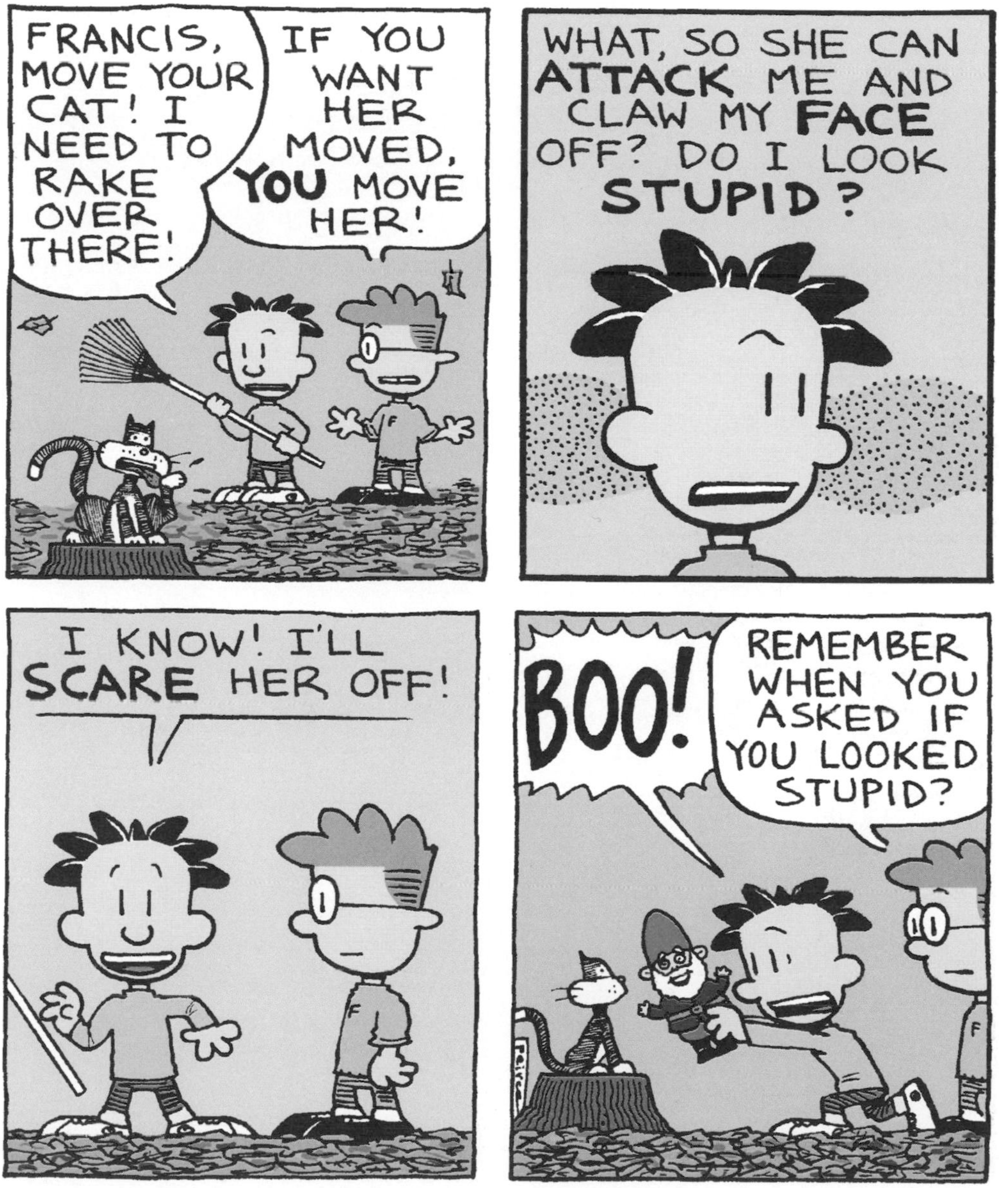
FRANCIS, MOVE YOUR CAT! I NEED TO RAKE OVER THERE!
IF YOU WANT HER MOVED, **YOU** MOVE HER!
WHAT, SO SHE CAN **ATTACK** ME AND CLAW MY **FACE** OFF? DO I LOOK **STUPID**?
I KNOW! I'LL **SCARE** HER OFF!
BOO!
REMEMBER WHEN YOU ASKED IF YOU LOOKED STUPID?
Peirce

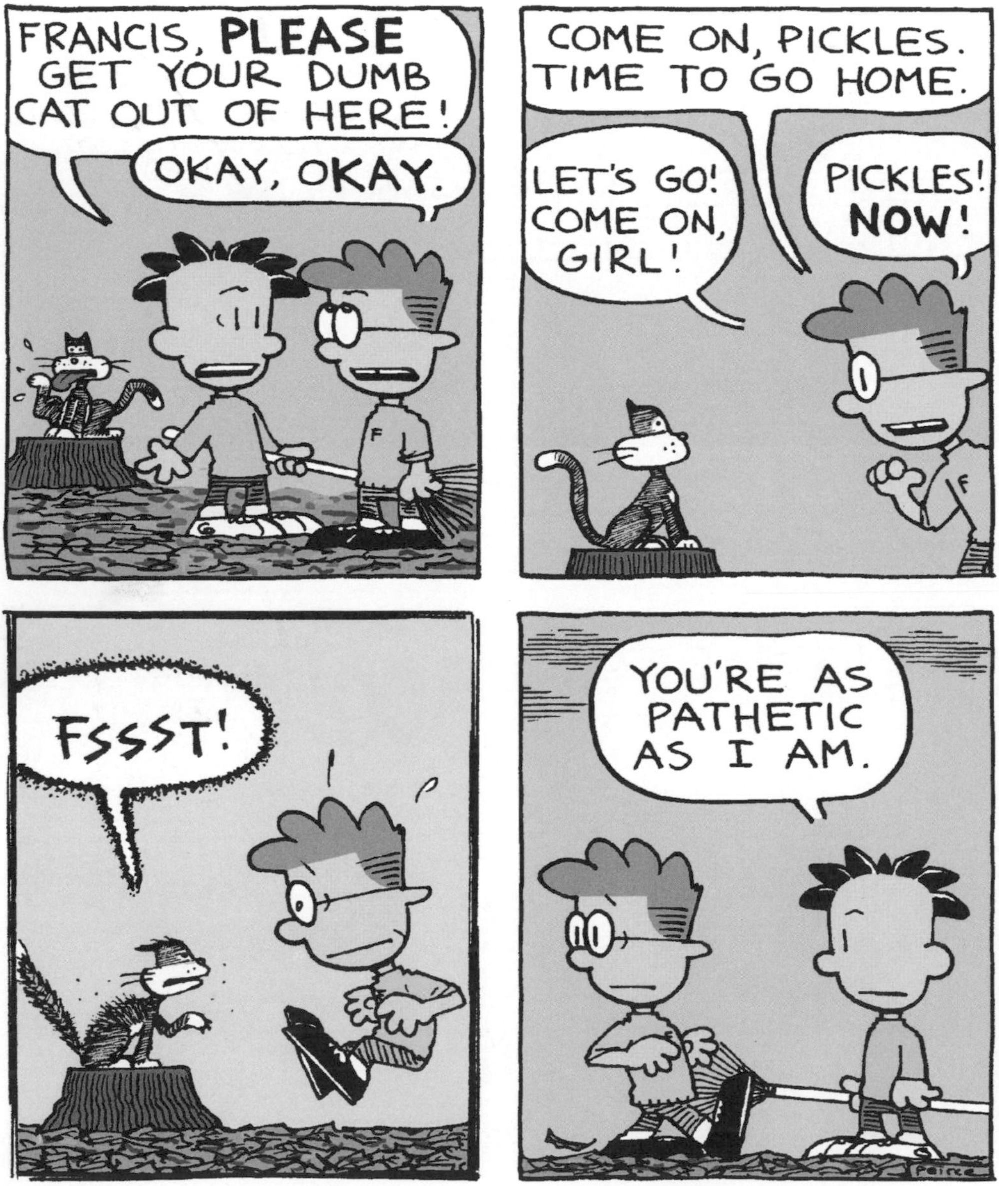
FRANCIS, PLEASE GET YOUR DUMB CAT OUT OF HERE!
OKAY, OKAY.
COME ON, PICKLES. TIME TO GO HOME.
LET'S GO! COME ON, GIRL!
PICKLES! NOW!
FSSST!
YOU'RE AS PATHETIC AS I AM.
Peirce

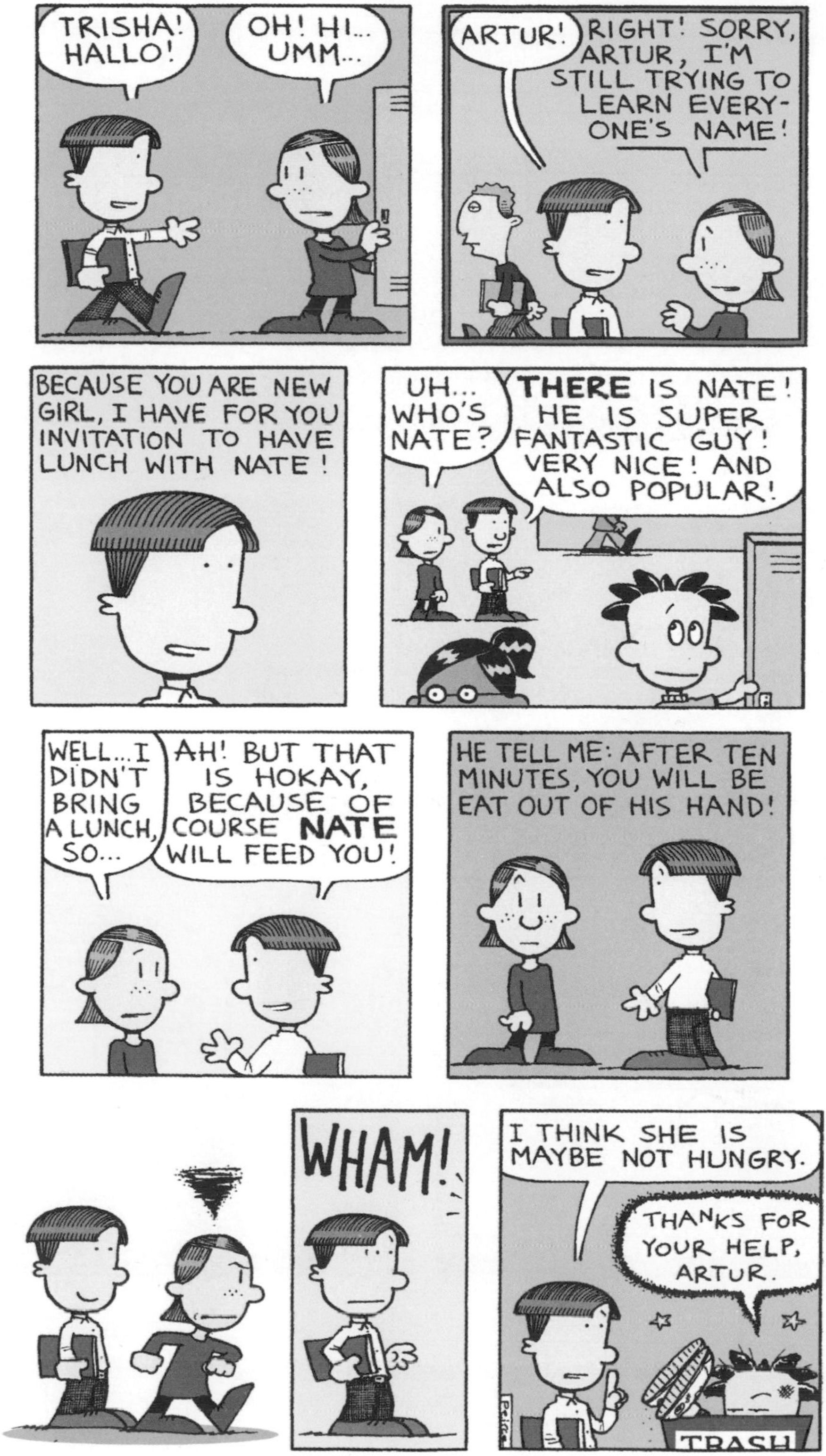
TRISHA! HALLO!
OH! HI... UMM...
ARTUR!
RIGHT! SORRY, ARTUR, I'M STILL TRYING TO LEARN EVERY-ONE'S NAME!
BECAUSE YOU ARE NEW GIRL, I HAVE FOR YOU INVITATION TO HAVE LUNCH WITH NATE!
UH... WHO'S NATE?
THERE IS NATE! HE IS SUPER FANTASTIC GUY! VERY NICE! AND ALSO POPULAR!
WELL...I DIDN'T BRING A LUNCH, SO...
AH! BUT THAT IS HOKAY, BECAUSE OF COURSE NATE WILL FEED YOU!
HE TELL ME: AFTER TEN MINUTES, YOU WILL BE EAT OUT OF HIS HAND!
WHAM!
I THINK SHE IS MAYBE NOT HUNGRY.
THANKS FOR YOUR HELP, ARTUR.
TRASH

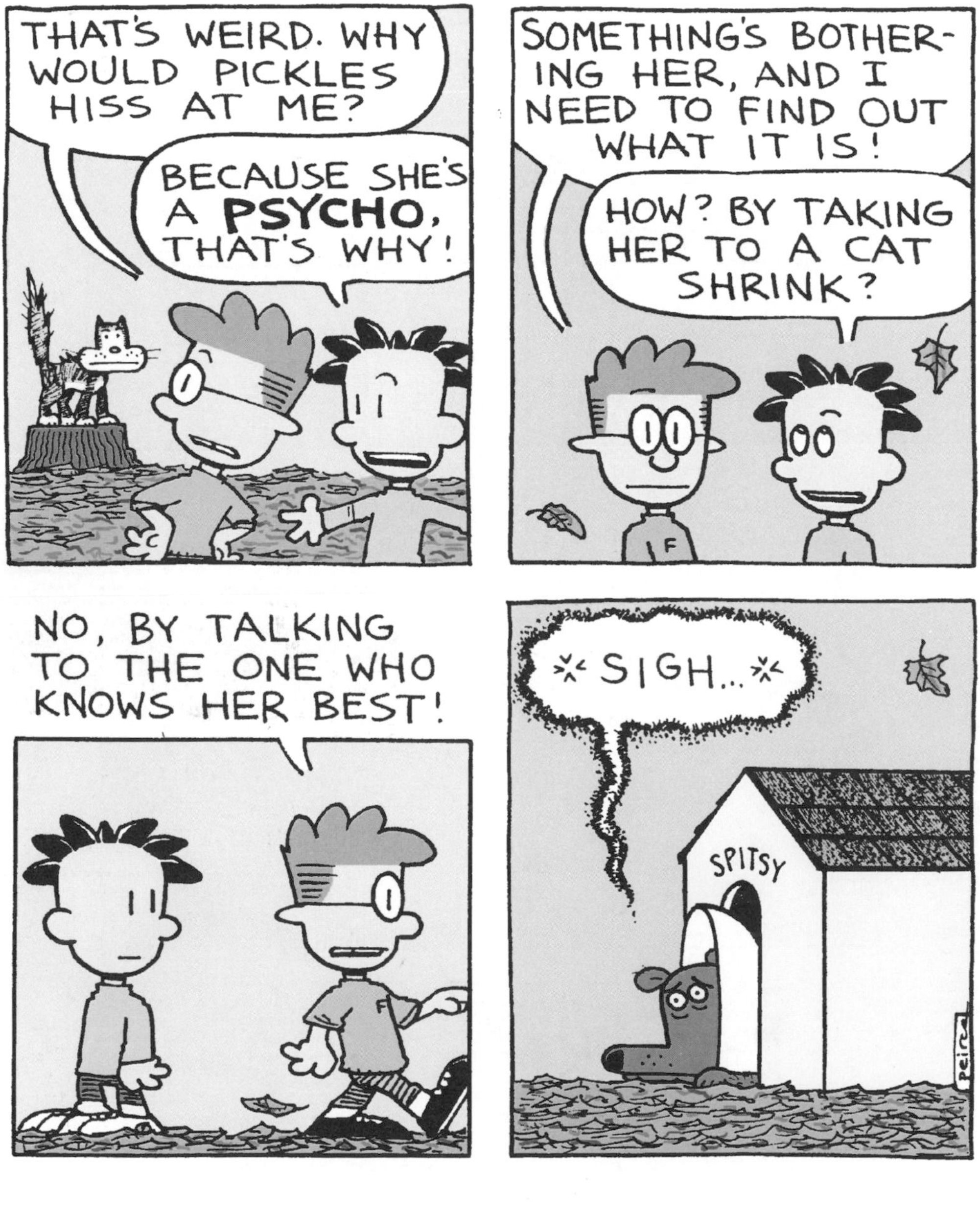
THAT'S WEIRD. WHY WOULD PICKLES HISS AT ME?
BECAUSE SHE'S A **PSYCHO**, THAT'S WHY!
SOMETHING'S BOTHER-ING HER, AND I NEED TO FIND OUT WHAT IT IS!
HOW? BY TAKING HER TO A CAT SHRINK?
NO, BY TALKING TO THE ONE WHO KNOWS HER BEST!
SIGH...
SPITSY
peirce

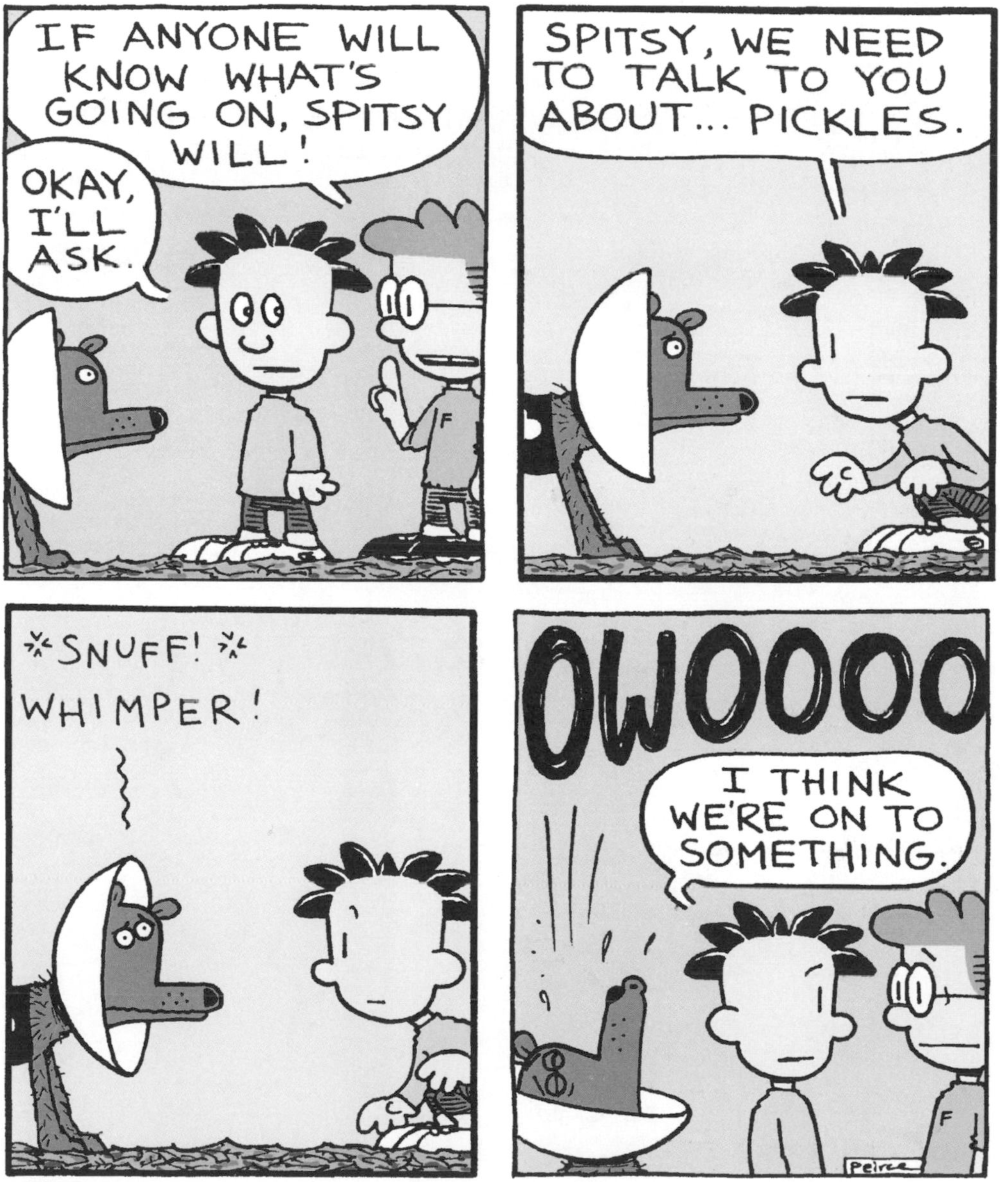
IF ANYONE WILL KNOW WHAT'S GOING ON, SPITSY WILL!
OKAY, I'LL ASK.
SPITSY, WE NEED TO TALK TO YOU ABOUT... PICKLES.
SNUFF!
WHIMPER!
OWOOOO
I THINK WE'RE ON TO SOMETHING.
Peirce

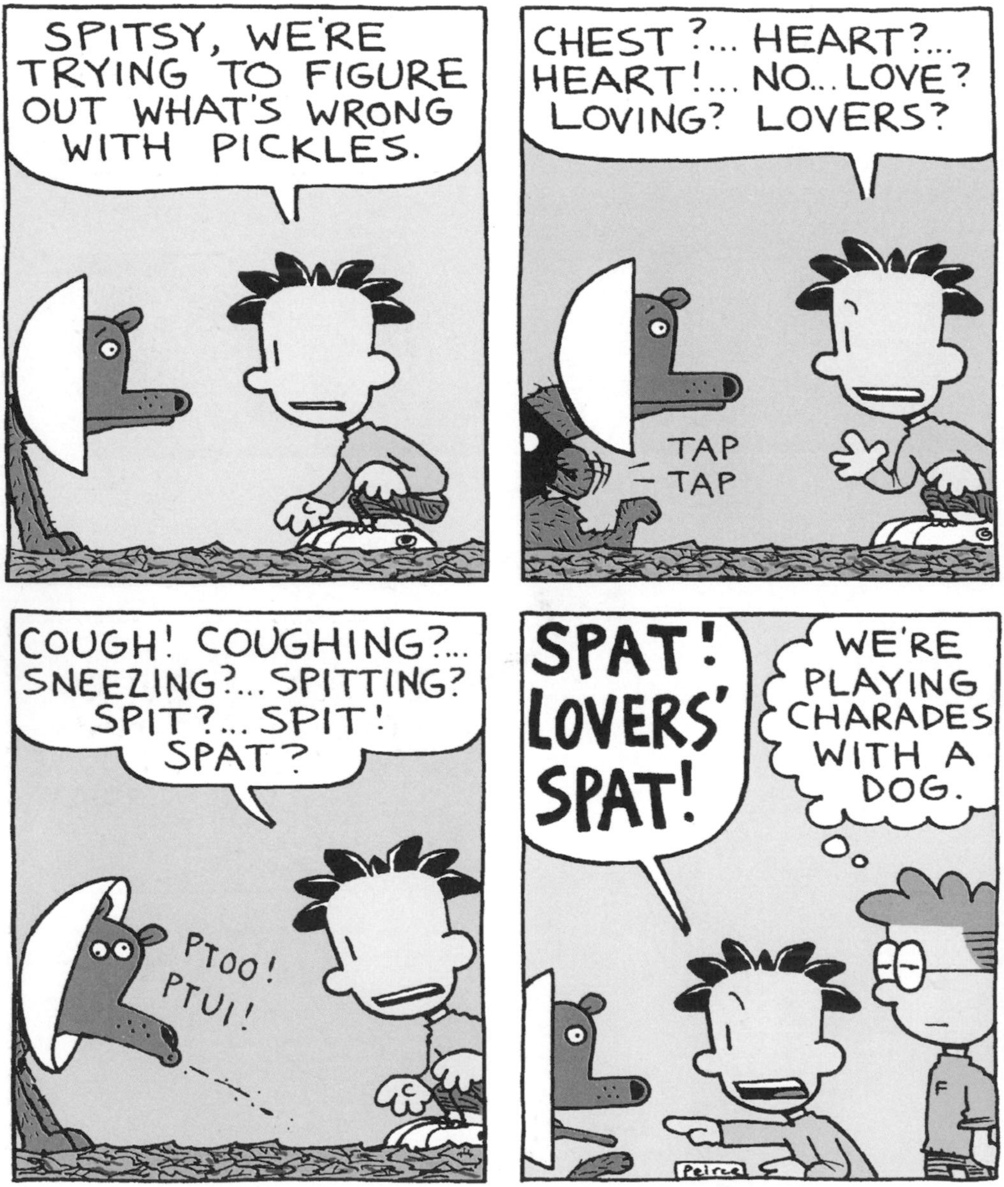
SPITSY, WE'RE TRYING TO FIGURE OUT WHAT'S WRONG WITH PICKLES.
CHEST?... HEART?... HEART!... NO... LOVE? LOVING? LOVERS?
TAP TAP
COUGH! COUGHING?... SNEEZING?... SPITTING? SPIT?... SPIT! SPAT?
PTOO! PTUI!
SPAT! LOVERS' SPAT!
WE'RE PLAYING CHARADES WITH A DOG.
F
Peirce

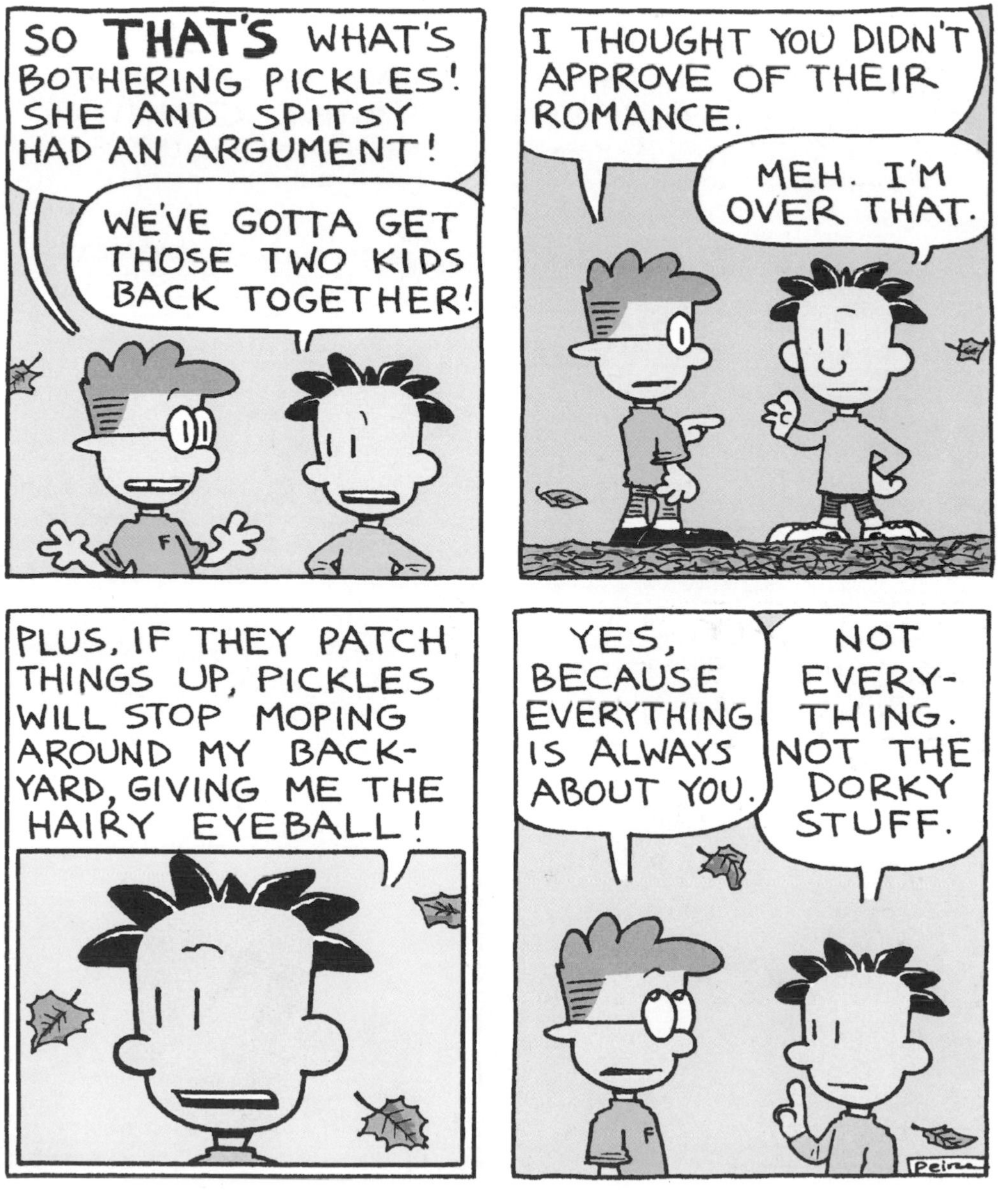
SO THAT'S WHAT'S BOTHERING PICKLES! SHE AND SPITSY HAD AN ARGUMENT!
WE'VE GOTTA GET THOSE TWO KIDS BACK TOGETHER!
I THOUGHT YOU DIDN'T APPROVE OF THEIR ROMANCE.
MEH. I'M OVER THAT.
PLUS, IF THEY PATCH THINGS UP, PICKLES WILL STOP MOPING AROUND MY BACK-YARD, GIVING ME THE HAIRY EYEBALL!
YES, BECAUSE EVERYTHING IS ALWAYS ABOUT YOU.
NOT EVERY-THING. NOT THE DORKY STUFF.
F
F
Peirce

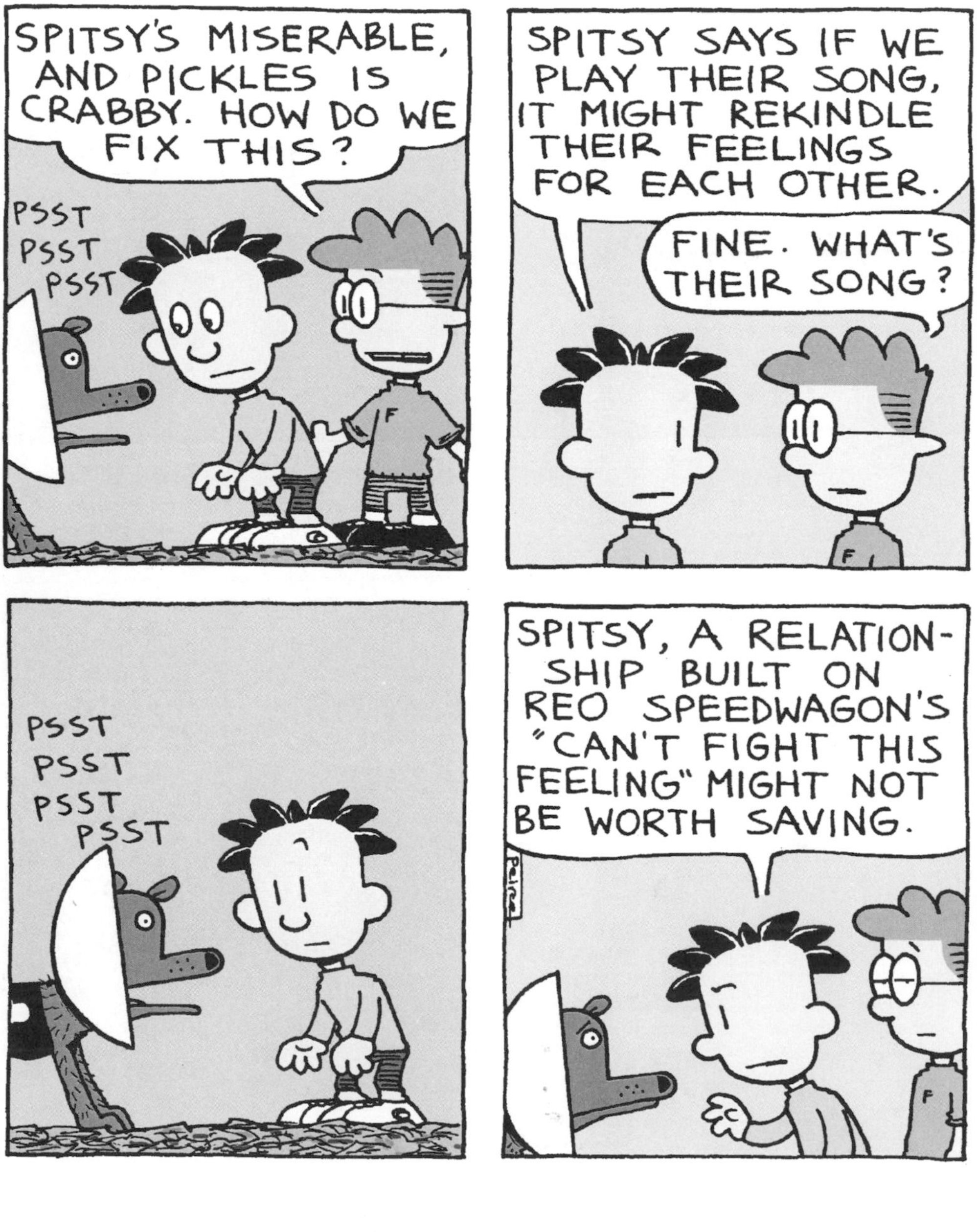
SPITSY'S MISERABLE, AND PICKLES IS CRABBY. HOW DO WE FIX THIS?
PSST PSST PSST
SPITSY SAYS IF WE PLAY THEIR SONG, IT MIGHT REKINDLE THEIR FEELINGS FOR EACH OTHER.
FINE. WHAT'S THEIR SONG?
PSST PSST PSST PSST
SPITSY, A RELATION-SHIP BUILT ON REO SPEEDWAGON'S "CAN'T FIGHT THIS FEELING" MIGHT NOT BE WORTH SAVING.
Peirce

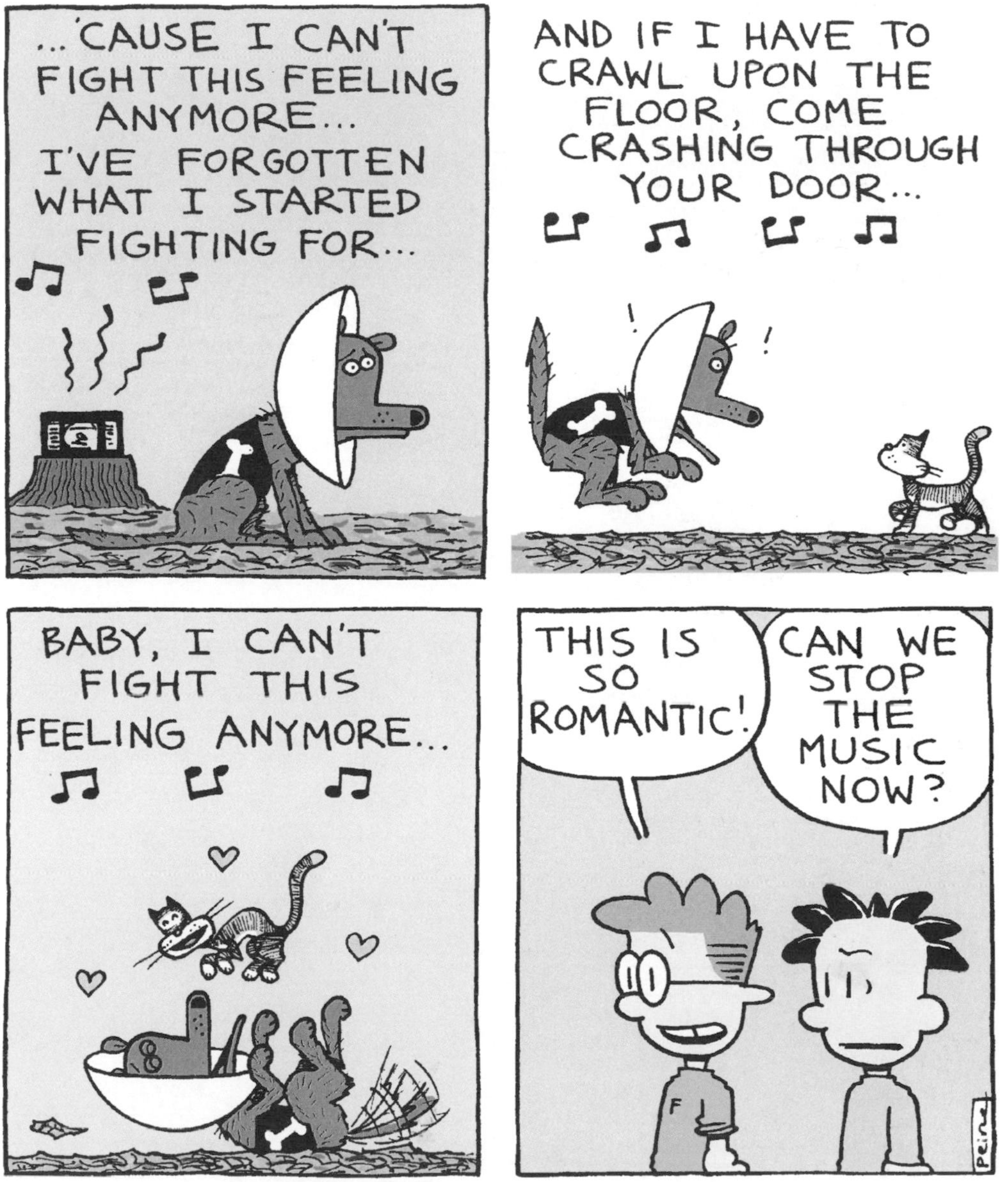

...'CAUSE I CAN'T FIGHT THIS FEELING ANYMORE...
I'VE FORGOTTEN WHAT I STARTED FIGHTING FOR...
AND IF I HAVE TO CRAWL UPON THE FLOOR, COME CRASHING THROUGH YOUR DOOR...
!
!
BABY, I CAN'T FIGHT THIS FEELING ANYMORE...
THIS IS SO ROMANTIC!
CAN WE STOP THE MUSIC NOW?
F
Peirce

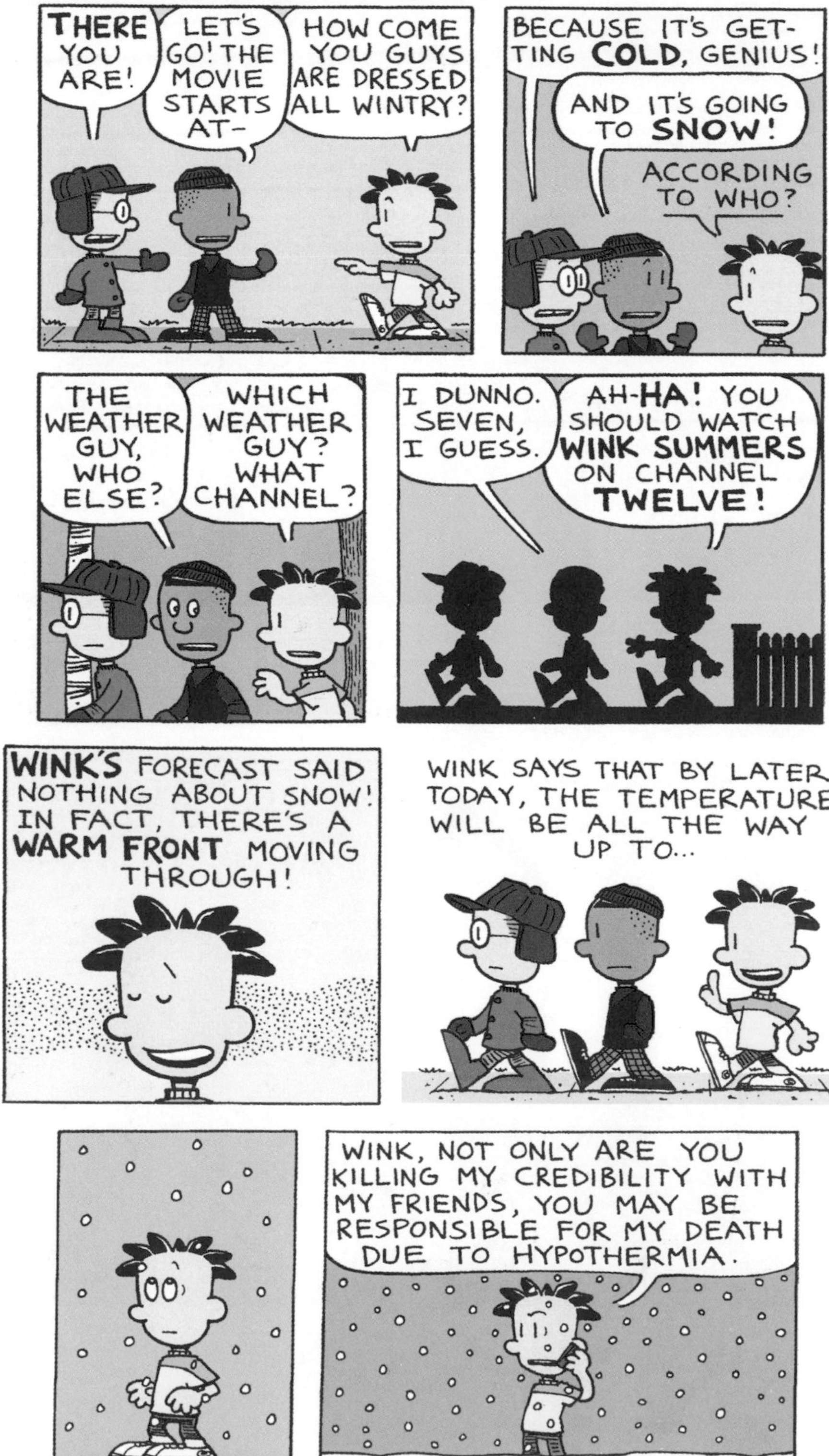
THERE YOU ARE!
LET'S GO! THE MOVIE STARTS AT-
HOW COME YOU GUYS ARE DRESSED ALL WINTRY?
BECAUSE IT'S GETTING COLD, GENIUS!
AND IT'S GOING TO SNOW!
ACCORDING TO WHO?
THE WEATHER GUY, WHO ELSE?
WHICH WEATHER GUY? WHAT CHANNEL?
I DUNNO. SEVEN, I GUESS.
AH-HA! YOU SHOULD WATCH WINK SUMMERS ON CHANNEL TWELVE!
WINK'S FORECAST SAID NOTHING ABOUT SNOW! IN FACT, THERE'S A WARM FRONT MOVING THROUGH!
WINK SAYS THAT BY LATER TODAY, THE TEMPERATURE WILL BE ALL THE WAY UP TO...
WINK, NOT ONLY ARE YOU KILLING MY CREDIBILITY WITH MY FRIENDS, YOU MAY BE RESPONSIBLE FOR MY DEATH DUE TO HYPOTHERMIA.

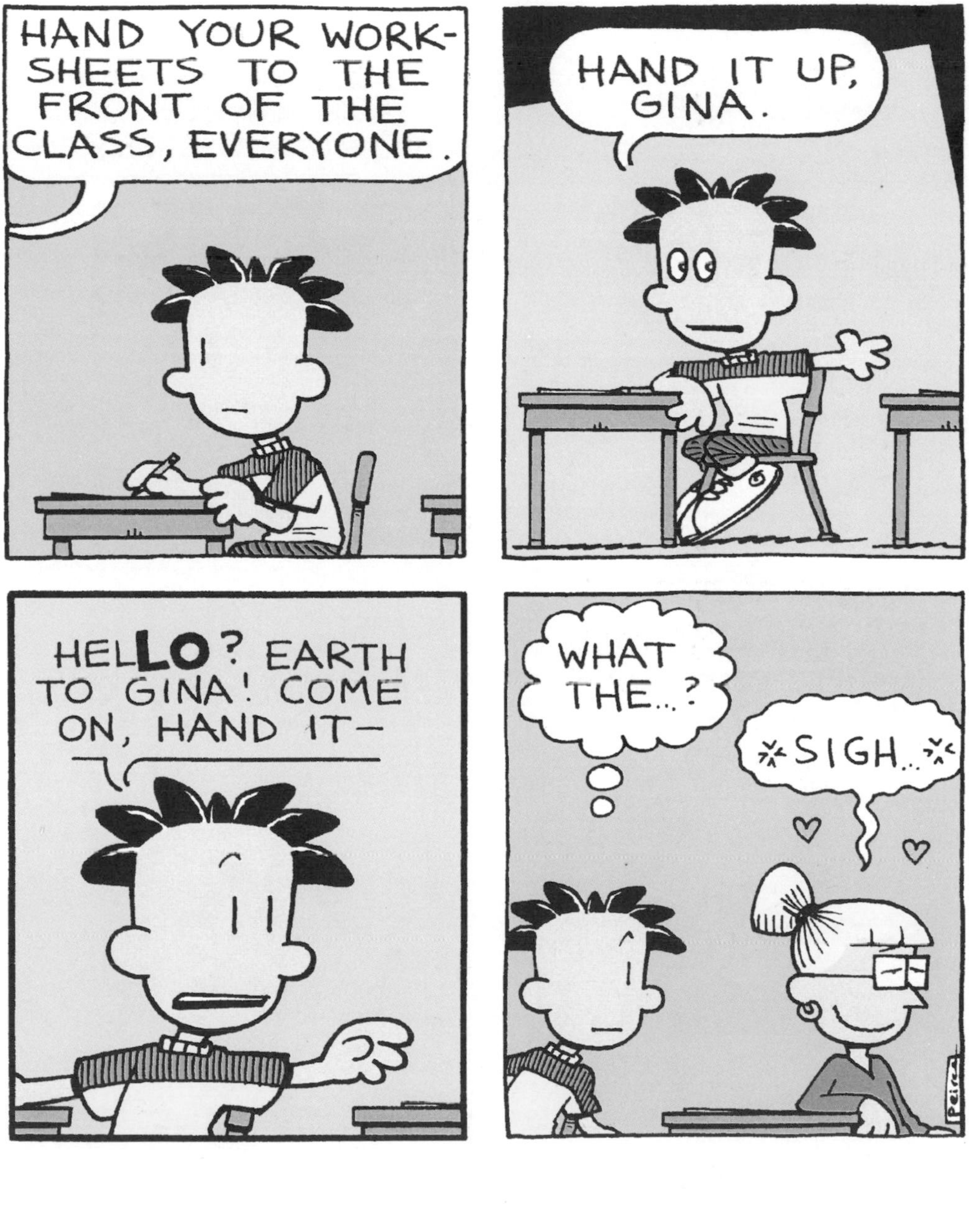
HAND YOUR WORK-SHEETS TO THE FRONT OF THE CLASS, EVERYONE.
HAND IT UP, GINA.
HELLO? EARTH TO GINA! COME ON, HAND IT—
WHAT THE...?
SIGH...

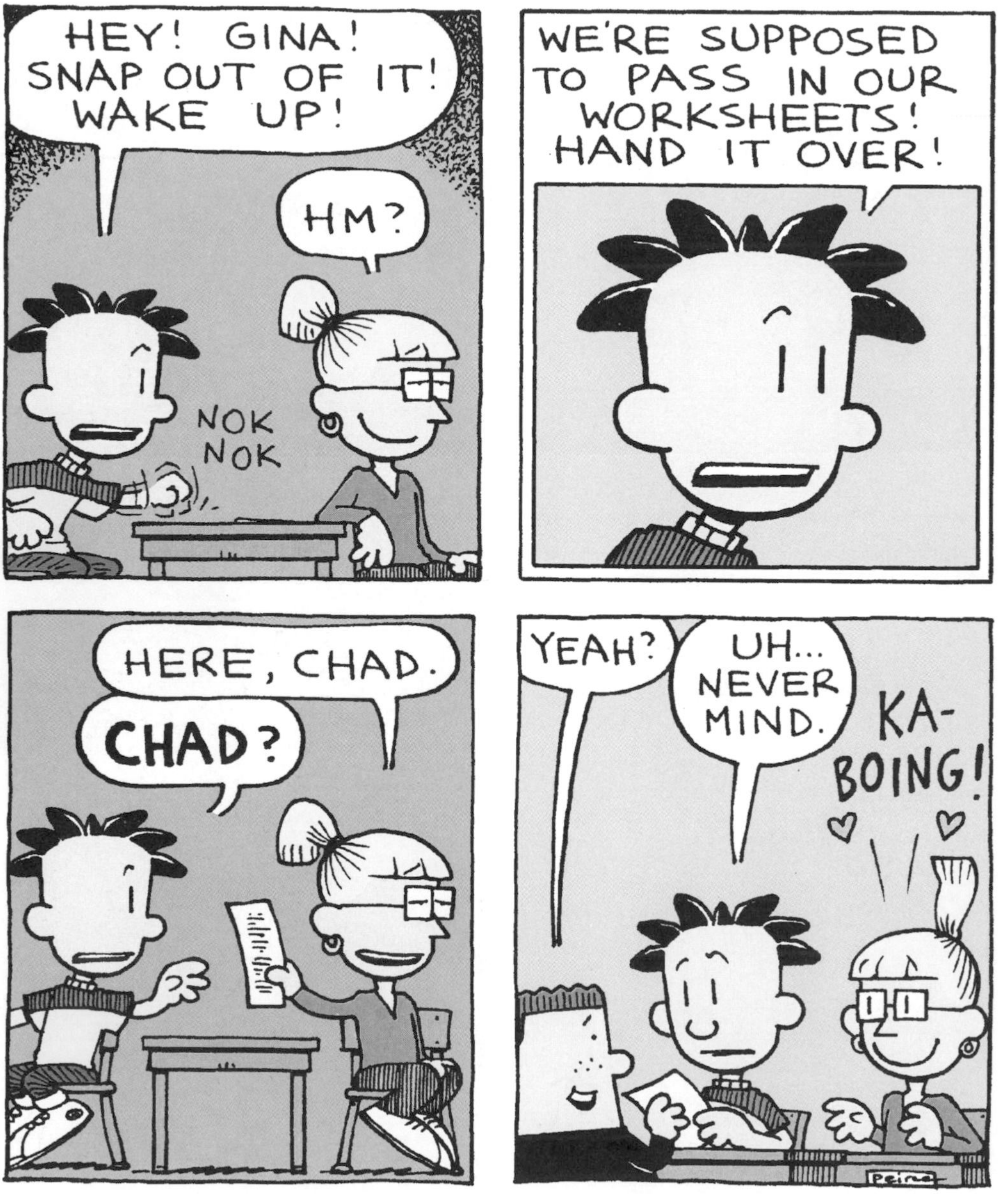
HEY! GINA! SNAP OUT OF IT! WAKE UP!
HM?
NOK NOK
WE'RE SUPPOSED TO PASS IN OUR WORKSHEETS! HAND IT OVER!
HERE, CHAD.
CHAD?
YEAH?
UH... NEVER MIND.
KA-BOING!

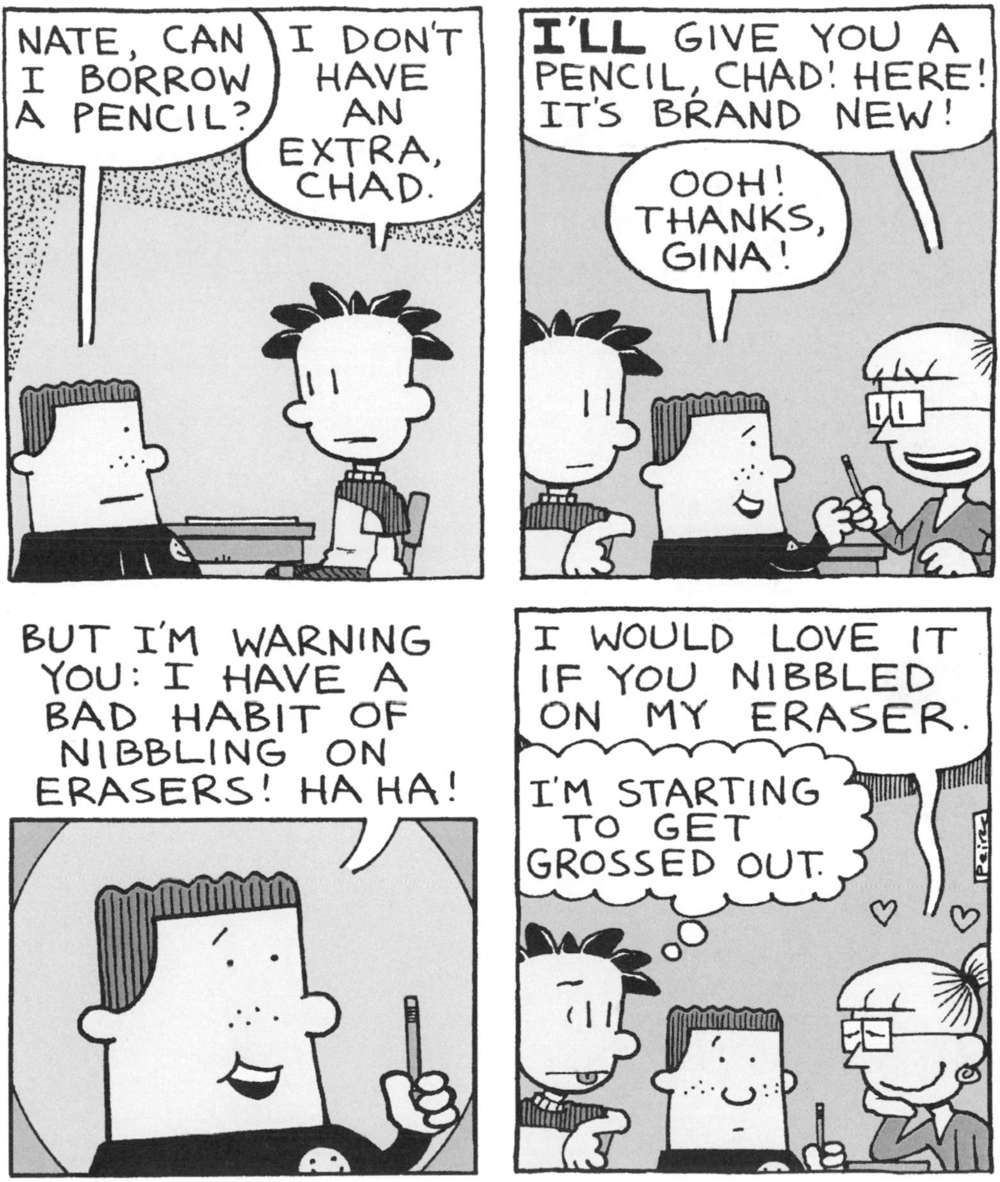
NATE, CAN I BORROW A PENCIL?
I DON'T HAVE AN EXTRA, CHAD.
I'LL GIVE YOU A PENCIL, CHAD! HERE! IT'S BRAND NEW!
OOH! THANKS, GINA!
BUT I'M WARNING YOU: I HAVE A BAD HABIT OF NIBBLING ON ERASERS! HA HA!
I WOULD LOVE IT IF YOU NIBBLED ON MY ERASER.
I'M STARTING TO GET GROSSED OUT.

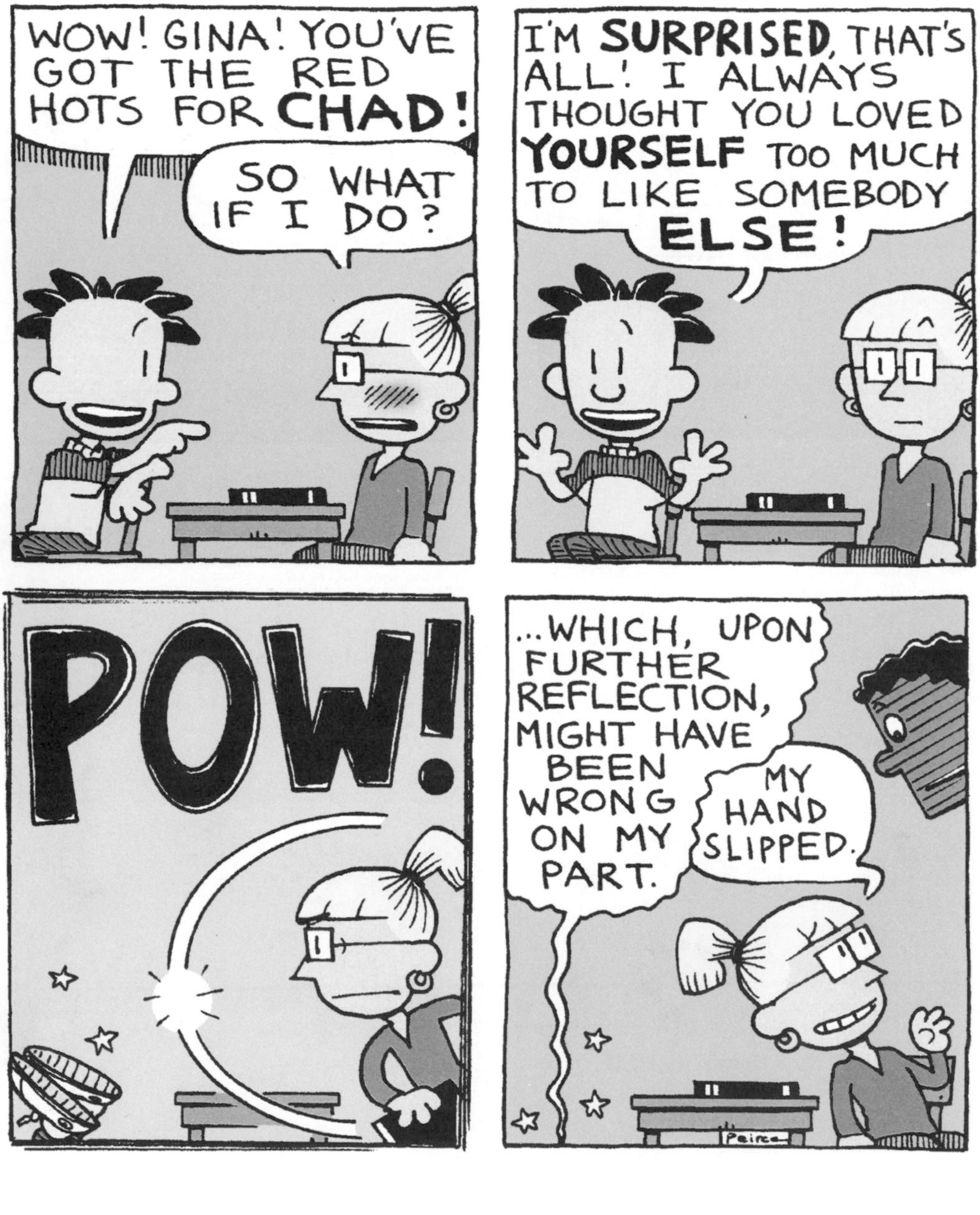
WOW! GINA! YOU'VE GOT THE RED HOTS FOR CHAD!
SO WHAT IF I DO?
I'M SURPRISED, THAT'S ALL! I ALWAYS THOUGHT YOU LOVED YOURSELF TOO MUCH TO LIKE SOMEBODY ELSE!
POW!
...WHICH, UPON FURTHER REFLECTION, MIGHT HAVE BEEN WRONG ON MY PART.
MY HAND SLIPPED.
Peirce

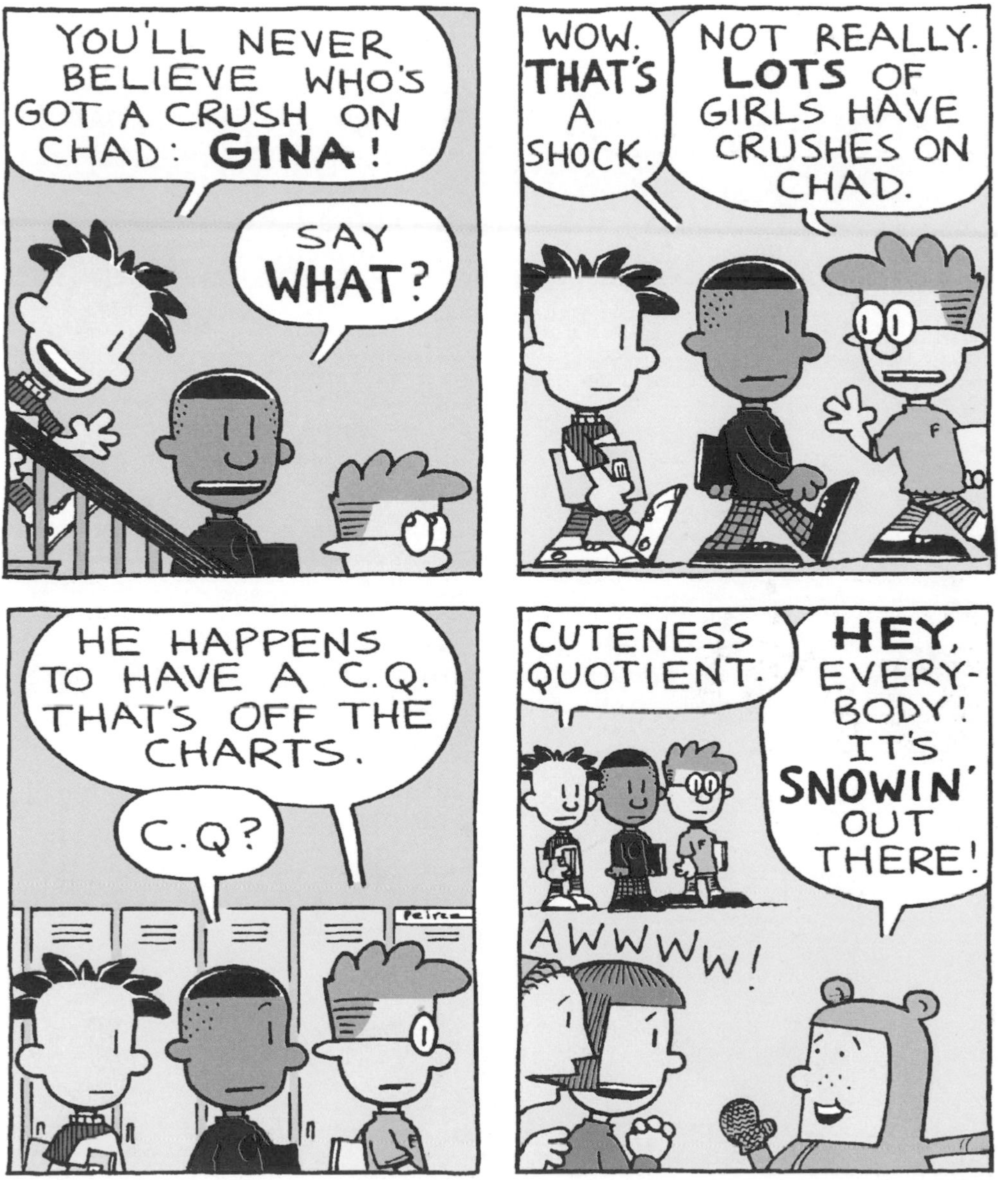
YOU'LL NEVER BELIEVE WHO'S GOT A CRUSH ON CHAD: GINA!
SAY WHAT?
WOW. THAT'S A SHOCK.
NOT REALLY. LOTS OF GIRLS HAVE CRUSHES ON CHAD.
HE HAPPENS TO HAVE A C.Q. THAT'S OFF THE CHARTS.
C.Q?
CUTENESS QUOTIENT.
HEY, EVERY-BODY! IT'S SNOWIN' OUT THERE!
AWWWWW!

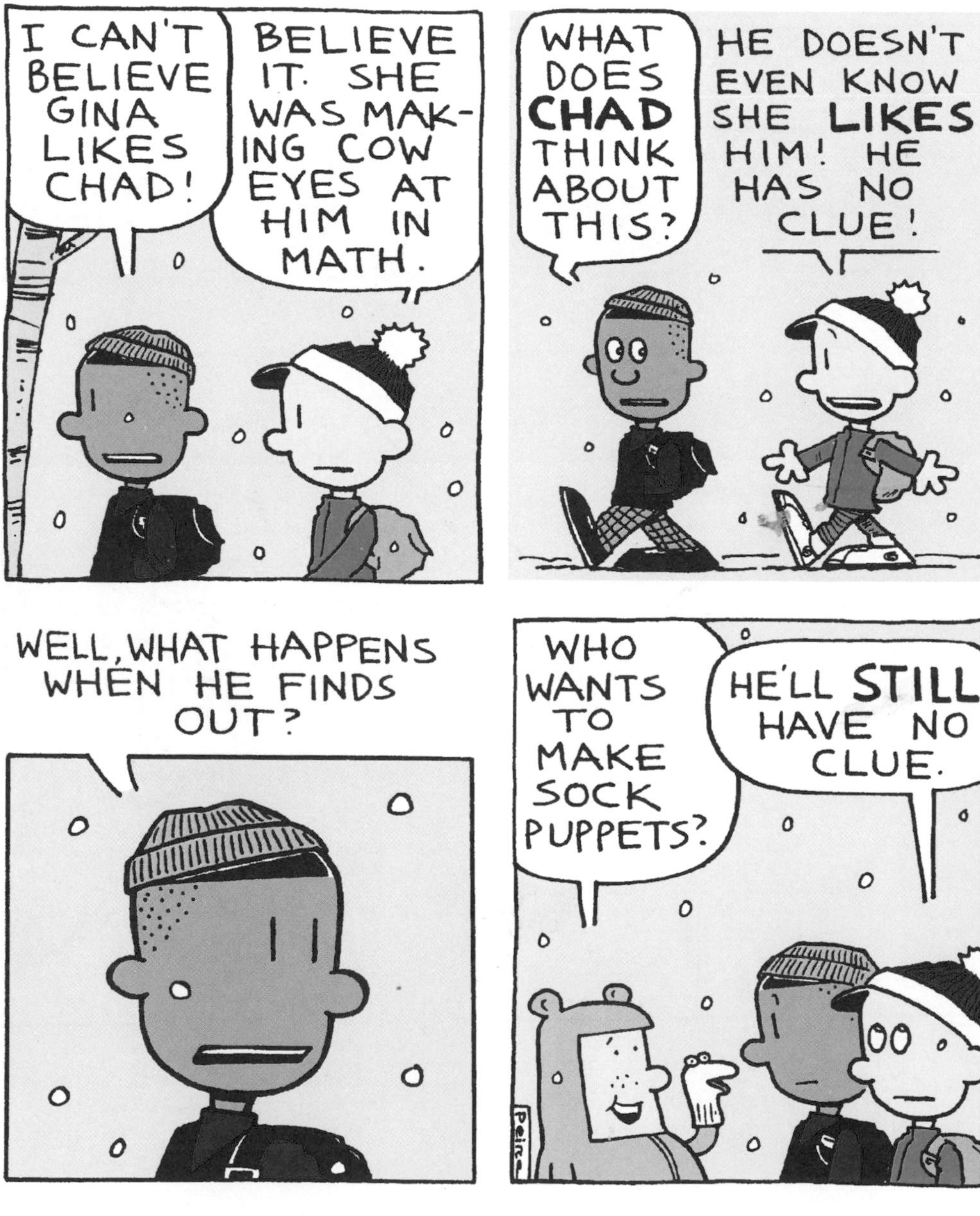
I CAN'T BELIEVE GINA LIKES CHAD!
BELIEVE IT. SHE WAS MAKING COW EYES AT HIM IN MATH.
WHAT DOES **CHAD** THINK ABOUT THIS?
HE DOESN'T EVEN KNOW SHE **LIKES** HIM! HE HAS NO CLUE!
WELL, WHAT HAPPENS WHEN HE FINDS OUT?
WHO WANTS TO MAKE SOCK PUPPETS?
HE'LL **STILL** HAVE NO CLUE.
Peirce

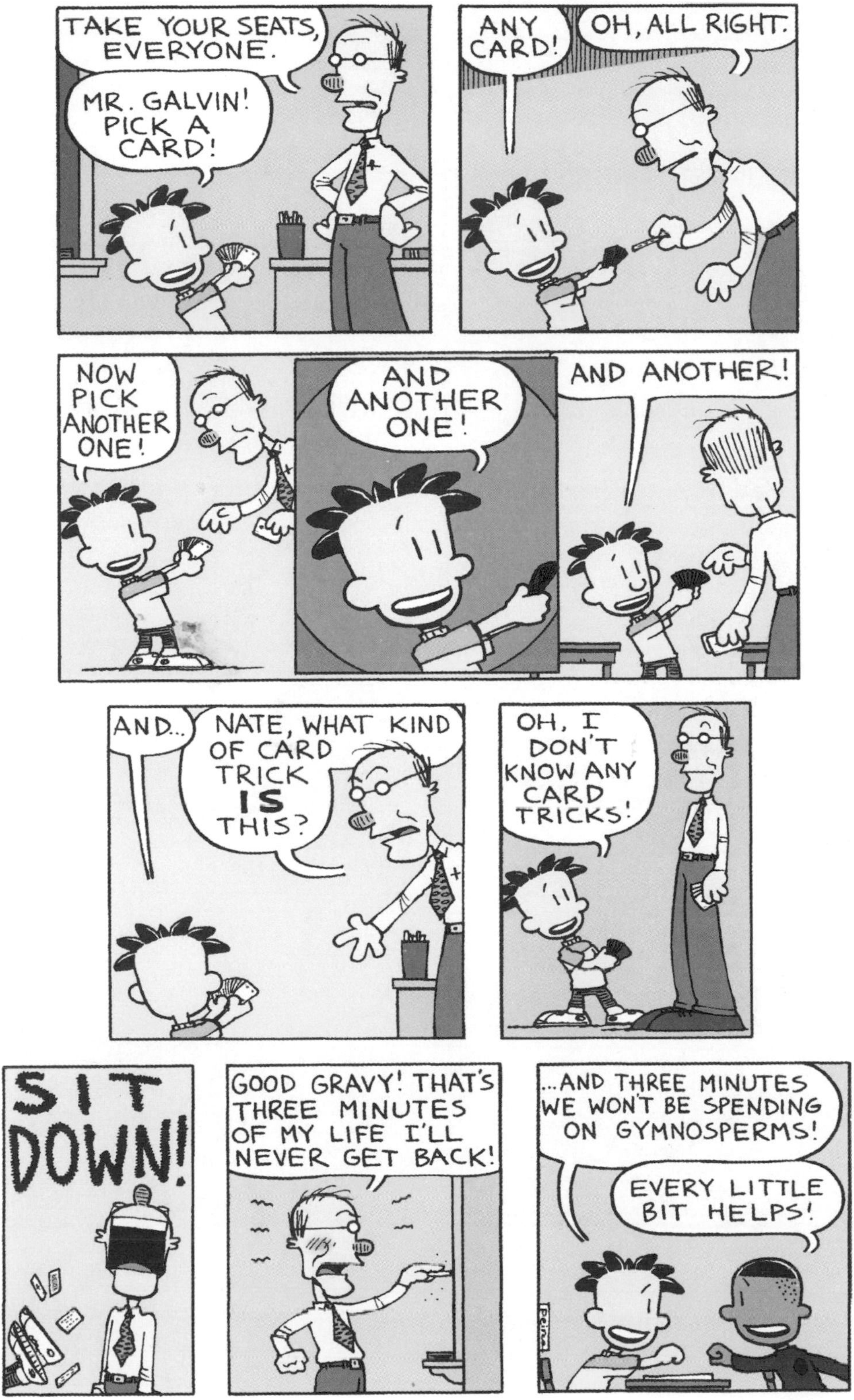
TAKE YOUR SEATS, EVERYONE.
MR. GALVIN! PICK A CARD!
ANY CARD!
OH, ALL RIGHT.
NOW PICK ANOTHER ONE!
AND ANOTHER ONE!
AND ANOTHER!
AND...
NATE, WHAT KIND OF CARD TRICK **IS** THIS?
OH, I DON'T KNOW ANY CARD TRICKS!
SIT DOWN!
GOOD GRAVY! THAT'S THREE MINUTES OF MY LIFE I'LL NEVER GET BACK!
...AND THREE MINUTES WE WON'T BE SPENDING ON GYMNOSPERMS!
EVERY LITTLE BIT HELPS!
Peirce

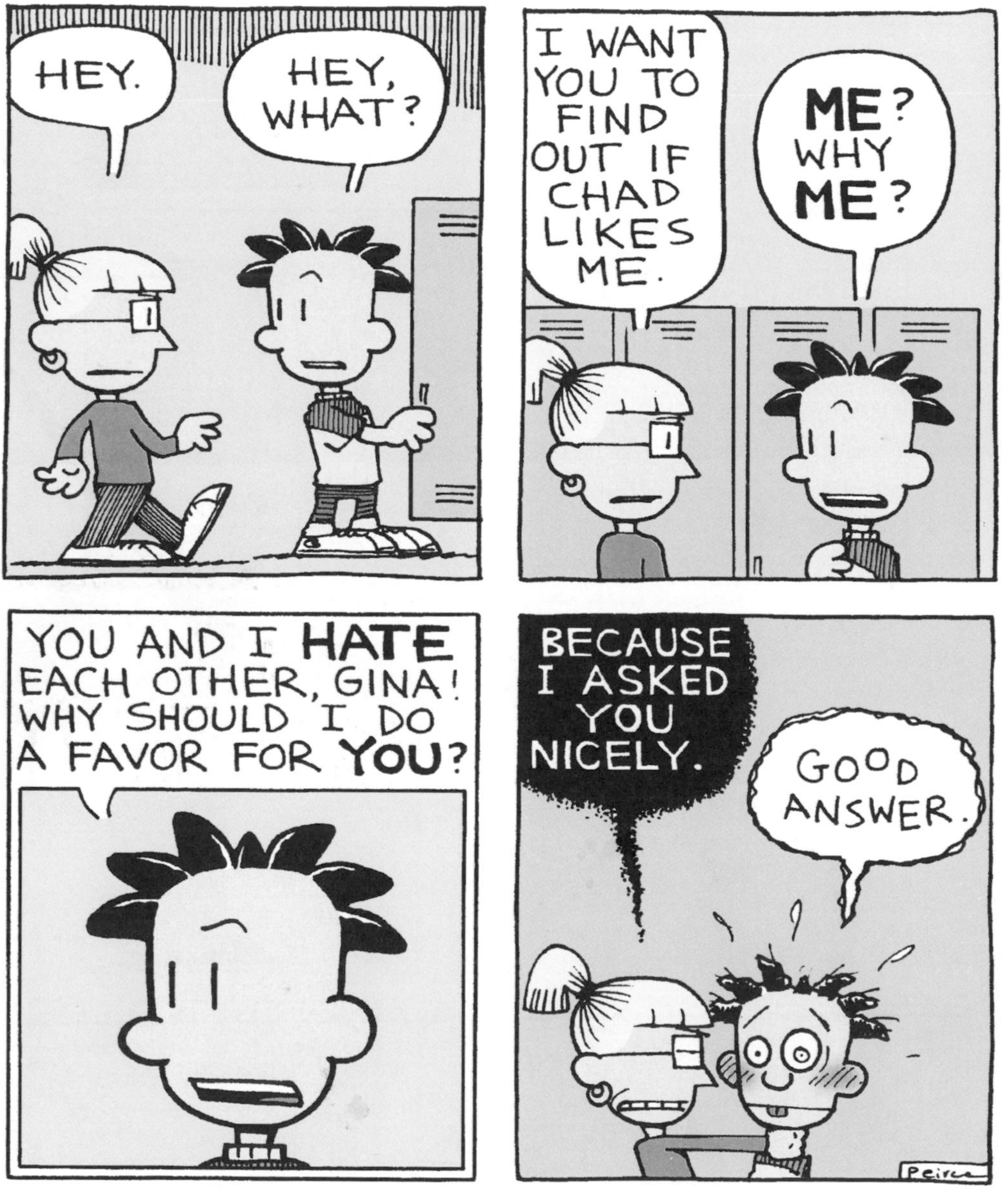
HEY.
HEY, WHAT?
I WANT YOU TO FIND OUT IF CHAD LIKES ME.
ME? WHY ME?
YOU AND I HATE EACH OTHER, GINA! WHY SHOULD I DO A FAVOR FOR YOU?
BECAUSE I ASKED YOU NICELY.
GOOD ANSWER.
Peirce

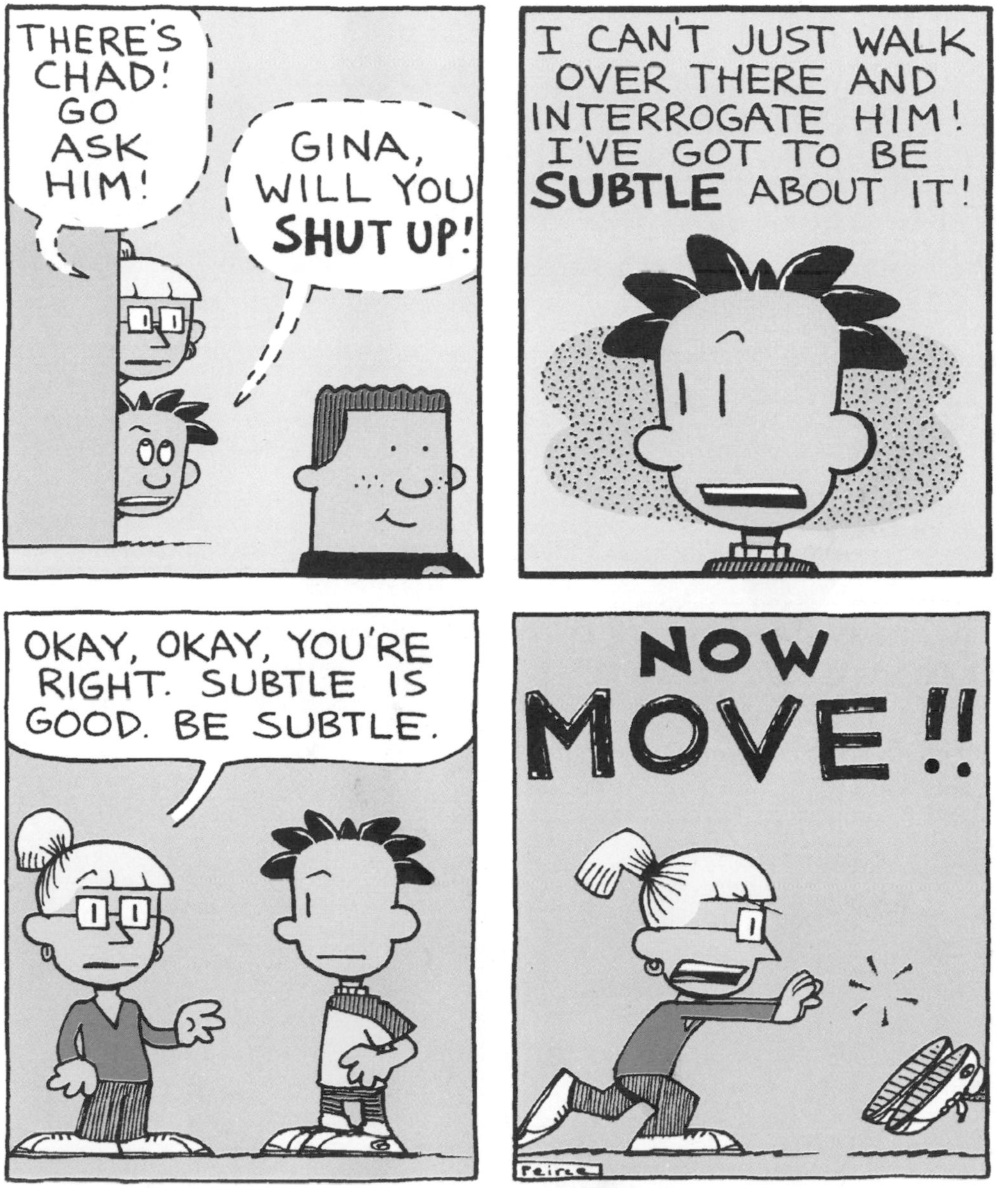
THERE'S CHAD! GO ASK HIM!
GINA, WILL YOU SHUT UP!
I CAN'T JUST WALK OVER THERE AND INTERROGATE HIM! I'VE GOT TO BE SUBTLE ABOUT IT!
OKAY, OKAY, YOU'RE RIGHT. SUBTLE IS GOOD. BE SUBTLE.
NOW MOVE!!
Peirce

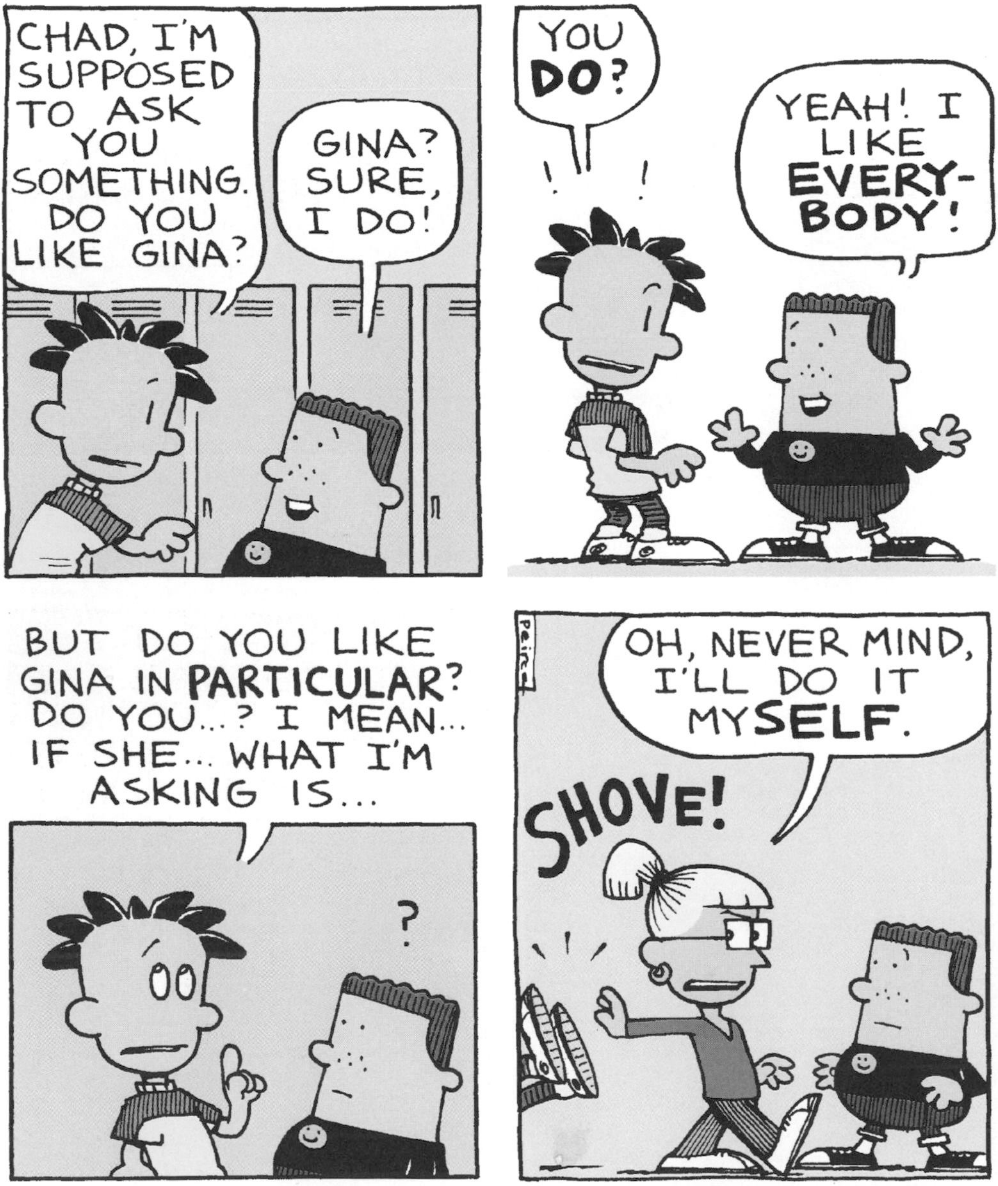
CHAD, I'M SUPPOSED TO ASK YOU SOMETHING. DO YOU LIKE GINA?
GINA? SURE, I DO!
YOU **DO**?
YEAH! I LIKE **EVERY-BODY**!
BUT DO YOU LIKE GINA IN **PARTICULAR**? DO YOU...? I MEAN... IF SHE... WHAT I'M ASKING IS...
?
SHOVE!
OH, NEVER MIND, I'LL DO IT MY**SELF**.
Peirce

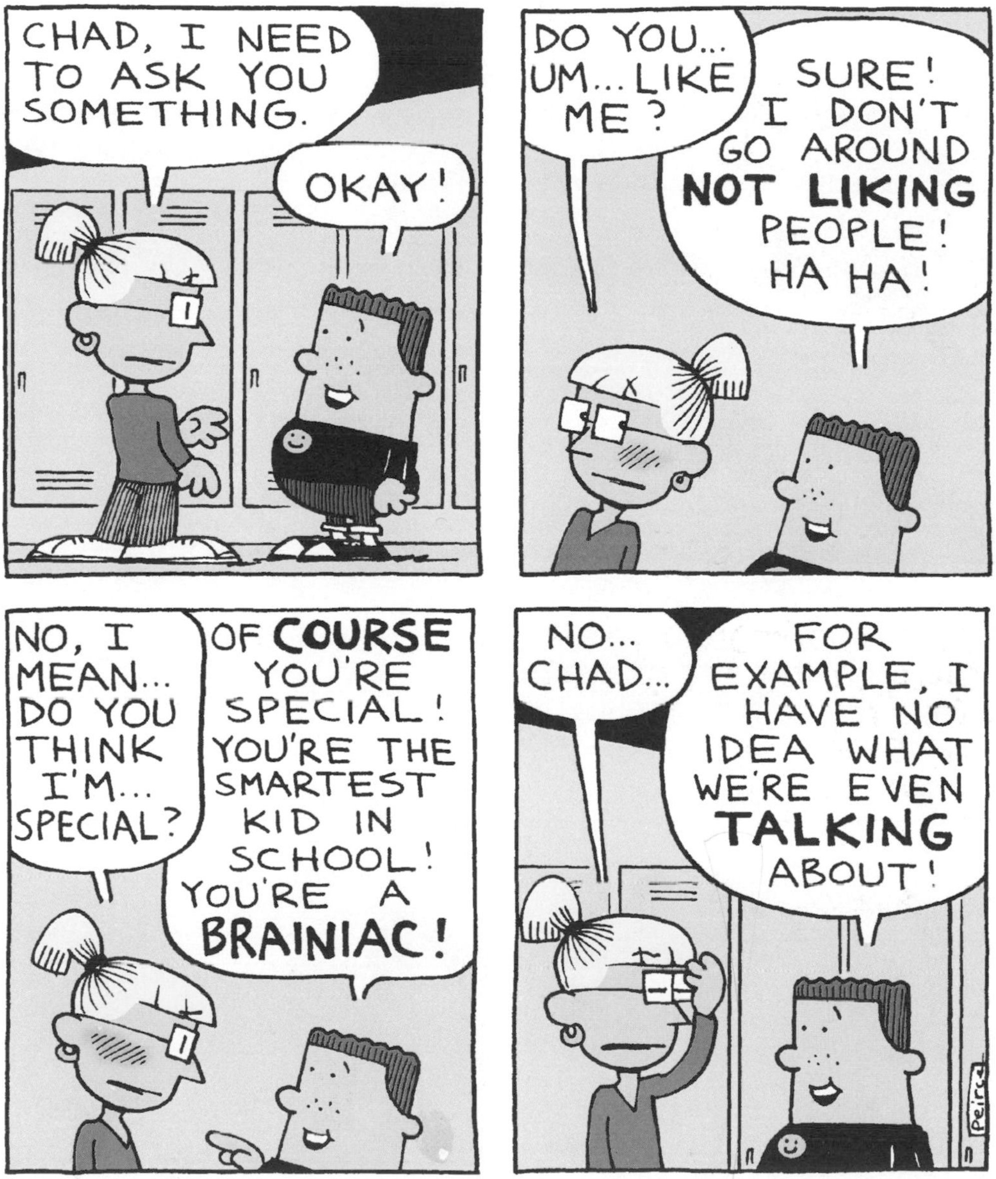
CHAD, I NEED TO ASK YOU SOMETHING.
OKAY!
DO YOU... UM... LIKE ME?
SURE! I DON'T GO AROUND NOT LIKING PEOPLE! HA HA!
NO, I MEAN... DO YOU THINK I'M... SPECIAL?
OF COURSE YOU'RE SPECIAL! YOU'RE THE SMARTEST KID IN SCHOOL! YOU'RE A BRAINIAC!
NO... CHAD...
FOR EXAMPLE, I HAVE NO IDEA WHAT WE'RE EVEN TALKING ABOUT!
Peirce

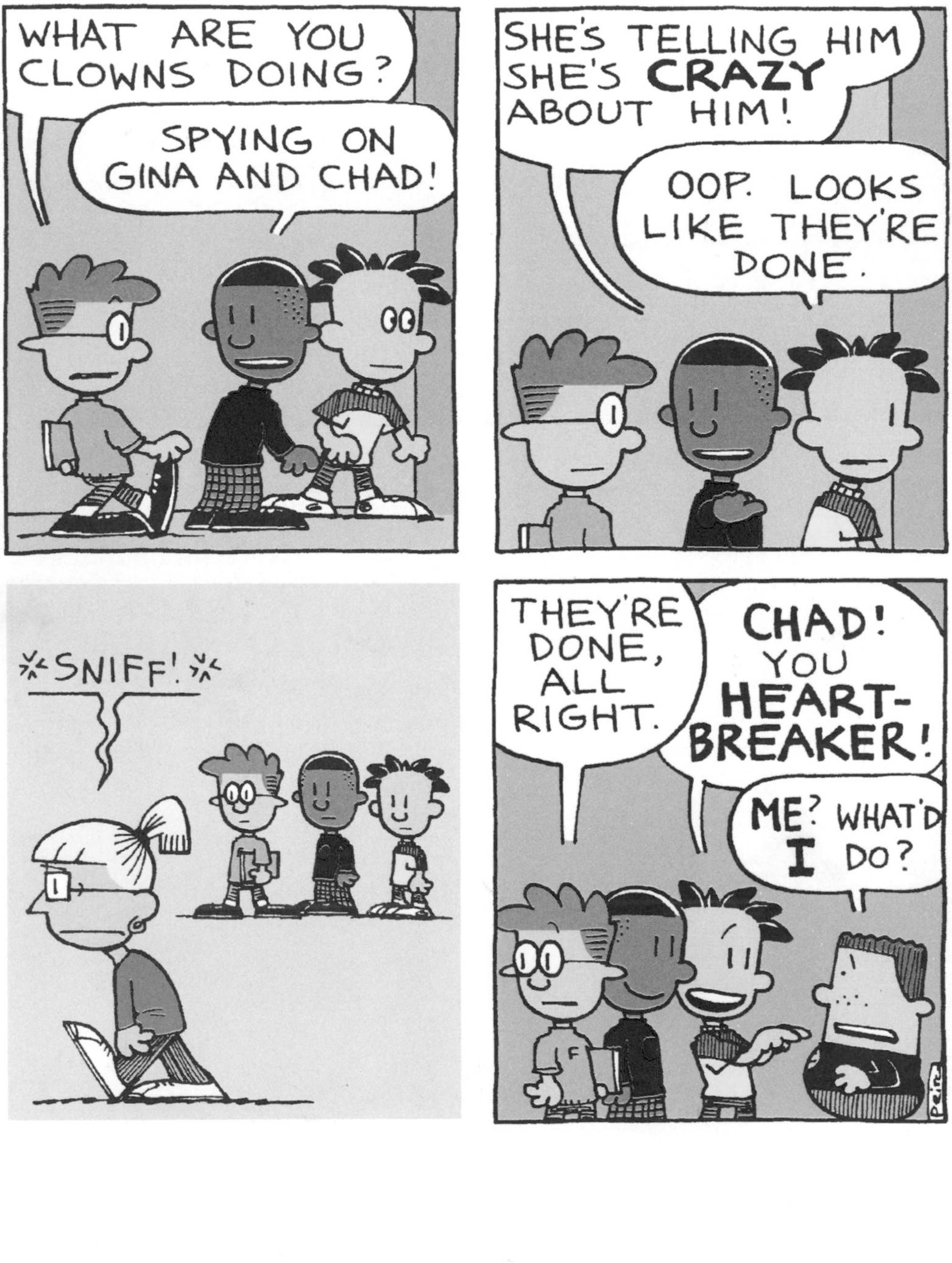
WHAT ARE YOU CLOWNS DOING?
SPYING ON GINA AND CHAD!
SHE'S TELLING HIM SHE'S **CRAZY** ABOUT HIM!
OOP. LOOKS LIKE THEY'RE DONE.
SNIFF!
THEY'RE DONE, ALL RIGHT.
CHAD! YOU **HEART-BREAKER!**
ME? WHAT'D **I** DO?
PEIRCE

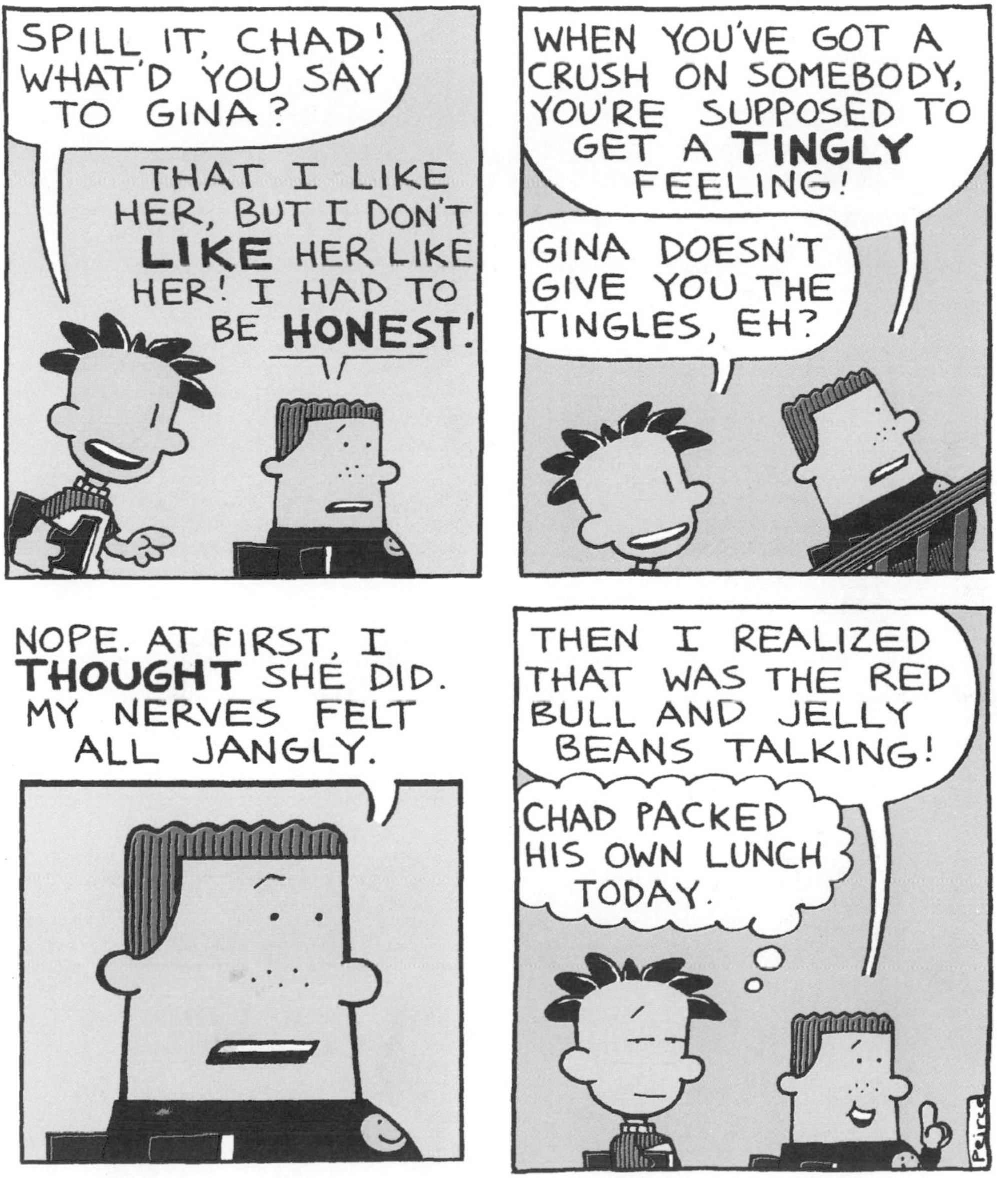
SPILL IT, CHAD! WHAT'D YOU SAY TO GINA?
THAT I LIKE HER, BUT I DON'T **LIKE** HER LIKE HER! I HAD TO BE **HONEST**!
WHEN YOU'VE GOT A CRUSH ON SOMEBODY, YOU'RE SUPPOSED TO GET A **TINGLY** FEELING!
GINA DOESN'T GIVE YOU THE TINGLES, EH?
NOPE. AT FIRST, I **THOUGHT** SHE DID. MY NERVES FELT ALL JANGLY.
THEN I REALIZED THAT WAS THE RED BULL AND JELLY BEANS TALKING!
CHAD PACKED HIS OWN LUNCH TODAY.
Peirce

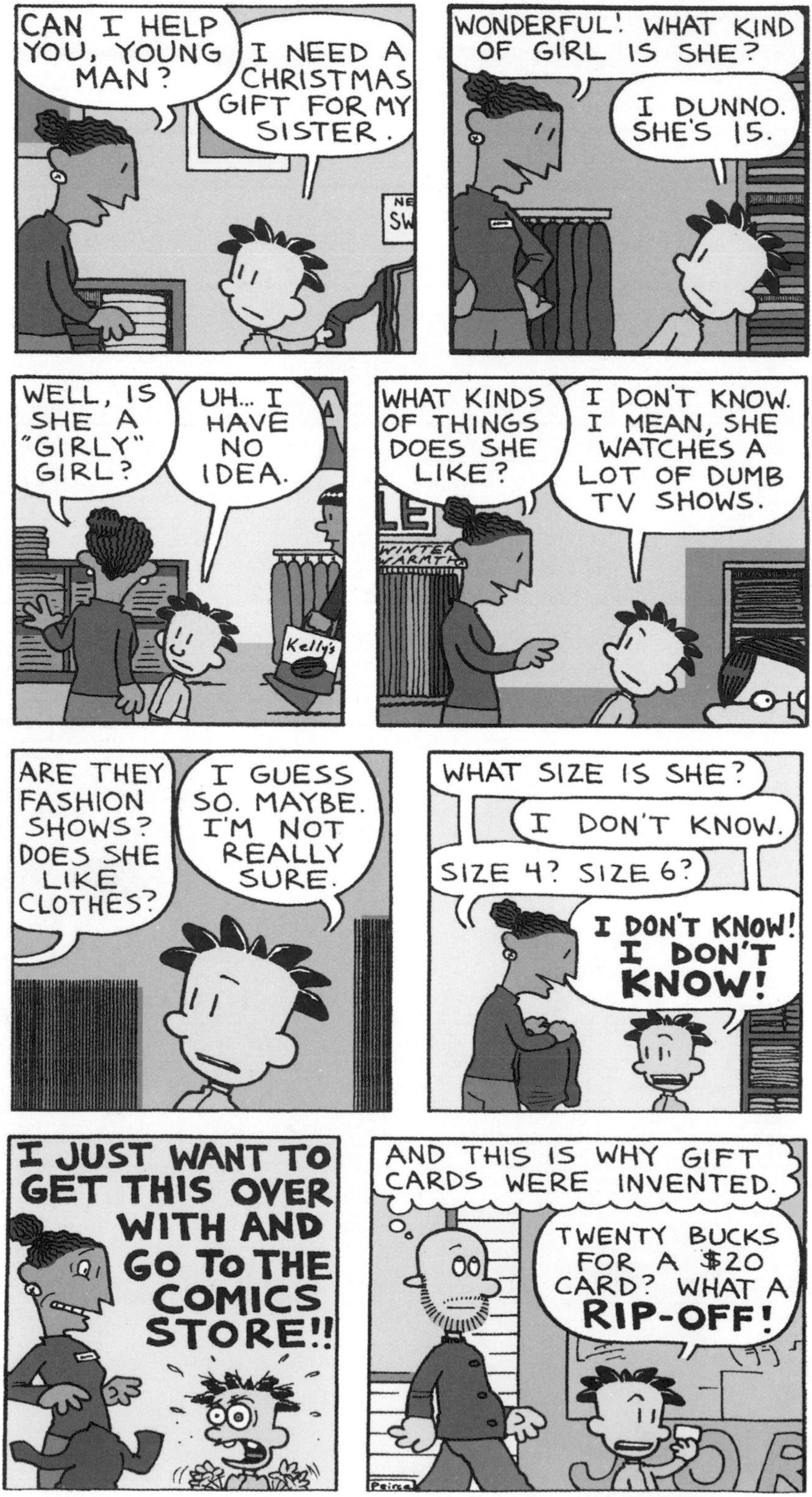
CAN I HELP YOU, YOUNG MAN?
I NEED A CHRISTMAS GIFT FOR MY SISTER.
WONDERFUL! WHAT KIND OF GIRL IS SHE?
I DUNNO. SHE'S 15.
WELL, IS SHE A "GIRLY" GIRL?
UH... I HAVE NO IDEA.
Kelly's
WHAT KINDS OF THINGS DOES SHE LIKE?
I DON'T KNOW. I MEAN, SHE WATCHES A LOT OF DUMB TV SHOWS.
WINTER WARMTH
ARE THEY FASHION SHOWS? DOES SHE LIKE CLOTHES?
I GUESS SO. MAYBE. I'M NOT REALLY SURE.
WHAT SIZE IS SHE?
I DON'T KNOW.
SIZE 4? SIZE 6?
I DON'T KNOW! I DON'T KNOW!
I JUST WANT TO GET THIS OVER WITH AND GO TO THE COMICS STORE!!
AND THIS IS WHY GIFT CARDS WERE INVENTED.
TWENTY BUCKS FOR A $20 CARD? WHAT A RIP-OFF!
Peirce

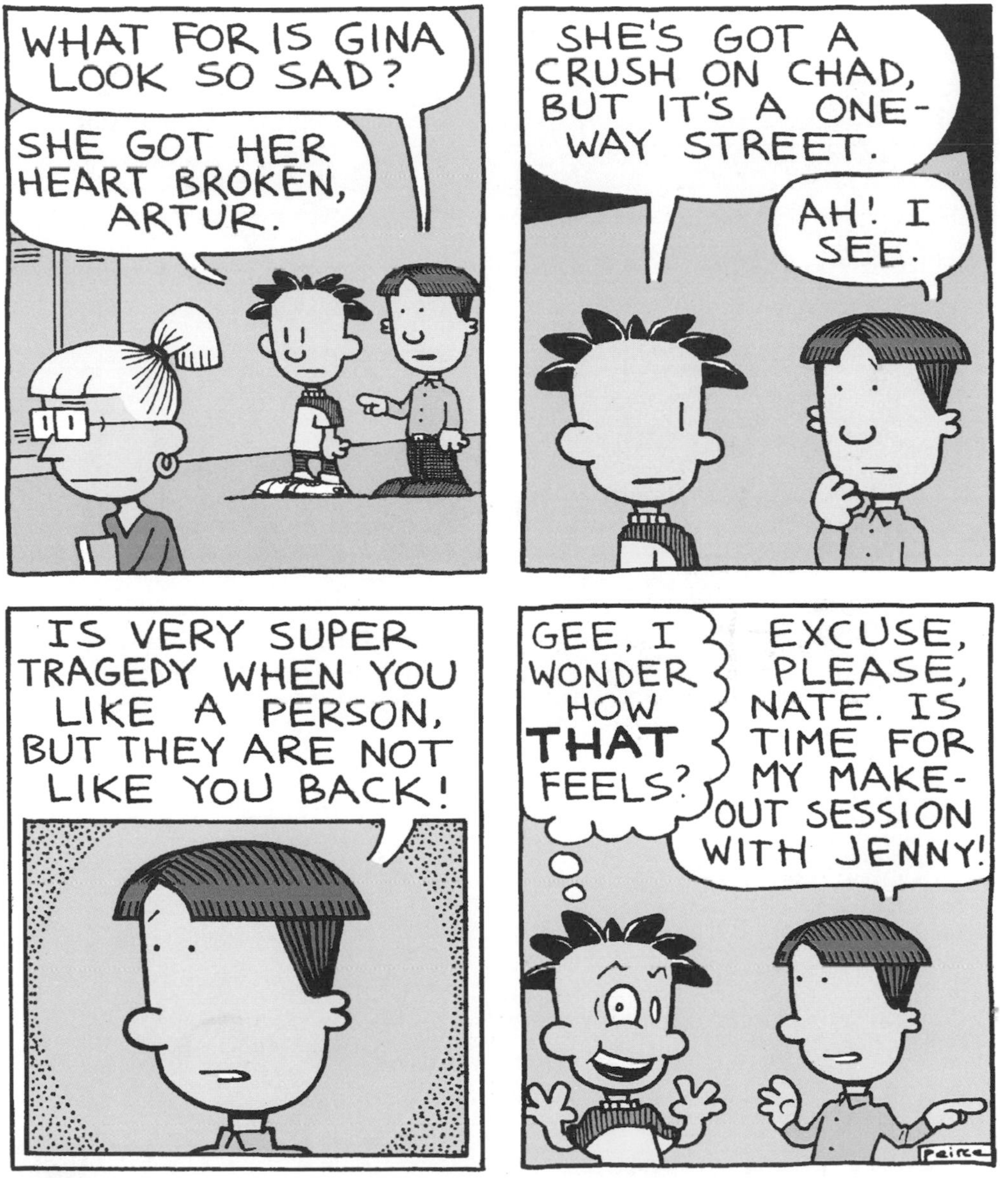
WHAT FOR IS GINA LOOK SO SAD?
SHE GOT HER HEART BROKEN, ARTUR.
SHE'S GOT A CRUSH ON CHAD, BUT IT'S A ONE-WAY STREET.
AH! I SEE.
IS VERY SUPER TRAGEDY WHEN YOU LIKE A PERSON, BUT THEY ARE NOT LIKE YOU BACK!
GEE, I WONDER HOW **THAT** FEELS?
EXCUSE, PLEASE, NATE. IS TIME FOR MY MAKE-OUT SESSION WITH JENNY!
peirce

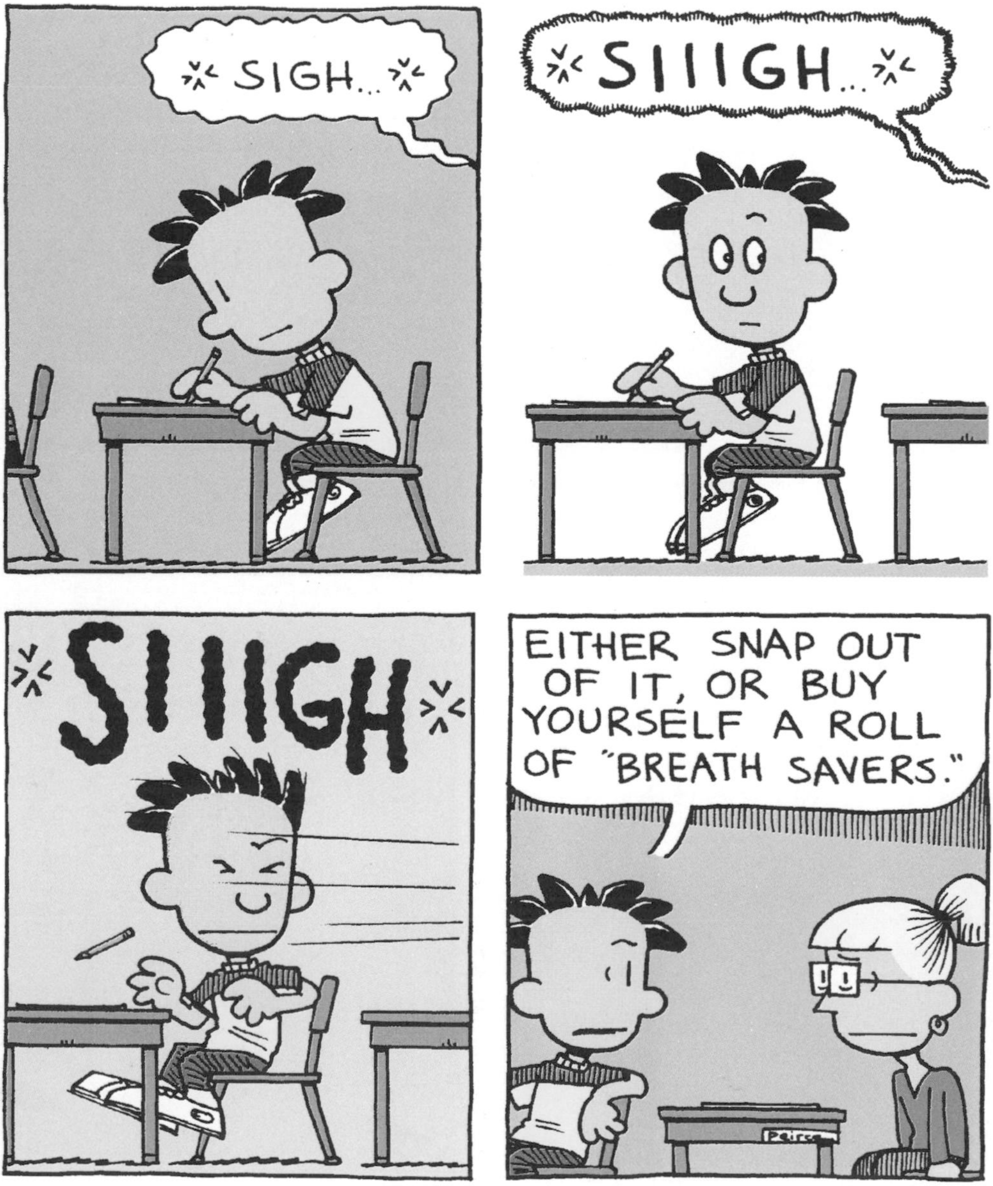
SIGH...
SIIIGH...
SIIIGH
EITHER SNAP OUT OF IT, OR BUY YOURSELF A ROLL OF "BREATH SAVERS."
Peirce

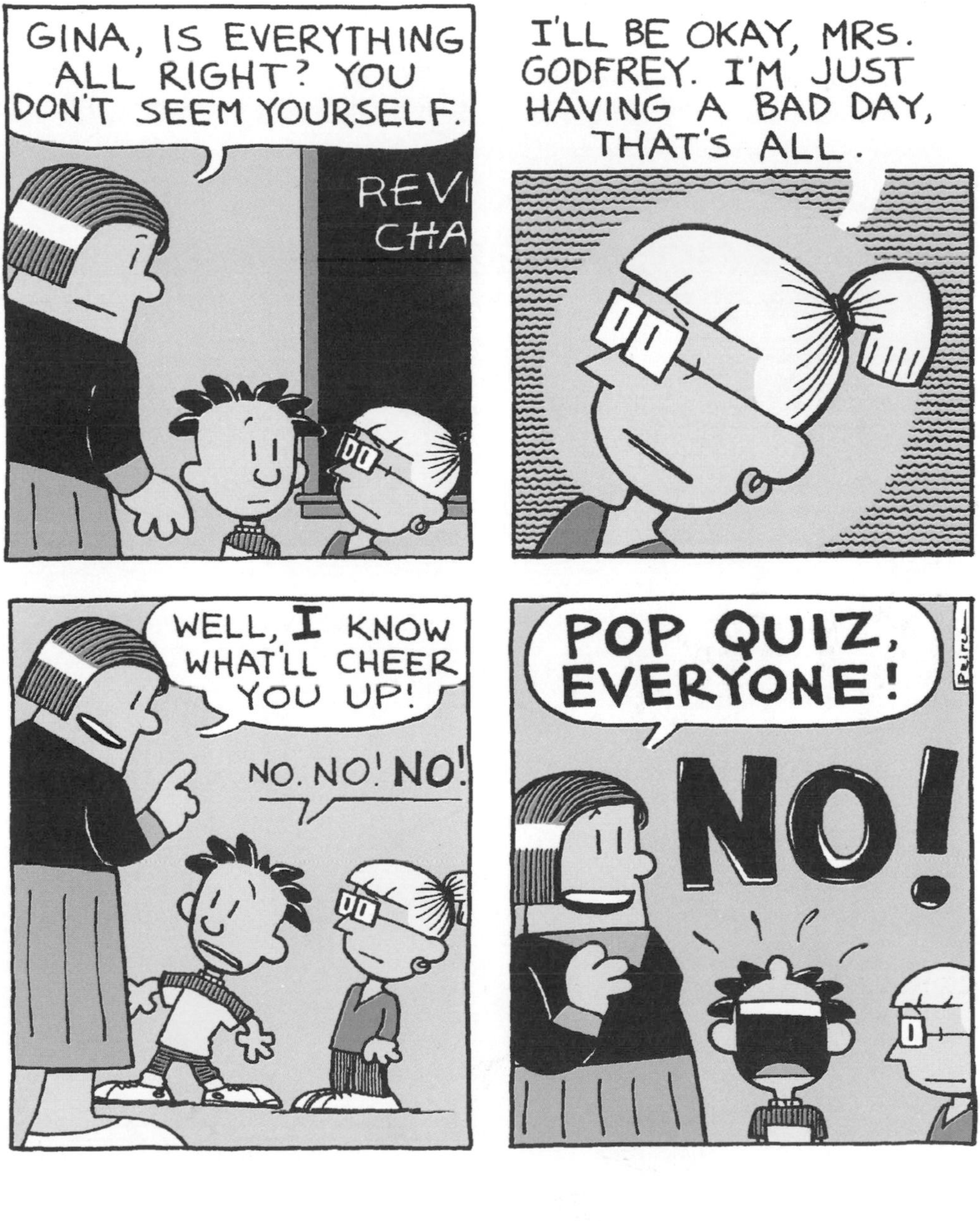
GINA, IS EVERYTHING ALL RIGHT? YOU DON'T SEEM YOURSELF.
REVI
CHA
I'LL BE OKAY, MRS. GODFREY. I'M JUST HAVING A BAD DAY, THAT'S ALL.
WELL, I KNOW WHAT'LL CHEER YOU UP!
NO. NO! NO!
POP QUIZ, EVERYONE!
NO!
Peirce

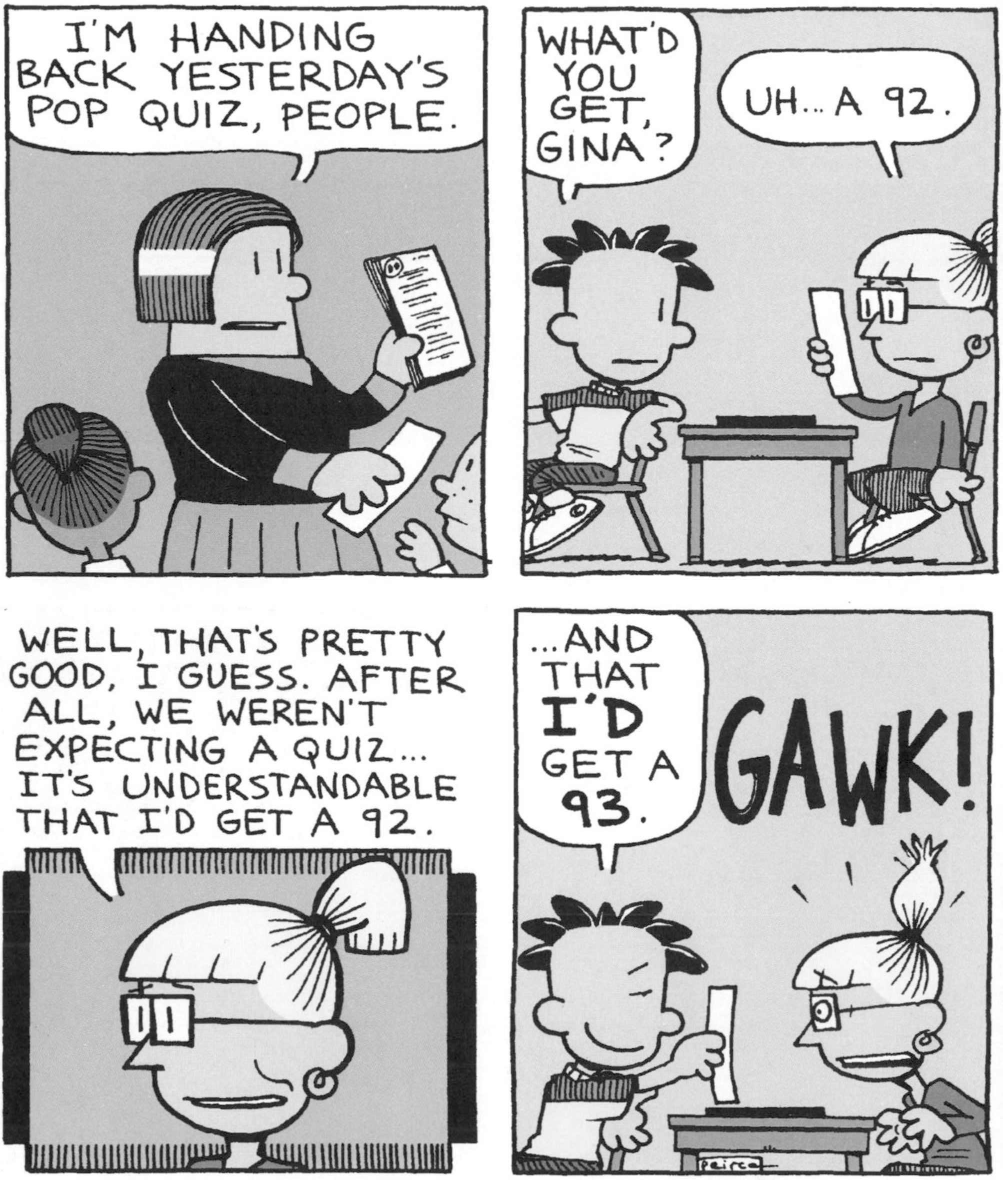
I'M HANDING BACK YESTERDAY'S POP QUIZ, PEOPLE.
WHAT'D YOU GET, GINA?
UH... A 92.
WELL, THAT'S PRETTY GOOD, I GUESS. AFTER ALL, WE WEREN'T EXPECTING A QUIZ... IT'S UNDERSTANDABLE THAT I'D GET A 92.
...AND THAT **I'D** GET A 93.
GAWK!
Peirce

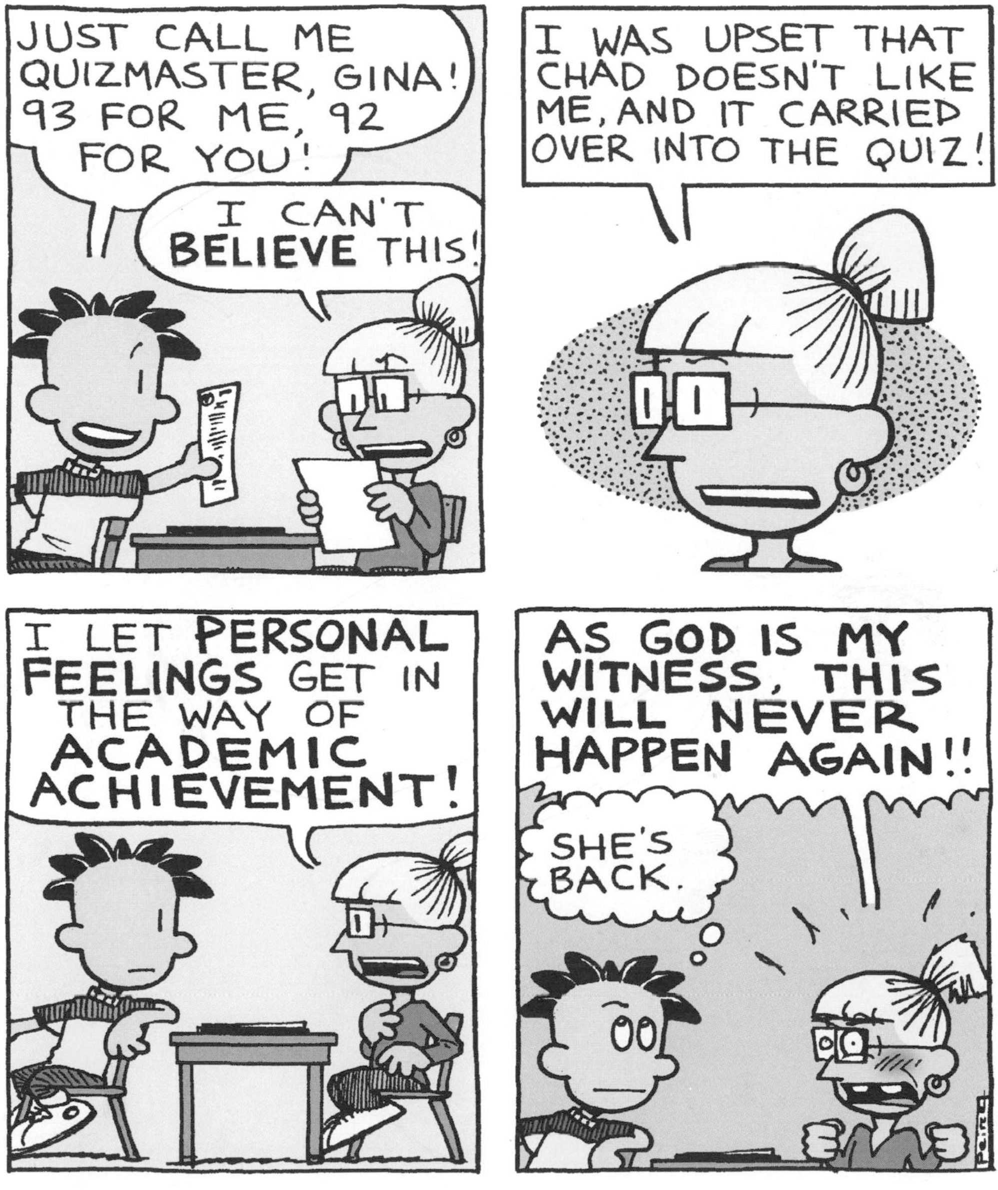
JUST CALL ME QUIZMASTER, GINA! 93 FOR ME, 92 FOR YOU!
I CAN'T **BELIEVE** THIS!
I WAS UPSET THAT CHAD DOESN'T LIKE ME, AND IT CARRIED OVER INTO THE QUIZ!
I LET **PERSONAL FEELINGS** GET IN THE WAY OF **ACADEMIC ACHIEVEMENT**!
AS GOD IS MY WITNESS, THIS WILL NEVER HAPPEN AGAIN!!
SHE'S BACK.

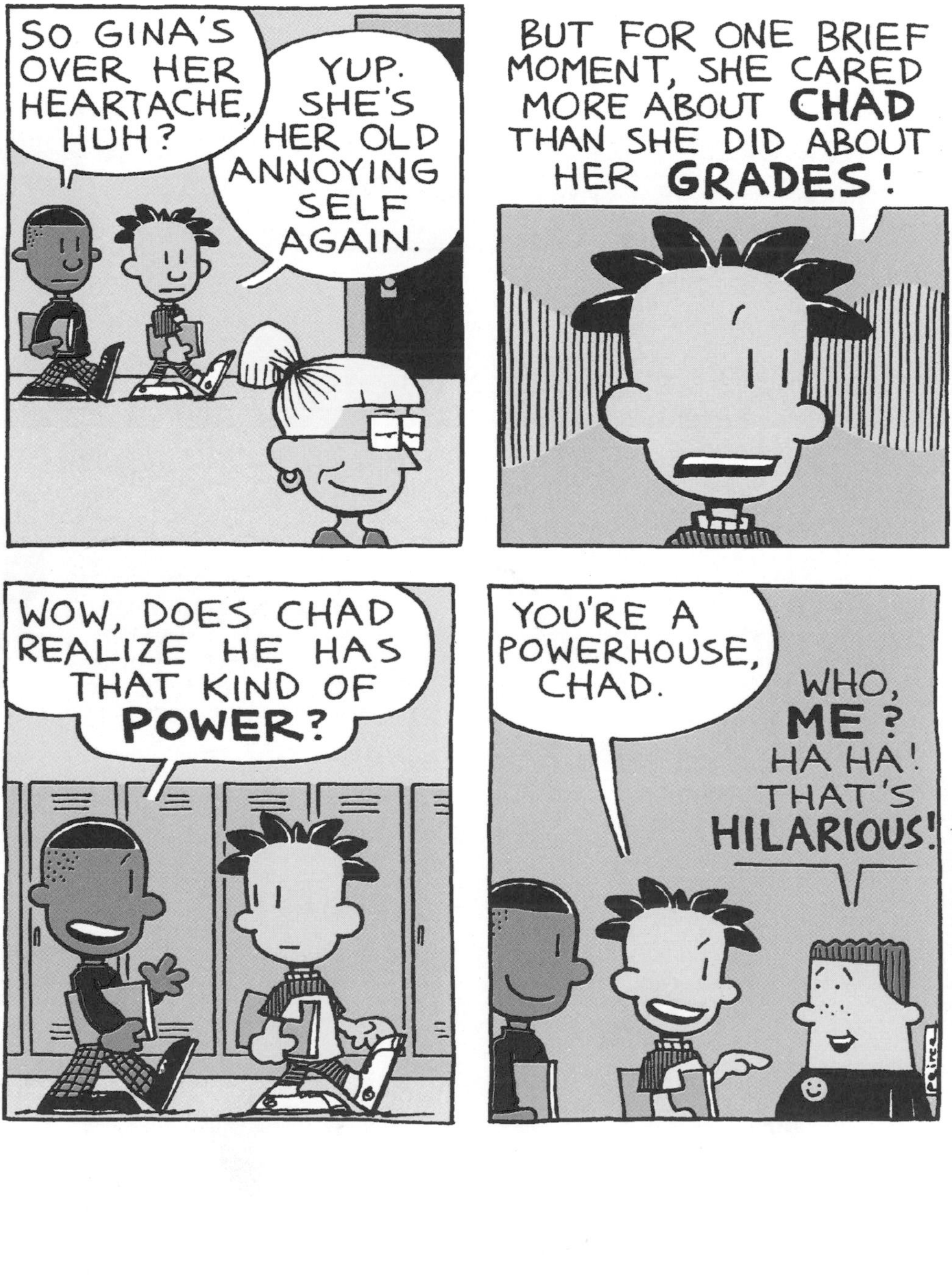
SO GINA'S OVER HER HEARTACHE, HUH?
YUP. SHE'S HER OLD ANNOYING SELF AGAIN.
BUT FOR ONE BRIEF MOMENT, SHE CARED MORE ABOUT **CHAD** THAN SHE DID ABOUT HER **GRADES**!
WOW, DOES CHAD REALIZE HE HAS THAT KIND OF **POWER**?
YOU'RE A POWERHOUSE, CHAD.
WHO, **ME**? HA HA! THAT'S **HILARIOUS**!

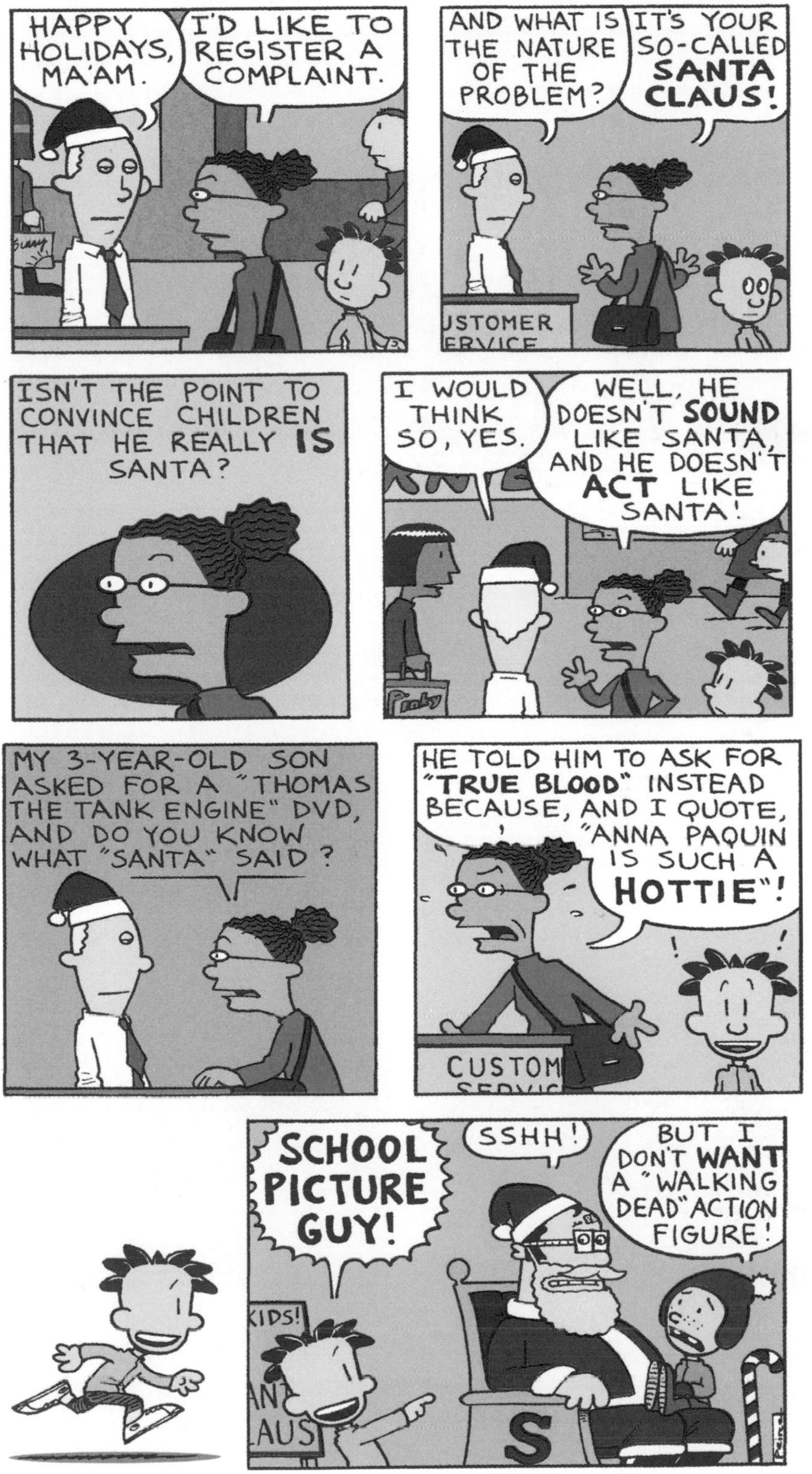
HAPPY HOLIDAYS, MA'AM.
I'D LIKE TO REGISTER A COMPLAINT.
AND WHAT IS THE NATURE OF THE PROBLEM?
IT'S YOUR SO-CALLED **SANTA CLAUS**!
USTOMER
ISN'T THE POINT TO CONVINCE CHILDREN THAT HE REALLY **IS** SANTA?
I WOULD THINK SO, YES.
WELL, HE DOESN'T **SOUND** LIKE SANTA, AND HE DOESN'T **ACT** LIKE SANTA!
MY 3-YEAR-OLD SON ASKED FOR A "THOMAS THE TANK ENGINE" DVD, AND DO YOU KNOW WHAT "SANTA" SAID?
HE TOLD HIM TO ASK FOR "**TRUE BLOOD**" INSTEAD BECAUSE, AND I QUOTE, "ANNA PAQUIN IS SUCH A **HOTTIE**"!
! !
CUSTOM
SCHOOL PICTURE GUY!
SSHH!
BUT I DON'T **WANT** A "WALKING DEAD" ACTION FIGURE!
KIDS!
S

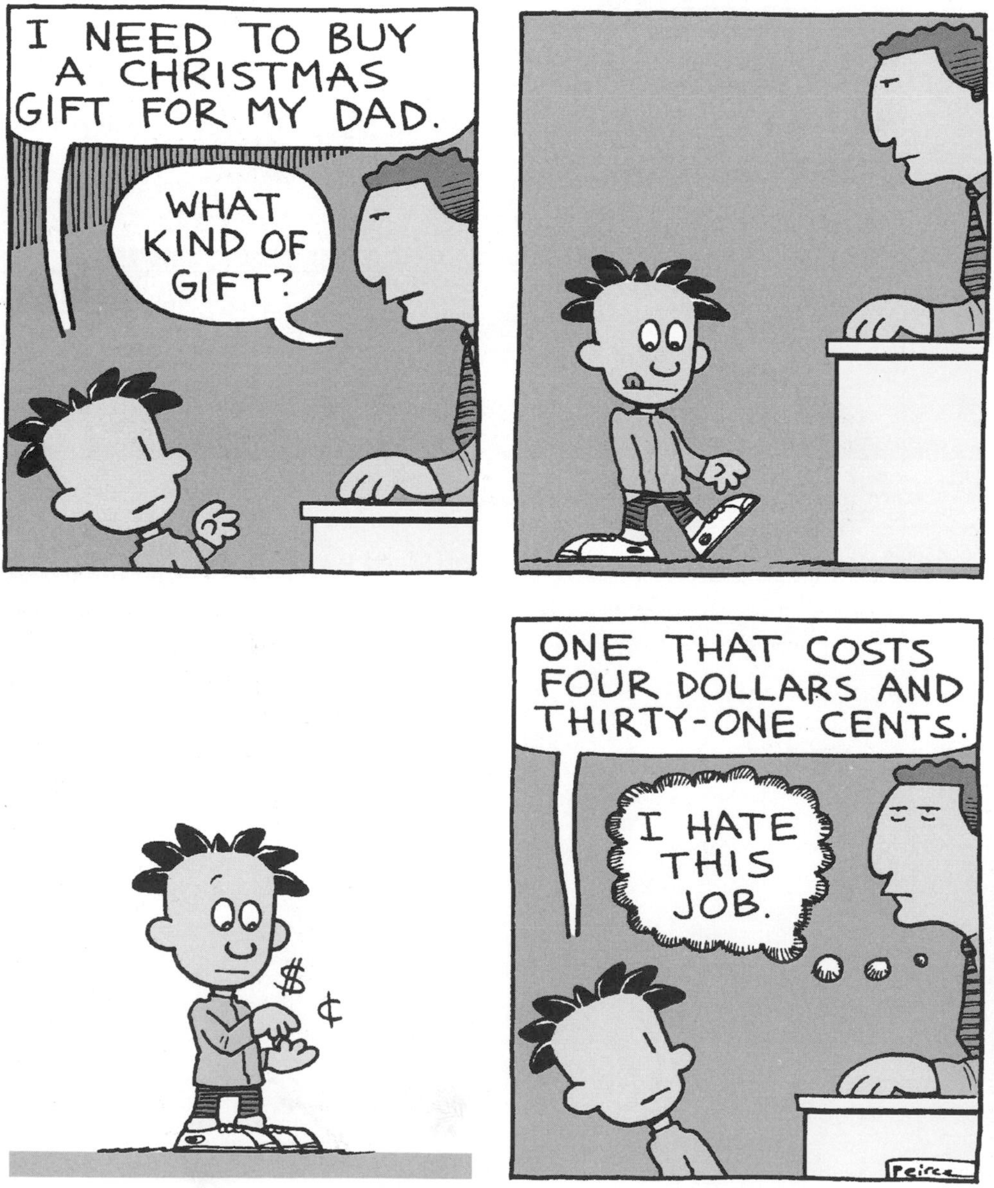
I NEED TO BUY A CHRISTMAS GIFT FOR MY DAD.
WHAT KIND OF GIFT?
ONE THAT COSTS FOUR DOLLARS AND THIRTY-ONE CENTS.
I HATE THIS JOB.
Peirce

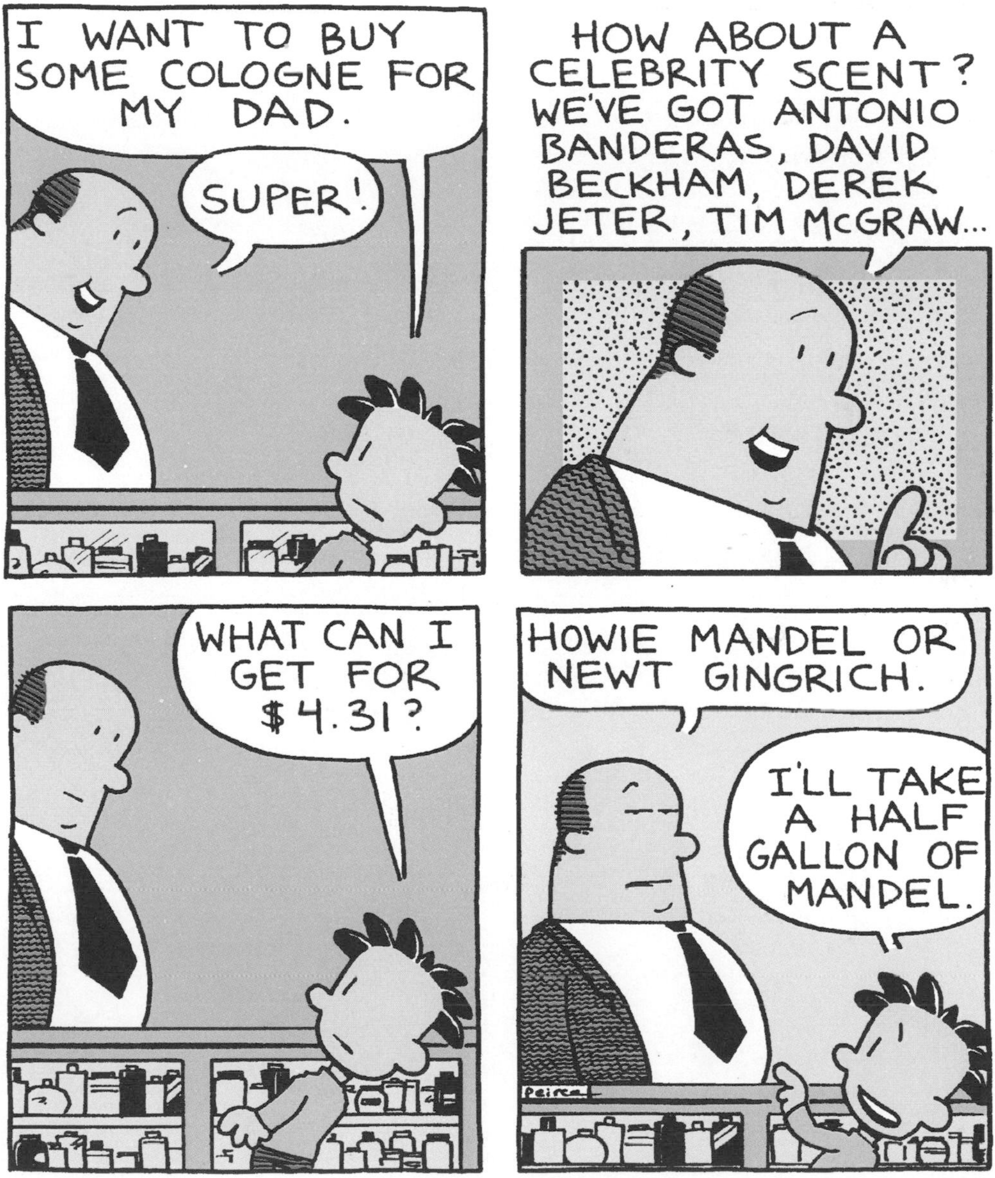
I WANT TO BUY SOME COLOGNE FOR MY DAD.
SUPER!
HOW ABOUT A CELEBRITY SCENT? WE'VE GOT ANTONIO BANDERAS, DAVID BECKHAM, DEREK JETER, TIM McGRAW...
WHAT CAN I GET FOR $4.31?
HOWIE MANDEL OR NEWT GINGRICH.
I'LL TAKE A HALF GALLON OF MANDEL.
Peirce

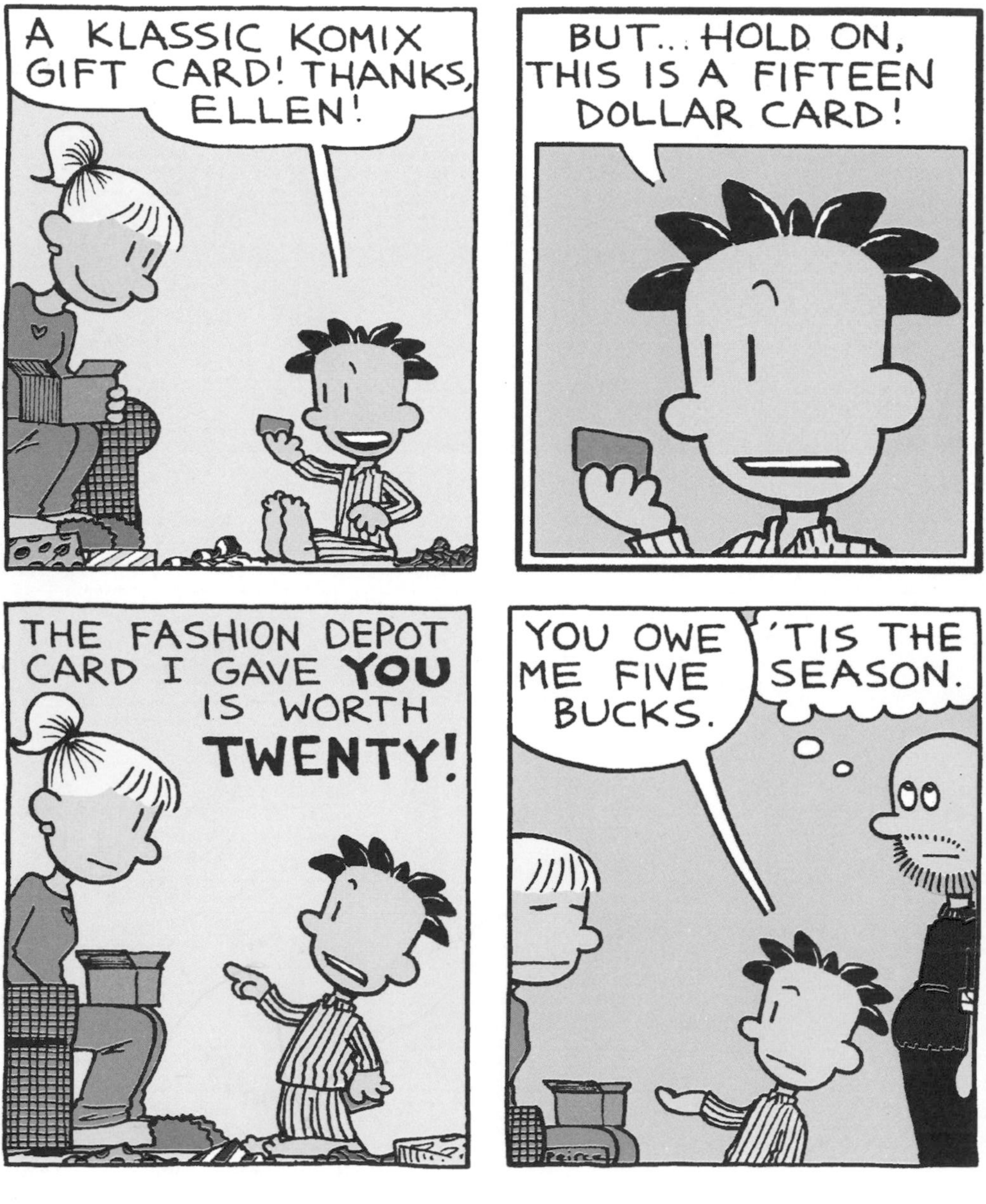
A KLASSIC KOMIX GIFT CARD! THANKS, ELLEN!
BUT... HOLD ON, THIS IS A FIFTEEN DOLLAR CARD!
THE FASHION DEPOT CARD I GAVE **YOU** IS WORTH **TWENTY!**
YOU OWE ME FIVE BUCKS.
'TIS THE SEASON.

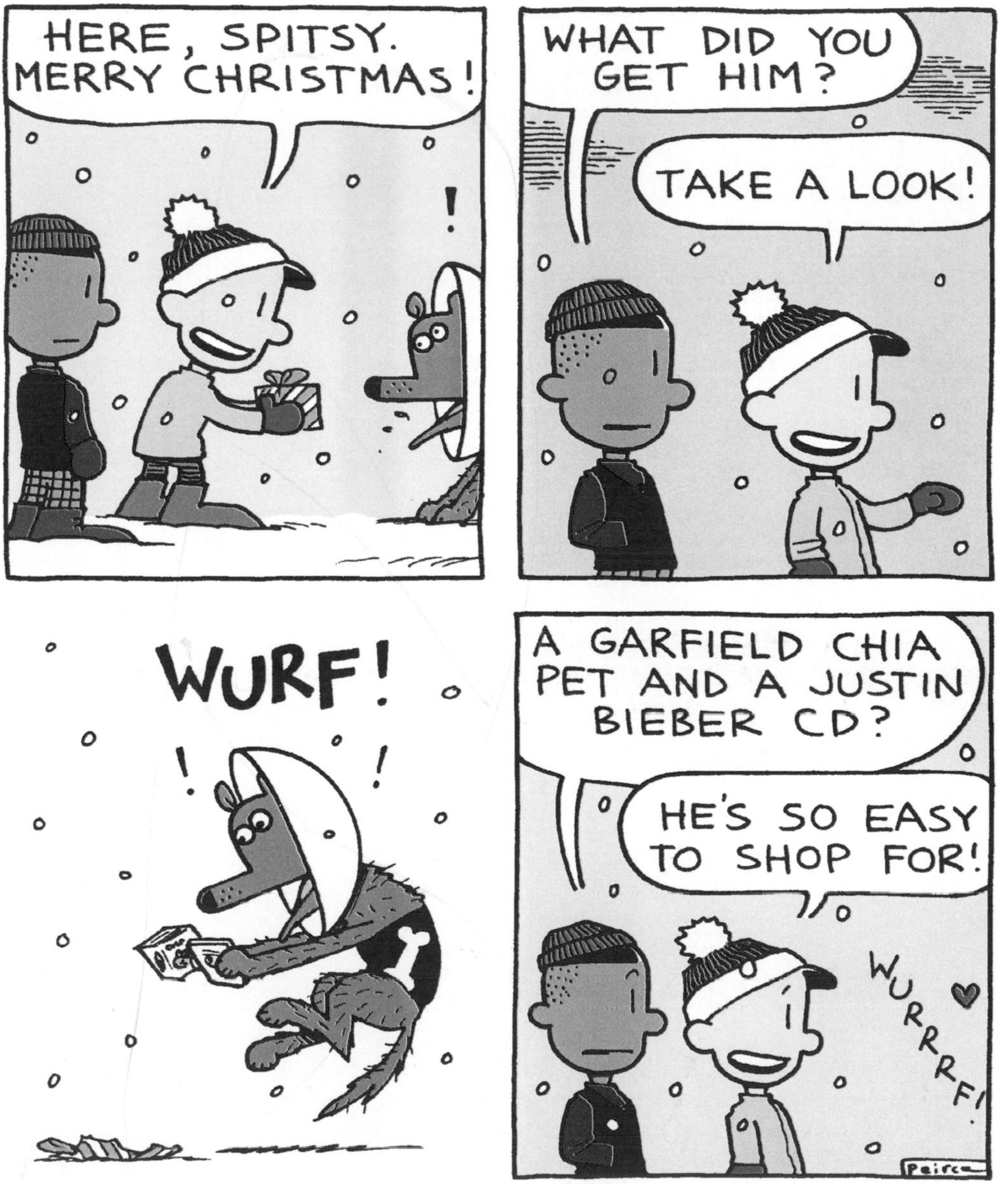
HERE, SPITSY. MERRY CHRISTMAS!
!
WHAT DID YOU GET HIM?
TAKE A LOOK!
WURF!
! !
A GARFIELD CHIA PET AND A JUSTIN BIEBER CD?
HE'S SO EASY TO SHOP FOR!
WURRRRF!
Peirce

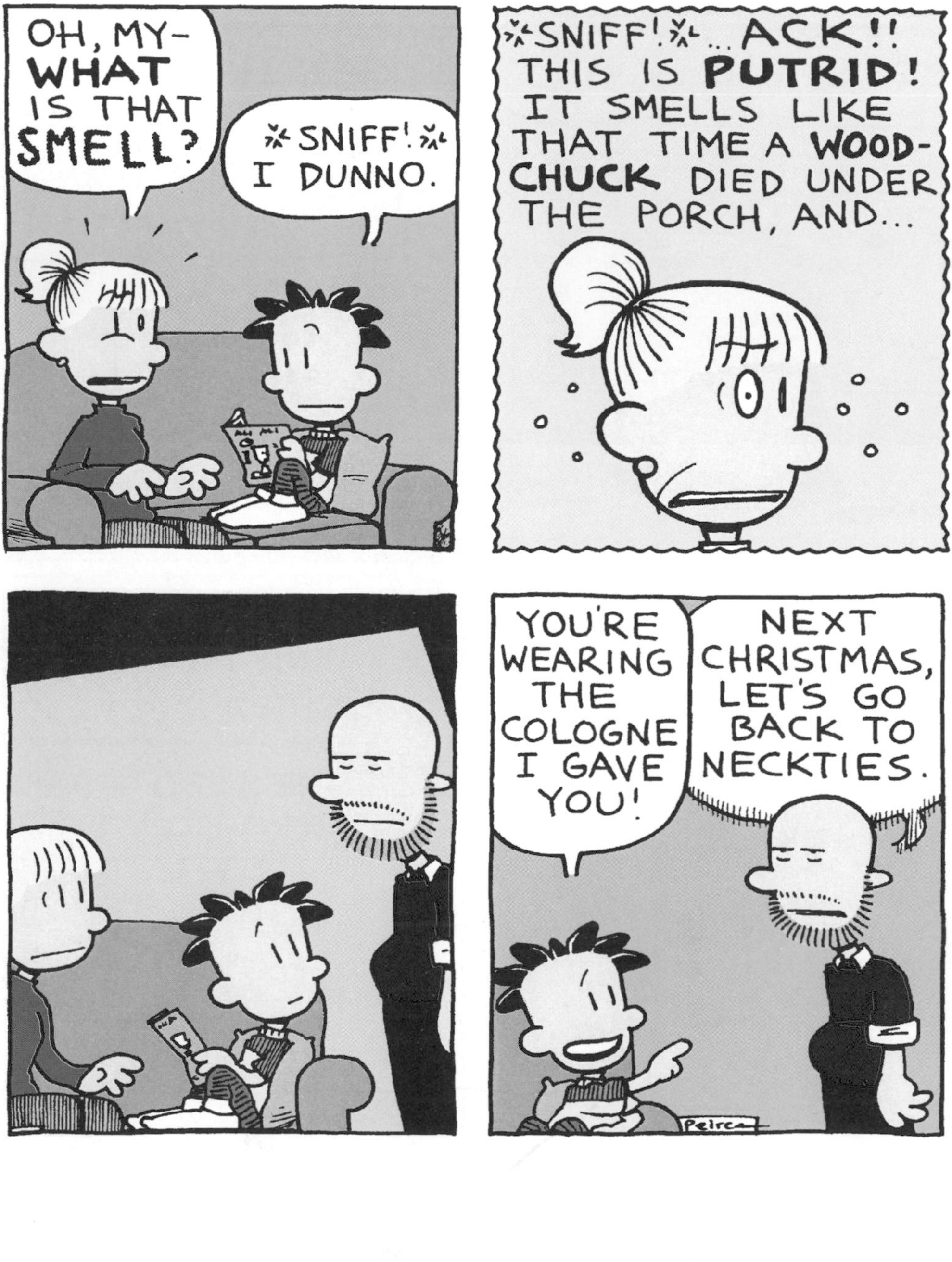
OH, MY- WHAT IS THAT SMELL?
SNIFF! I DUNNO.
SNIFF! ... ACK!! THIS IS PUTRID! IT SMELLS LIKE THAT TIME A WOOD-CHUCK DIED UNDER THE PORCH, AND...
YOU'RE WEARING THE COLOGNE I GAVE YOU!
NEXT CHRISTMAS, LET'S GO BACK TO NECKTIES.
Peirce

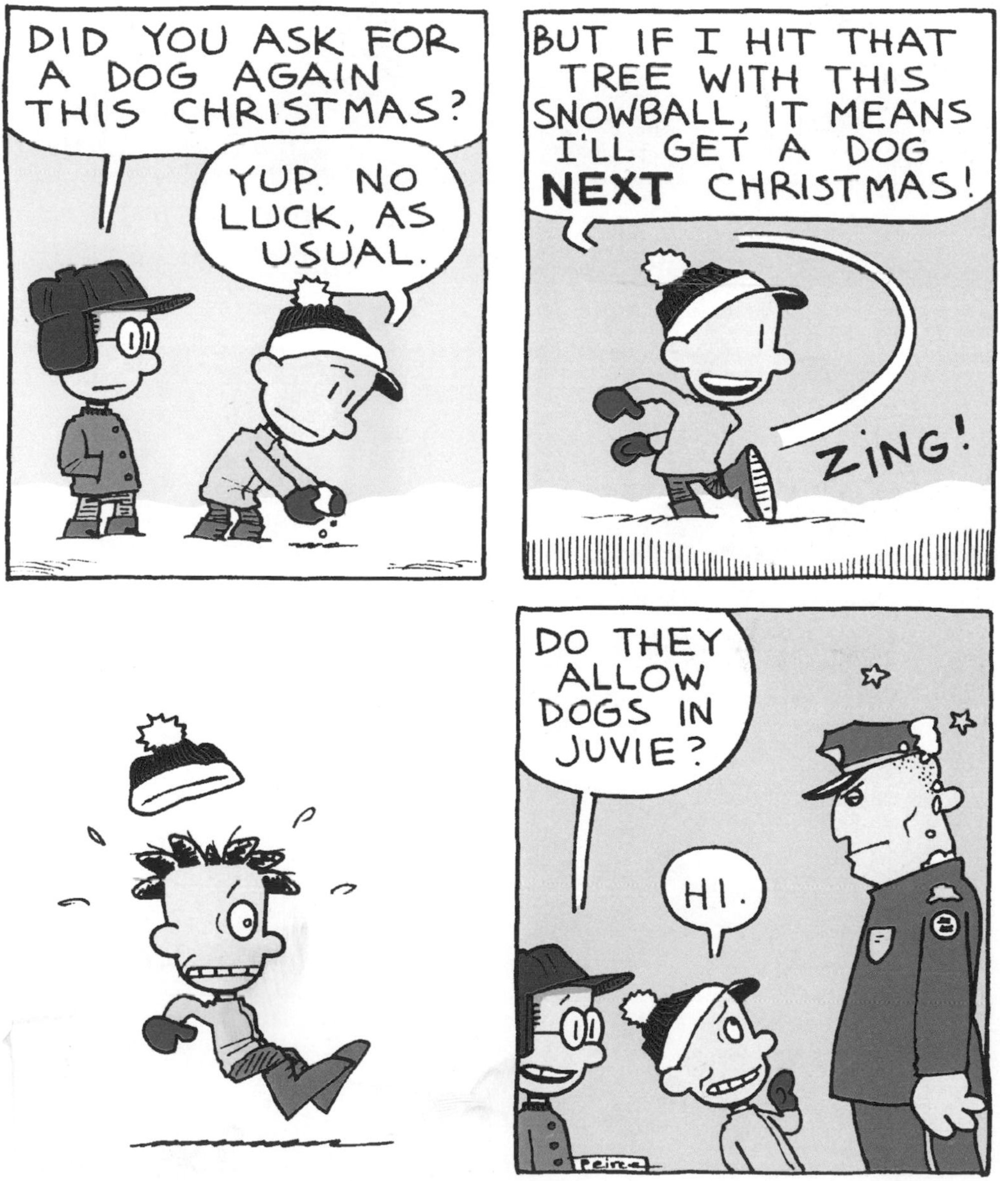
DID YOU ASK FOR A DOG AGAIN THIS CHRISTMAS?
YUP. NO LUCK, AS USUAL.
BUT IF I HIT THAT TREE WITH THIS SNOWBALL, IT MEANS I'LL GET A DOG **NEXT** CHRISTMAS!
ZING!
DO THEY ALLOW DOGS IN JUVIE?
HI.
PEIRCE

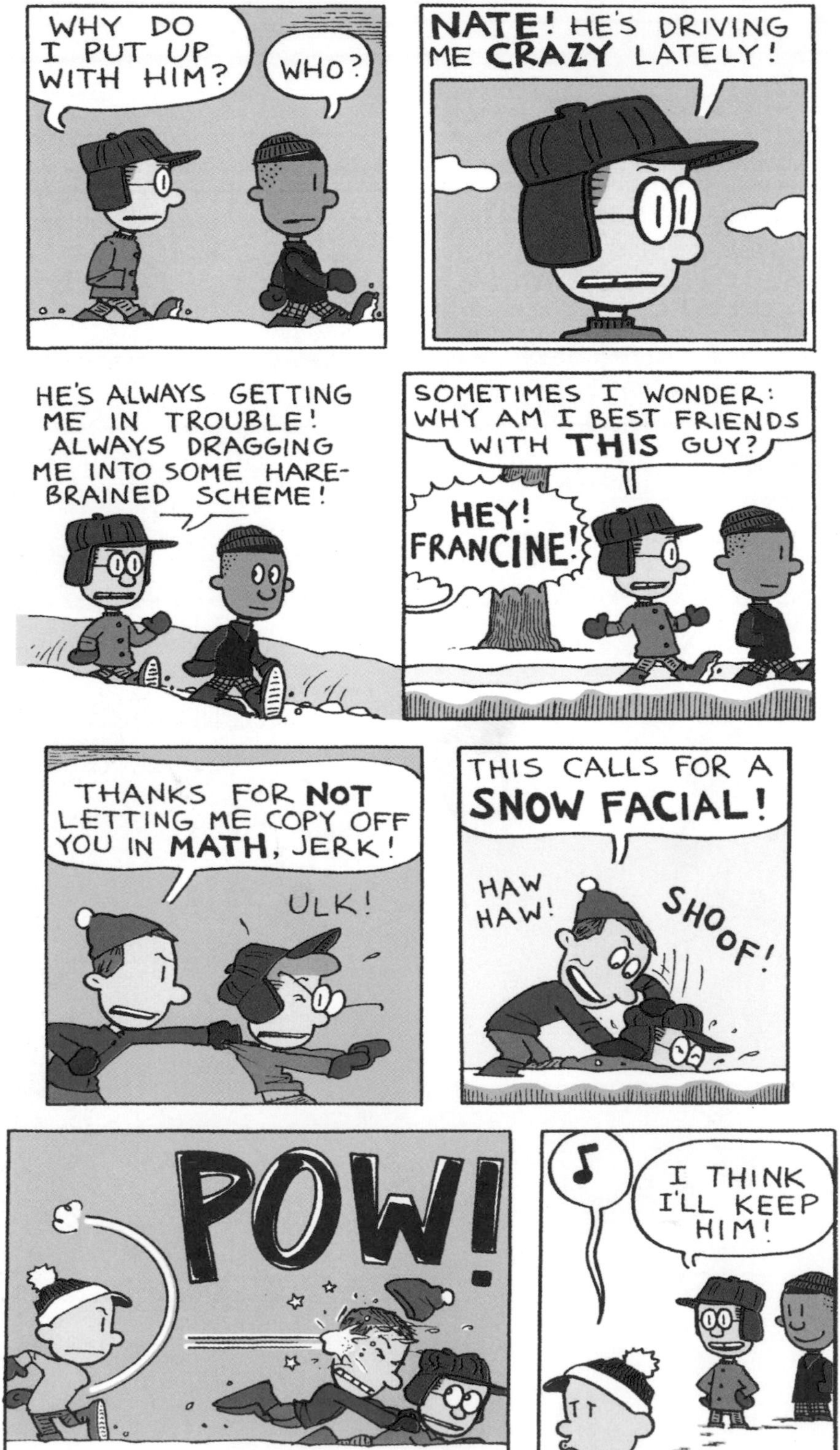
WHY DO I PUT UP WITH HIM?
WHO?
NATE! HE'S DRIVING ME CRAZY LATELY!
HE'S ALWAYS GETTING ME IN TROUBLE! ALWAYS DRAGGING ME INTO SOME HARE-BRAINED SCHEME!
SOMETIMES I WONDER: WHY AM I BEST FRIENDS WITH THIS GUY?
HEY! FRANCINE!
THANKS FOR NOT LETTING ME COPY OFF YOU IN MATH, JERK!
ULK!
THIS CALLS FOR A SNOW FACIAL!
HAW HAW!
SHOOF!
POW!
I THINK I'LL KEEP HIM!
Peirce

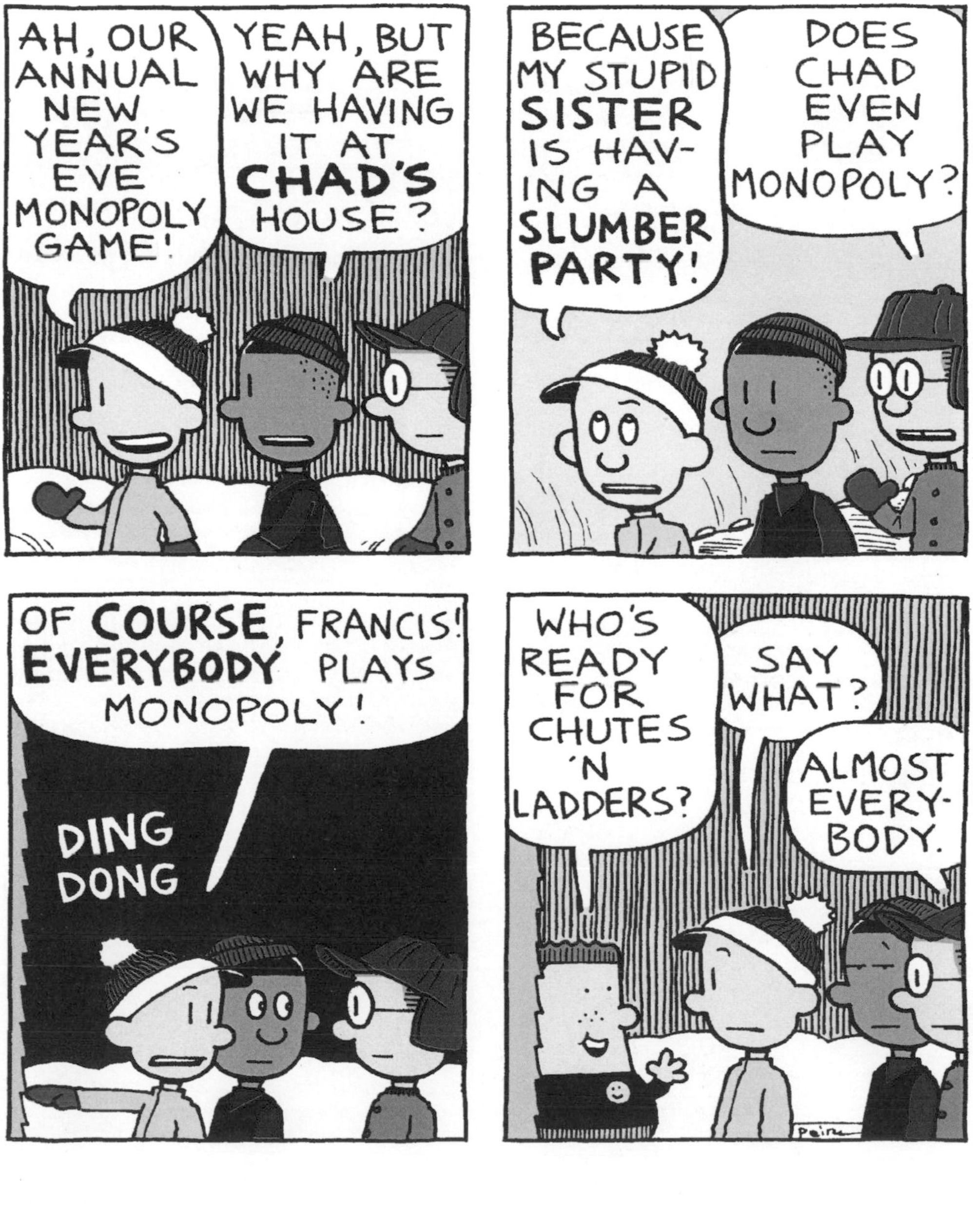
AH, OUR ANNUAL NEW YEAR'S EVE MONOPOLY GAME!
YEAH, BUT WHY ARE WE HAVING IT AT **CHAD'S** HOUSE?
BECAUSE MY STUPID **SISTER** IS HAVING A **SLUMBER PARTY**!
DOES CHAD EVEN PLAY MONOPOLY?
OF **COURSE**, FRANCIS! **EVERYBODY** PLAYS MONOPOLY!
DING DONG
WHO'S READY FOR CHUTES 'N LADDERS?
SAY WHAT?
ALMOST EVERYBODY.
Peirce

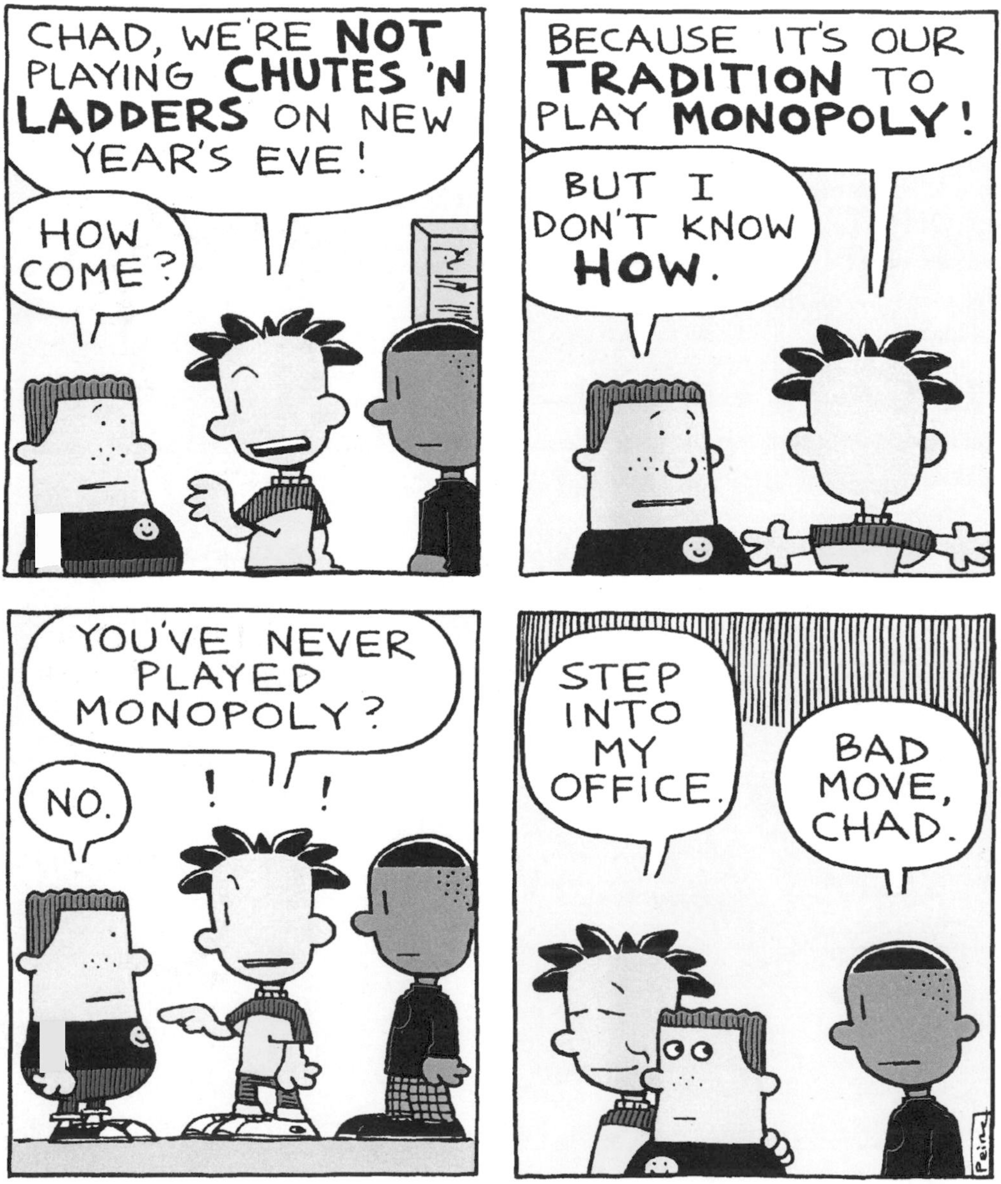
CHAD, WE'RE **NOT** PLAYING **CHUTES 'N LADDERS** ON NEW YEAR'S EVE!
HOW COME?
BECAUSE IT'S OUR **TRADITION** TO PLAY **MONOPOLY**!
BUT I DON'T KNOW **HOW**.
YOU'VE NEVER PLAYED MONOPOLY?
NO.
! !
STEP INTO MY OFFICE.
BAD MOVE, CHAD.
Peirce

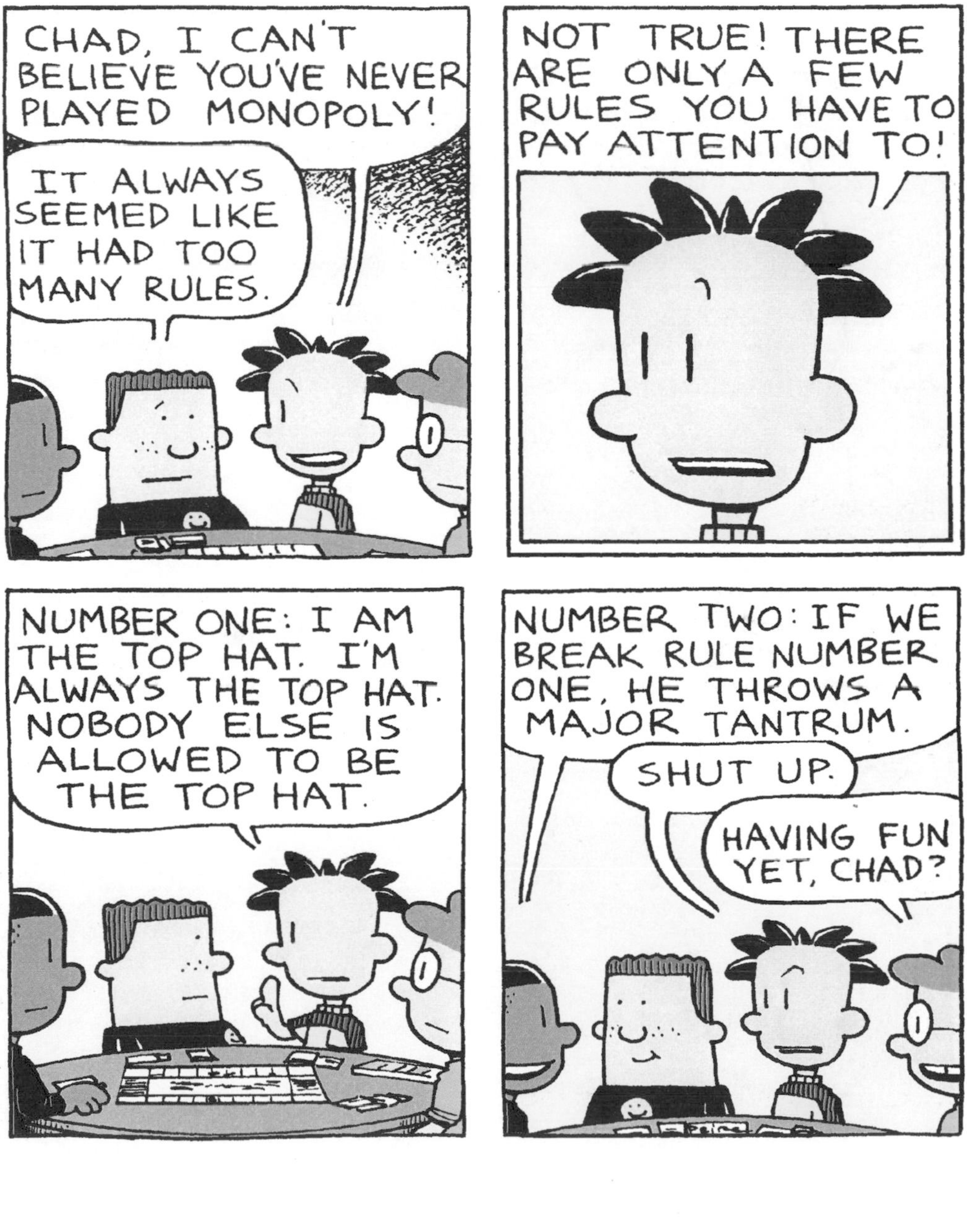
CHAD, I CAN'T BELIEVE YOU'VE NEVER PLAYED MONOPOLY!
IT ALWAYS SEEMED LIKE IT HAD TOO MANY RULES.
NOT TRUE! THERE ARE ONLY A FEW RULES YOU HAVE TO PAY ATTENTION TO!
NUMBER ONE: I AM THE TOP HAT. I'M ALWAYS THE TOP HAT. NOBODY ELSE IS ALLOWED TO BE THE TOP HAT.
NUMBER TWO: IF WE BREAK RULE NUMBER ONE, HE THROWS A MAJOR TANTRUM.
SHUT UP.
HAVING FUN YET, CHAD?

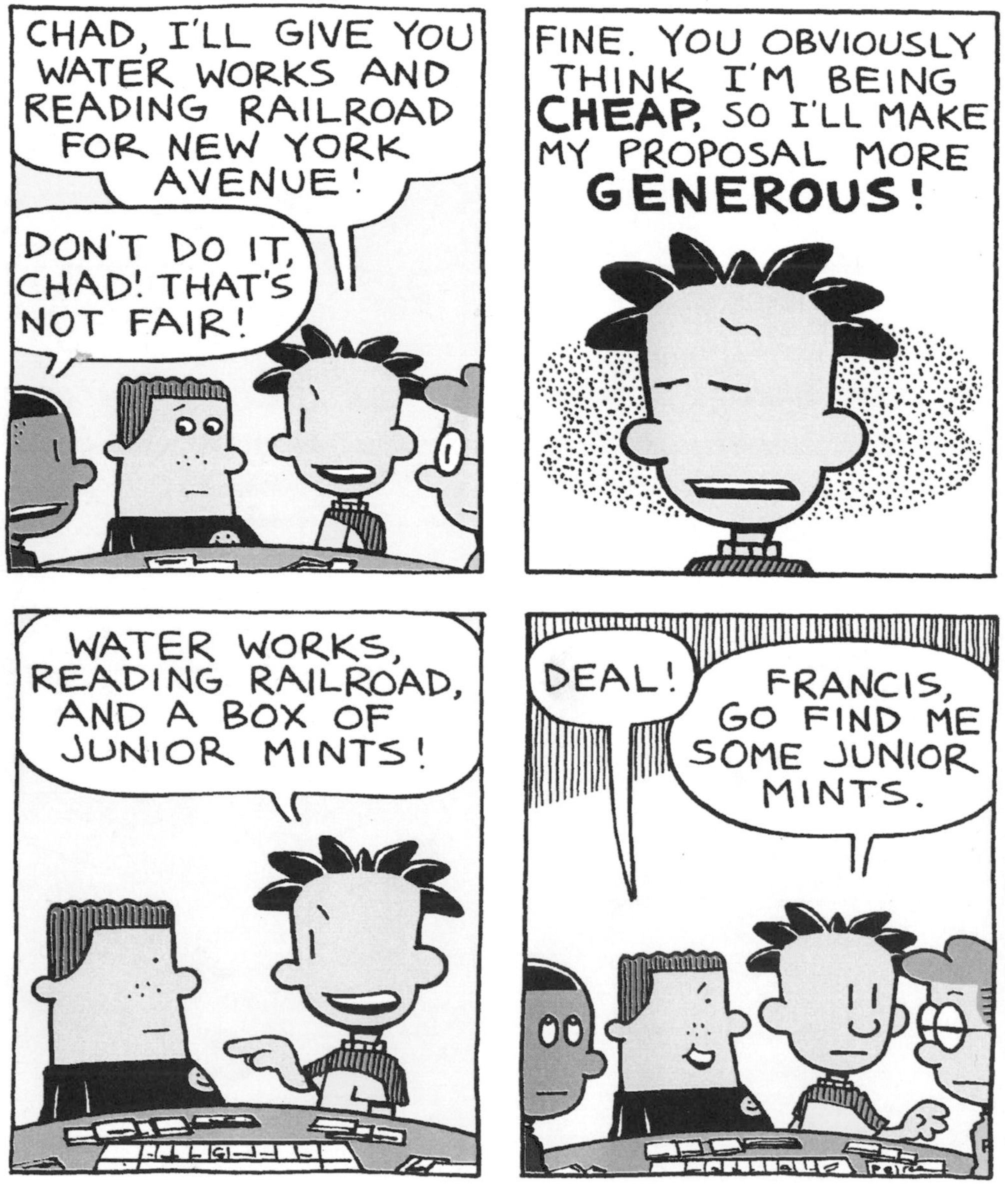

CHAD, I'LL GIVE YOU WATER WORKS AND READING RAILROAD FOR NEW YORK AVENUE!
DON'T DO IT, CHAD! THAT'S NOT FAIR!
FINE. YOU OBVIOUSLY THINK I'M BEING **CHEAP**, SO I'LL MAKE MY PROPOSAL MORE **GENEROUS!**
WATER WORKS, READING RAILROAD, AND A BOX OF JUNIOR MINTS!
DEAL!
FRANCIS, GO FIND ME SOME JUNIOR MINTS.

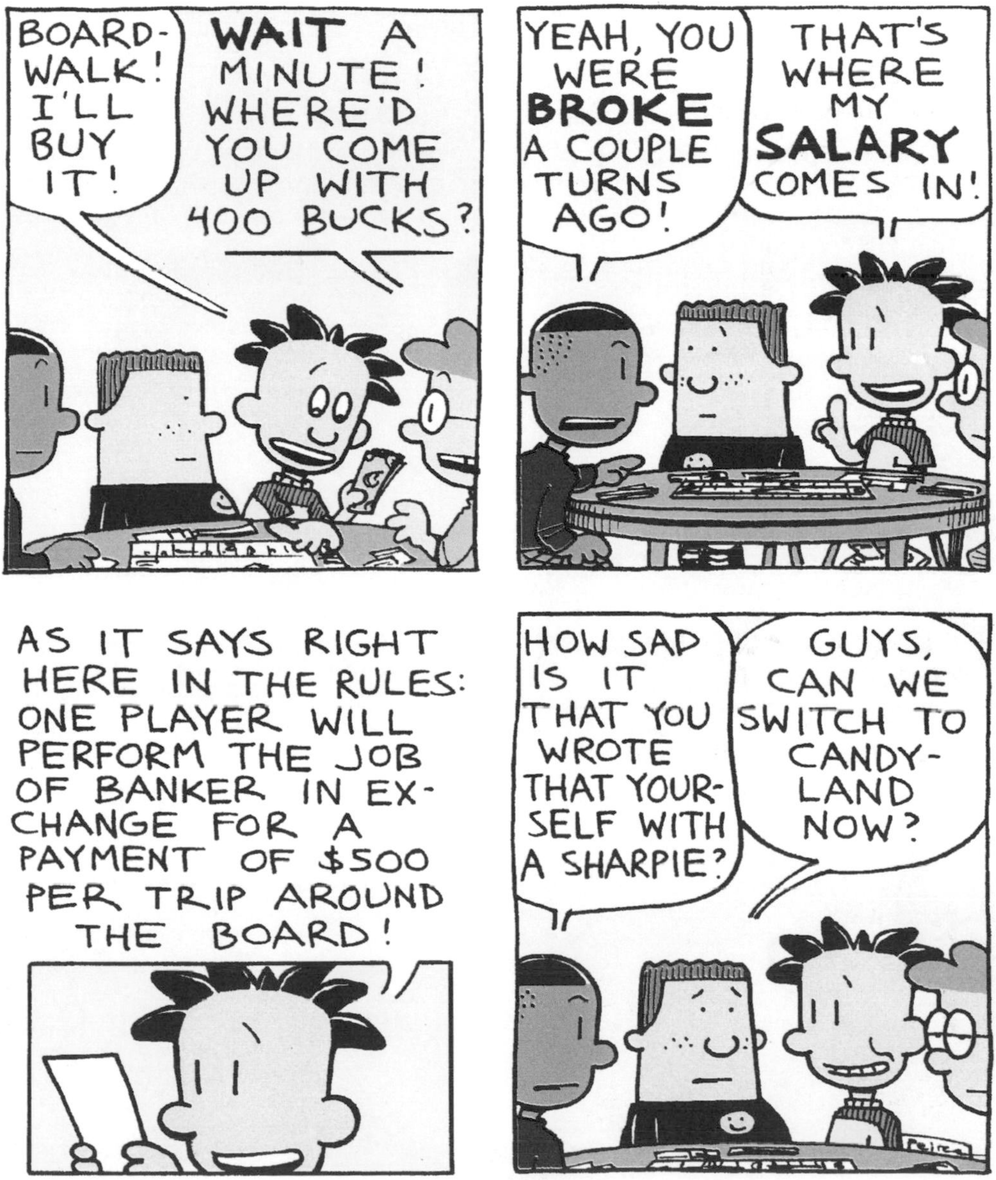
BOARD-WALK! I'LL BUY IT!
WAIT A MINUTE! WHERE'D YOU COME UP WITH 400 BUCKS?
YEAH, YOU WERE BROKE A COUPLE TURNS AGO!
THAT'S WHERE MY SALARY COMES IN!
AS IT SAYS RIGHT HERE IN THE RULES: ONE PLAYER WILL PERFORM THE JOB OF BANKER IN EX-CHANGE FOR A PAYMENT OF $500 PER TRIP AROUND THE BOARD!
HOW SAD IS IT THAT YOU WROTE THAT YOUR-SELF WITH A SHARPIE?
GUYS, CAN WE SWITCH TO CANDY-LAND NOW?

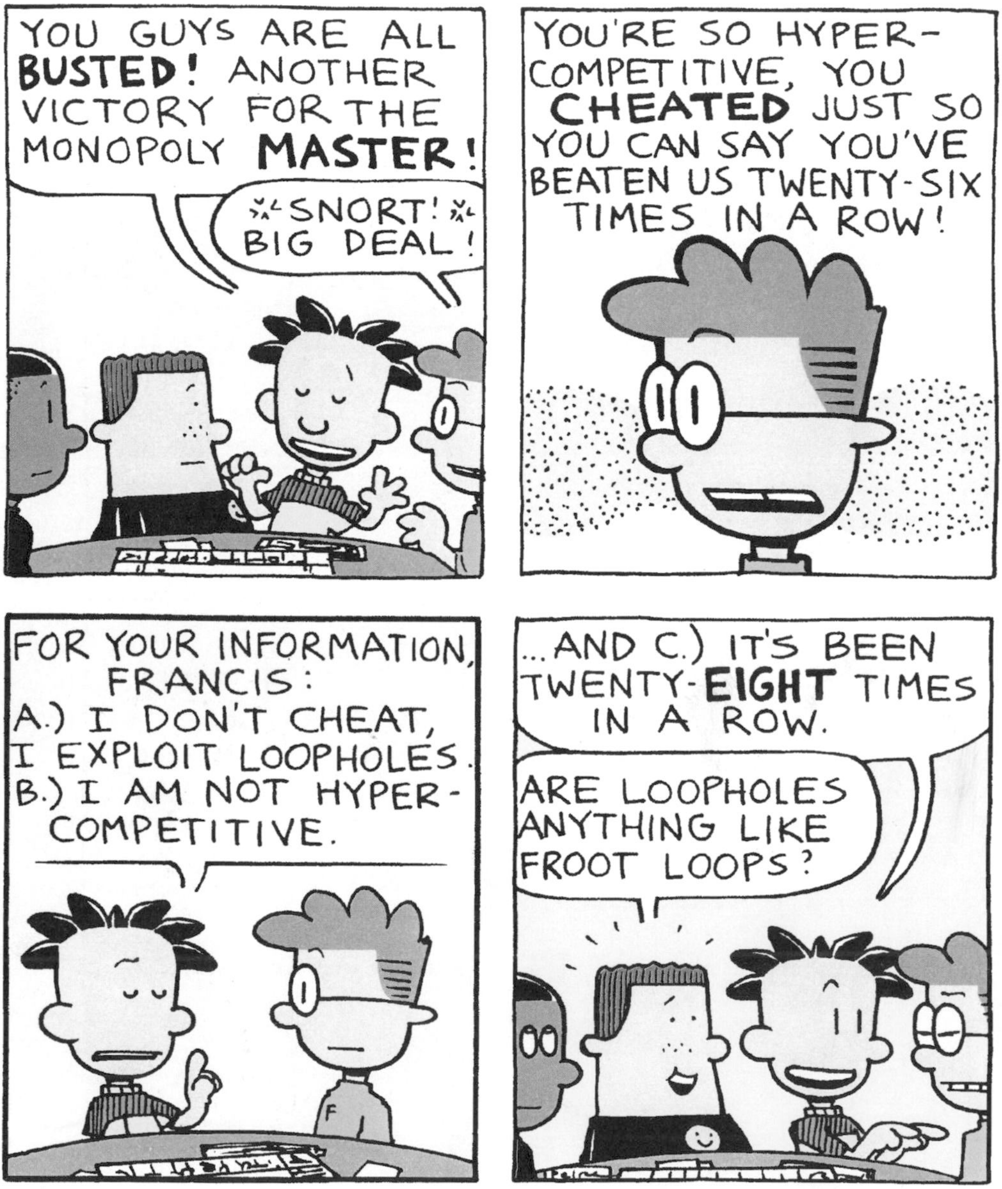
YOU GUYS ARE ALL BUSTED! ANOTHER VICTORY FOR THE MONOPOLY MASTER!
SNORT! BIG DEAL!
YOU'RE SO HYPER-COMPETITIVE, YOU CHEATED JUST SO YOU CAN SAY YOU'VE BEATEN US TWENTY-SIX TIMES IN A ROW!
FOR YOUR INFORMATION, FRANCIS: A.) I DON'T CHEAT, I EXPLOIT LOOPHOLES. B.) I AM NOT HYPER-COMPETITIVE.
...AND C.) IT'S BEEN TWENTY-EIGHT TIMES IN A ROW.
ARE LOOPHOLES ANYTHING LIKE FROOT LOOPS?

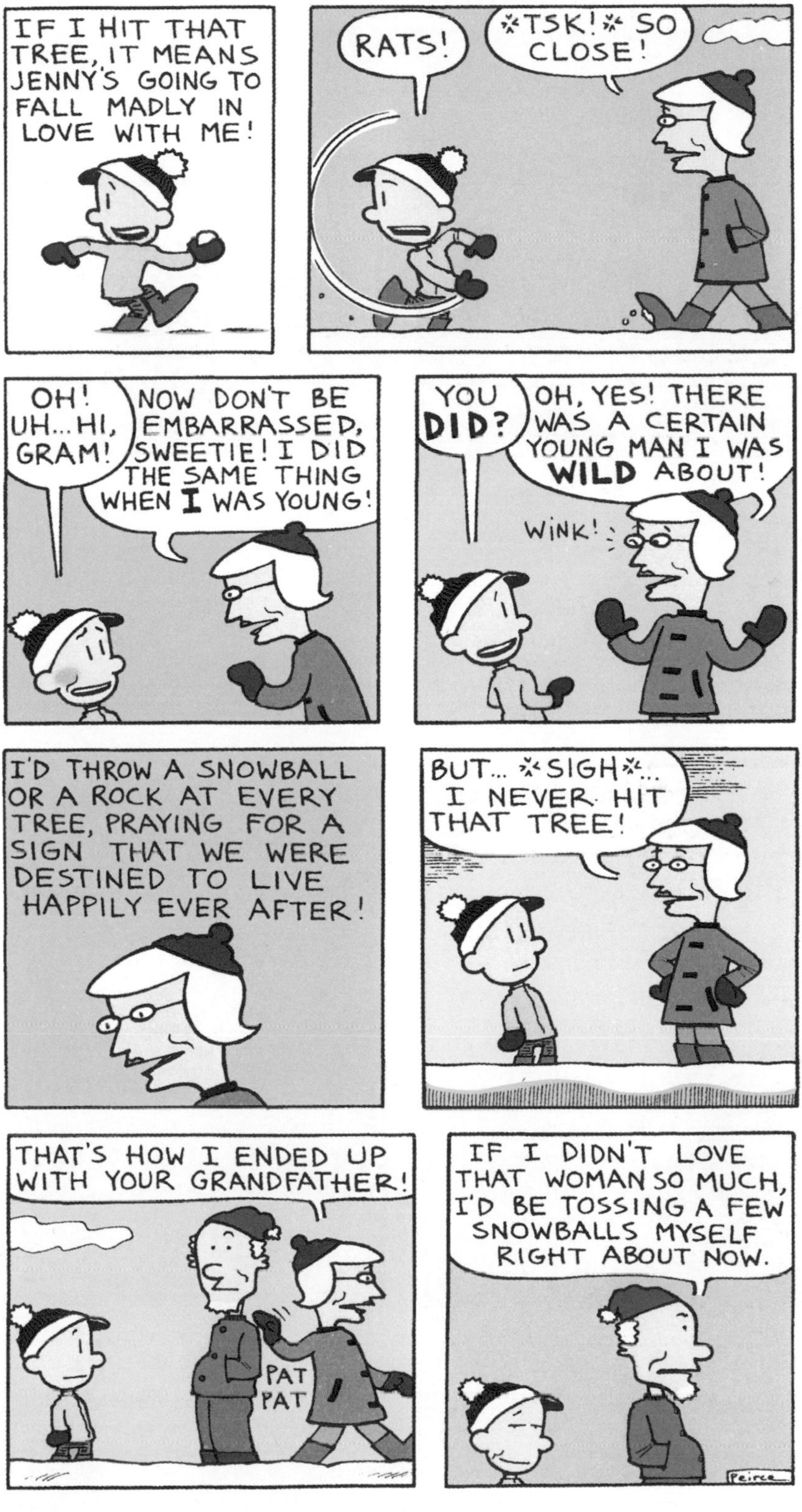
IF I HIT THAT TREE, IT MEANS JENNY'S GOING TO FALL MADLY IN LOVE WITH ME!
RATS!
TSK! SO CLOSE!
OH! UH... HI, GRAM!
NOW DON'T BE EMBARRASSED, SWEETIE! I DID THE SAME THING WHEN I WAS YOUNG!
YOU DID?
OH, YES! THERE WAS A CERTAIN YOUNG MAN I WAS WILD ABOUT!
WINK!
I'D THROW A SNOWBALL OR A ROCK AT EVERY TREE, PRAYING FOR A SIGN THAT WE WERE DESTINED TO LIVE HAPPILY EVER AFTER!
BUT... *SIGH*... I NEVER HIT THAT TREE!
THAT'S HOW I ENDED UP WITH YOUR GRANDFATHER!
PAT PAT
IF I DIDN'T LOVE THAT WOMAN SO MUCH, I'D BE TOSSING A FEW SNOWBALLS MYSELF RIGHT ABOUT NOW.
Peirce

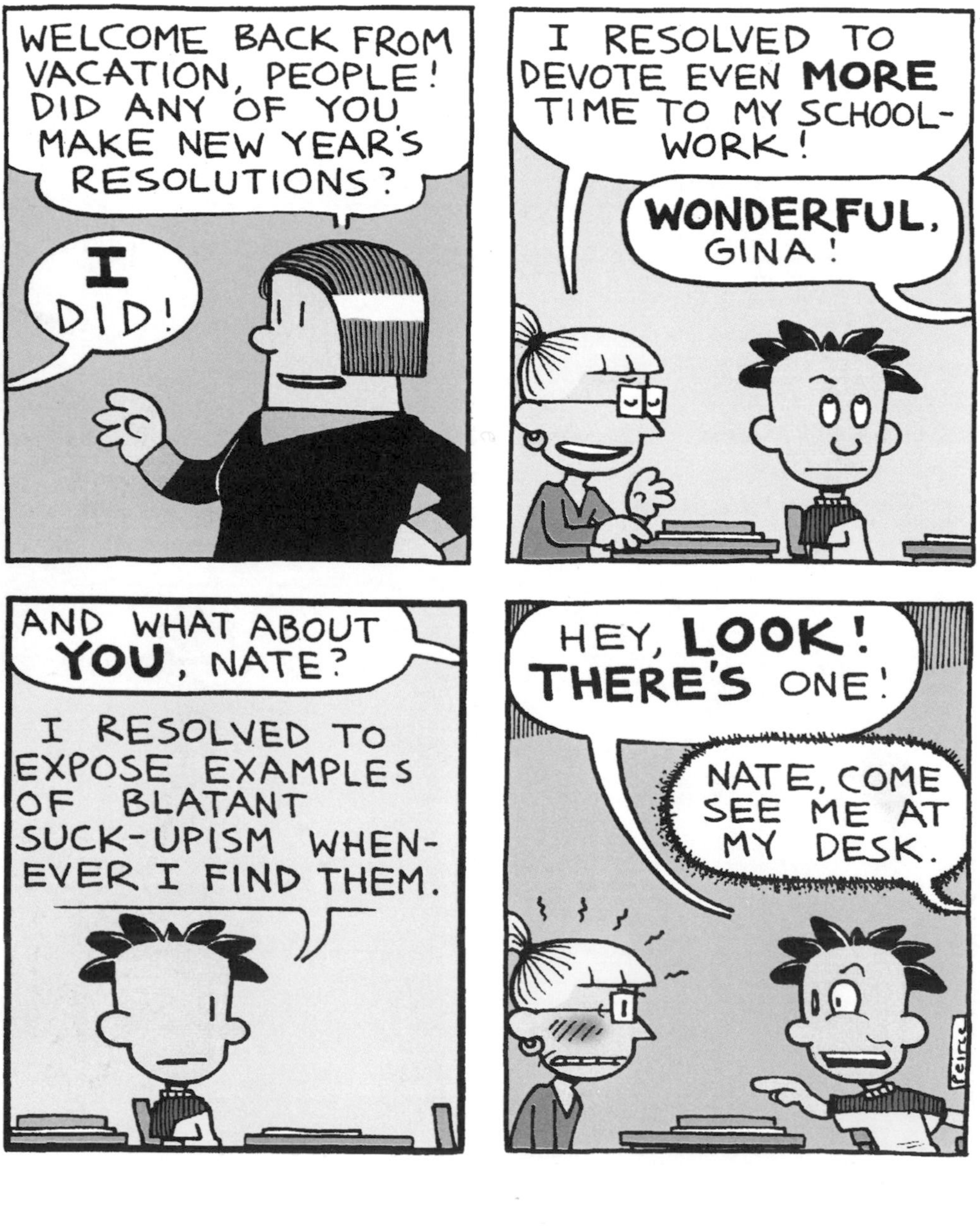
WELCOME BACK FROM VACATION, PEOPLE! DID ANY OF YOU MAKE NEW YEAR'S RESOLUTIONS?
I DID!
I RESOLVED TO DEVOTE EVEN MORE TIME TO MY SCHOOL-WORK!
WONDERFUL, GINA!
AND WHAT ABOUT YOU, NATE?
I RESOLVED TO EXPOSE EXAMPLES OF BLATANT SUCK-UPISM WHENEVER I FIND THEM.
HEY, LOOK! THERE'S ONE!
NATE, COME SEE ME AT MY DESK.
PEIRCE

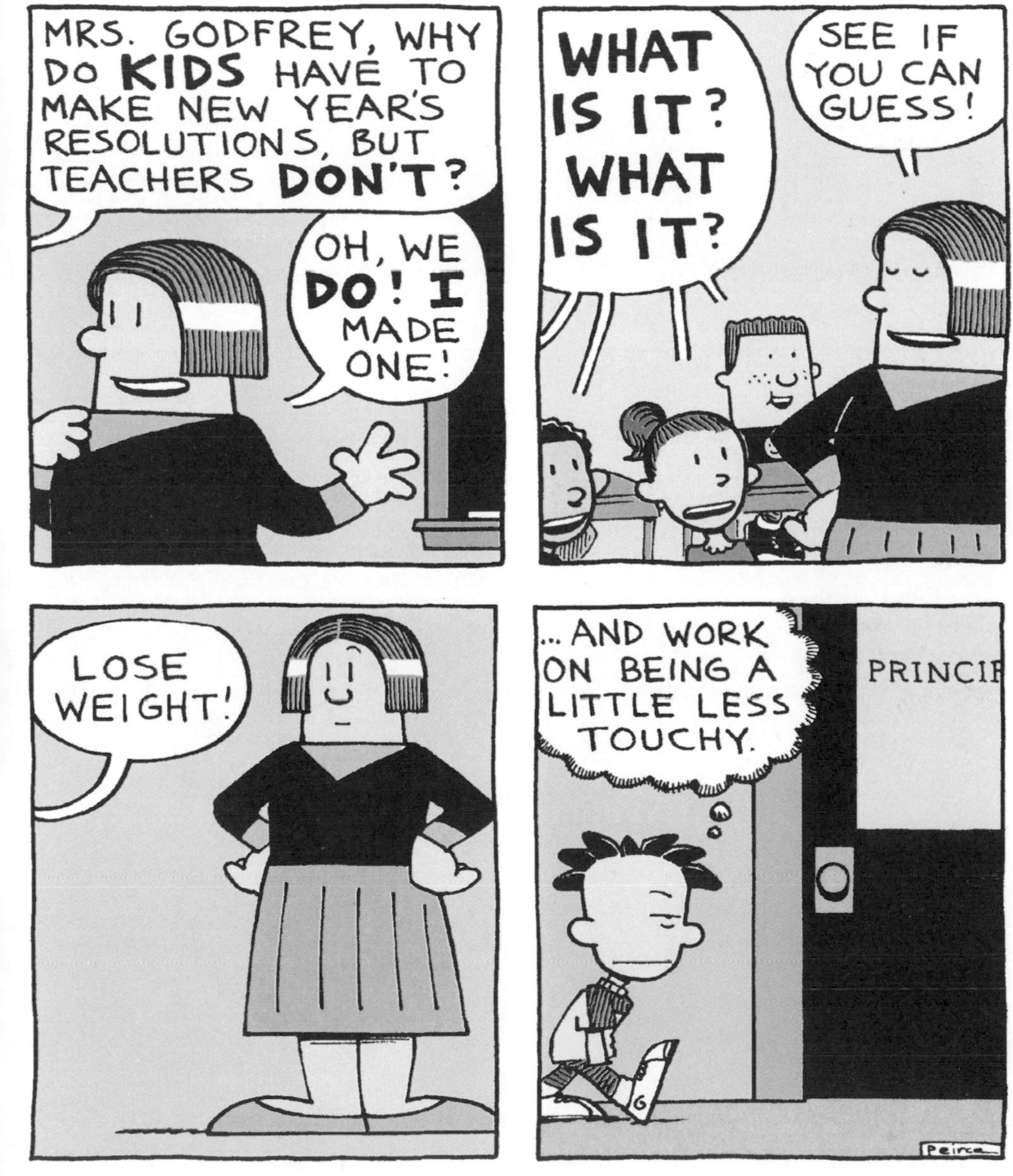

MRS. GODFREY, WHY DO KIDS HAVE TO MAKE NEW YEAR'S RESOLUTIONS, BUT TEACHERS DON'T?
OH, WE DO! I MADE ONE!
WHAT IS IT? WHAT IS IT?
SEE IF YOU CAN GUESS!
LOSE WEIGHT!
... AND WORK ON BEING A LITTLE LESS TOUCHY.
PRINCIP
Peirce

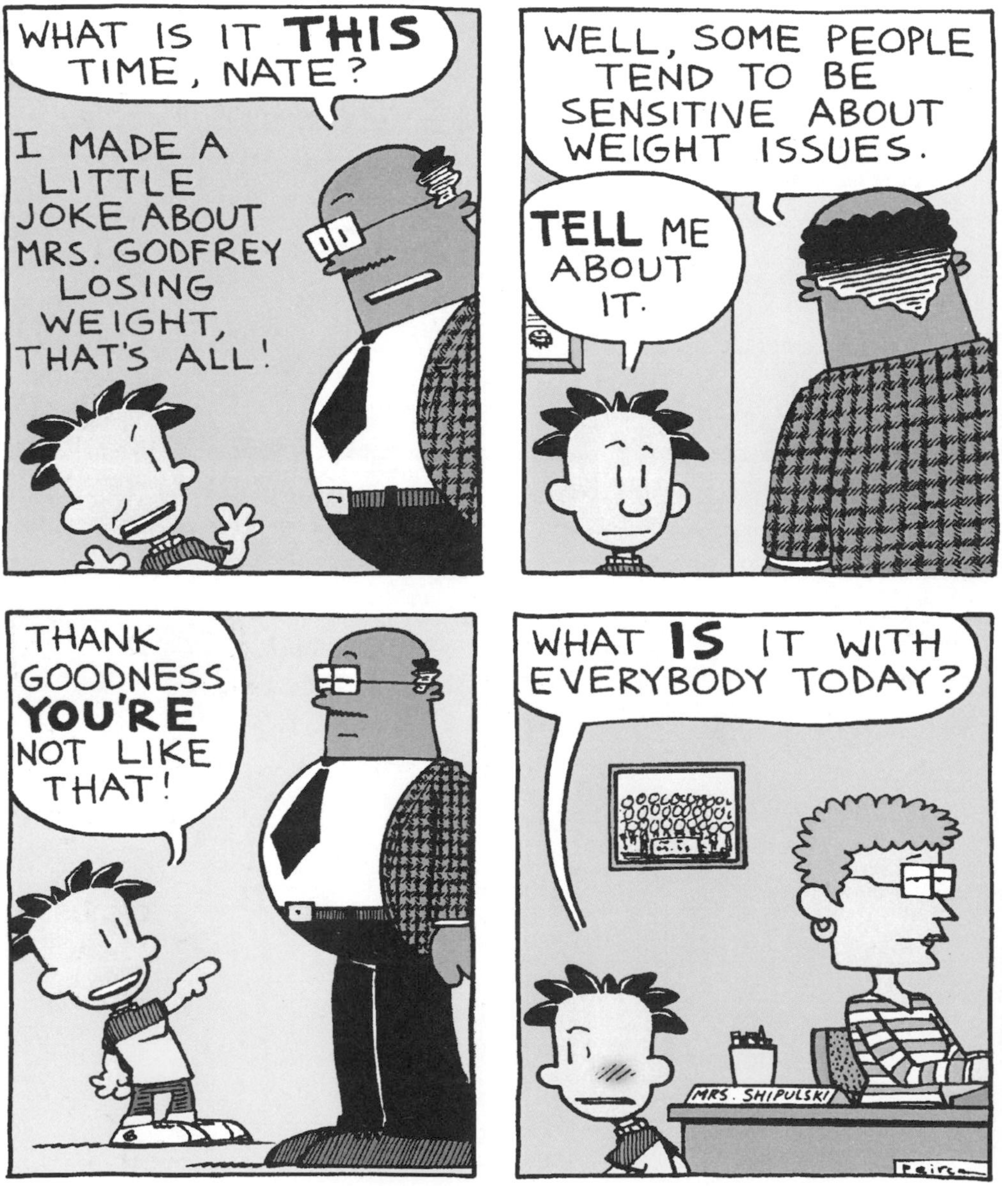
WHAT IS IT **THIS** TIME, NATE?
I MADE A LITTLE JOKE ABOUT MRS. GODFREY LOSING WEIGHT, THAT'S ALL!
WELL, SOME PEOPLE TEND TO BE SENSITIVE ABOUT WEIGHT ISSUES.
TELL ME ABOUT IT.
THANK GOODNESS **YOU'RE** NOT LIKE THAT!
WHAT **IS** IT WITH EVERYBODY TODAY?
MRS. SHIPULSKI

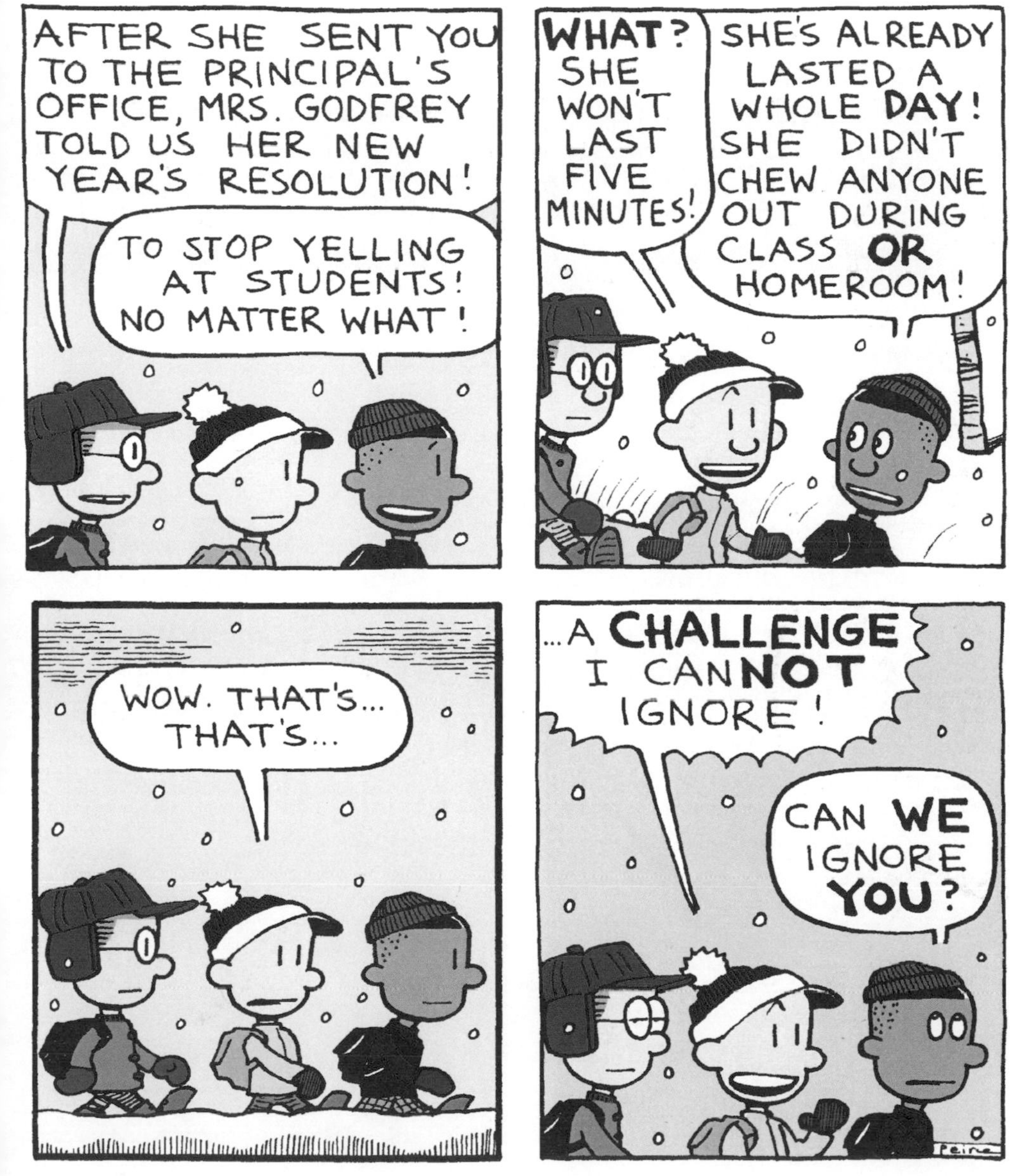
AFTER SHE SENT YOU TO THE PRINCIPAL'S OFFICE, MRS. GODFREY TOLD US HER NEW YEAR'S RESOLUTION!
TO STOP YELLING AT STUDENTS! NO MATTER WHAT!
WHAT? SHE WON'T LAST FIVE MINUTES!
SHE'S ALREADY LASTED A WHOLE DAY! SHE DIDN'T CHEW ANYONE OUT DURING CLASS OR HOMEROOM!
WOW. THAT'S... THAT'S...
...A CHALLENGE I CANNOT IGNORE!
CAN WE IGNORE YOU?
peirce

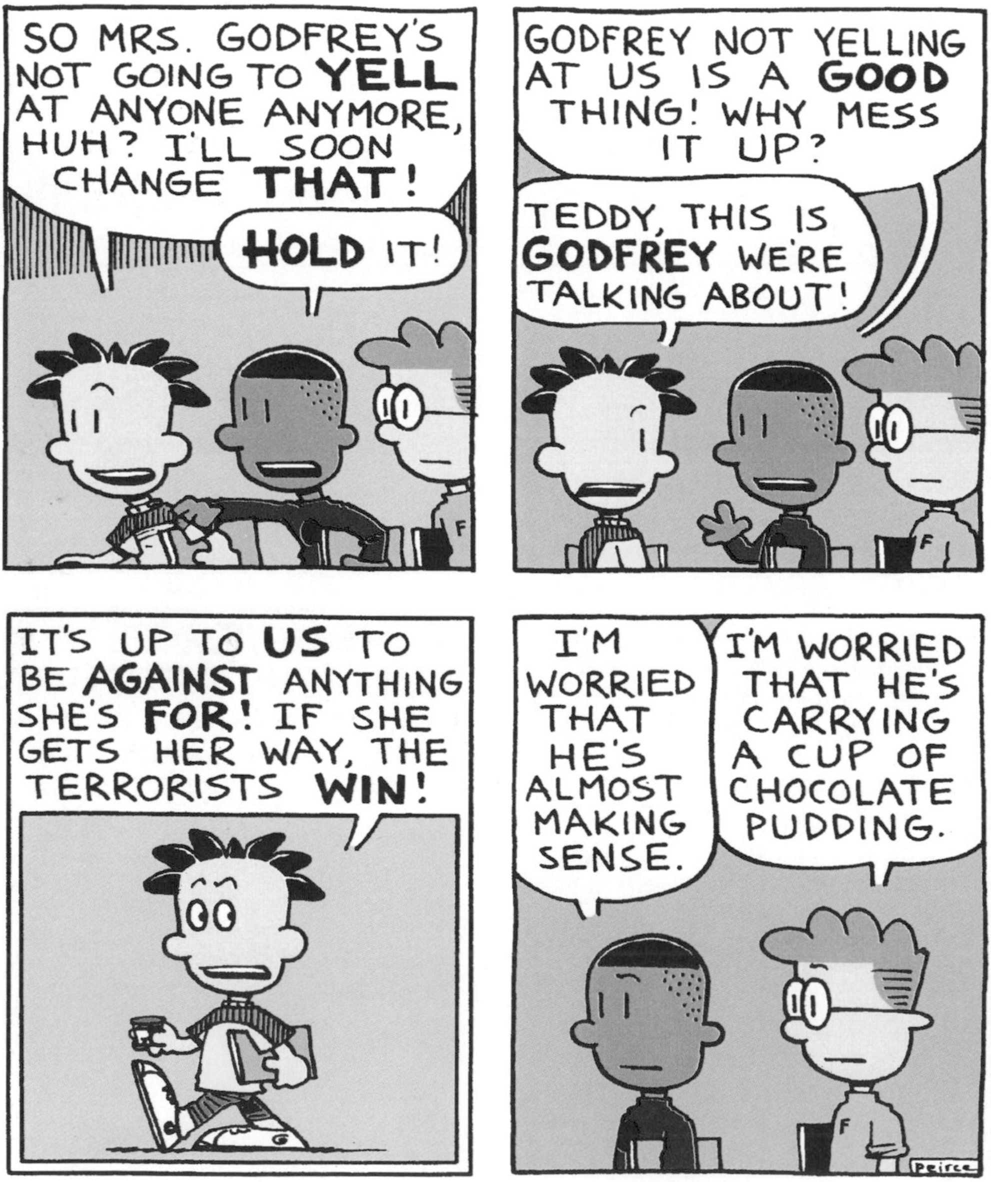
SO MRS. GODFREY'S NOT GOING TO YELL AT ANYONE ANYMORE, HUH? I'LL SOON CHANGE THAT!
HOLD IT!
GODFREY NOT YELLING AT US IS A GOOD THING! WHY MESS IT UP?
TEDDY, THIS IS GODFREY WE'RE TALKING ABOUT!
IT'S UP TO US TO BE AGAINST ANYTHING SHE'S FOR! IF SHE GETS HER WAY, THE TERRORISTS WIN!
I'M WORRIED THAT HE'S ALMOST MAKING SENSE.
I'M WORRIED THAT HE'S CARRYING A CUP OF CHOCOLATE PUDDING.
PEIRCE

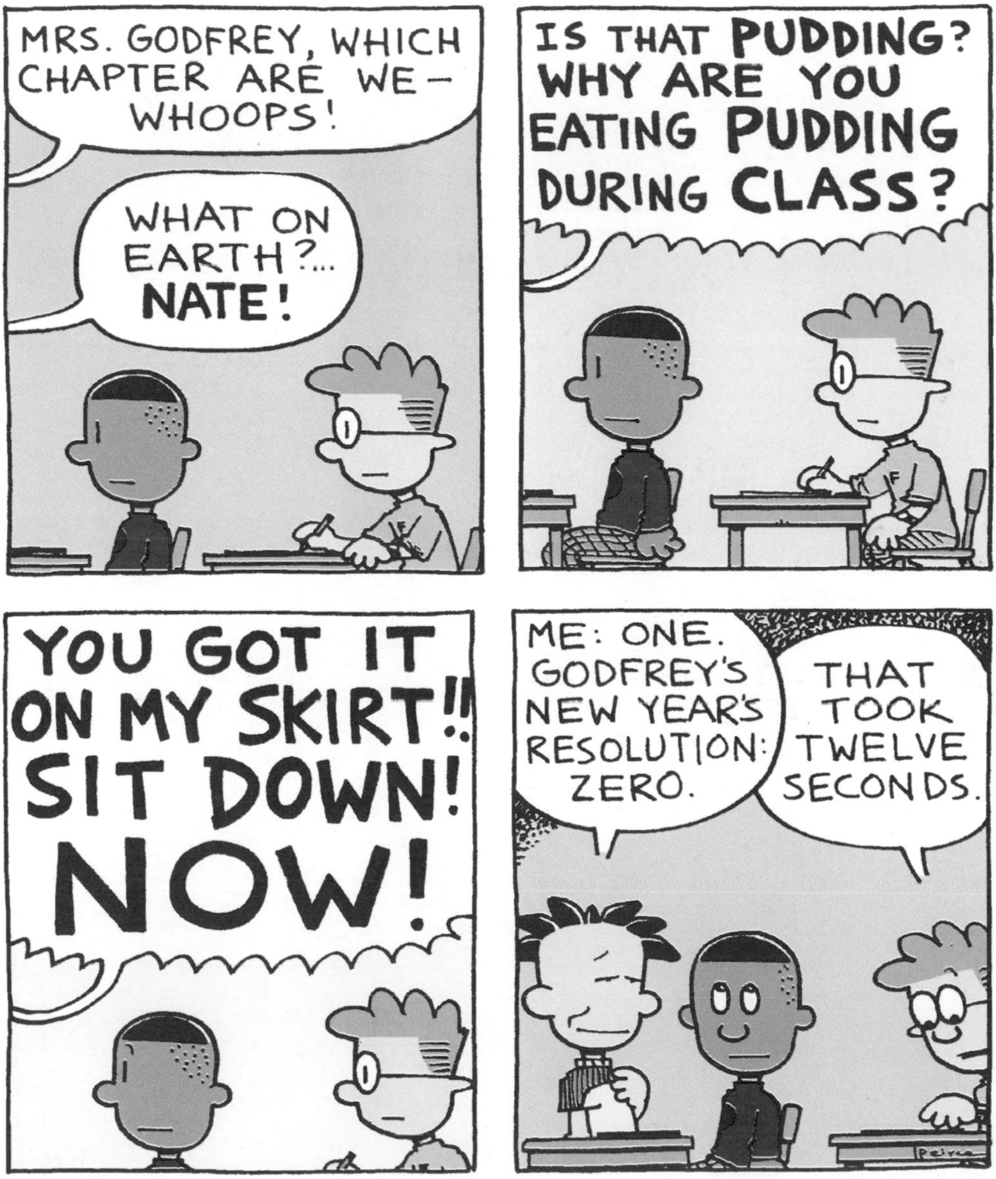
MRS. GODFREY, WHICH CHAPTER ARE WE— WHOOPS!
WHAT ON EARTH?... NATE!
IS THAT PUDDING? WHY ARE YOU EATING PUDDING DURING CLASS?
YOU GOT IT ON MY SKIRT!! SIT DOWN! NOW!
ME: ONE. GODFREY'S NEW YEAR'S RESOLUTION: ZERO.
THAT TOOK TWELVE SECONDS.

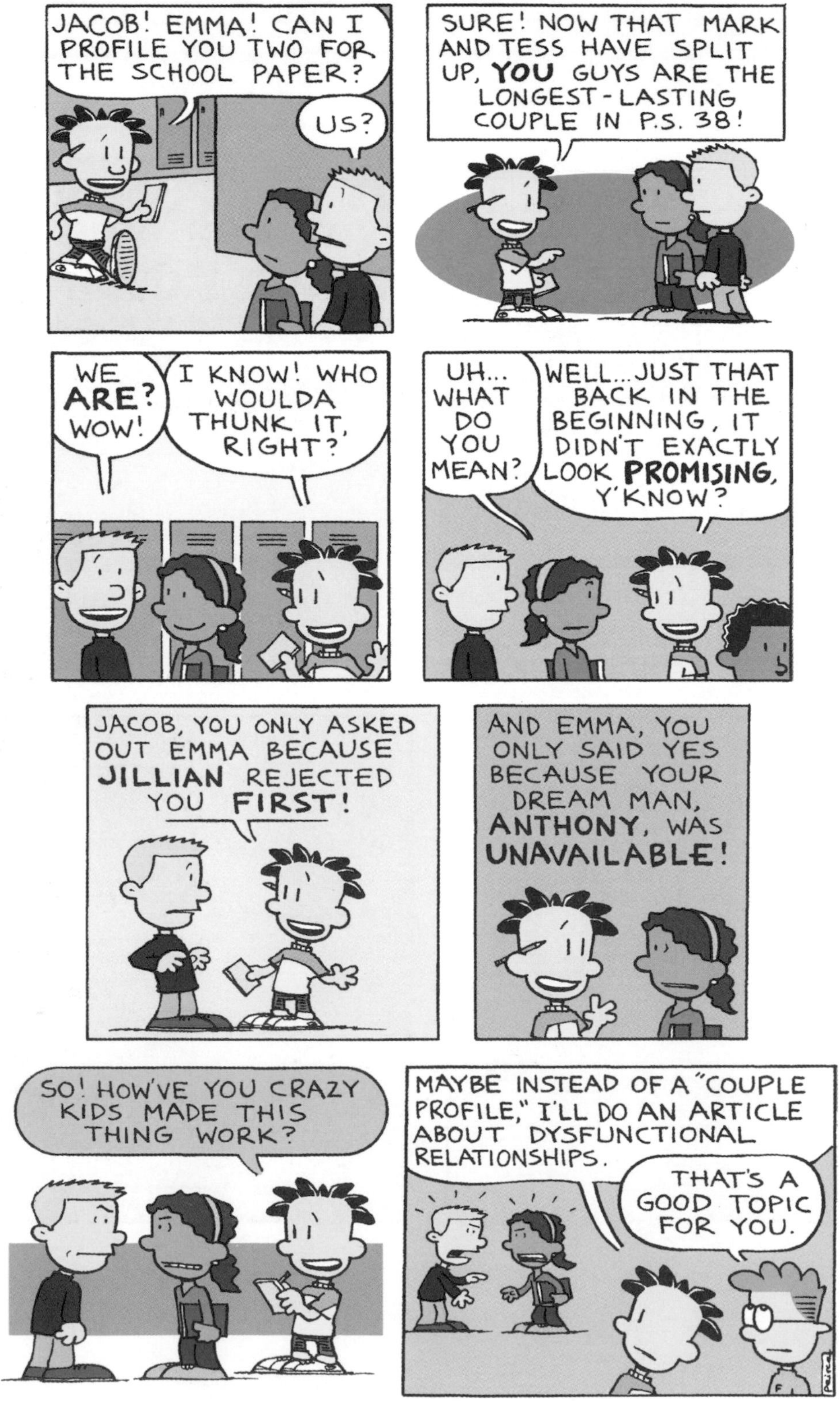
JACOB! EMMA! CAN I PROFILE YOU TWO FOR THE SCHOOL PAPER?
US?
SURE! NOW THAT MARK AND TESS HAVE SPLIT UP, YOU GUYS ARE THE LONGEST-LASTING COUPLE IN P.S. 38!
WE ARE? WOW!
I KNOW! WHO WOULDA THUNK IT, RIGHT?
UH... WHAT DO YOU MEAN?
WELL...JUST THAT BACK IN THE BEGINNING, IT DIDN'T EXACTLY LOOK PROMISING, Y'KNOW?
JACOB, YOU ONLY ASKED OUT EMMA BECAUSE JILLIAN REJECTED YOU FIRST!
AND EMMA, YOU ONLY SAID YES BECAUSE YOUR DREAM MAN, ANTHONY, WAS UNAVAILABLE!
SO! HOW'VE YOU CRAZY KIDS MADE THIS THING WORK?
MAYBE INSTEAD OF A "COUPLE PROFILE," I'LL DO AN ARTICLE ABOUT DYSFUNCTIONAL RELATIONSHIPS.
THAT'S A GOOD TOPIC FOR YOU.

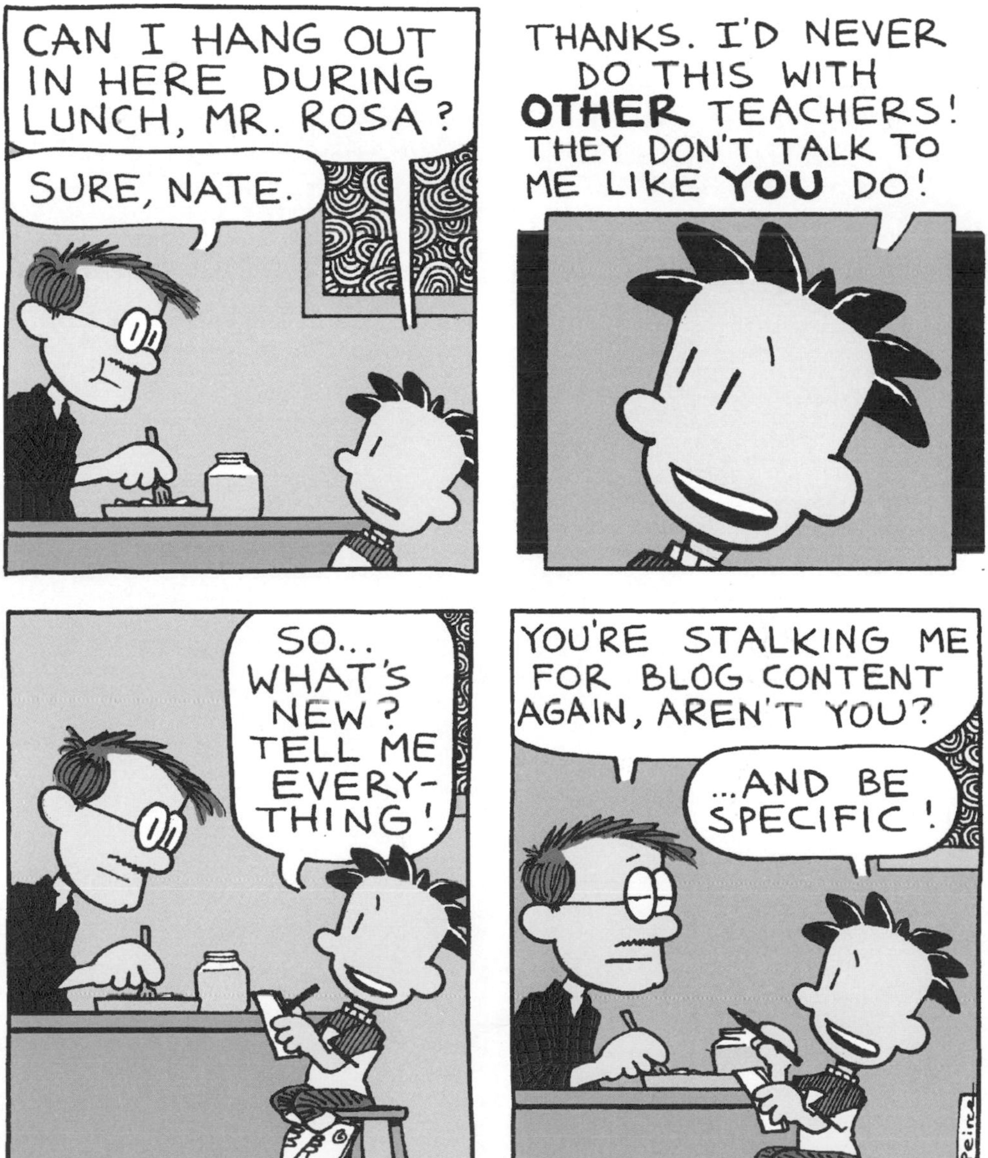
CAN I HANG OUT IN HERE DURING LUNCH, MR. ROSA?
SURE, NATE.
THANKS. I'D NEVER DO THIS WITH **OTHER** TEACHERS! THEY DON'T TALK TO ME LIKE **YOU** DO!
SO... WHAT'S NEW? TELL ME EVERY-THING!
YOU'RE STALKING ME FOR BLOG CONTENT AGAIN, AREN'T YOU?
...AND BE SPECIFIC!
Peirce

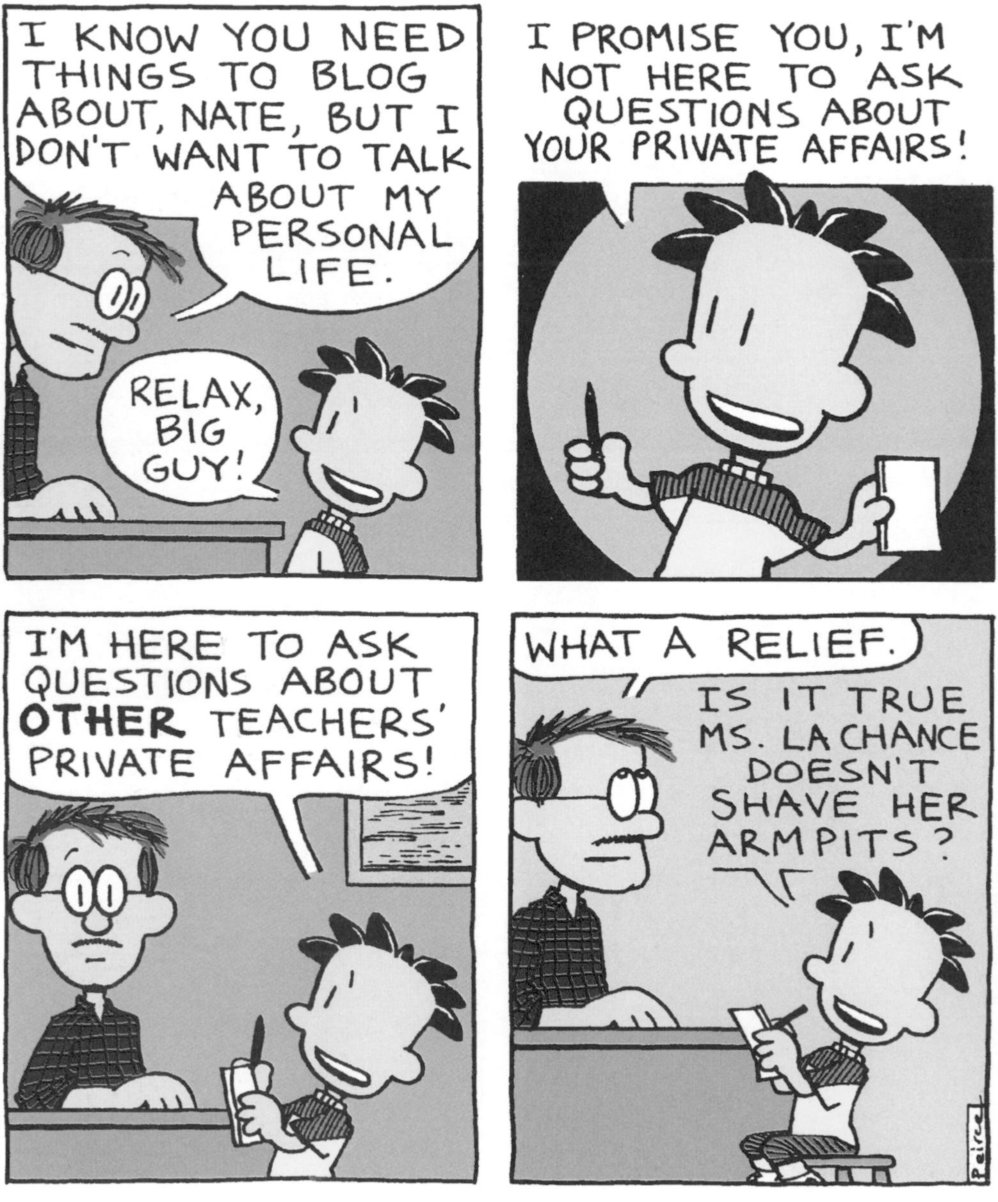
I KNOW YOU NEED THINGS TO BLOG ABOUT, NATE, BUT I DON'T WANT TO TALK ABOUT MY PERSONAL LIFE.
RELAX, BIG GUY!
I PROMISE YOU, I'M NOT HERE TO ASK QUESTIONS ABOUT YOUR PRIVATE AFFAIRS!
I'M HERE TO ASK QUESTIONS ABOUT **OTHER** TEACHERS' PRIVATE AFFAIRS!
WHAT A RELIEF.
IS IT TRUE MS. LACHANCE DOESN'T SHAVE HER ARMPITS?
Peirce

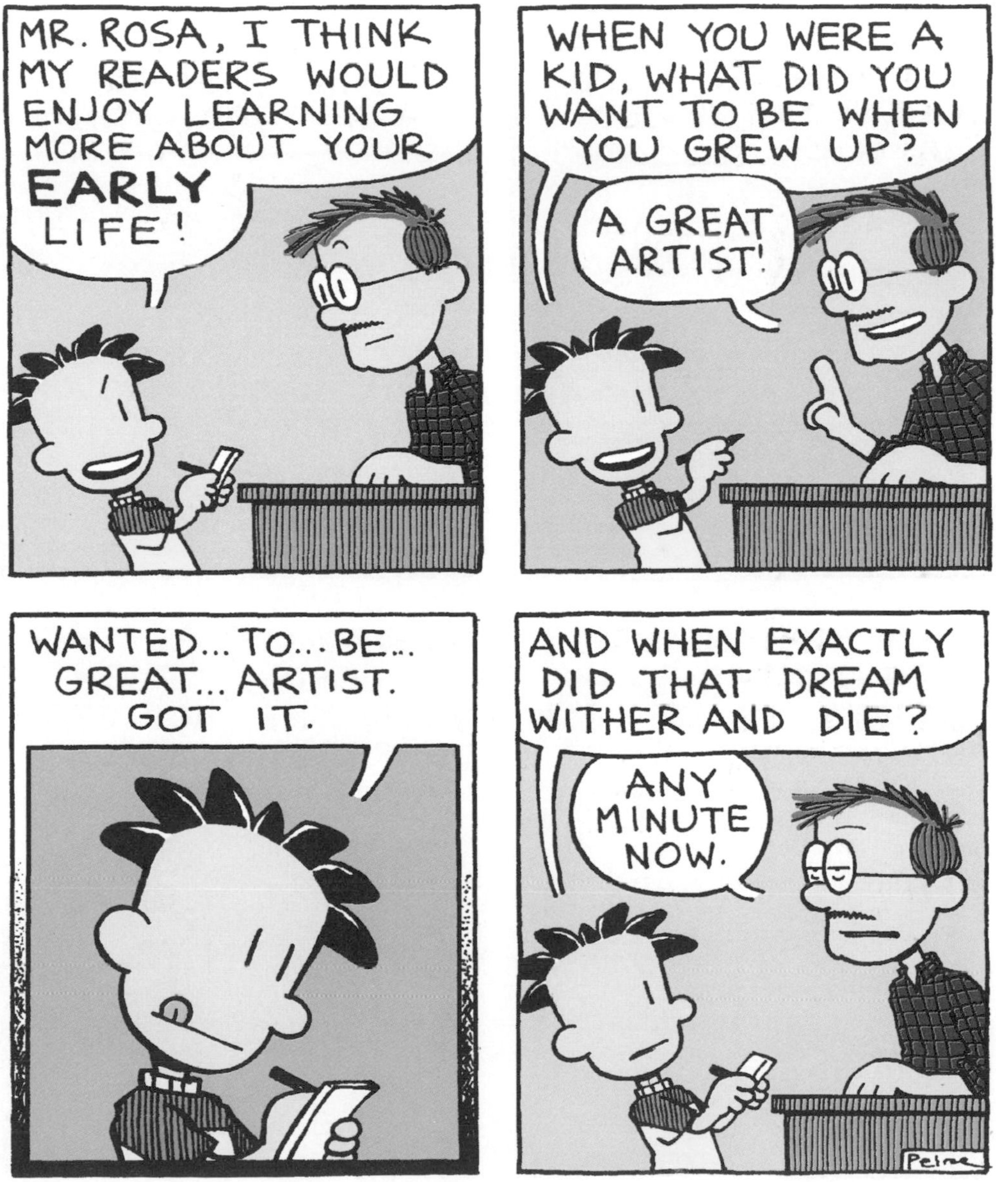
MR. ROSA, I THINK MY READERS WOULD ENJOY LEARNING MORE ABOUT YOUR **EARLY** LIFE!
WHEN YOU WERE A KID, WHAT DID YOU WANT TO BE WHEN YOU GREW UP?
A GREAT ARTIST!
WANTED... TO... BE... GREAT... ARTIST. GOT IT.
AND WHEN EXACTLY DID THAT DREAM WITHER AND DIE?
ANY MINUTE NOW.
Peirce

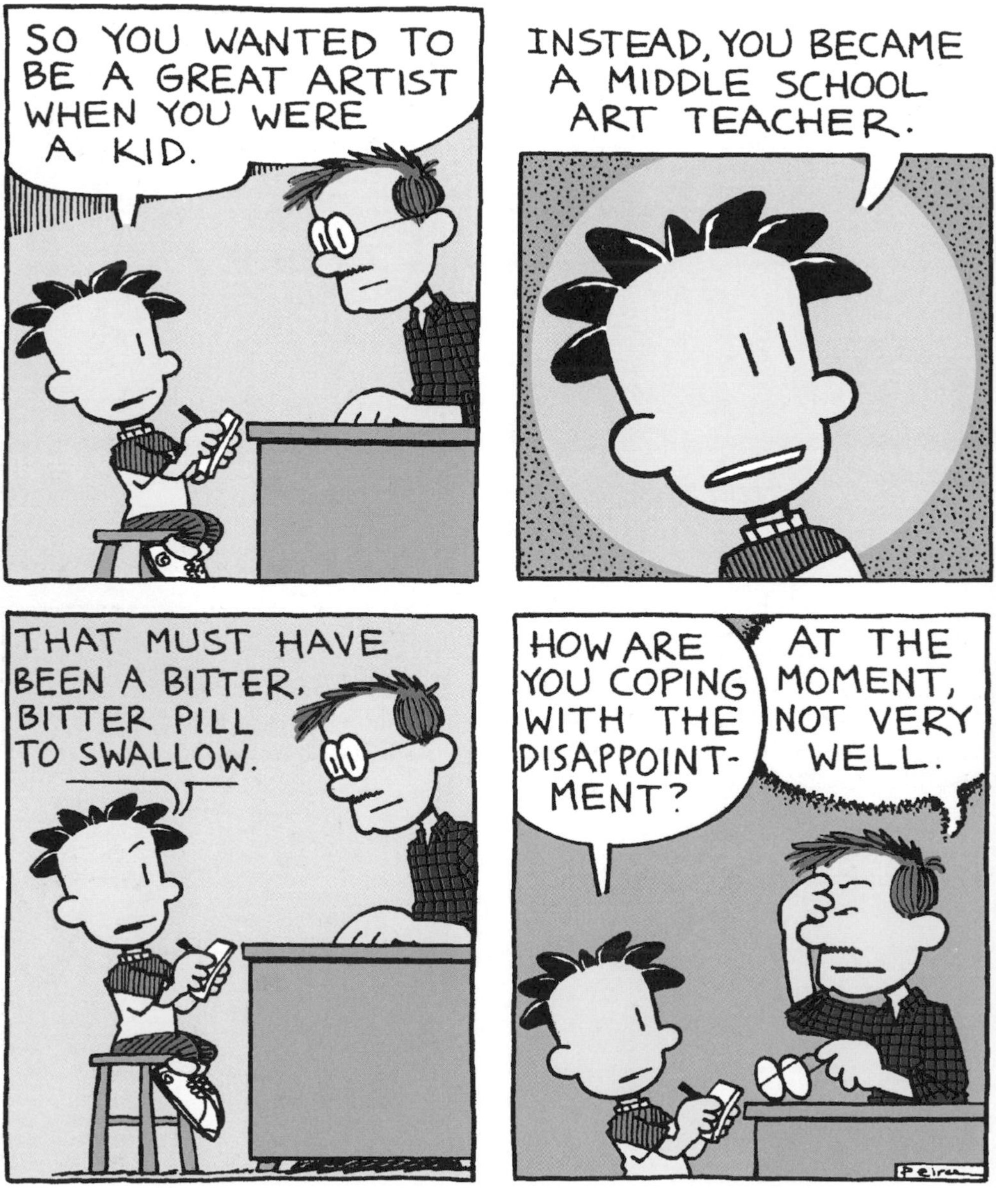
SO YOU WANTED TO BE A GREAT ARTIST WHEN YOU WERE A KID.
INSTEAD, YOU BECAME A MIDDLE SCHOOL ART TEACHER.
THAT MUST HAVE BEEN A BITTER, BITTER PILL TO SWALLOW.
HOW ARE YOU COPING WITH THE DISAPPOINTMENT?
AT THE MOMENT, NOT VERY WELL.

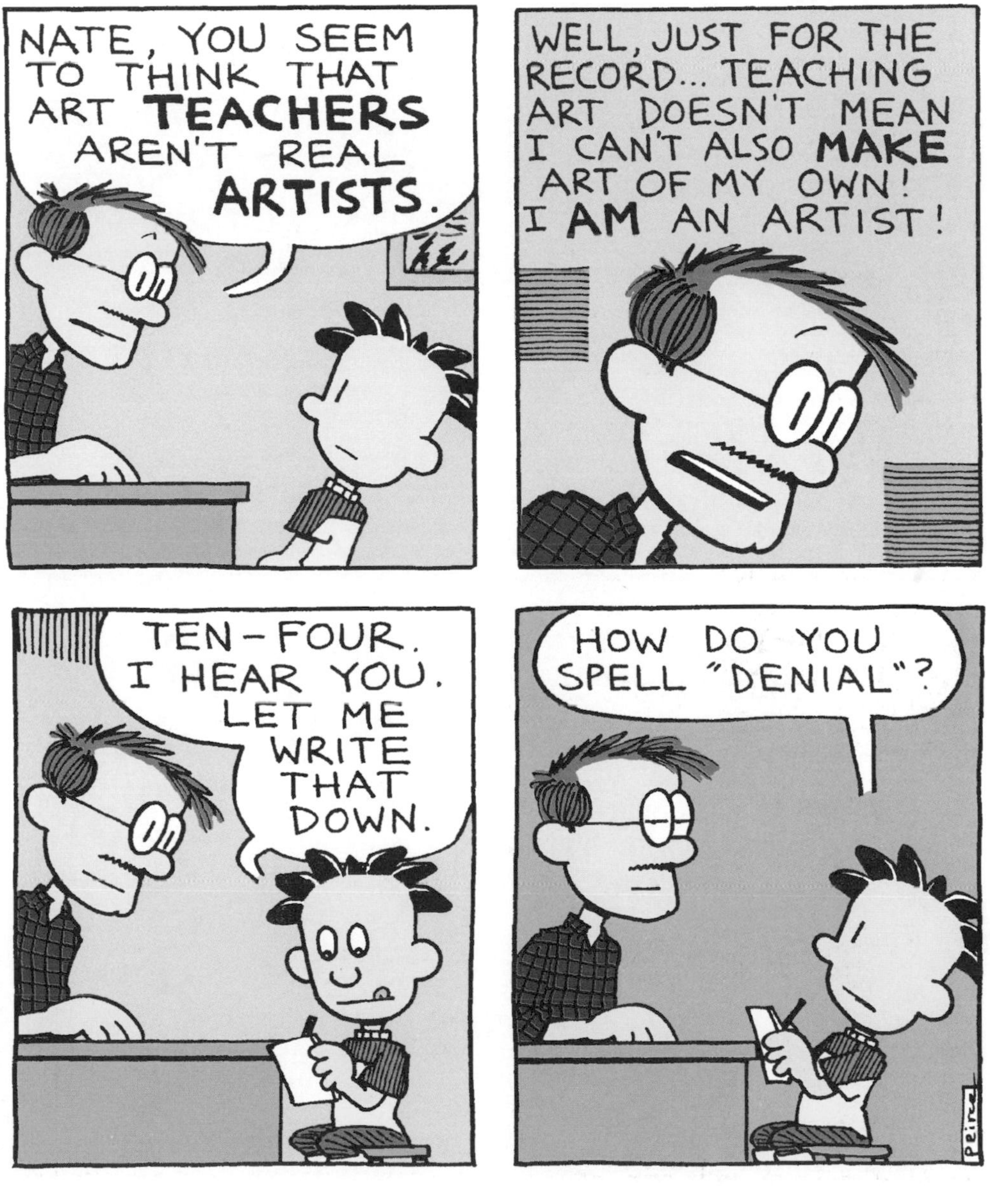
NATE, YOU SEEM TO THINK THAT ART **TEACHERS** AREN'T REAL **ARTISTS**.
WELL, JUST FOR THE RECORD... TEACHING ART DOESN'T MEAN I CAN'T ALSO **MAKE** ART OF MY OWN! I **AM** AN ARTIST!
TEN-FOUR. I HEAR YOU. LET ME WRITE THAT DOWN.
HOW DO YOU SPELL "DENIAL"?
Peirce

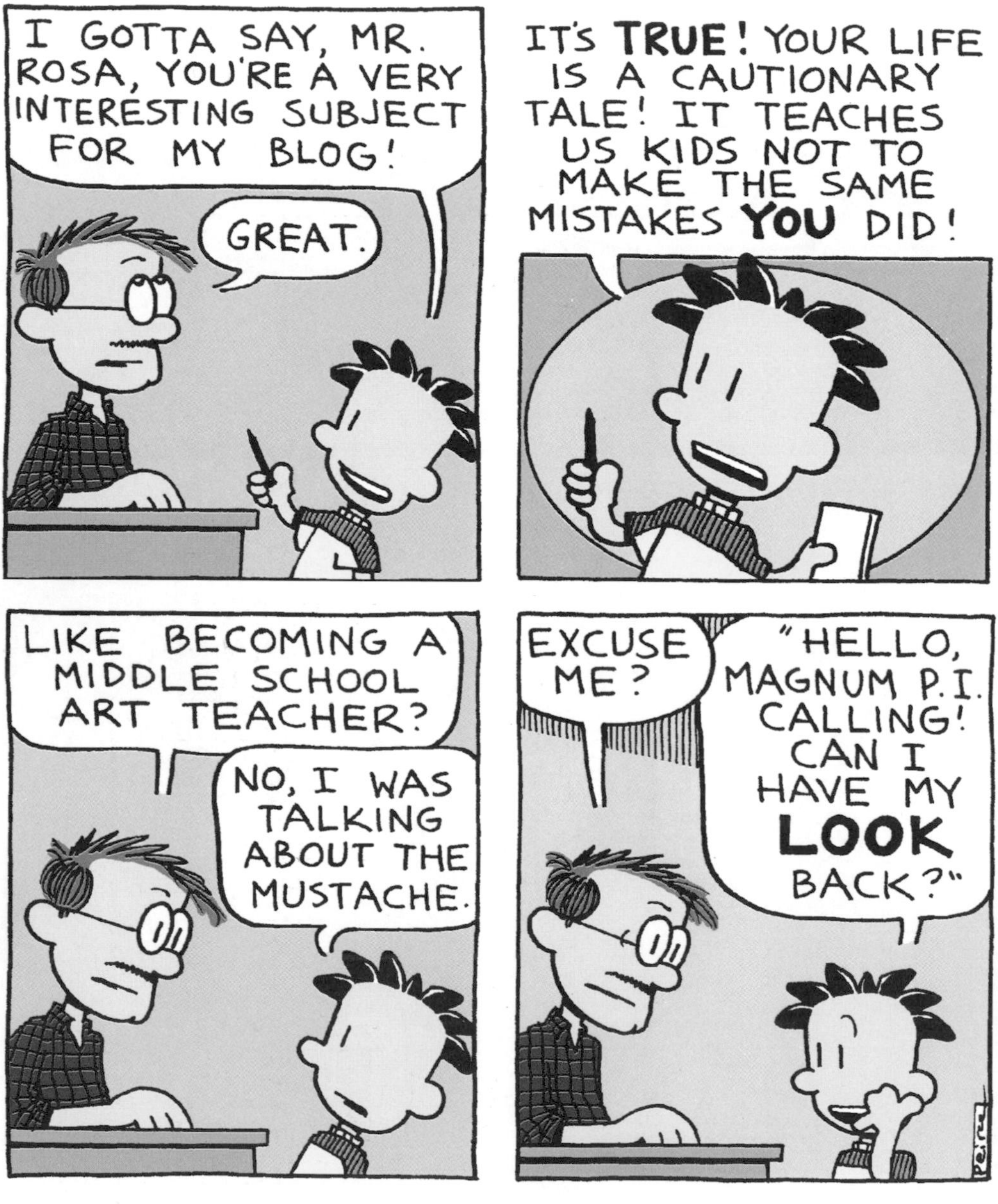
I GOTTA SAY, MR. ROSA, YOU'RE A VERY INTERESTING SUBJECT FOR MY BLOG!
GREAT.
IT'S **TRUE**! YOUR LIFE IS A CAUTIONARY TALE! IT TEACHES US KIDS NOT TO MAKE THE SAME MISTAKES **YOU** DID!
LIKE BECOMING A MIDDLE SCHOOL ART TEACHER?
NO, I WAS TALKING ABOUT THE MUSTACHE.
EXCUSE ME?
"HELLO, MAGNUM P.I. CALLING! CAN I HAVE MY **LOOK** BACK?"

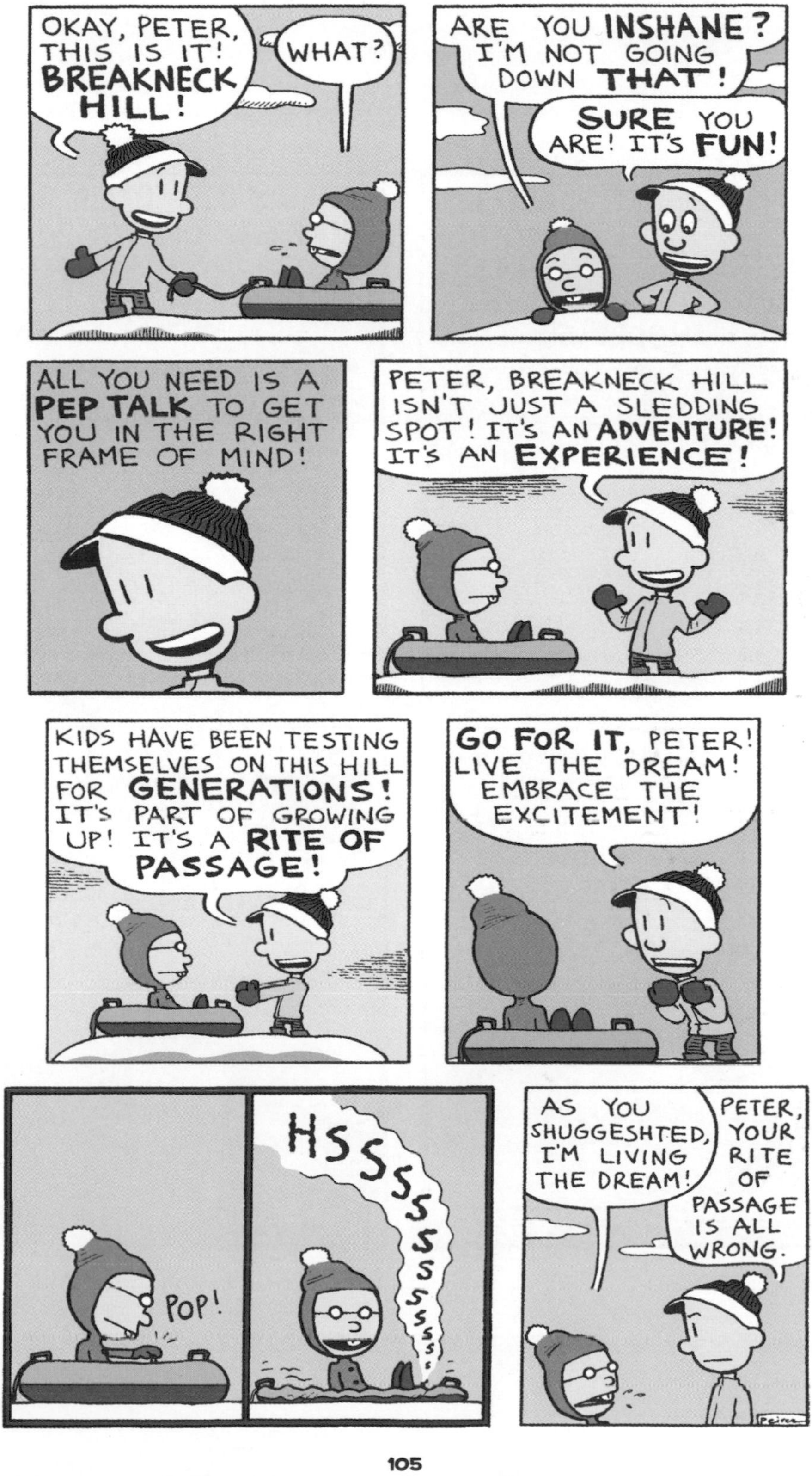
OKAY, PETER, THIS IS IT! BREAKNECK HILL!
WHAT?
ARE YOU INSHANE? I'M NOT GOING DOWN THAT!
SURE YOU ARE! IT'S FUN!
ALL YOU NEED IS A PEP TALK TO GET YOU IN THE RIGHT FRAME OF MIND!
PETER, BREAKNECK HILL ISN'T JUST A SLEDDING SPOT! IT'S AN ADVENTURE! IT'S AN EXPERIENCE!
KIDS HAVE BEEN TESTING THEMSELVES ON THIS HILL FOR GENERATIONS! IT'S PART OF GROWING UP! IT'S A RITE OF PASSAGE!
GO FOR IT, PETER! LIVE THE DREAM! EMBRACE THE EXCITEMENT!
POP!
HSSSSSSSSSSS
AS YOU SHUGGESHTED, I'M LIVING THE DREAM!
PETER, YOUR RITE OF PASSAGE IS ALL WRONG.

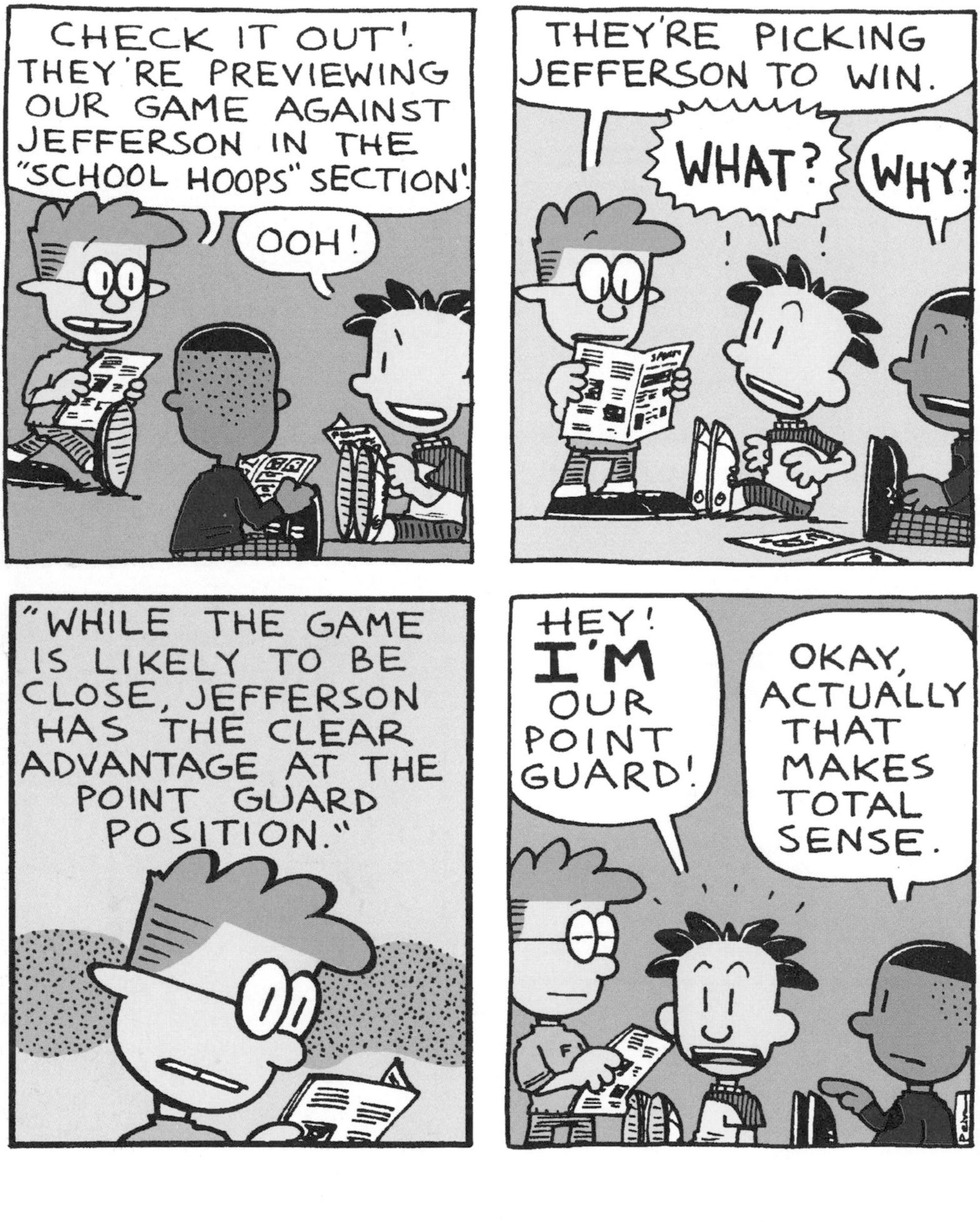
CHECK IT OUT! THEY'RE PREVIEWING OUR GAME AGAINST JEFFERSON IN THE "SCHOOL HOOPS" SECTION!
OOH!
THEY'RE PICKING JEFFERSON TO WIN.
WHAT?
WHY?
"WHILE THE GAME IS LIKELY TO BE CLOSE, JEFFERSON HAS THE CLEAR ADVANTAGE AT THE POINT GUARD POSITION."
HEY! I'M OUR POINT GUARD!
OKAY, ACTUALLY THAT MAKES TOTAL SENSE.

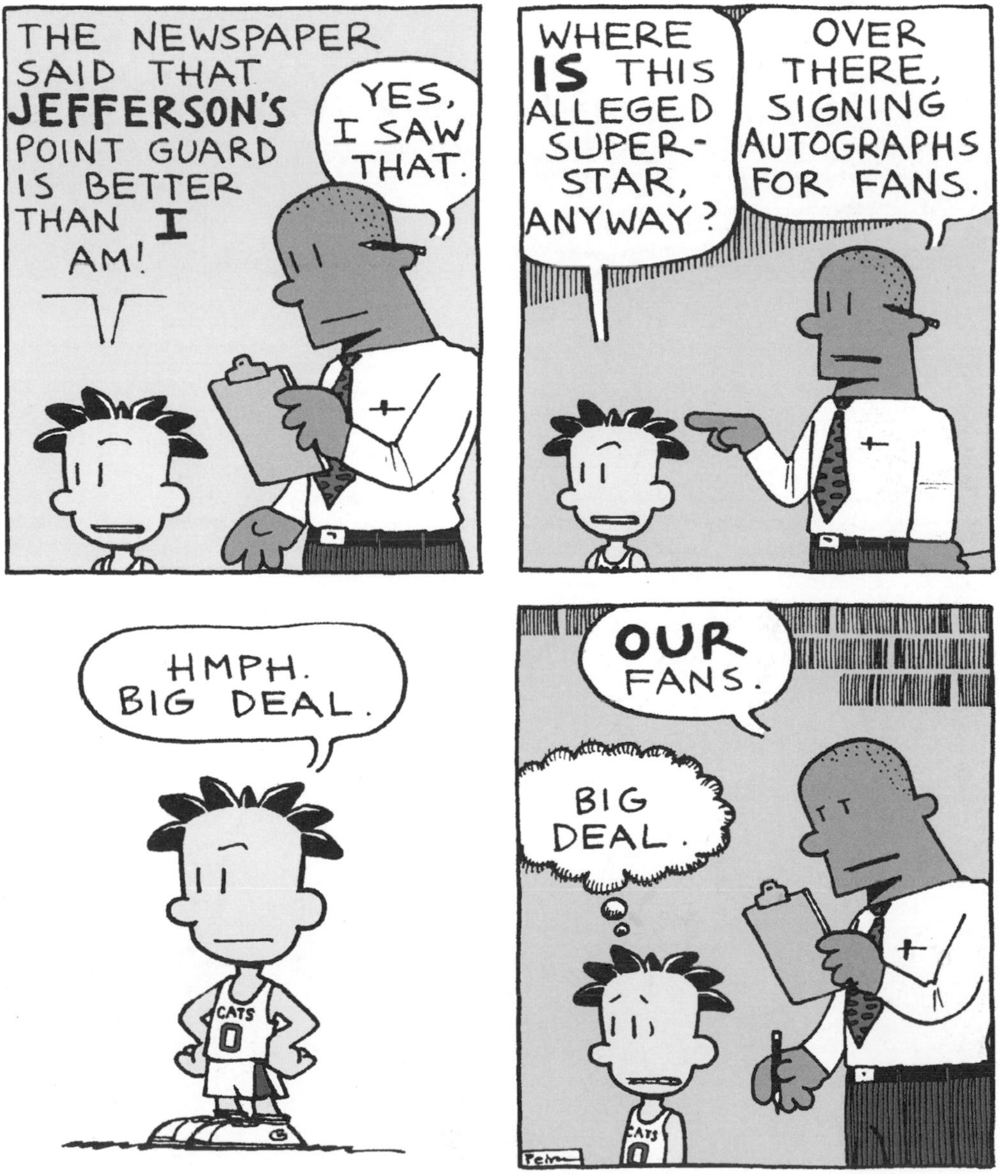
THE NEWSPAPER SAID THAT JEFFERSON'S POINT GUARD IS BETTER THAN I AM!
YES, I SAW THAT.
WHERE IS THIS ALLEGED SUPER-STAR, ANYWAY?
OVER THERE, SIGNING AUTOGRAPHS FOR FANS.
HMPH. BIG DEAL.
OUR FANS.
BIG DEAL.
CATS
0

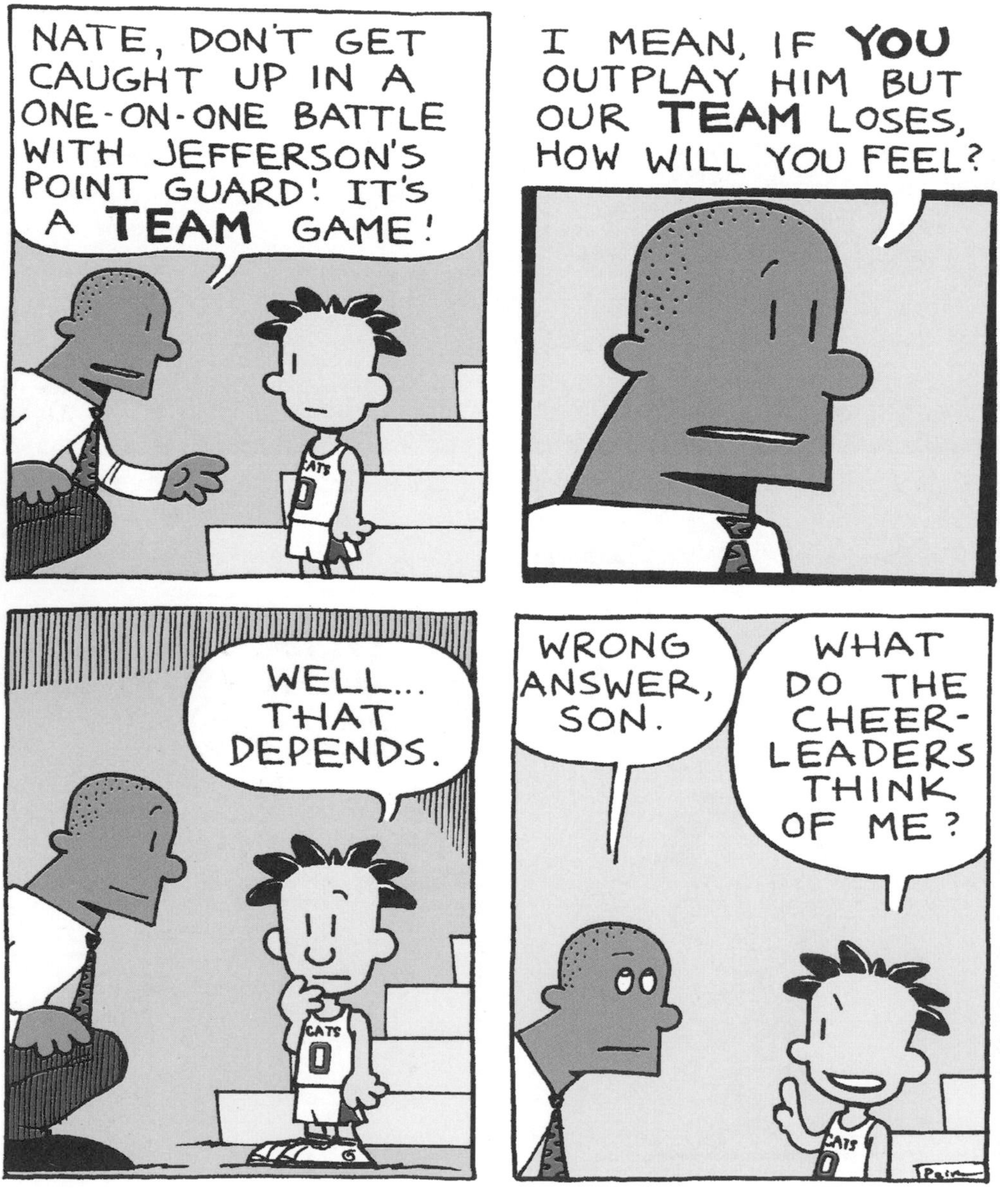
NATE, DON'T GET CAUGHT UP IN A ONE-ON-ONE BATTLE WITH JEFFERSON'S POINT GUARD! IT'S A **TEAM** GAME!
CATS 0
I MEAN, IF **YOU** OUTPLAY HIM BUT OUR **TEAM** LOSES, HOW WILL YOU FEEL?
WELL... THAT DEPENDS.
CATS 0
WRONG ANSWER, SON.
WHAT DO THE CHEER-LEADERS THINK OF ME?
CATS 0

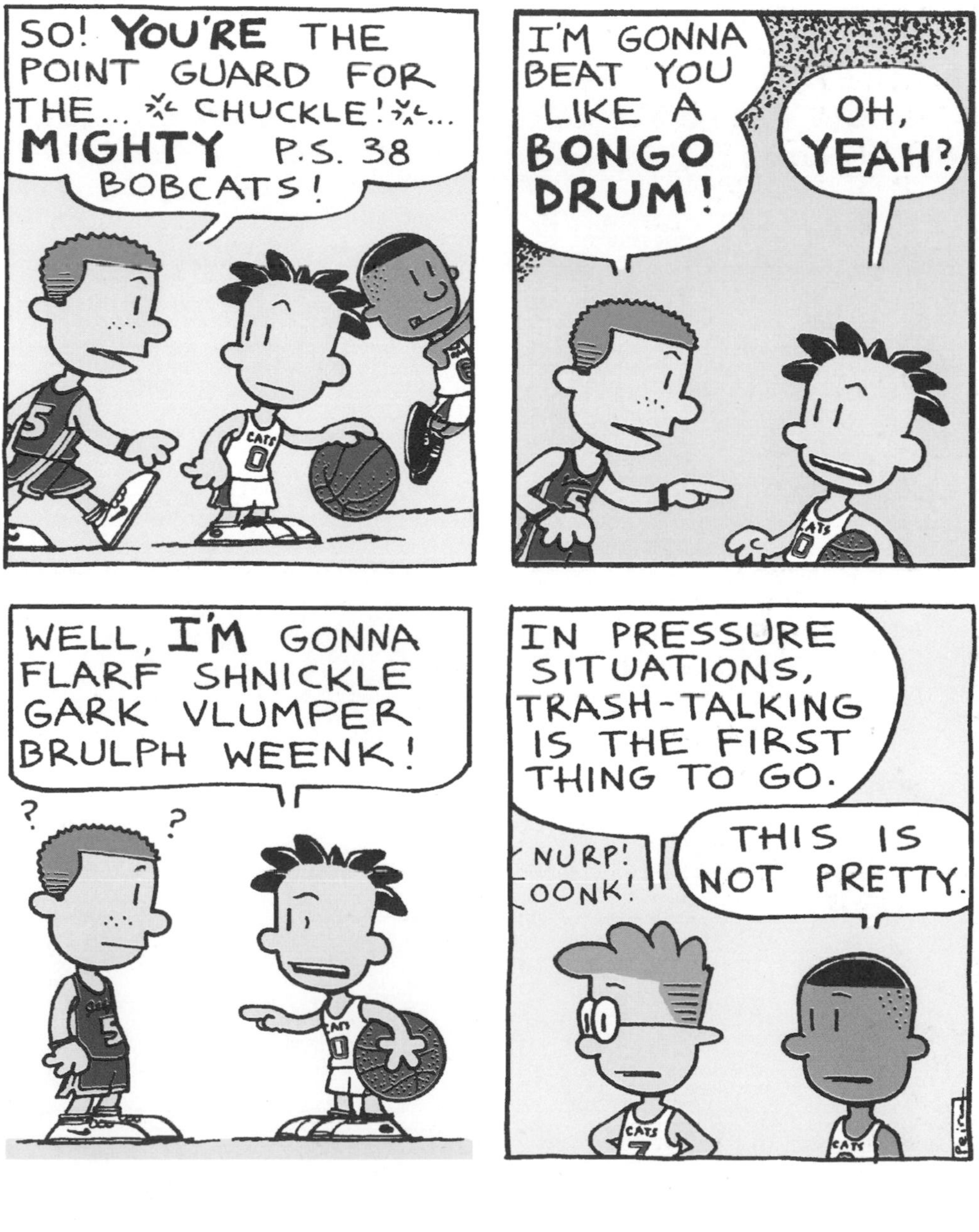

SO! YOU'RE THE POINT GUARD FOR THE... CHUCKLE!... MIGHTY P.S. 38 BOBCATS!
I'M GONNA BEAT YOU LIKE A BONGO DRUM!
OH, YEAH?
WELL, I'M GONNA FLARF SHNICKLE GARK VLUMPER BRULPH WEENK!
? ?
IN PRESSURE SITUATIONS, TRASH-TALKING IS THE FIRST THING TO GO.
NURP! OONK!
THIS IS NOT PRETTY.

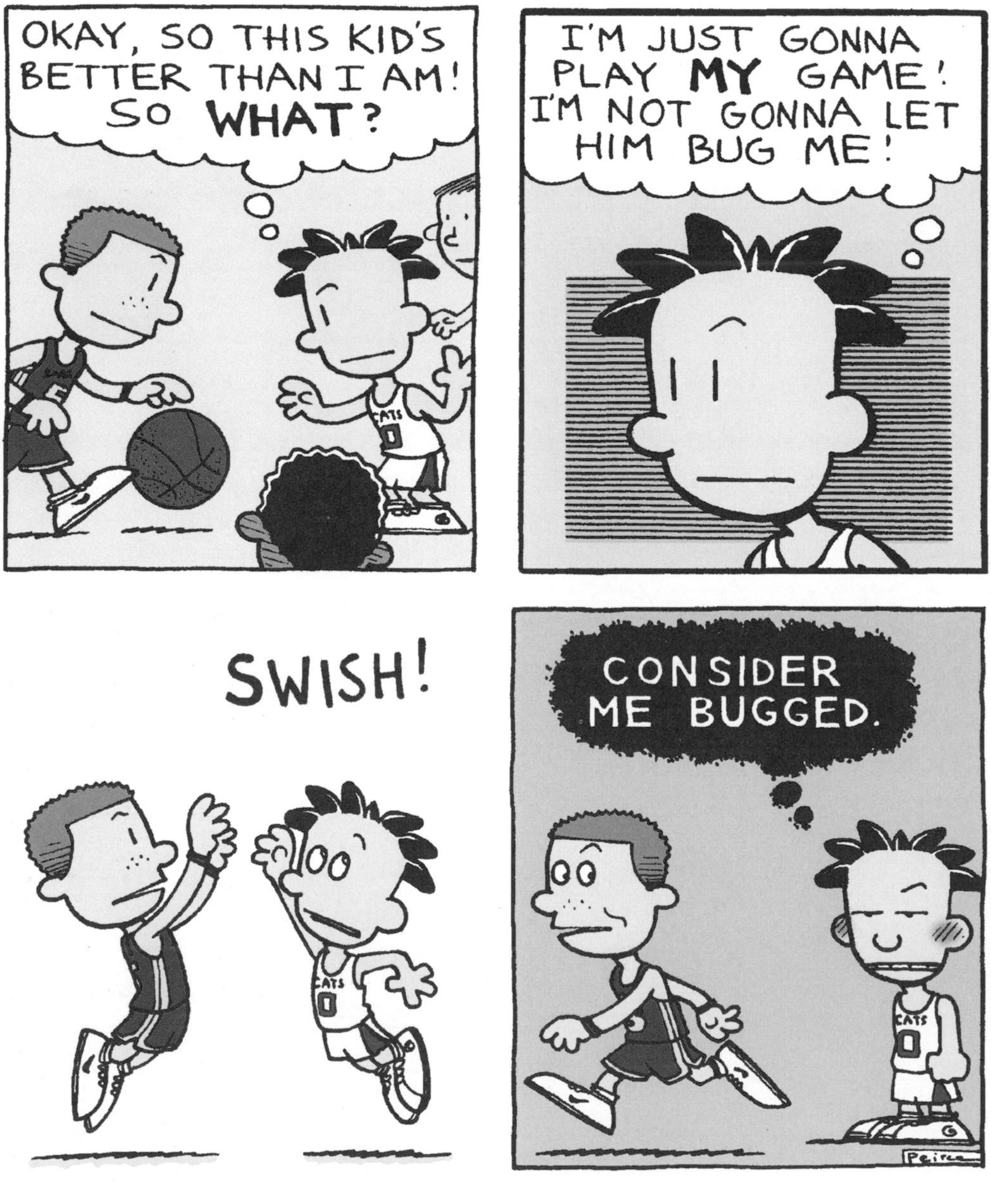
OKAY, SO THIS KID'S BETTER THAN I AM! SO WHAT?
I'M JUST GONNA PLAY MY GAME! I'M NOT GONNA LET HIM BUG ME!
SWISH!
CONSIDER ME BUGGED.
Peirce

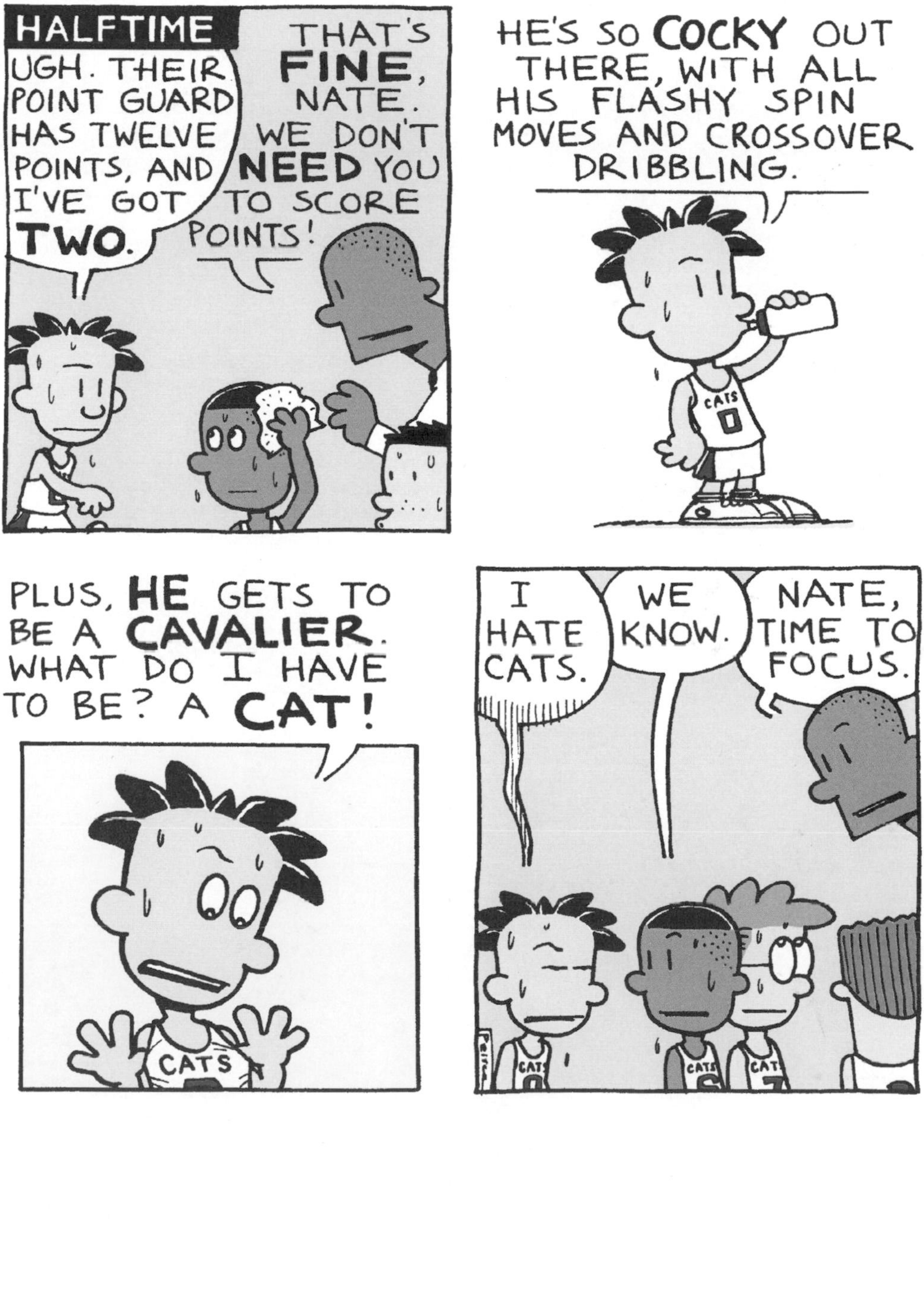
HALFTIME
UGH. THEIR POINT GUARD HAS TWELVE POINTS, AND I'VE GOT TWO.
THAT'S FINE, NATE. WE DON'T NEED YOU TO SCORE POINTS!
HE'S SO COCKY OUT THERE, WITH ALL HIS FLASHY SPIN MOVES AND CROSSOVER DRIBBLING.
CATS
PLUS, HE GETS TO BE A CAVALIER. WHAT DO I HAVE TO BE? A CAT!
CATS
I HATE CATS.
WE KNOW.
NATE, TIME TO FOCUS.

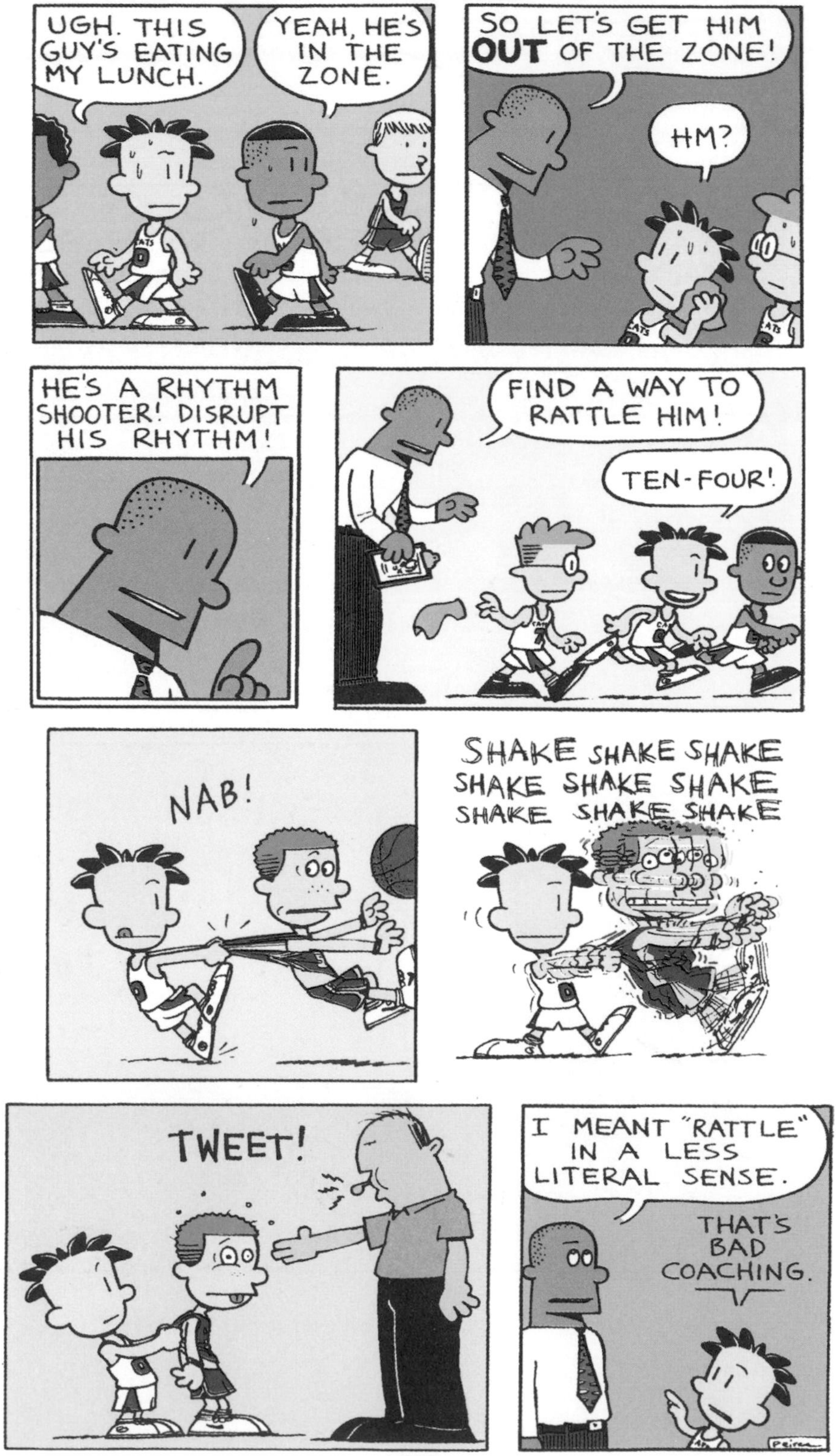
UGH. THIS GUY'S EATING MY LUNCH.
YEAH, HE'S IN THE ZONE.
SO LET'S GET HIM **OUT** OF THE ZONE!
HM?
HE'S A RHYTHM SHOOTER! DISRUPT HIS RHYTHM!
FIND A WAY TO RATTLE HIM!
TEN-FOUR!
NAB!
SHAKE SHAKE SHAKE SHAKE SHAKE SHAKE SHAKE SHAKE SHAKE
TWEET!
I MEANT "RATTLE" IN A LESS LITERAL SENSE.
THAT'S BAD COACHING.

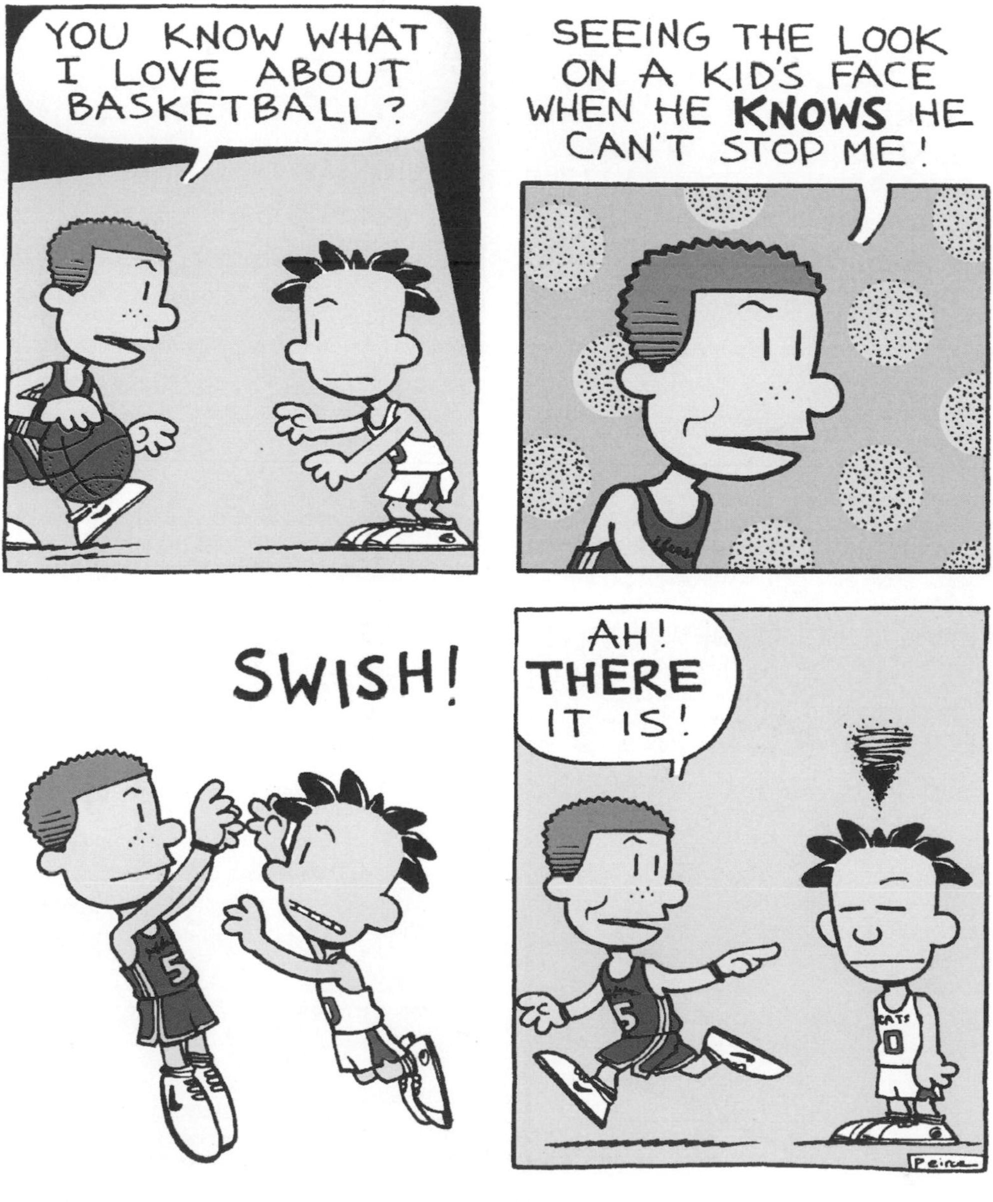
YOU KNOW WHAT I LOVE ABOUT BASKETBALL?
SEEING THE LOOK ON A KID'S FACE WHEN HE **KNOWS** HE CAN'T STOP ME!
SWISH!
AH! **THERE** IT IS!
Peirce

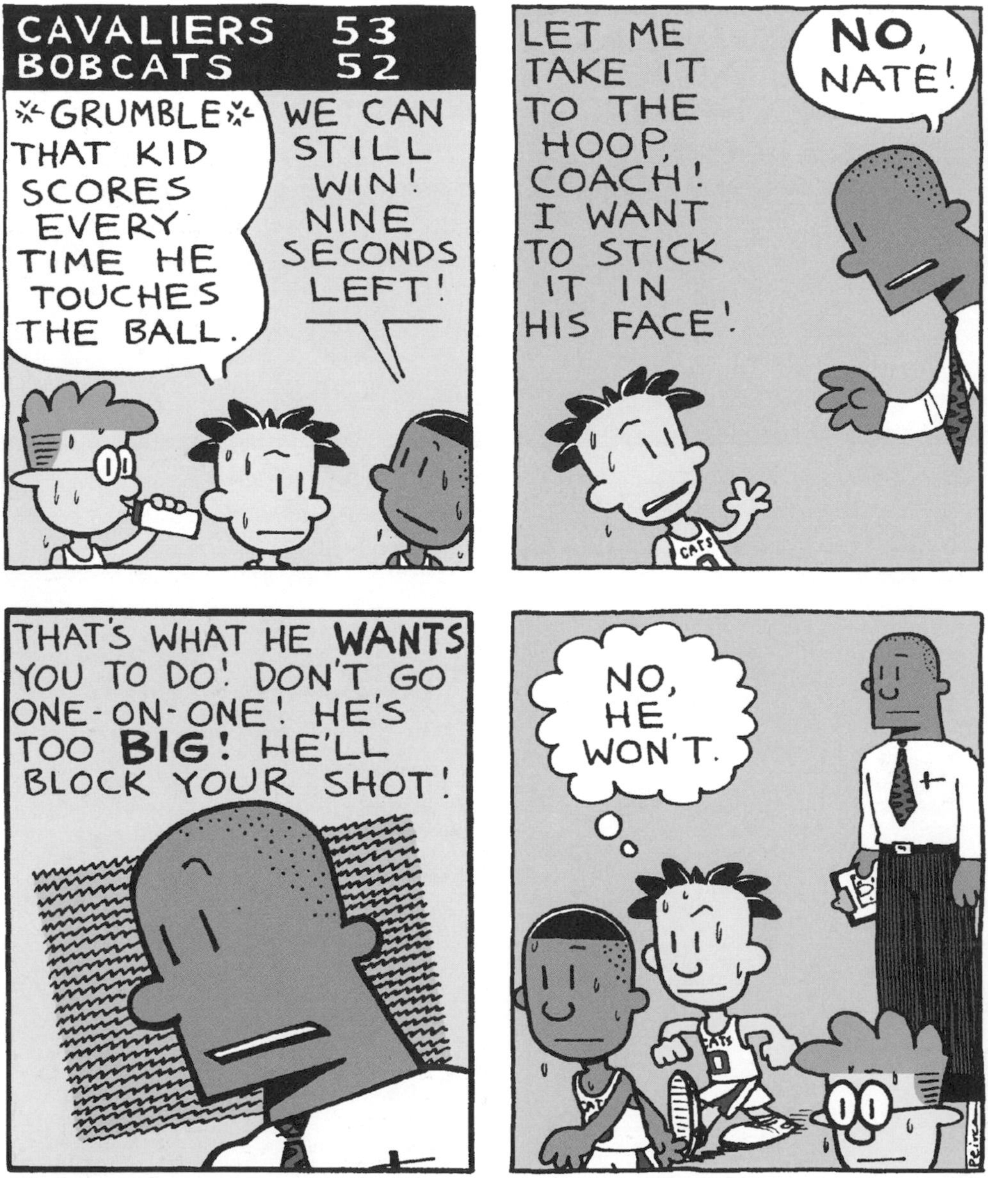
CAVALIERS 53
BOBCATS 52
GRUMBLE THAT KID SCORES EVERY TIME HE TOUCHES THE BALL.
WE CAN STILL WIN! NINE SECONDS LEFT!
LET ME TAKE IT TO THE HOOP, COACH! I WANT TO STICK IT IN HIS FACE!
NO, NATE!
THAT'S WHAT HE WANTS YOU TO DO! DON'T GO ONE-ON-ONE! HE'S TOO BIG! HE'LL BLOCK YOUR SHOT!
NO, HE WON'T.
PEIRCE

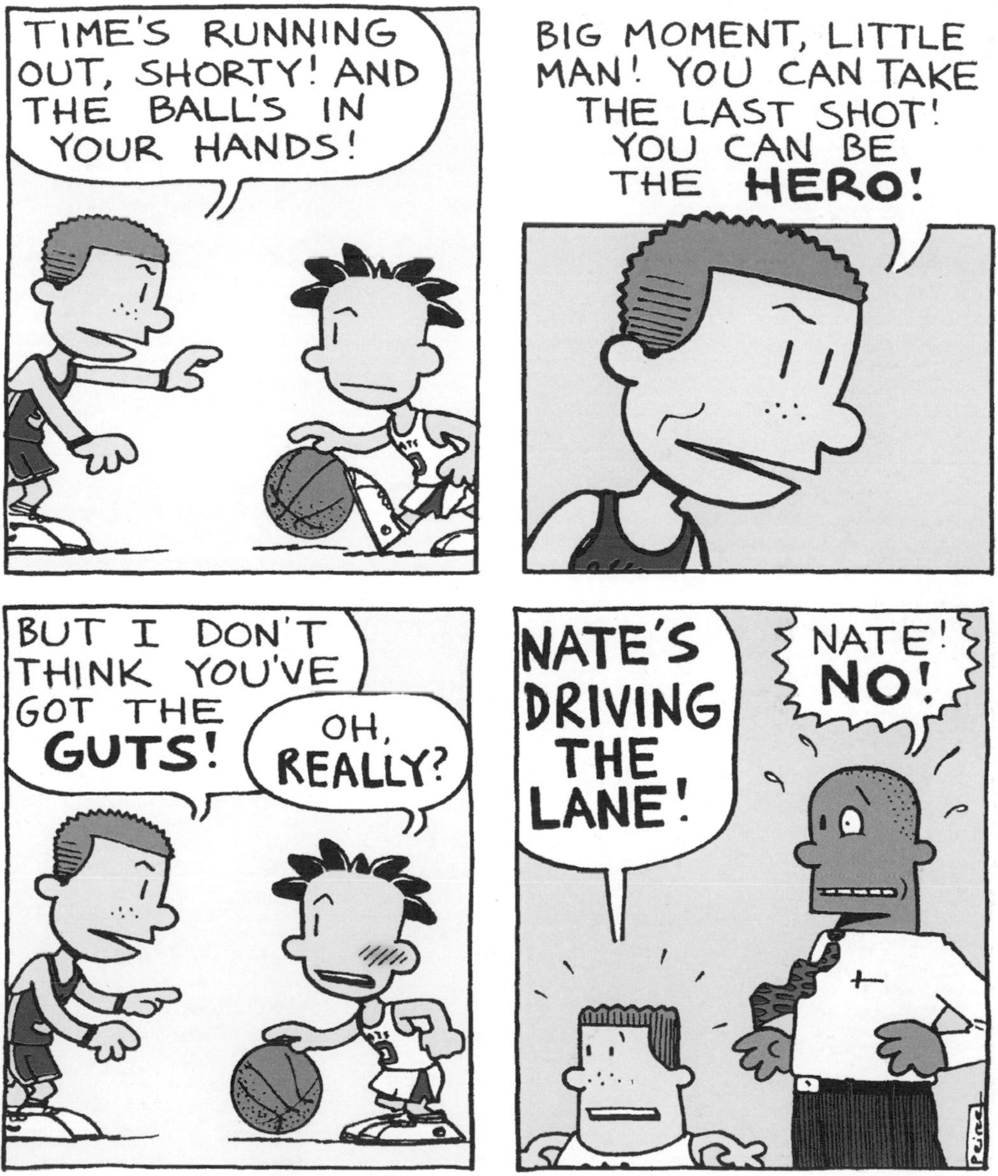
TIME'S RUNNING OUT, SHORTY! AND THE BALL'S IN YOUR HANDS!
BIG MOMENT, LITTLE MAN! YOU CAN TAKE THE LAST SHOT! YOU CAN BE THE **HERO**!
BUT I DON'T THINK YOU'VE GOT THE **GUTS**!
OH, REALLY?
NATE'S DRIVING THE LANE!
NATE! **NO!**
PEIRCE

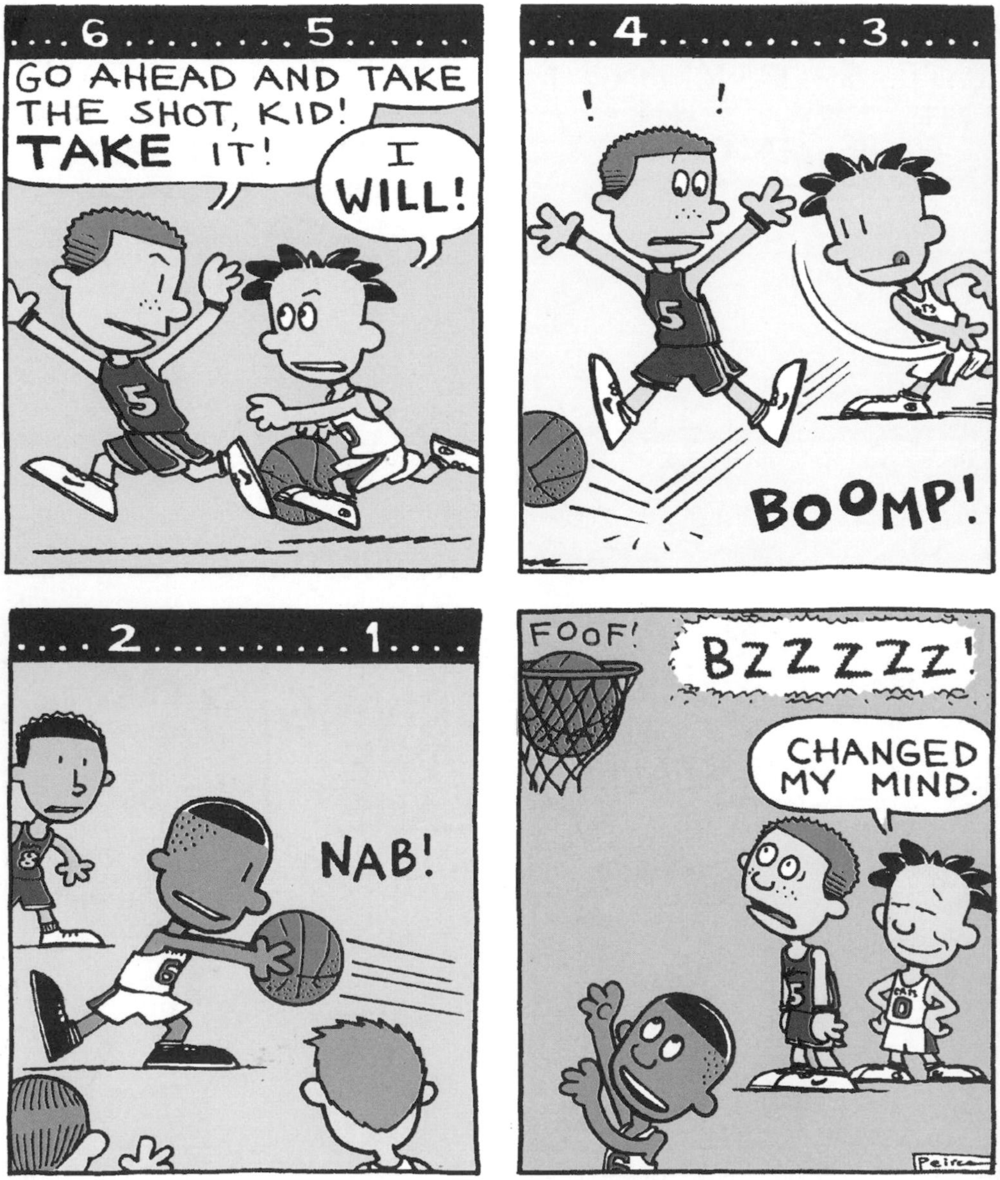
....6.........5......
GO AHEAD AND TAKE THE SHOT, KID! TAKE IT!
I WILL!
....4..........3....
! !
BOOMP!
....2...........1....
NAB!
FOOF!
BZZZZZ!
CHANGED MY MIND.
Peirce

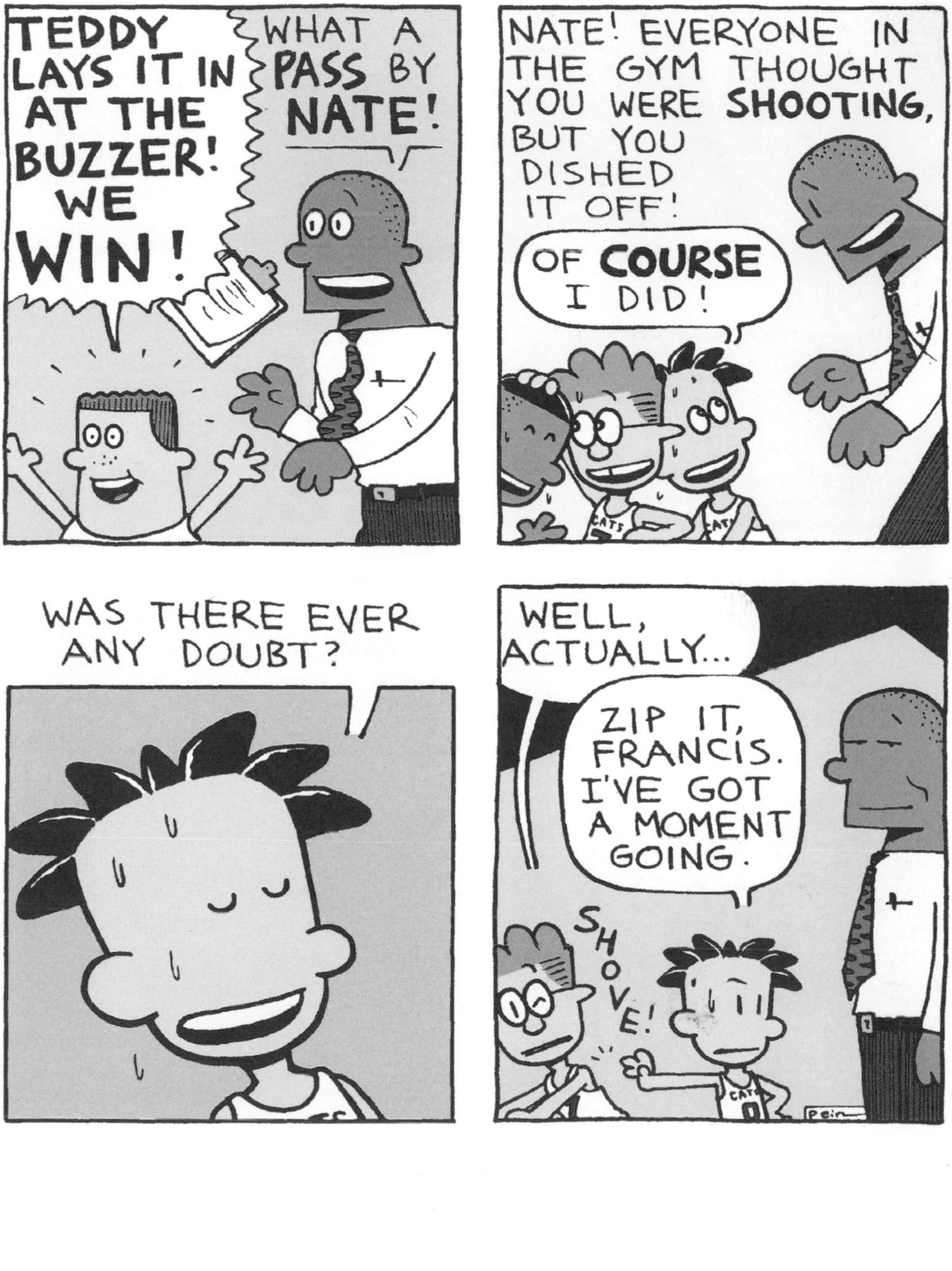
TEDDY LAYS IT IN AT THE BUZZER! WE WIN!
WHAT A PASS BY NATE!
NATE! EVERYONE IN THE GYM THOUGHT YOU WERE SHOOTING, BUT YOU DISHED IT OFF!
OF COURSE I DID!
WAS THERE EVER ANY DOUBT?
WELL, ACTUALLY...
ZIP IT, FRANCIS. I'VE GOT A MOMENT GOING.
SHOVE!

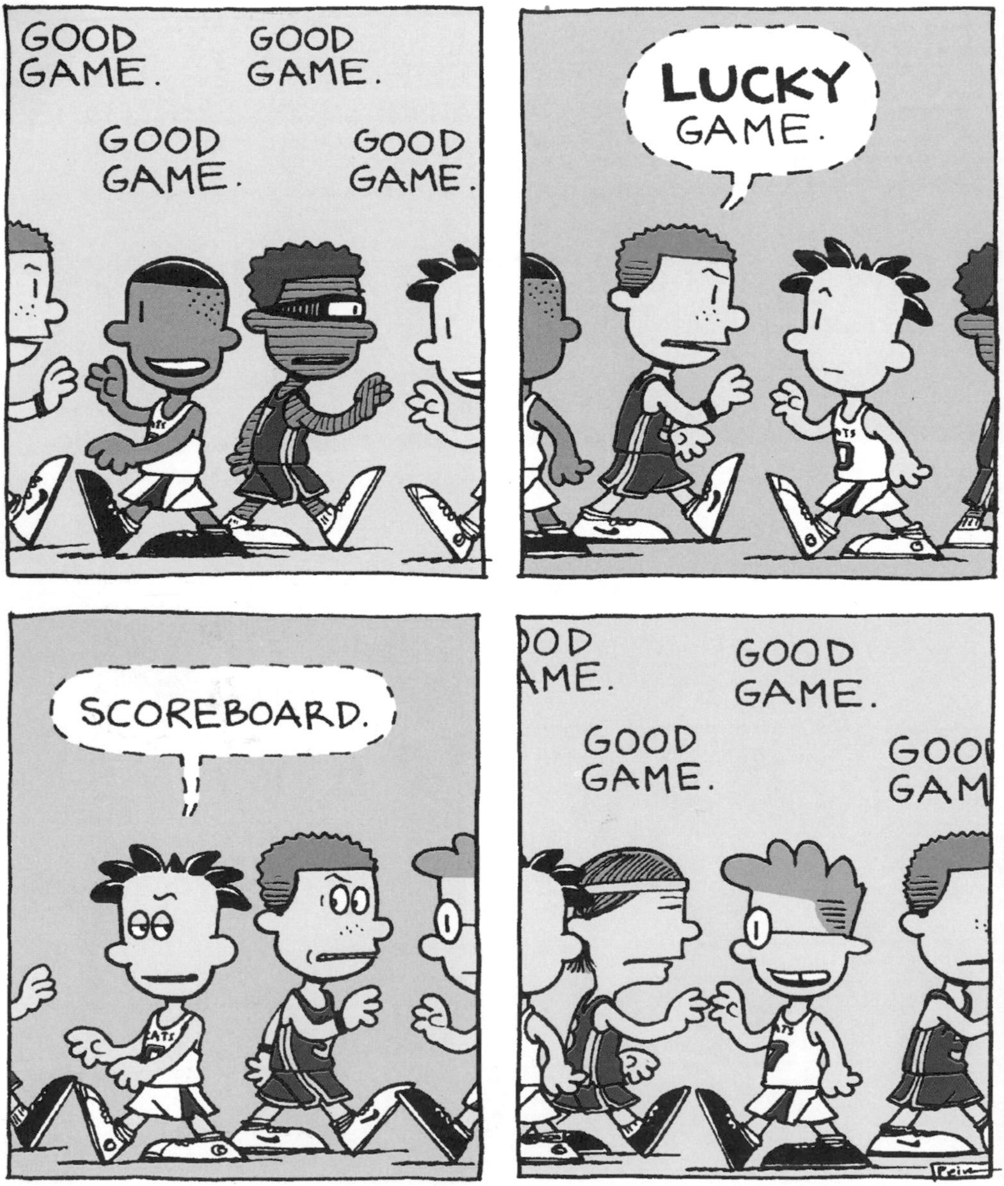
GOOD GAME.
GOOD GAME.
GOOD GAME.
GOOD GAME.
LUCKY GAME.
SCOREBOARD.
GOOD GAME.
GOOD GAME.

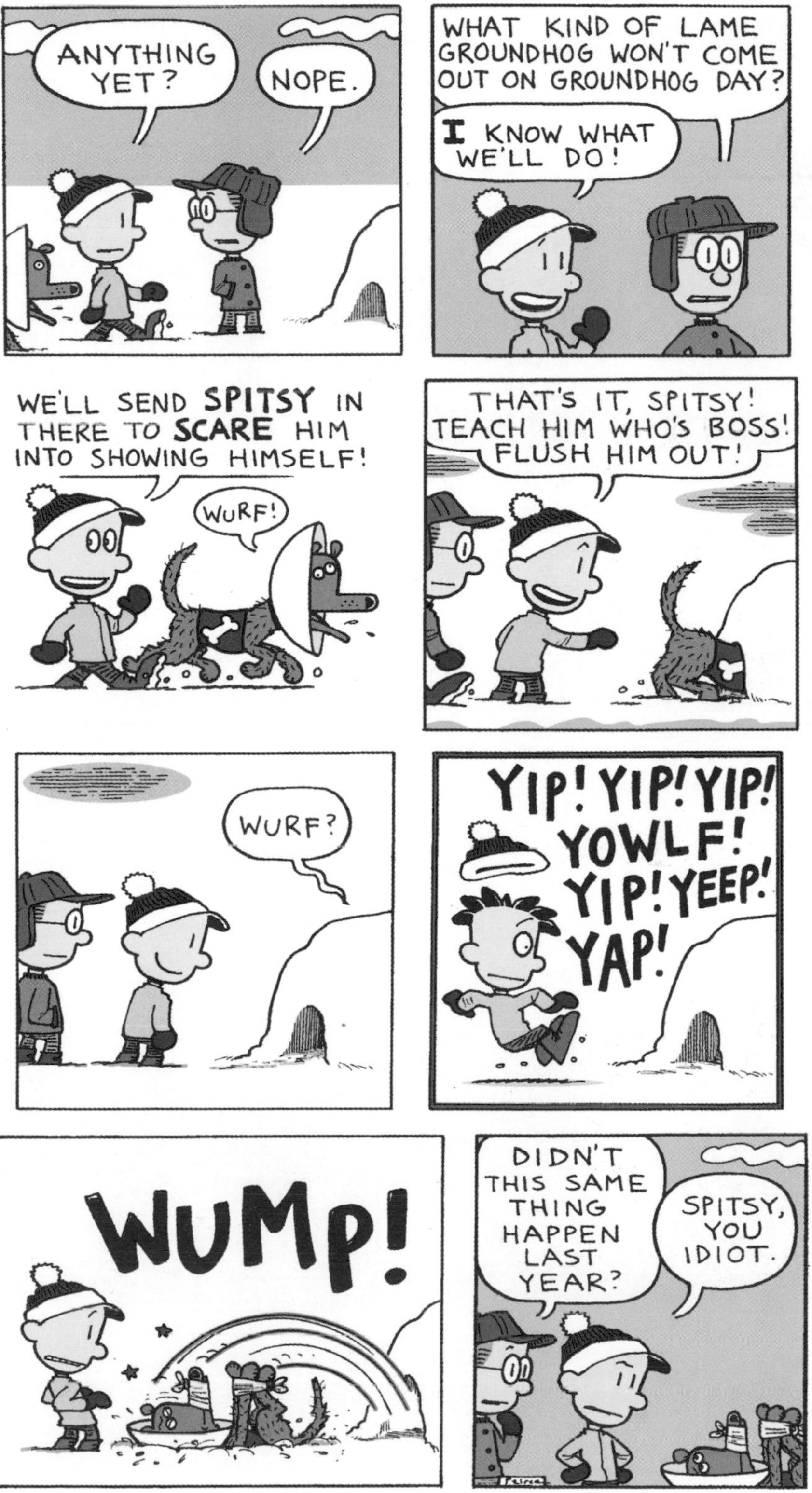
ANYTHING YET?
NOPE.
WHAT KIND OF LAME GROUNDHOG WON'T COME OUT ON GROUNDHOG DAY?
I KNOW WHAT WE'LL DO!
WE'LL SEND SPITSY IN THERE TO SCARE HIM INTO SHOWING HIMSELF!
WURF!
THAT'S IT, SPITSY! TEACH HIM WHO'S BOSS! FLUSH HIM OUT!
WURF?
YIP! YIP! YIP! YOWLF! YIP! YEEP! YAP!
WUMP!
DIDN'T THIS SAME THING HAPPEN LAST YEAR?
SPITSY, YOU IDIOT.

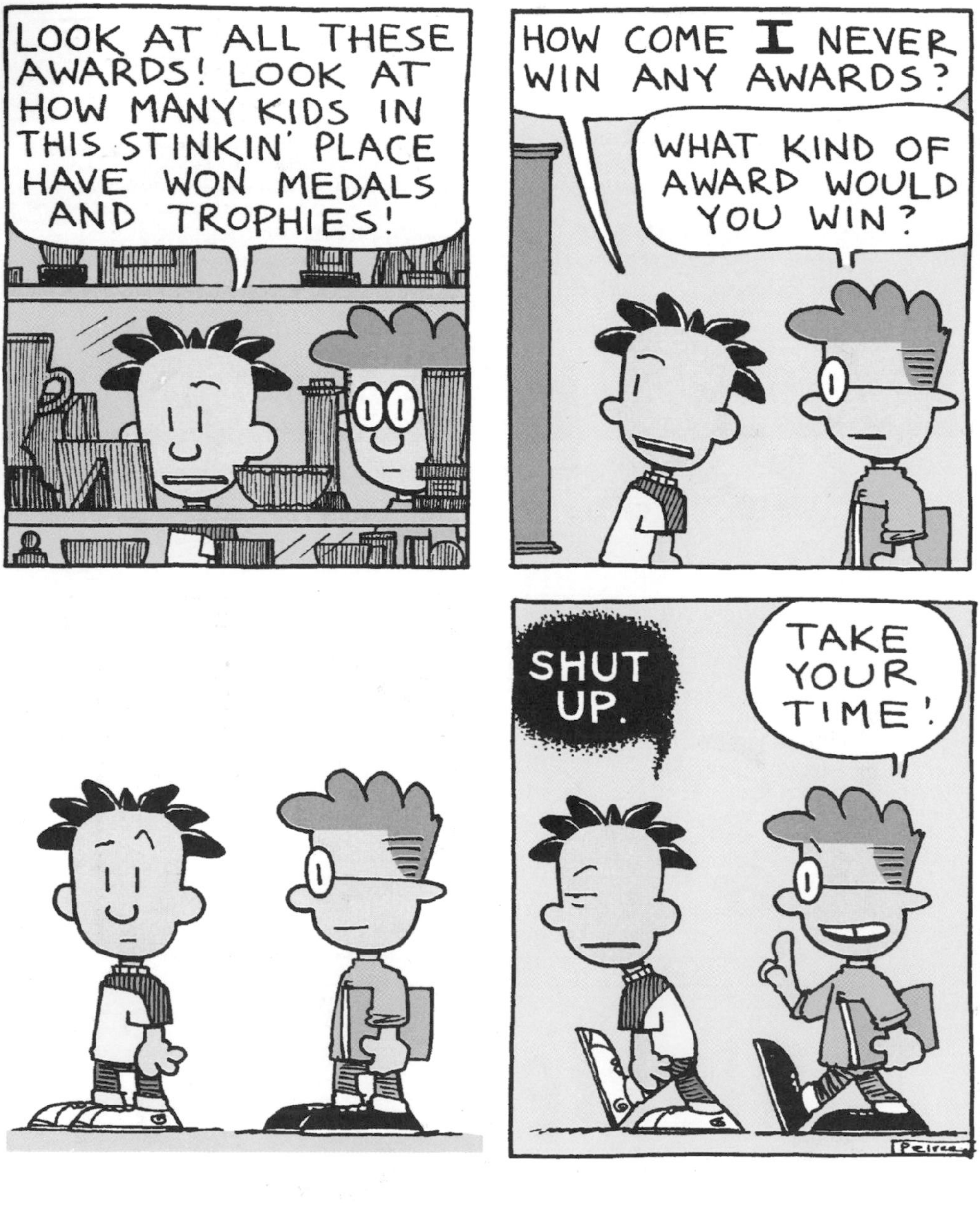
LOOK AT ALL THESE AWARDS! LOOK AT HOW MANY KIDS IN THIS STINKIN' PLACE HAVE WON MEDALS AND TROPHIES!
HOW COME I NEVER WIN ANY AWARDS?
WHAT KIND OF AWARD WOULD YOU WIN?
SHUT UP.
TAKE YOUR TIME!
Peirce

HERE'S AN AWARD I COULD WIN! "STUDENT OF THE MONTH"!

HUH? THAT'S FOR **BRAINIACS!**

NOT ALWAYS! SOMETIMES THEY GIVE IT TO KIDS THEY FEEL **SORRY** FOR!

IN JANUARY, ROBBIE WAS STUDENT OF THE MONTH BECAUSE OF HIS CHRONIC **EAR INFECTIONS!**

WHAT? **WHAT?**

IF I COME DOWN WITH CHICKEN POX OR SOMETHING, I'M A **SHOO-IN!**

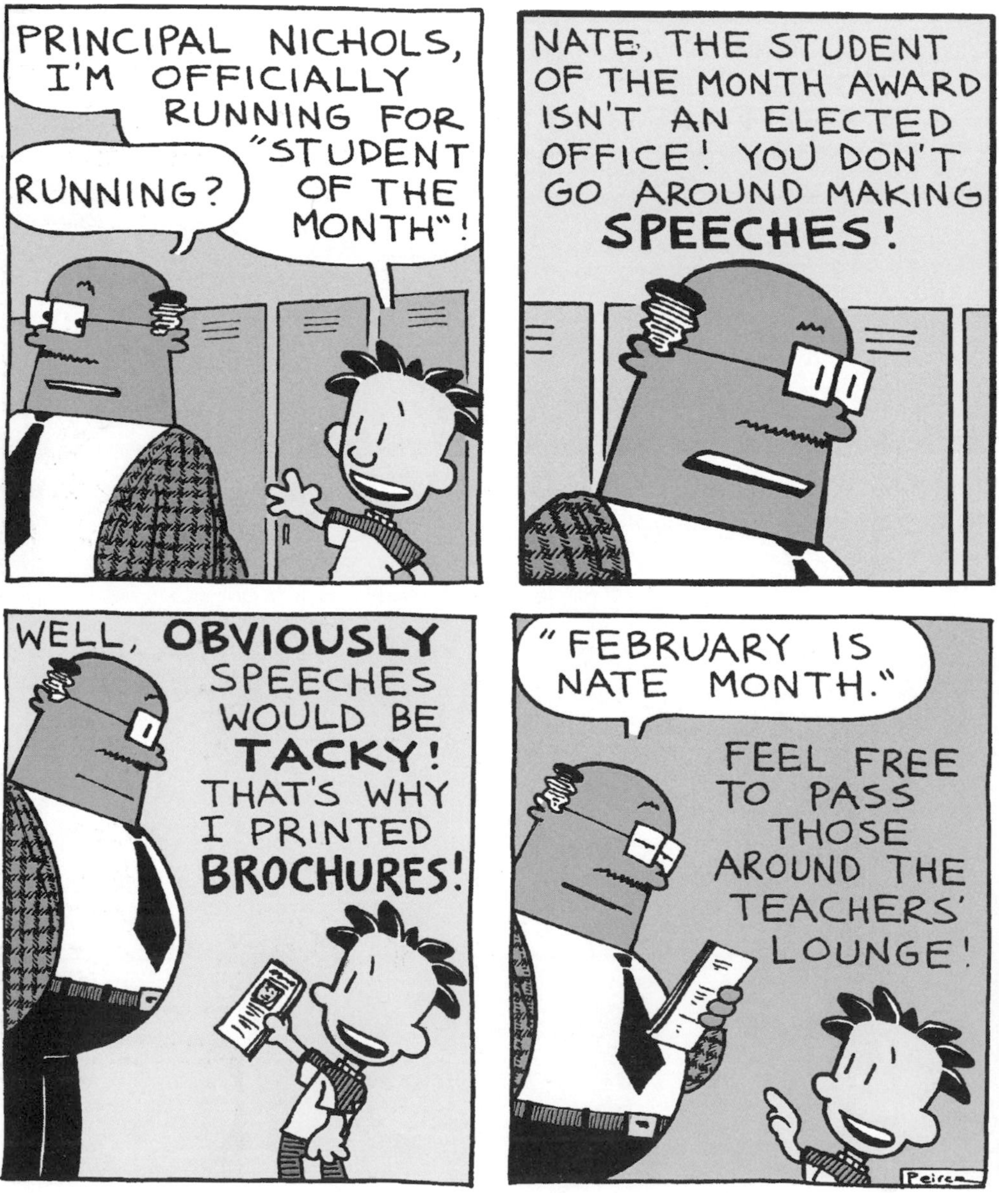
PRINCIPAL NICHOLS, I'M OFFICIALLY RUNNING FOR "STUDENT OF THE MONTH"!
RUNNING?
NATE, THE STUDENT OF THE MONTH AWARD ISN'T AN ELECTED OFFICE! YOU DON'T GO AROUND MAKING SPEECHES!
WELL, OBVIOUSLY SPEECHES WOULD BE TACKY! THAT'S WHY I PRINTED BROCHURES!
"FEBRUARY IS NATE MONTH."
FEEL FREE TO PASS THOSE AROUND THE TEACHERS' LOUNGE!
Peirce

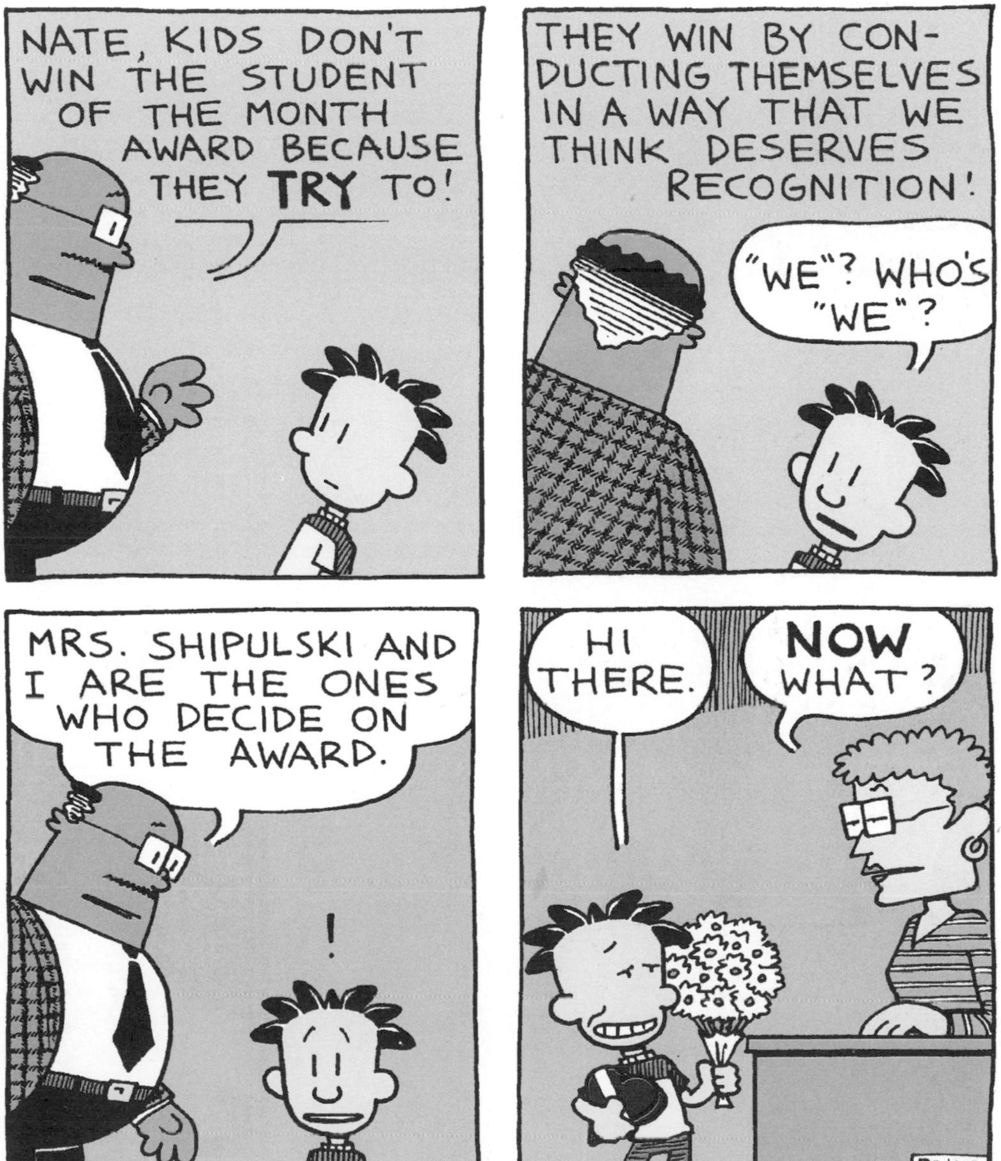
NATE, KIDS DON'T WIN THE STUDENT OF THE MONTH AWARD BECAUSE THEY **TRY** TO!
THEY WIN BY CONDUCTING THEMSELVES IN A WAY THAT WE THINK DESERVES RECOGNITION!
"WE"? WHO'S "WE"?
MRS. SHIPULSKI AND I ARE THE ONES WHO DECIDE ON THE AWARD.
!
HI THERE.
NOW WHAT?
Peirce

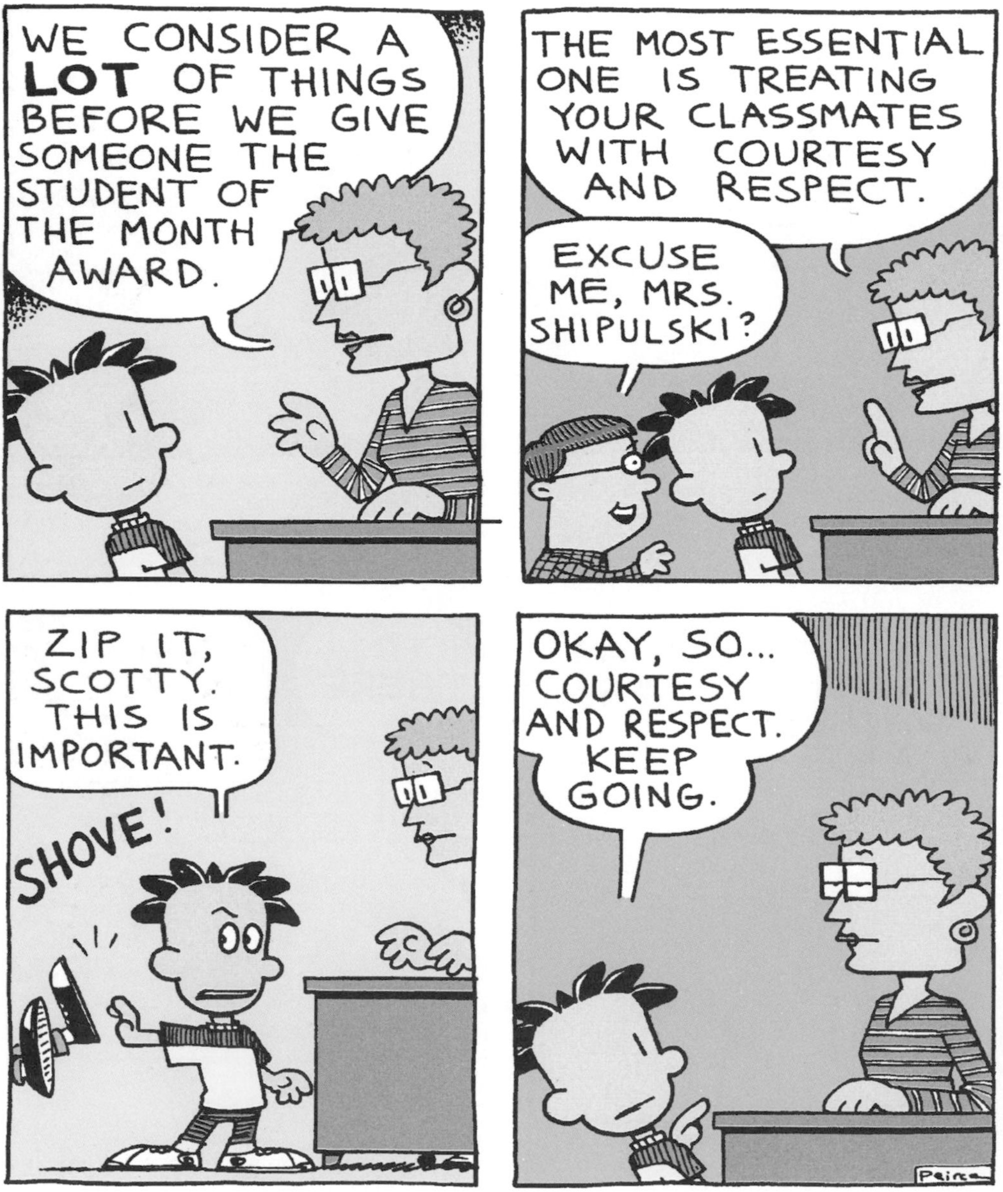
WE CONSIDER A **LOT** OF THINGS BEFORE WE GIVE SOMEONE THE STUDENT OF THE MONTH AWARD.
THE MOST ESSENTIAL ONE IS TREATING YOUR CLASSMATES WITH COURTESY AND RESPECT.
EXCUSE ME, MRS. SHIPULSKI?
ZIP IT, SCOTTY. THIS IS IMPORTANT.
SHOVE!
OKAY, SO... COURTESY AND RESPECT. KEEP GOING.
Peirce

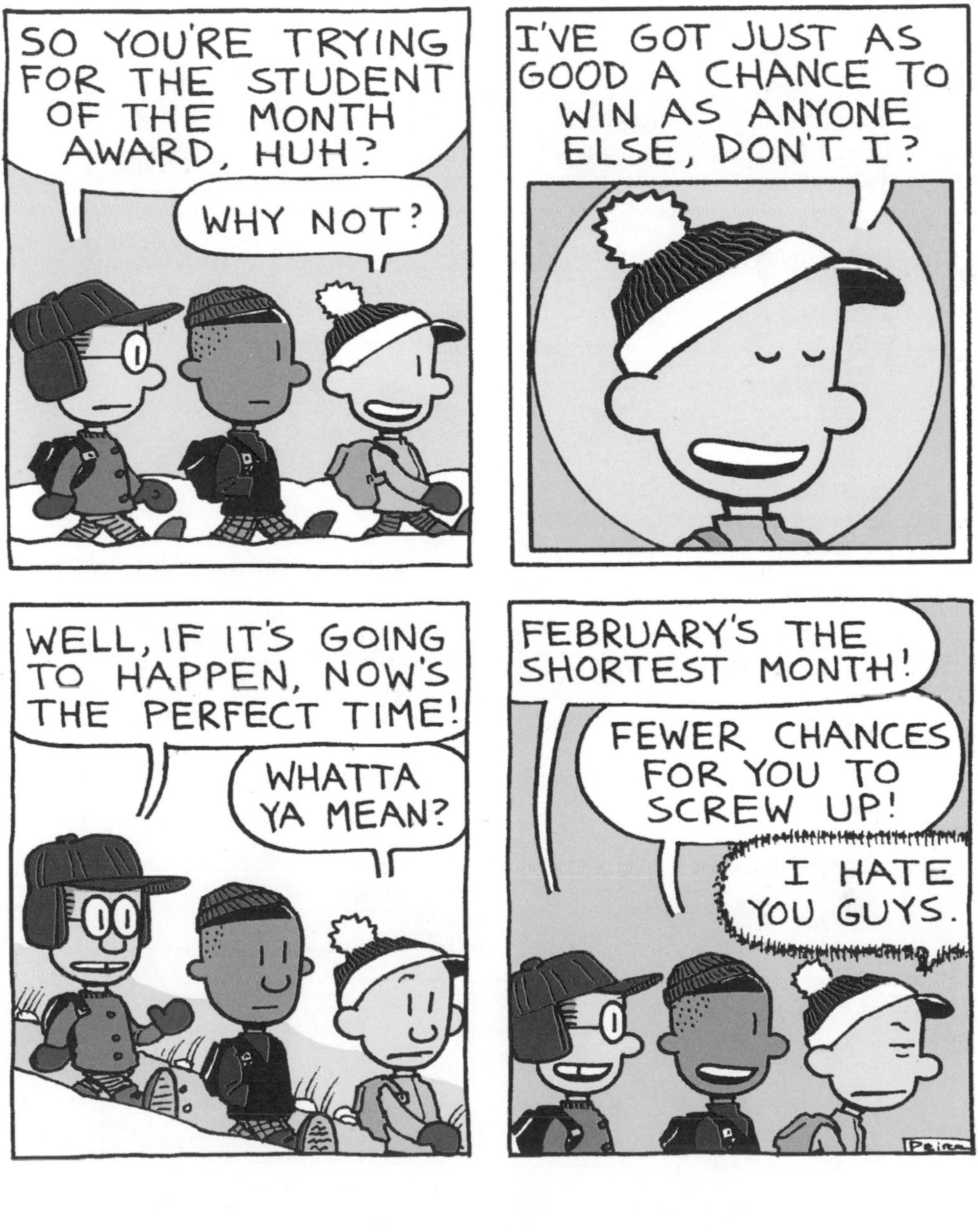
SO YOU'RE TRYING FOR THE STUDENT OF THE MONTH AWARD, HUH?
WHY NOT?
I'VE GOT JUST AS GOOD A CHANCE TO WIN AS ANYONE ELSE, DON'T I?
WELL, IF IT'S GOING TO HAPPEN, NOW'S THE PERFECT TIME!
WHATTA YA MEAN?
FEBRUARY'S THE SHORTEST MONTH!
FEWER CHANCES FOR YOU TO SCREW UP!
I HATE YOU GUYS.

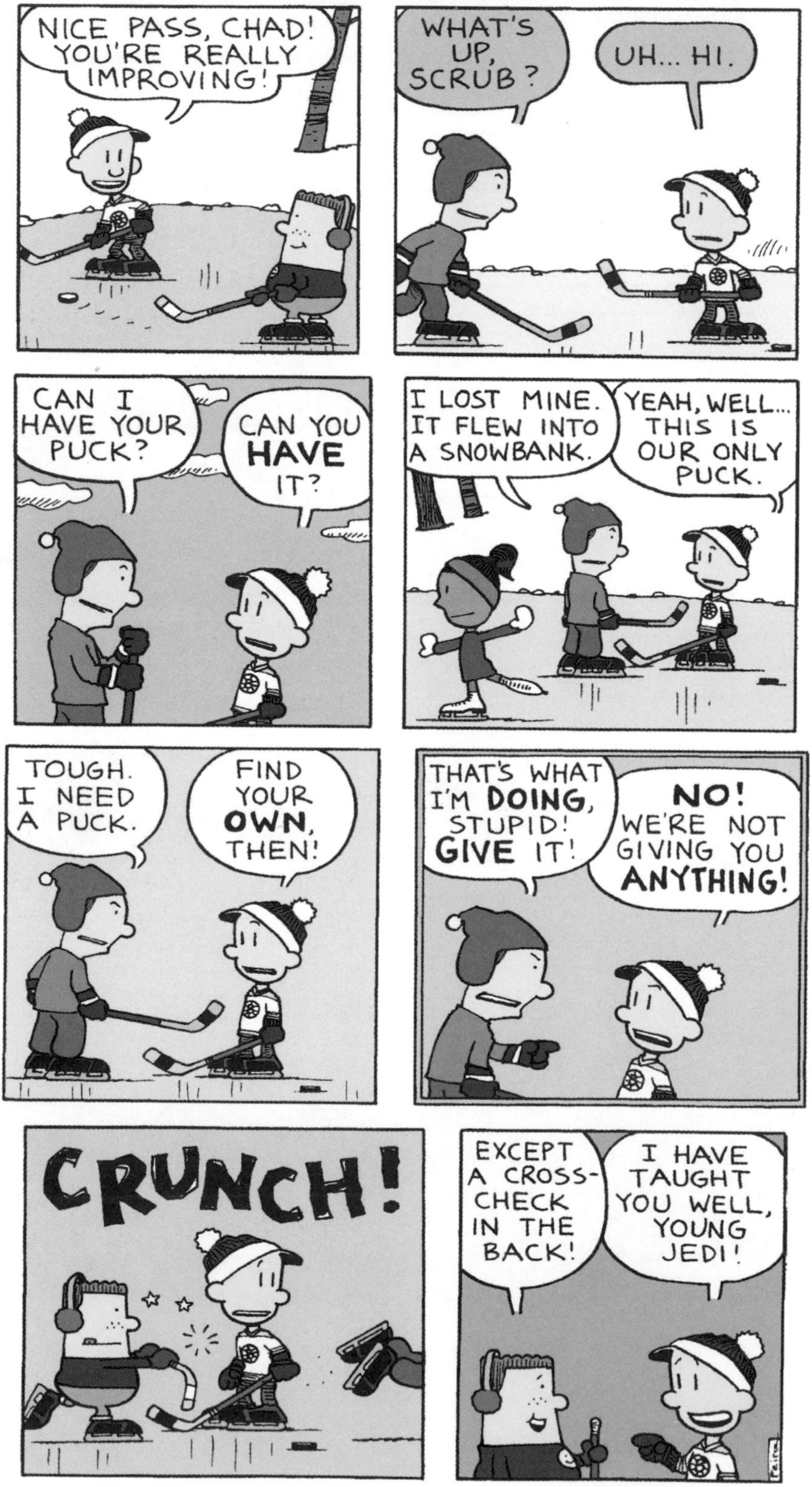
NICE PASS, CHAD! YOU'RE REALLY IMPROVING!
WHAT'S UP, SCRUB?
UH... HI.
CAN I HAVE YOUR PUCK?
CAN YOU **HAVE** IT?
I LOST MINE. IT FLEW INTO A SNOWBANK.
YEAH, WELL... THIS IS OUR ONLY PUCK.
TOUGH. I NEED A PUCK.
FIND YOUR **OWN**, THEN!
THAT'S WHAT I'M **DOING**, STUPID! **GIVE** IT!
NO! WE'RE NOT GIVING YOU **ANYTHING!**
CRUNCH!
EXCEPT A CROSS-CHECK IN THE BACK!
I HAVE TAUGHT YOU WELL, YOUNG JEDI!

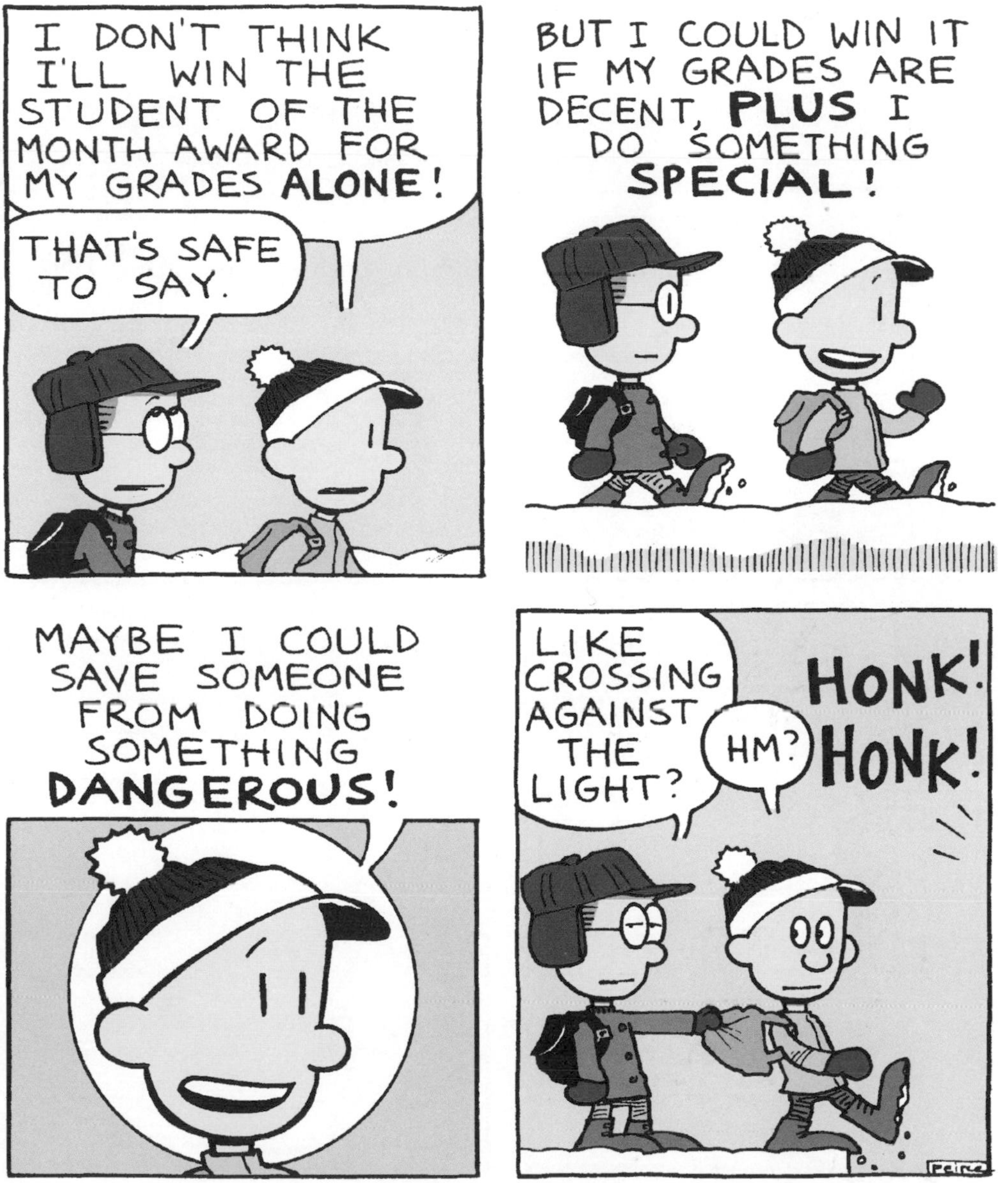
I DON'T THINK I'LL WIN THE STUDENT OF THE MONTH AWARD FOR MY GRADES **ALONE**!
THAT'S SAFE TO SAY.
BUT I COULD WIN IT IF MY GRADES ARE DECENT, **PLUS** I DO SOMETHING **SPECIAL**!
MAYBE I COULD SAVE SOMEONE FROM DOING SOMETHING **DANGEROUS**!
LIKE CROSSING AGAINST THE LIGHT?
HM?
HONK! HONK!

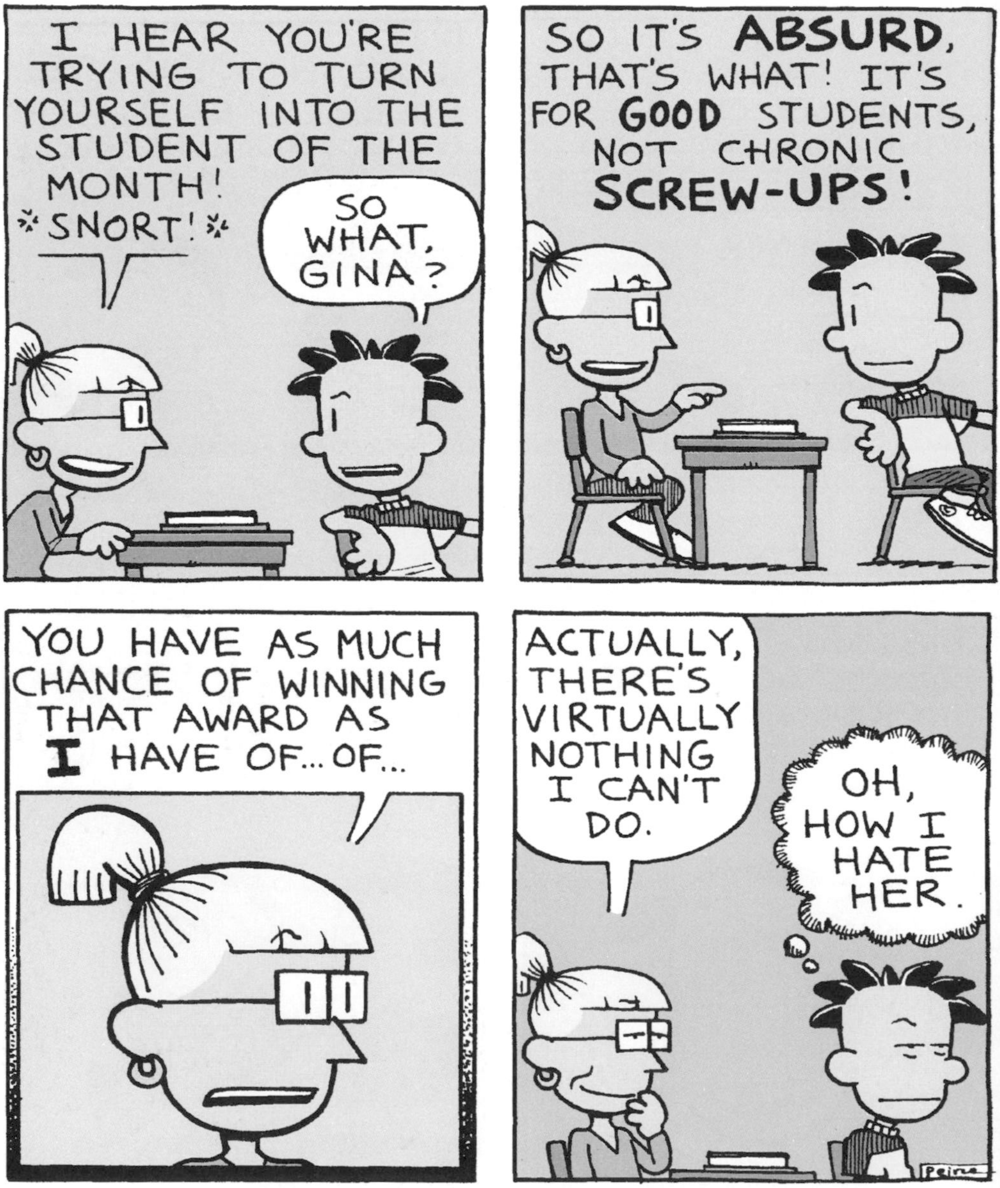
I HEAR YOU'RE TRYING TO TURN YOURSELF INTO THE STUDENT OF THE MONTH! *SNORT!*
SO WHAT, GINA?
SO IT'S **ABSURD**, THAT'S WHAT! IT'S FOR **GOOD** STUDENTS, NOT CHRONIC **SCREW-UPS**!
YOU HAVE AS MUCH CHANCE OF WINNING THAT AWARD AS **I** HAVE OF... OF...
ACTUALLY, THERE'S VIRTUALLY NOTHING I CAN'T DO.
OH, HOW I HATE HER.
Peirce

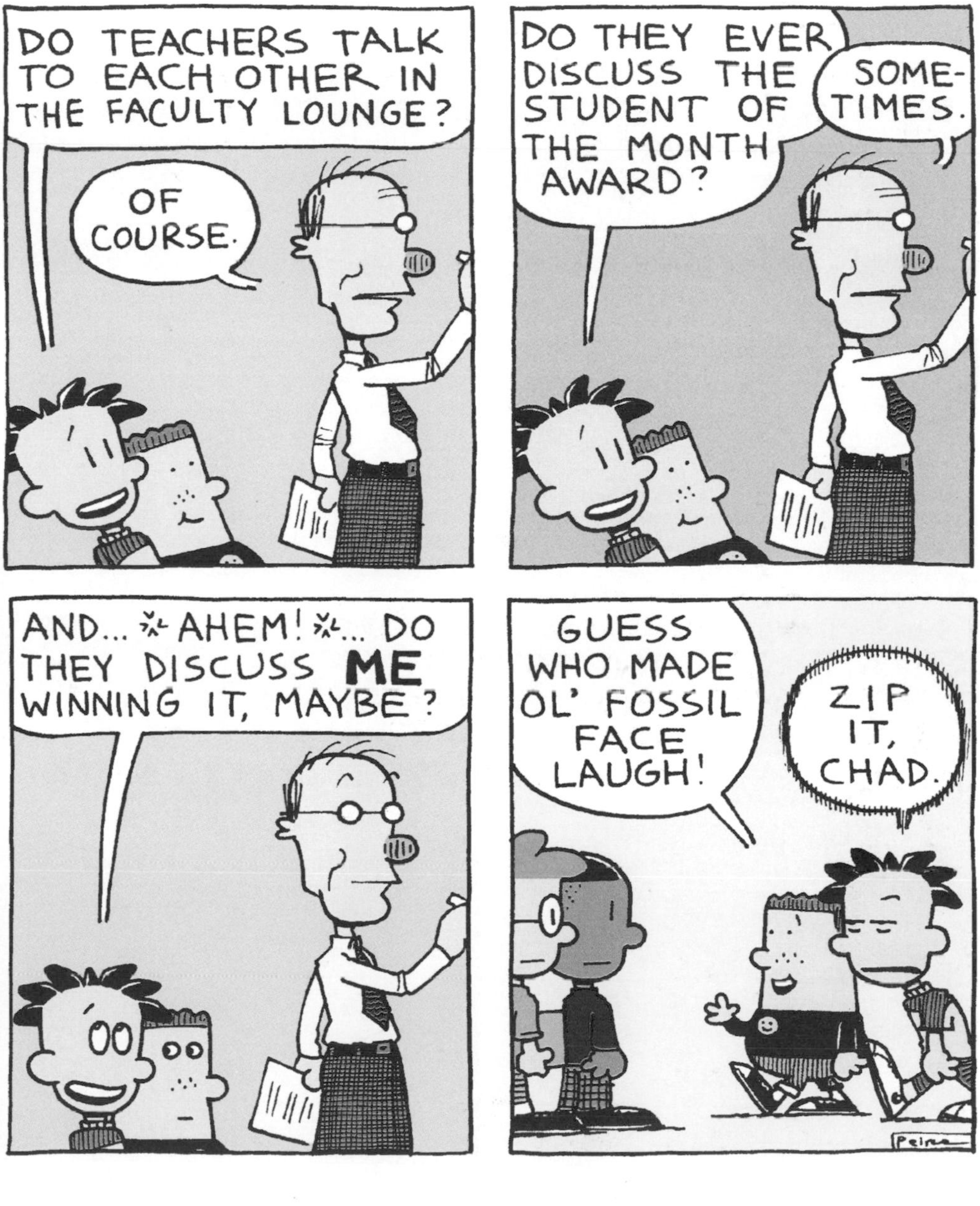
DO TEACHERS TALK TO EACH OTHER IN THE FACULTY LOUNGE?
OF COURSE.
DO THEY EVER DISCUSS THE STUDENT OF THE MONTH AWARD?
SOME-TIMES.
AND... AHEM!... DO THEY DISCUSS **ME** WINNING IT, MAYBE?
GUESS WHO MADE OL' FOSSIL FACE LAUGH!
ZIP IT, CHAD.
Peirce

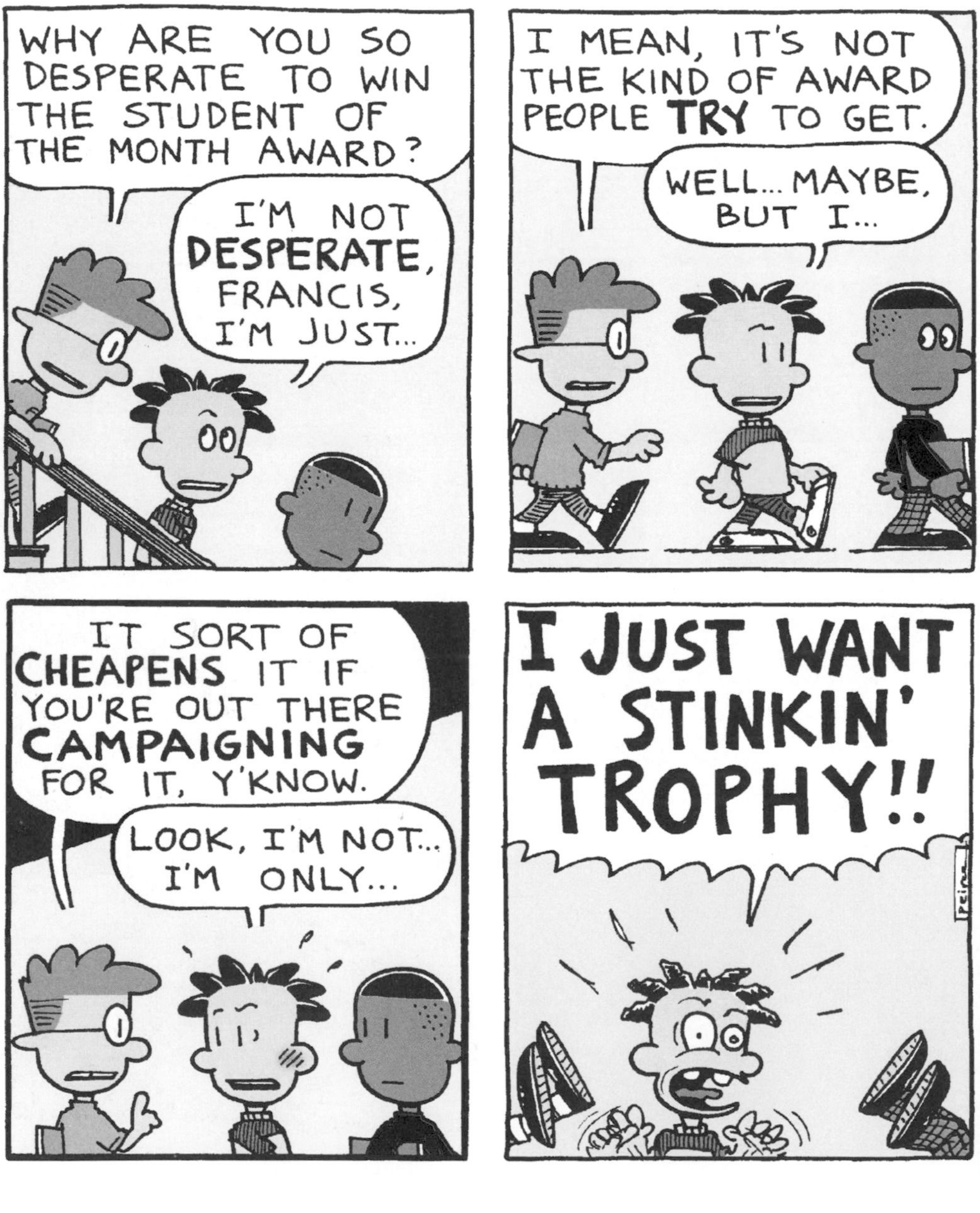
WHY ARE YOU SO DESPERATE TO WIN THE STUDENT OF THE MONTH AWARD?
I'M NOT **DESPERATE**, FRANCIS, I'M JUST...
I MEAN, IT'S NOT THE KIND OF AWARD PEOPLE **TRY** TO GET.
WELL... MAYBE, BUT I...
IT SORT OF **CHEAPENS** IT IF YOU'RE OUT THERE **CAMPAIGNING** FOR IT, Y'KNOW.
LOOK, I'M NOT... I'M ONLY...
I JUST WANT A STINKIN' TROPHY!!

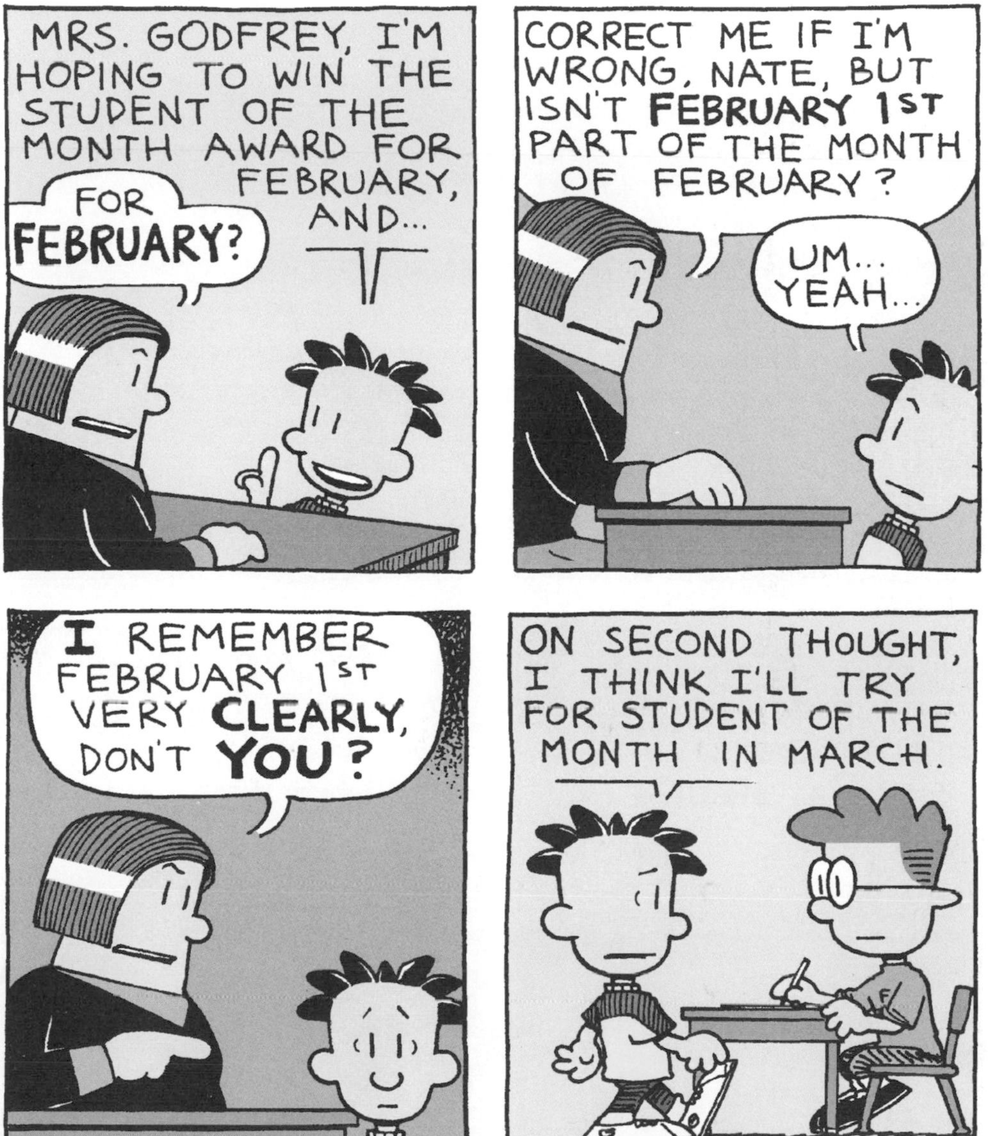
MRS. GODFREY, I'M HOPING TO WIN THE STUDENT OF THE MONTH AWARD FOR FEBRUARY, AND...
FOR **FEBRUARY**?
CORRECT ME IF I'M WRONG, NATE, BUT ISN'T **FEBRUARY 1ST** PART OF THE MONTH OF FEBRUARY?
UM... YEAH...
I REMEMBER FEBRUARY 1ST VERY **CLEARLY**, DON'T **YOU**?
ON SECOND THOUGHT, I THINK I'LL TRY FOR STUDENT OF THE MONTH IN MARCH.

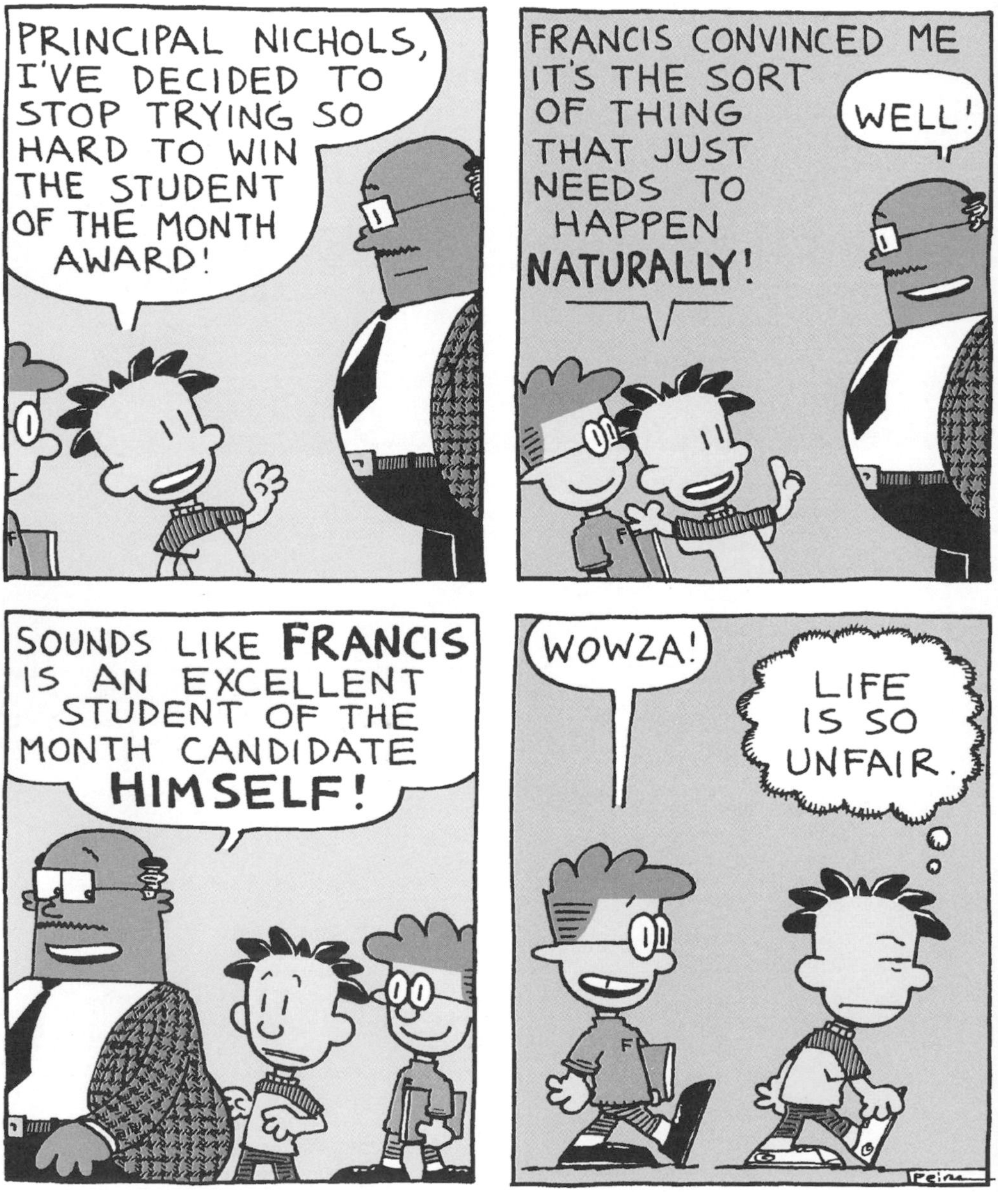
PRINCIPAL NICHOLS, I'VE DECIDED TO STOP TRYING SO HARD TO WIN THE STUDENT OF THE MONTH AWARD!
FRANCIS CONVINCED ME IT'S THE SORT OF THING THAT JUST NEEDS TO HAPPEN NATURALLY!
WELL!
SOUNDS LIKE FRANCIS IS AN EXCELLENT STUDENT OF THE MONTH CANDIDATE HIMSELF!
WOWZA!
LIFE IS SO UNFAIR.

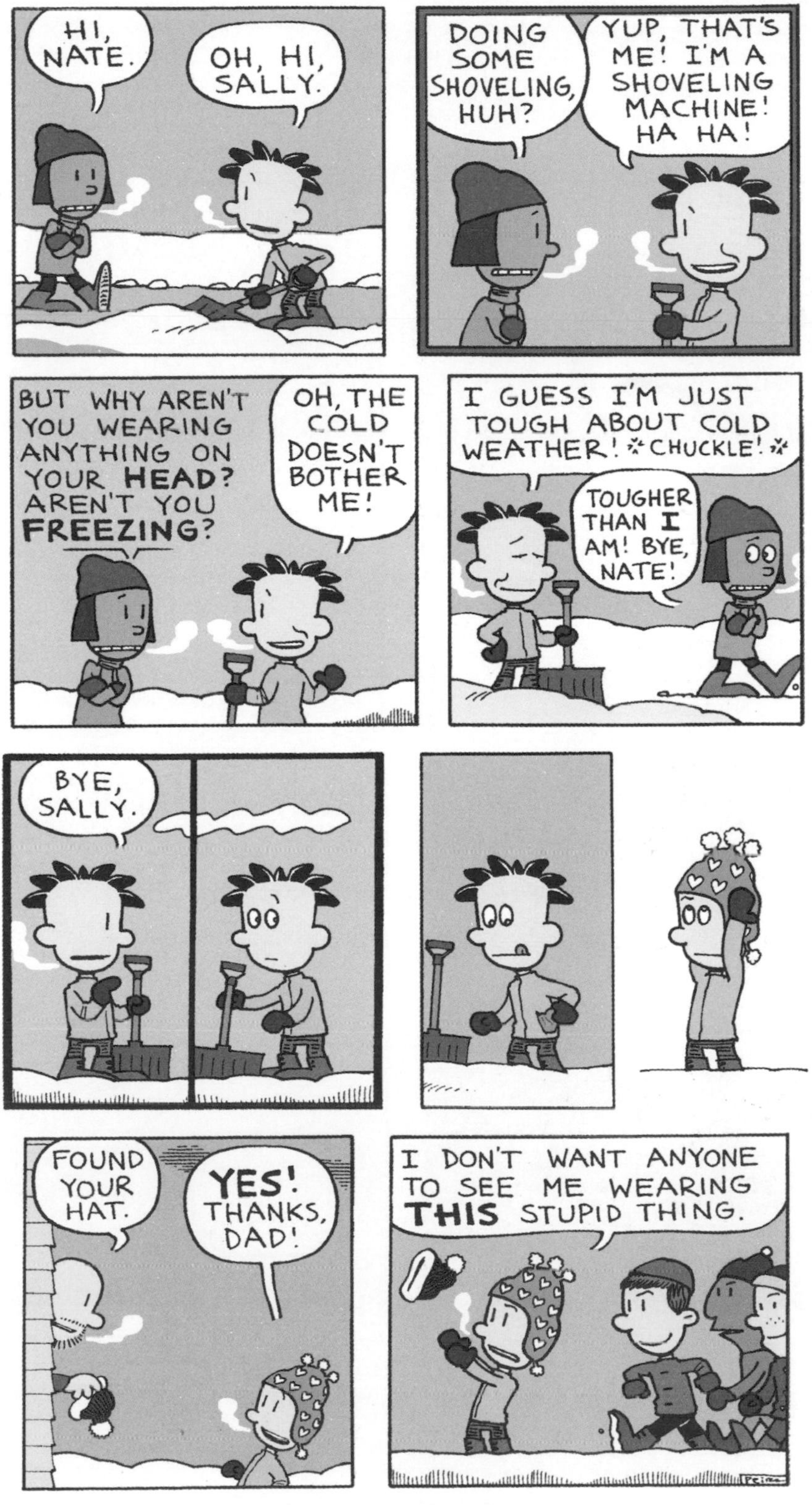
HI, NATE.
OH, HI, SALLY.
DOING SOME SHOVELING, HUH?
YUP, THAT'S ME! I'M A SHOVELING MACHINE! HA HA!
BUT WHY AREN'T YOU WEARING ANYTHING ON YOUR HEAD? AREN'T YOU FREEZING?
OH, THE COLD DOESN'T BOTHER ME!
I GUESS I'M JUST TOUGH ABOUT COLD WEATHER! *CHUCKLE!*
TOUGHER THAN I AM! BYE, NATE!
BYE, SALLY.
FOUND YOUR HAT.
YES! THANKS, DAD!
I DON'T WANT ANYONE TO SEE ME WEARING THIS STUPID THING.

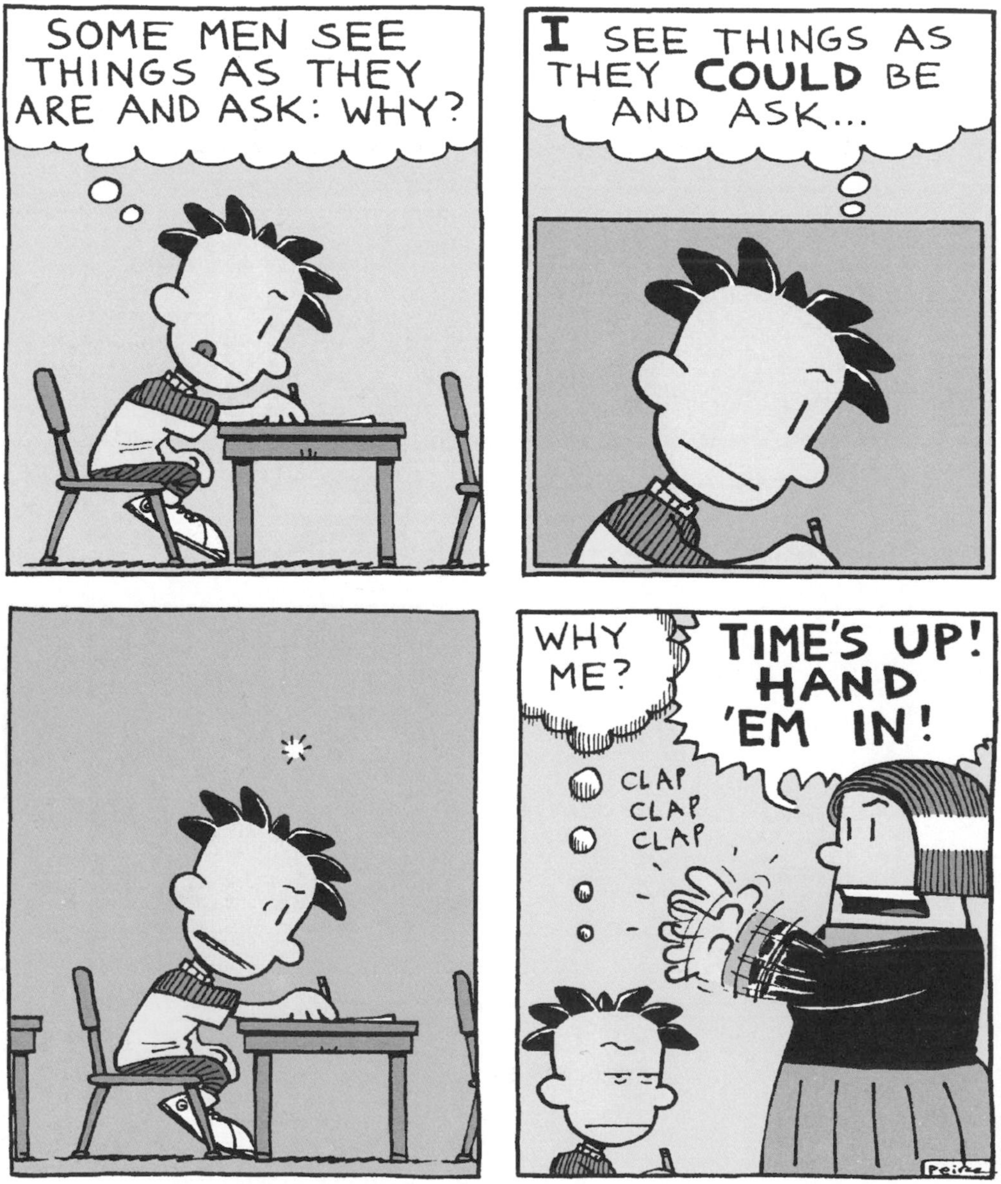
SOME MEN SEE THINGS AS THEY ARE AND ASK: WHY?
I SEE THINGS AS THEY COULD BE AND ASK...
WHY ME?
TIME'S UP! HAND 'EM IN!
CLAP CLAP CLAP
Peirce

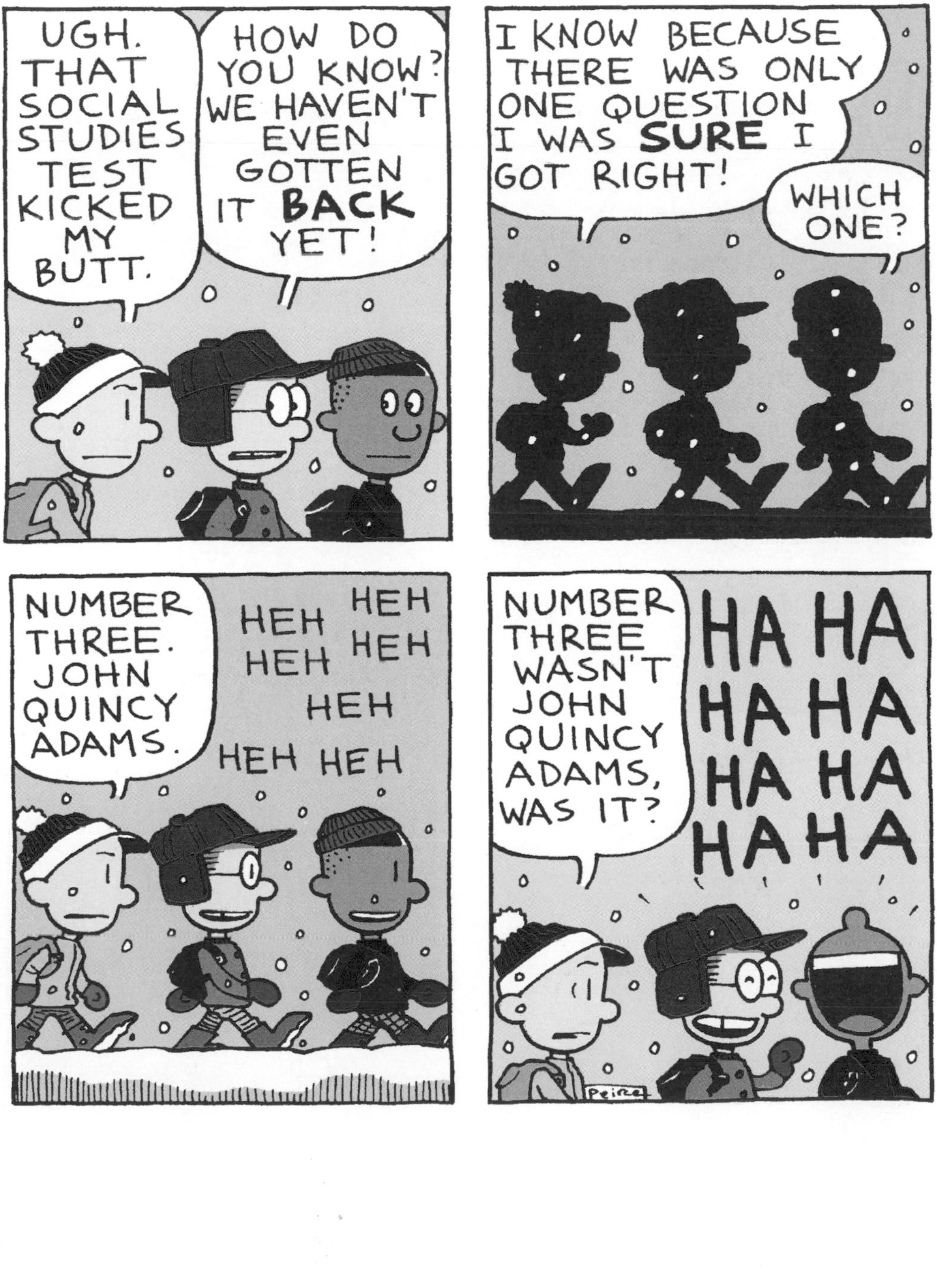
UGH. THAT SOCIAL STUDIES TEST KICKED MY BUTT.
HOW DO YOU KNOW? WE HAVEN'T EVEN GOTTEN IT BACK YET!
I KNOW BECAUSE THERE WAS ONLY ONE QUESTION I WAS SURE I GOT RIGHT!
WHICH ONE?
NUMBER THREE. JOHN QUINCY ADAMS.
HEH HEH HEH HEH HEH HEH HEH HEH
NUMBER THREE WASN'T JOHN QUINCY ADAMS, WAS IT?
HA HA HA HA HA HA HA HA
PEIRCE

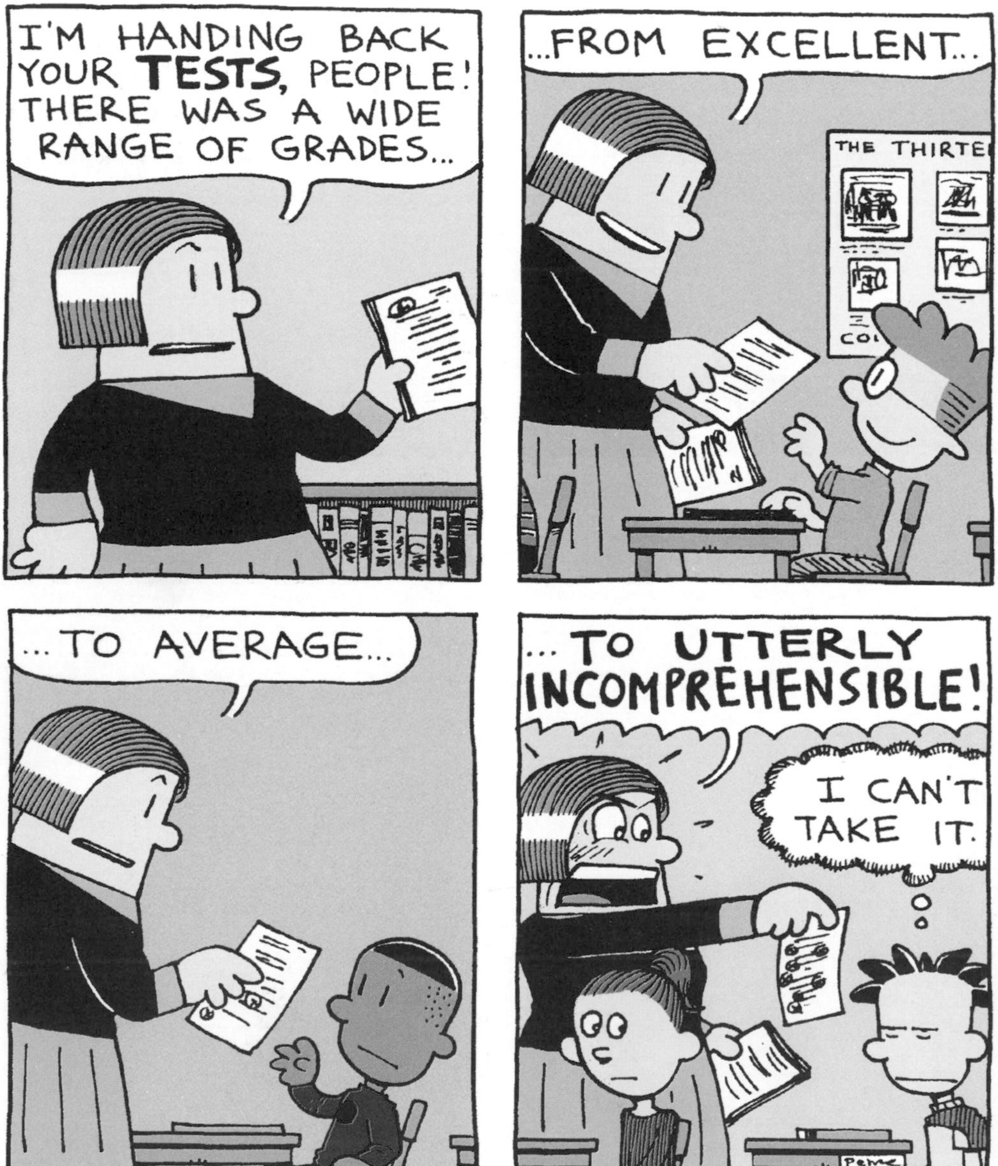
I'M HANDING BACK YOUR **TESTS**, PEOPLE! THERE WAS A WIDE RANGE OF GRADES...
...FROM EXCELLENT...
THE THIRTE
...TO AVERAGE...
...TO **UTTERLY INCOMPREHENSIBLE!**
I CAN'T TAKE IT.
PETIVE

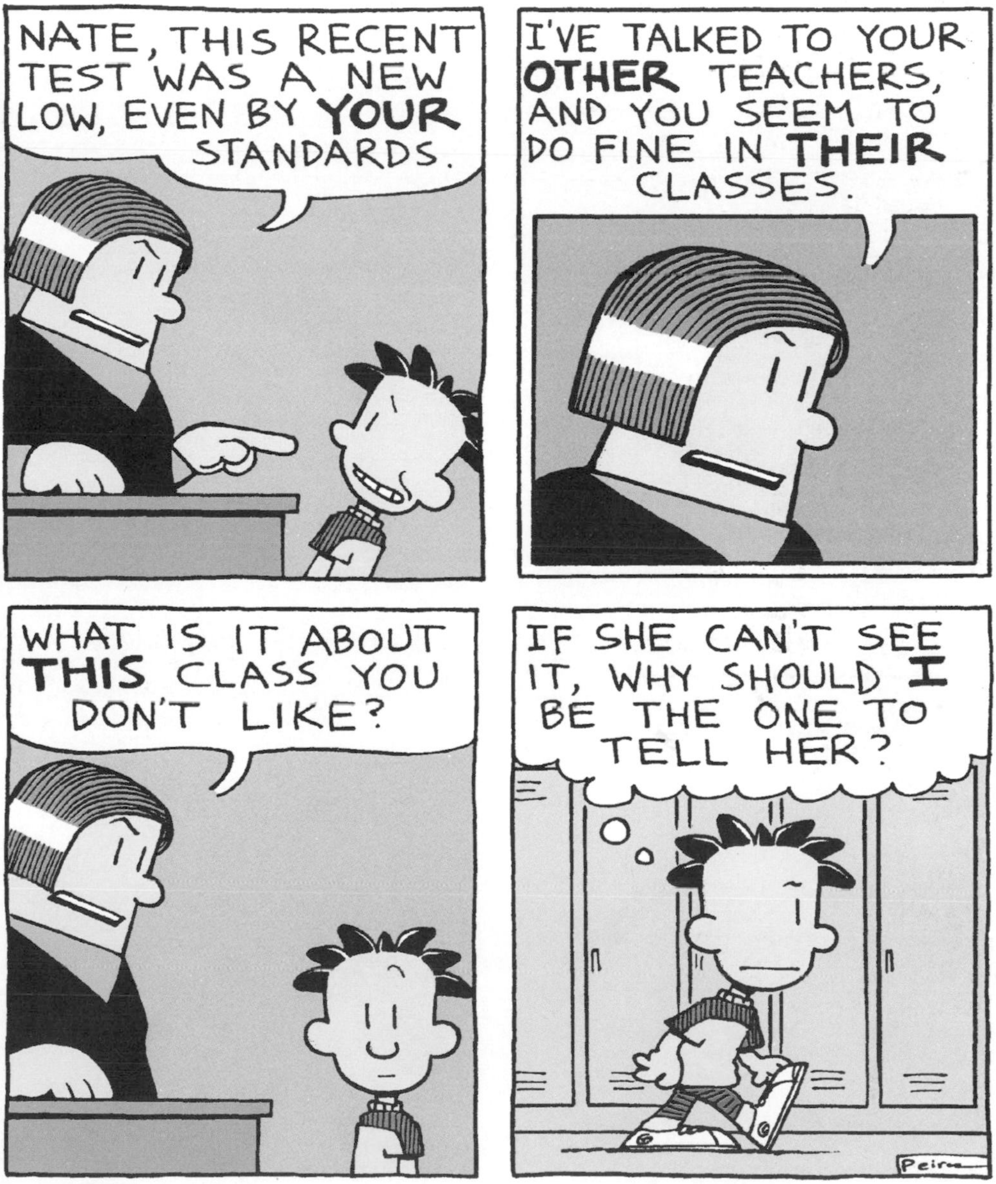
NATE, THIS RECENT TEST WAS A NEW LOW, EVEN BY **YOUR** STANDARDS.
I'VE TALKED TO YOUR **OTHER** TEACHERS, AND YOU SEEM TO DO FINE IN **THEIR** CLASSES.
WHAT IS IT ABOUT **THIS** CLASS YOU DON'T LIKE?
IF SHE CAN'T SEE IT, WHY SHOULD **I** BE THE ONE TO TELL HER?
Peirce

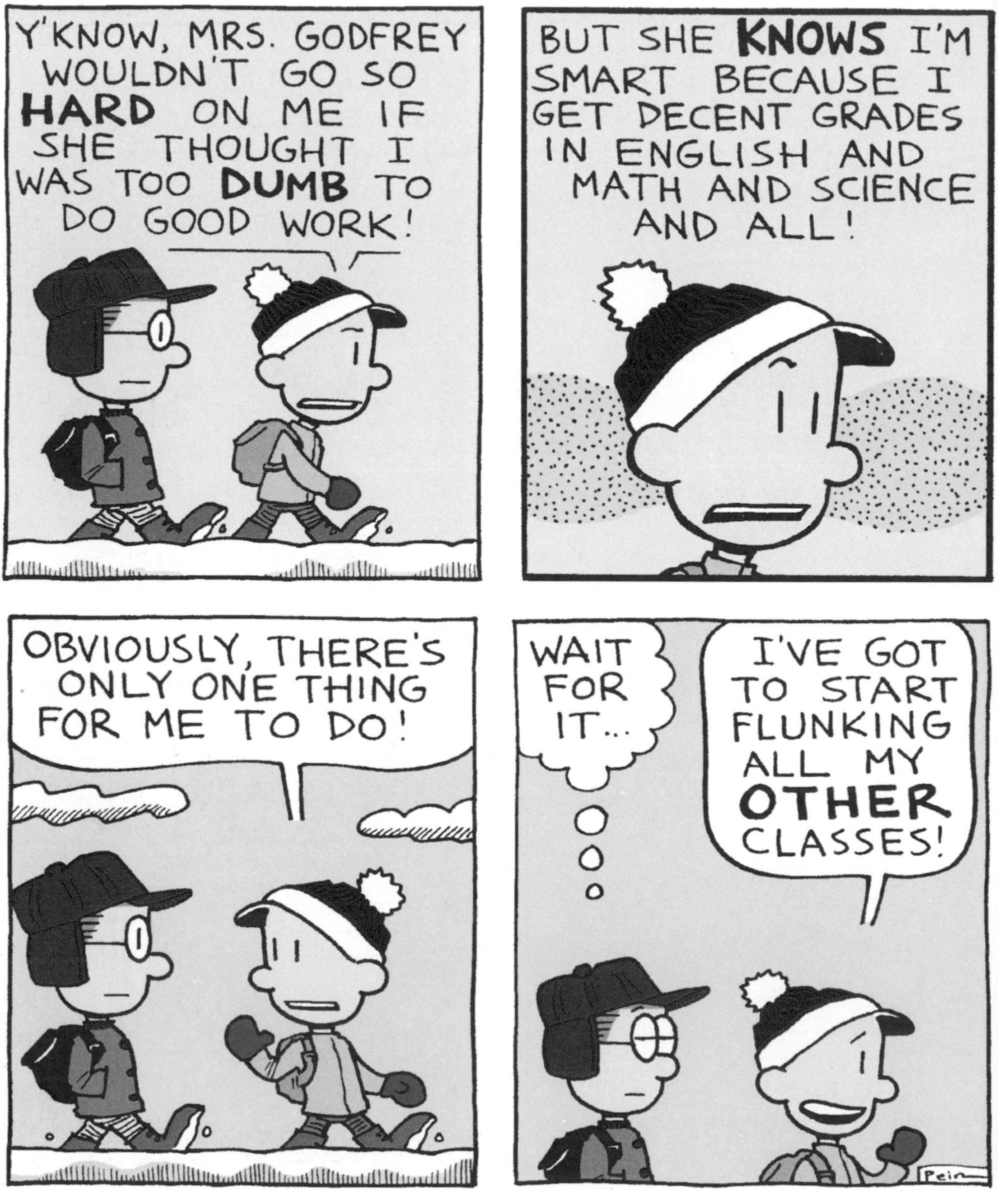
Y'KNOW, MRS. GODFREY WOULDN'T GO SO **HARD** ON ME IF SHE THOUGHT I WAS TOO **DUMB** TO DO GOOD WORK!
BUT SHE **KNOWS** I'M SMART BECAUSE I GET DECENT GRADES IN ENGLISH AND MATH AND SCIENCE AND ALL!
OBVIOUSLY, THERE'S ONLY ONE THING FOR ME TO DO!
WAIT FOR IT...
I'VE GOT TO START FLUNKING ALL MY **OTHER** CLASSES!
Peirce

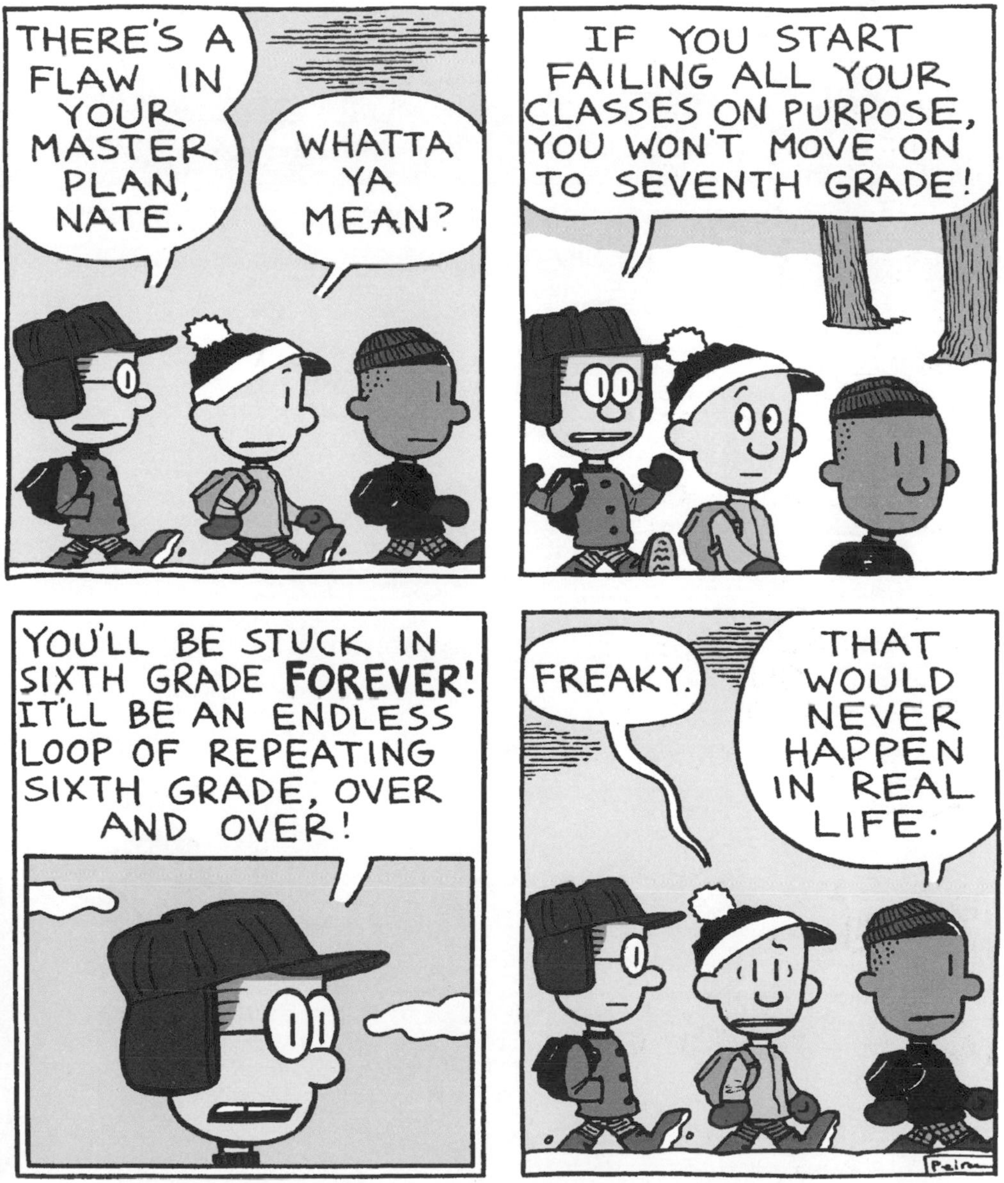

THERE'S A FLAW IN YOUR MASTER PLAN, NATE.
WHATTA YA MEAN?
IF YOU START FAILING ALL YOUR CLASSES ON PURPOSE, YOU WON'T MOVE ON TO SEVENTH GRADE!
YOU'LL BE STUCK IN SIXTH GRADE **FOREVER**! IT'LL BE AN ENDLESS LOOP OF REPEATING SIXTH GRADE, OVER AND OVER!
FREAKY.
THAT WOULD NEVER HAPPEN IN REAL LIFE.
Peirce

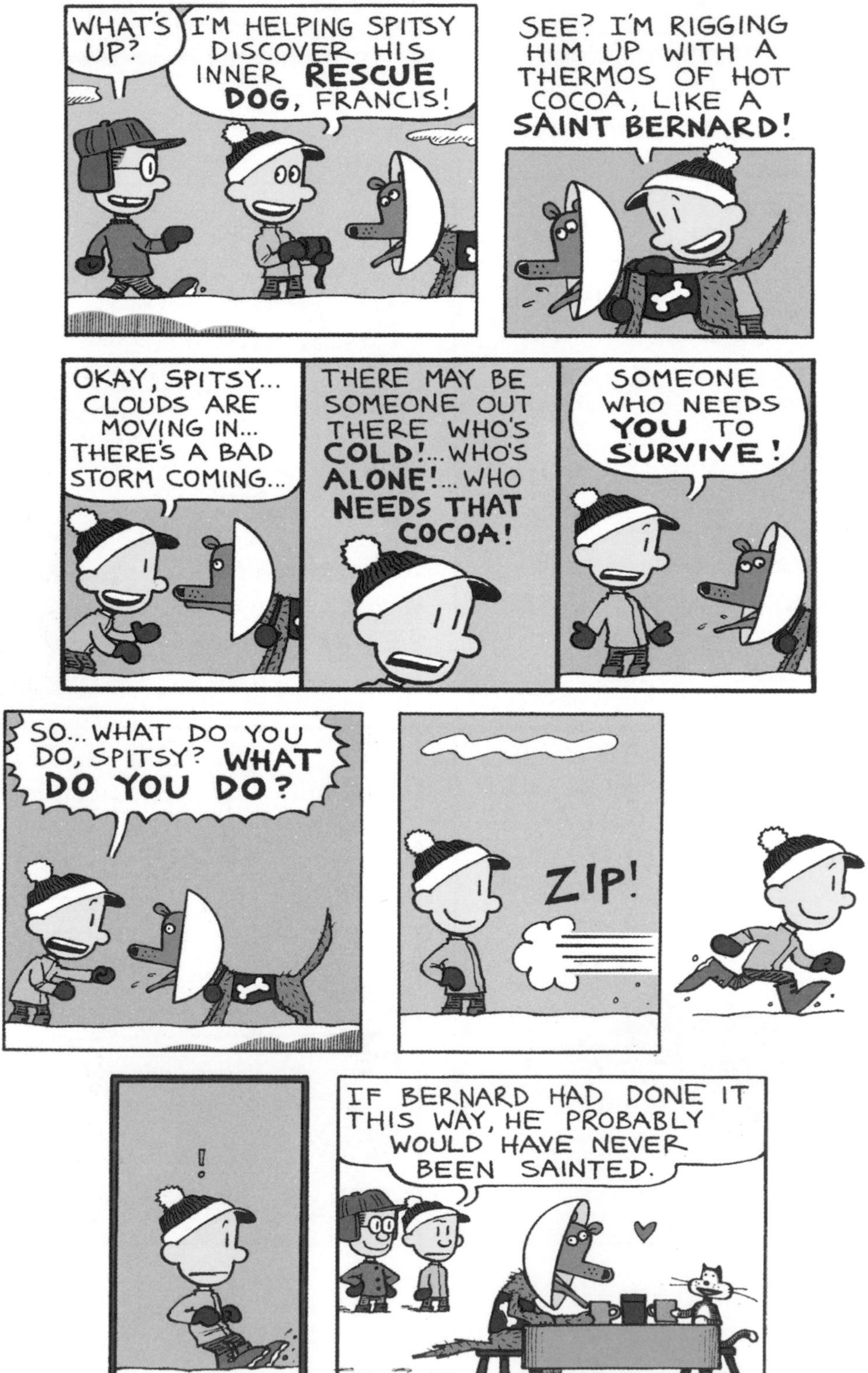
WHAT'S UP?
I'M HELPING SPITSY DISCOVER HIS INNER RESCUE DOG, FRANCIS!
SEE? I'M RIGGING HIM UP WITH A THERMOS OF HOT COCOA, LIKE A SAINT BERNARD!
OKAY, SPITSY... CLOUDS ARE MOVING IN... THERE'S A BAD STORM COMING...
THERE MAY BE SOMEONE OUT THERE WHO'S COLD!... WHO'S ALONE!... WHO NEEDS THAT COCOA!
SOMEONE WHO NEEDS YOU TO SURVIVE!
SO... WHAT DO YOU DO, SPITSY? WHAT DO YOU DO?
ZIP!
!
IF BERNARD HAD DONE IT THIS WAY, HE PROBABLY WOULD HAVE NEVER BEEN SAINTED.
Peirce

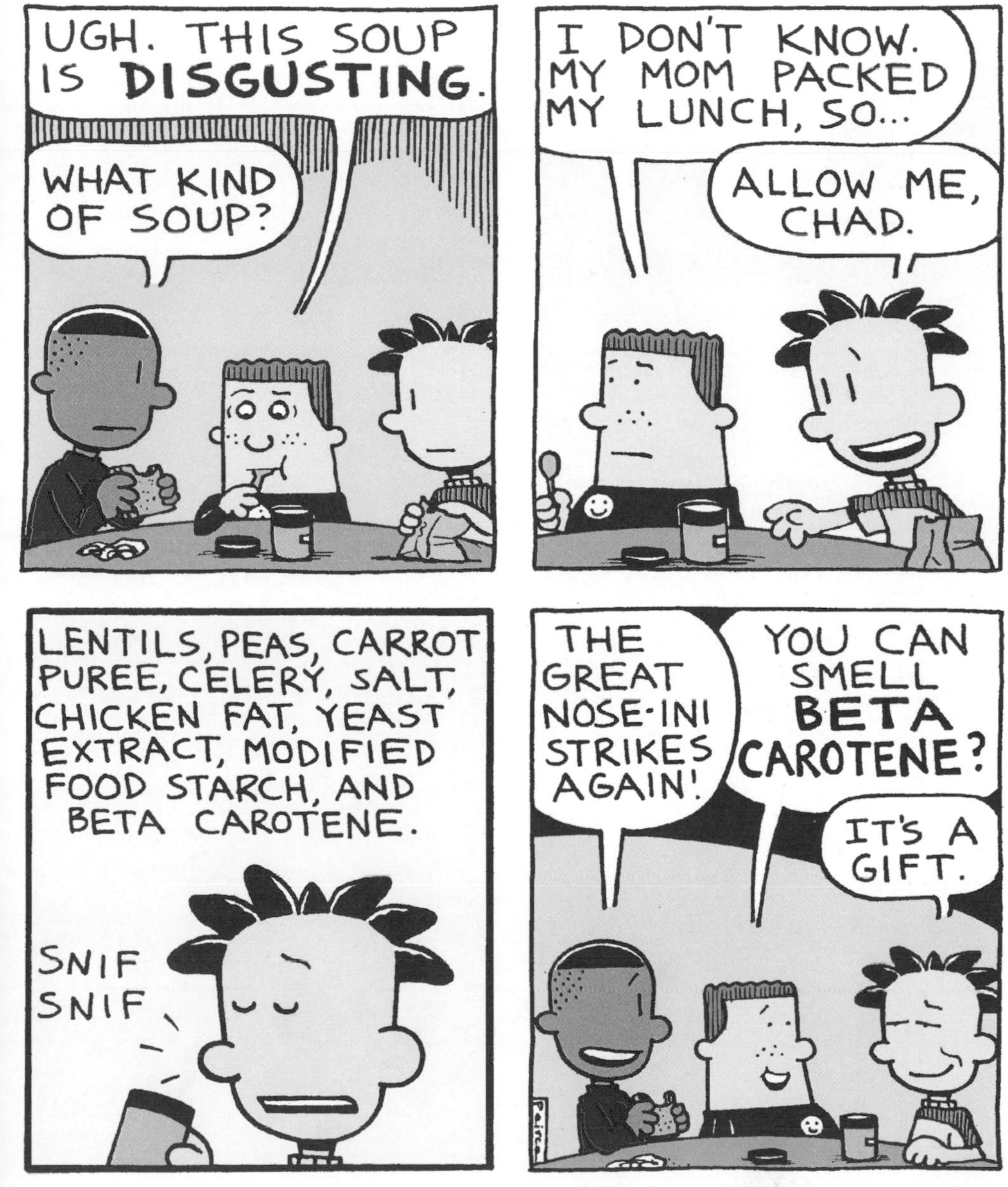
UGH. THIS SOUP IS **DISGUSTING**.
WHAT KIND OF SOUP?
I DON'T KNOW. MY MOM PACKED MY LUNCH, SO...
ALLOW ME, CHAD.
LENTILS, PEAS, CARROT PUREE, CELERY, SALT, CHICKEN FAT, YEAST EXTRACT, MODIFIED FOOD STARCH, AND BETA CAROTENE.
SNIF SNIF
THE GREAT NOSE-INI STRIKES AGAIN!
YOU CAN SMELL **BETA CAROTENE**?
IT'S A GIFT.

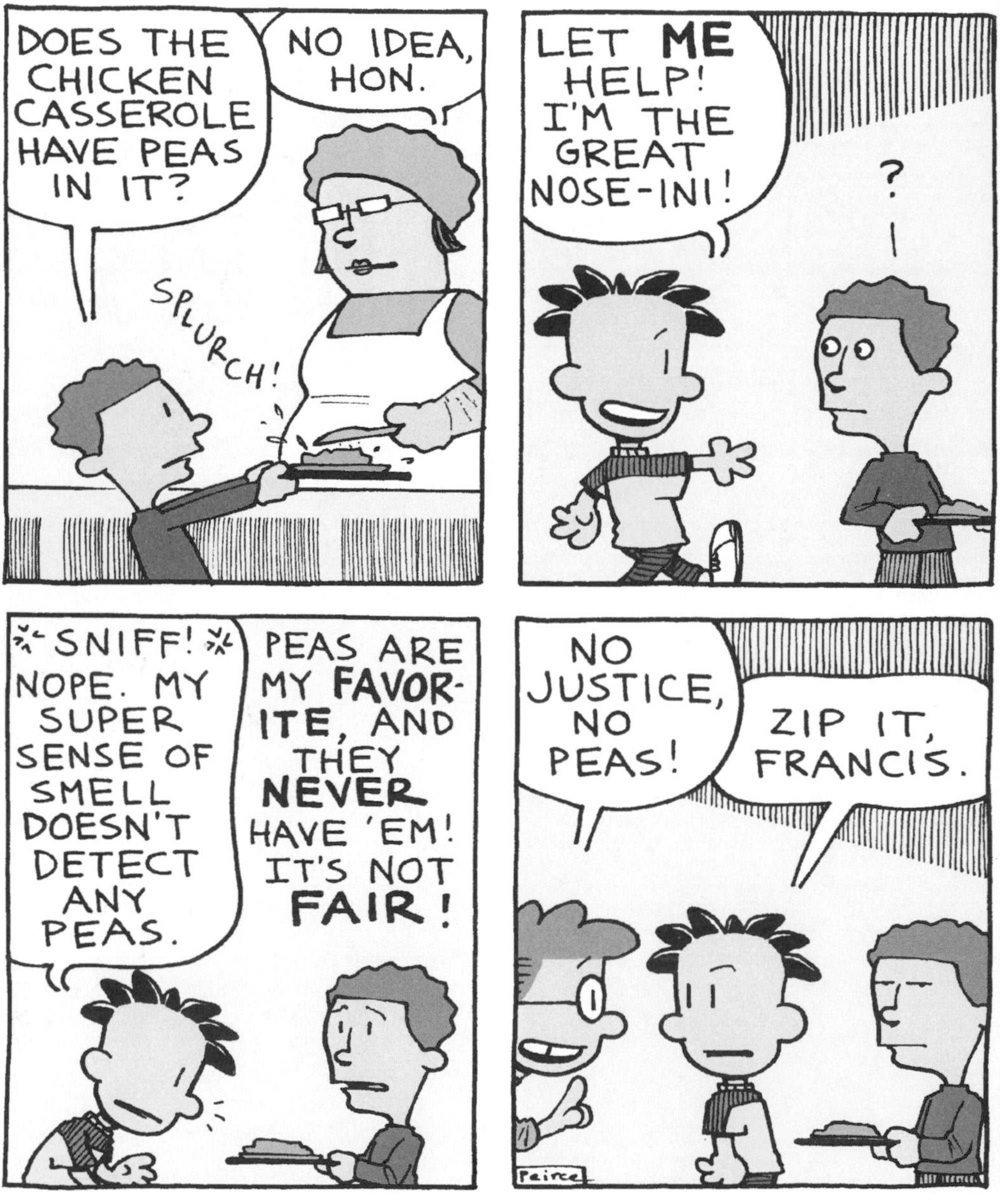
DOES THE CHICKEN CASSEROLE HAVE PEAS IN IT?
NO IDEA, HON.
SPLURCH!
LET **ME** HELP! I'M THE GREAT NOSE-INI!
?
SNIFF! NOPE. MY SUPER SENSE OF SMELL DOESN'T DETECT ANY PEAS.
PEAS ARE MY **FAVORITE**, AND THEY **NEVER** HAVE 'EM! IT'S NOT **FAIR**!
NO JUSTICE, NO PEAS!
ZIP IT, FRANCIS.
Peirce

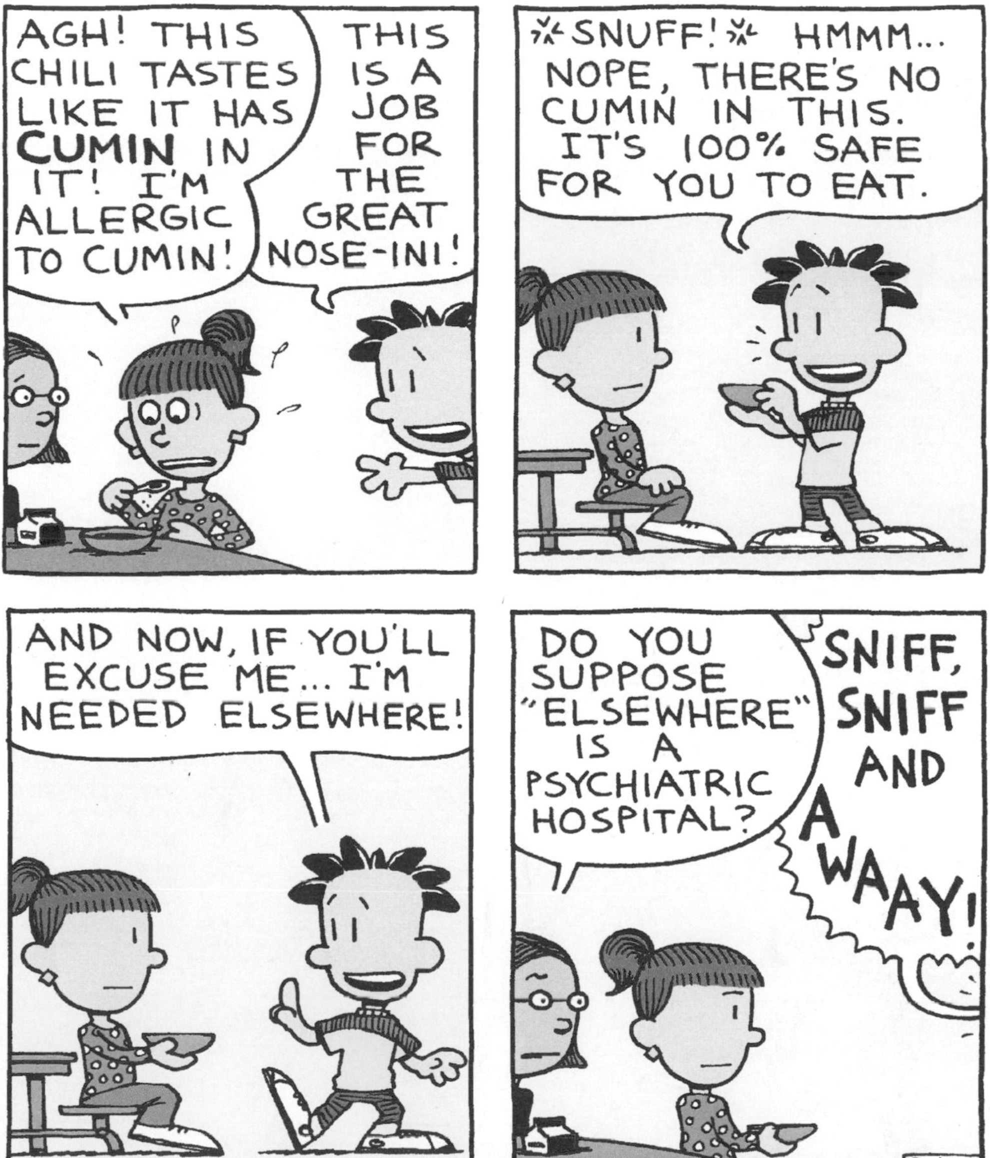
AGH! THIS CHILI TASTES LIKE IT HAS **CUMIN** IN IT! I'M ALLERGIC TO CUMIN!
THIS IS A JOB FOR THE GREAT NOSE-INI!
SNUFF! HMMM... NOPE, THERE'S NO CUMIN IN THIS. IT'S 100% SAFE FOR YOU TO EAT.
AND NOW, IF YOU'LL EXCUSE ME... I'M NEEDED ELSEWHERE!
DO YOU SUPPOSE "ELSEWHERE" IS A PSYCHIATRIC HOSPITAL?
SNIFF, SNIFF AND AWAAAY!
Peirce

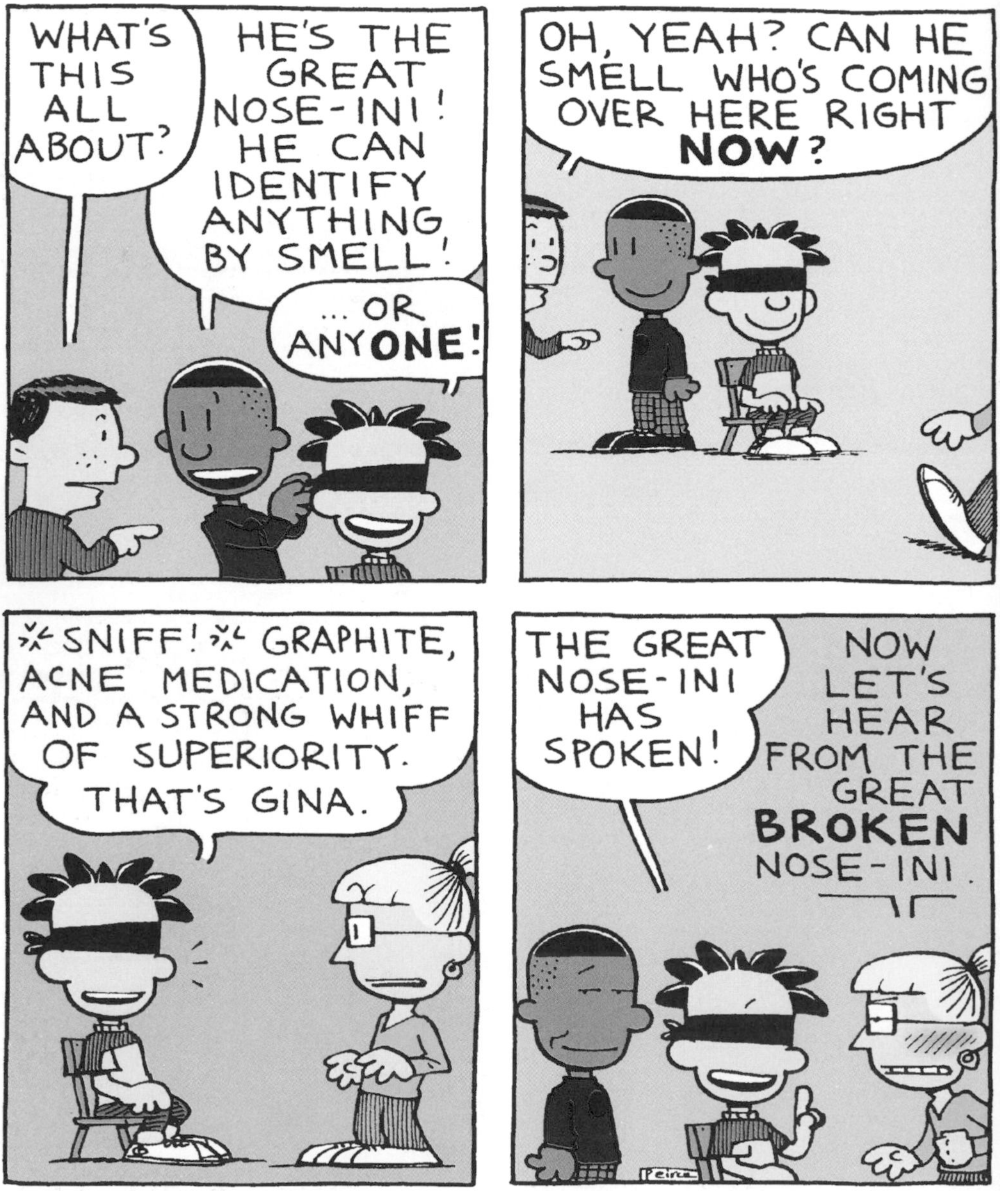
WHAT'S THIS ALL ABOUT?
HE'S THE GREAT NOSE-INI! HE CAN IDENTIFY ANYTHING BY SMELL!
...OR ANYONE!
OH, YEAH? CAN HE SMELL WHO'S COMING OVER HERE RIGHT NOW?
SNIFF! GRAPHITE, ACNE MEDICATION, AND A STRONG WHIFF OF SUPERIORITY. THAT'S GINA.
THE GREAT NOSE-INI HAS SPOKEN!
NOW LET'S HEAR FROM THE GREAT BROKEN NOSE-INI.
Peirce

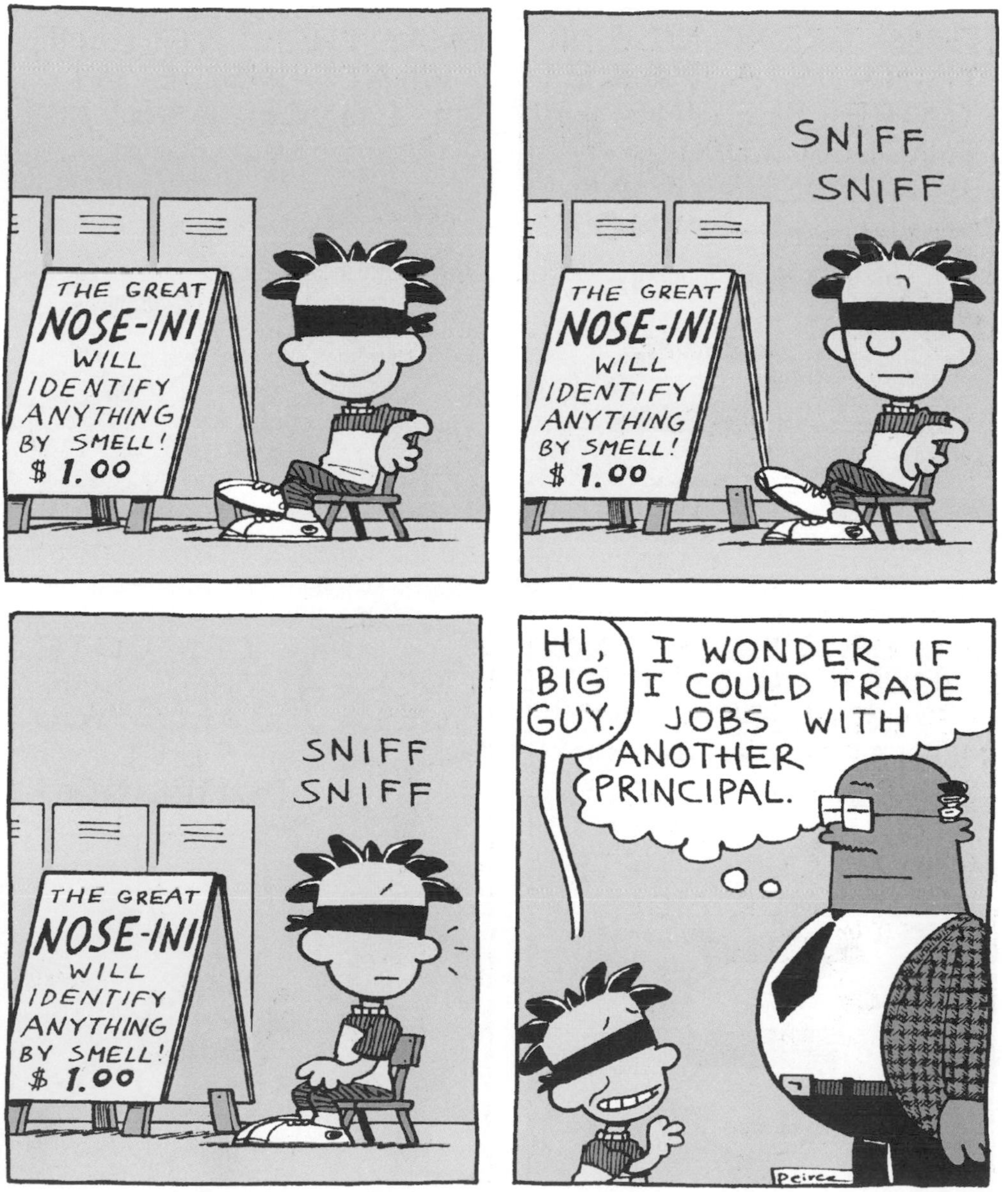
THE GREAT NOSE-INI WILL IDENTIFY ANYTHING BY SMELL! $ 1.00
SNIFF SNIFF
THE GREAT NOSE-INI WILL IDENTIFY ANYTHING BY SMELL! $ 1.00
SNIFF SNIFF
THE GREAT NOSE-INI WILL IDENTIFY ANYTHING BY SMELL! $ 1.00
HI, BIG GUY.
I WONDER IF I COULD TRADE JOBS WITH ANOTHER PRINCIPAL.
Peirce

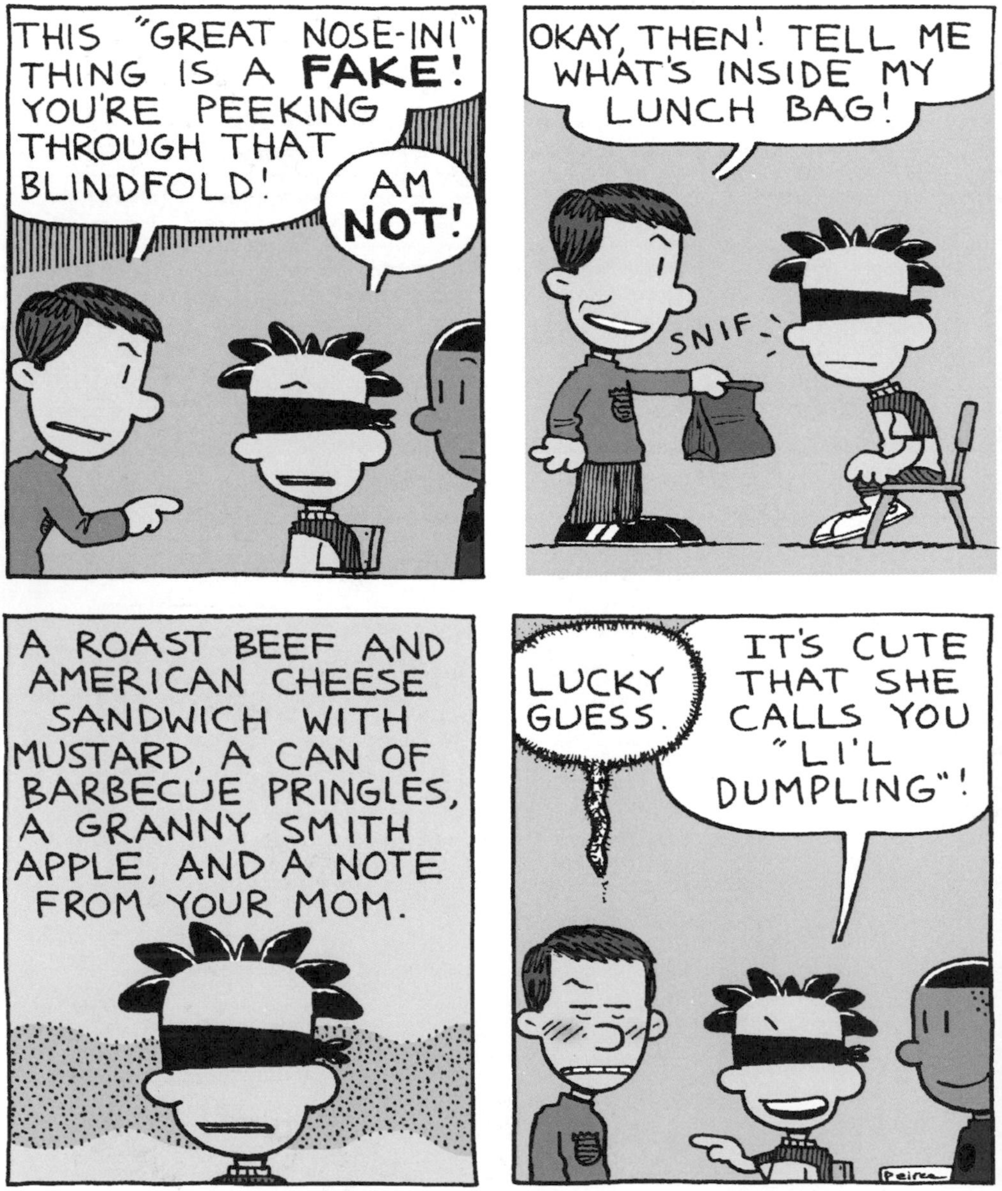
THIS "GREAT NOSE-INI" THING IS A **FAKE**! YOU'RE PEEKING THROUGH THAT BLINDFOLD!
AM **NOT**!
OKAY, THEN! TELL ME WHAT'S INSIDE MY LUNCH BAG!
SNIF
A ROAST BEEF AND AMERICAN CHEESE SANDWICH WITH MUSTARD, A CAN OF BARBECUE PRINGLES, A GRANNY SMITH APPLE, AND A NOTE FROM YOUR MOM.
LUCKY GUESS.
IT'S CUTE THAT SHE CALLS YOU "LI'L DUMPLING"!
Peirce

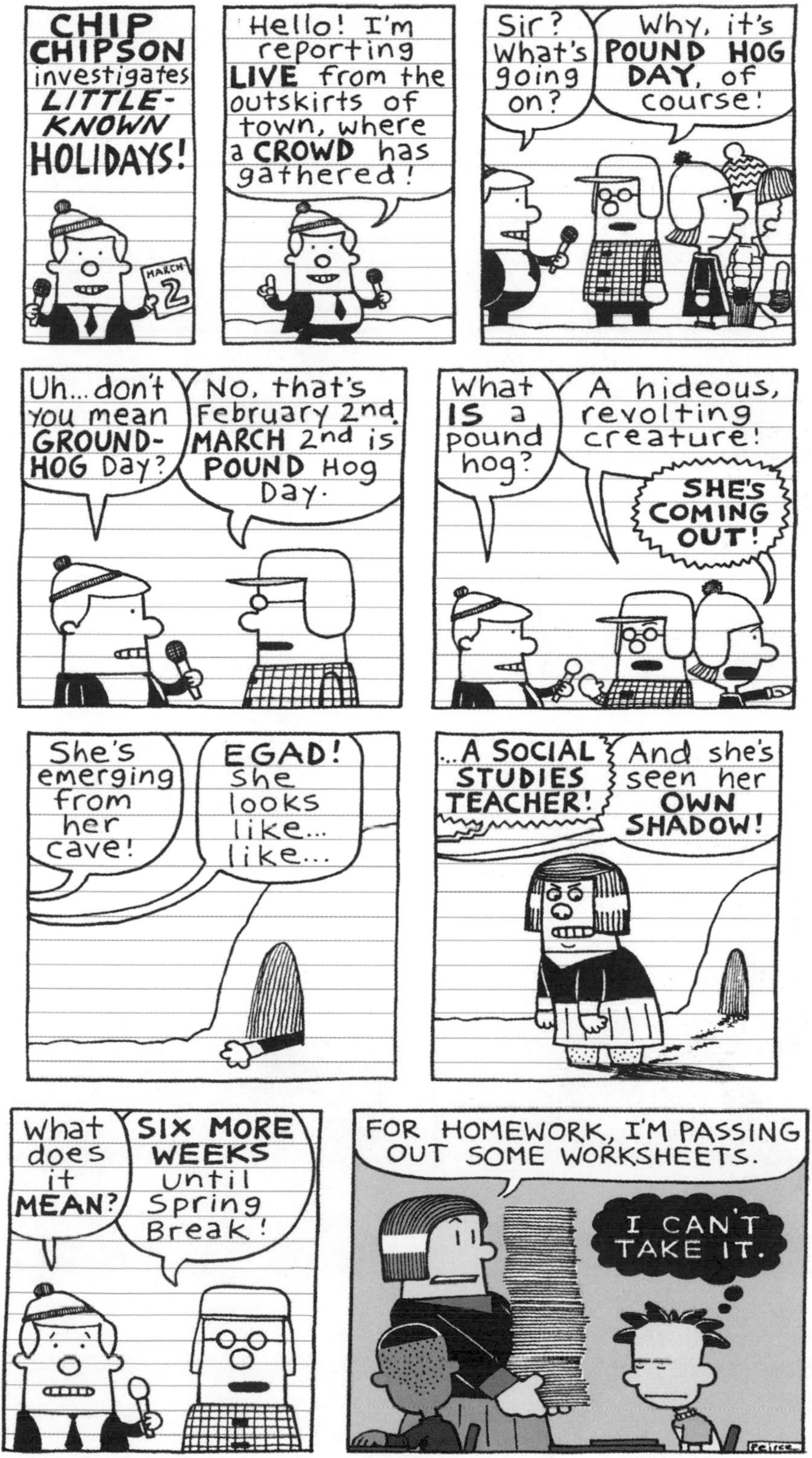
CHIP CHIPSON investigates LITTLE-KNOWN HOLIDAYS!
MARCH 2
Hello! I'm reporting LIVE from the outskirts of town, where a CROWD has gathered!
Sir? What's going on?
Why, it's POUND HOG DAY, of course!
Uh... don't you mean GROUND-HOG Day?
No, that's February 2nd. MARCH 2nd is POUND Hog Day.
What IS a pound hog?
A hideous, revolting creature!
SHE'S COMING OUT!
She's emerging from her cave!
EGAD! She looks like... like...
...A SOCIAL STUDIES TEACHER!
And she's seen her OWN SHADOW!
What does it MEAN?
SIX MORE WEEKS until Spring Break!
FOR HOMEWORK, I'M PASSING OUT SOME WORKSHEETS.
I CAN'T TAKE IT.
Peirce

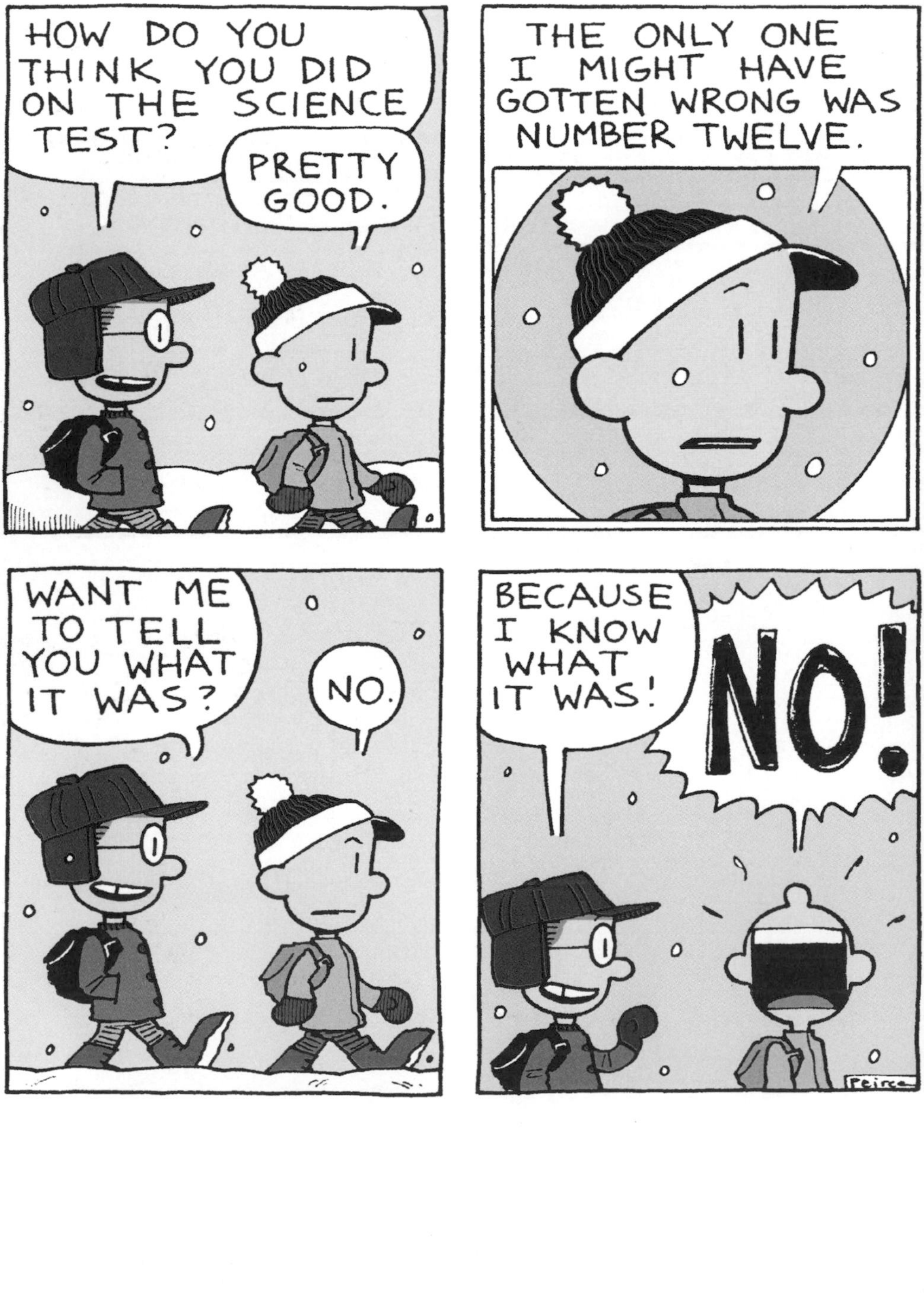
HOW DO YOU THINK YOU DID ON THE SCIENCE TEST?
PRETTY GOOD.
THE ONLY ONE I MIGHT HAVE GOTTEN WRONG WAS NUMBER TWELVE.
WANT ME TO TELL YOU WHAT IT WAS?
NO.
BECAUSE I KNOW WHAT IT WAS!
NO!
Peirce

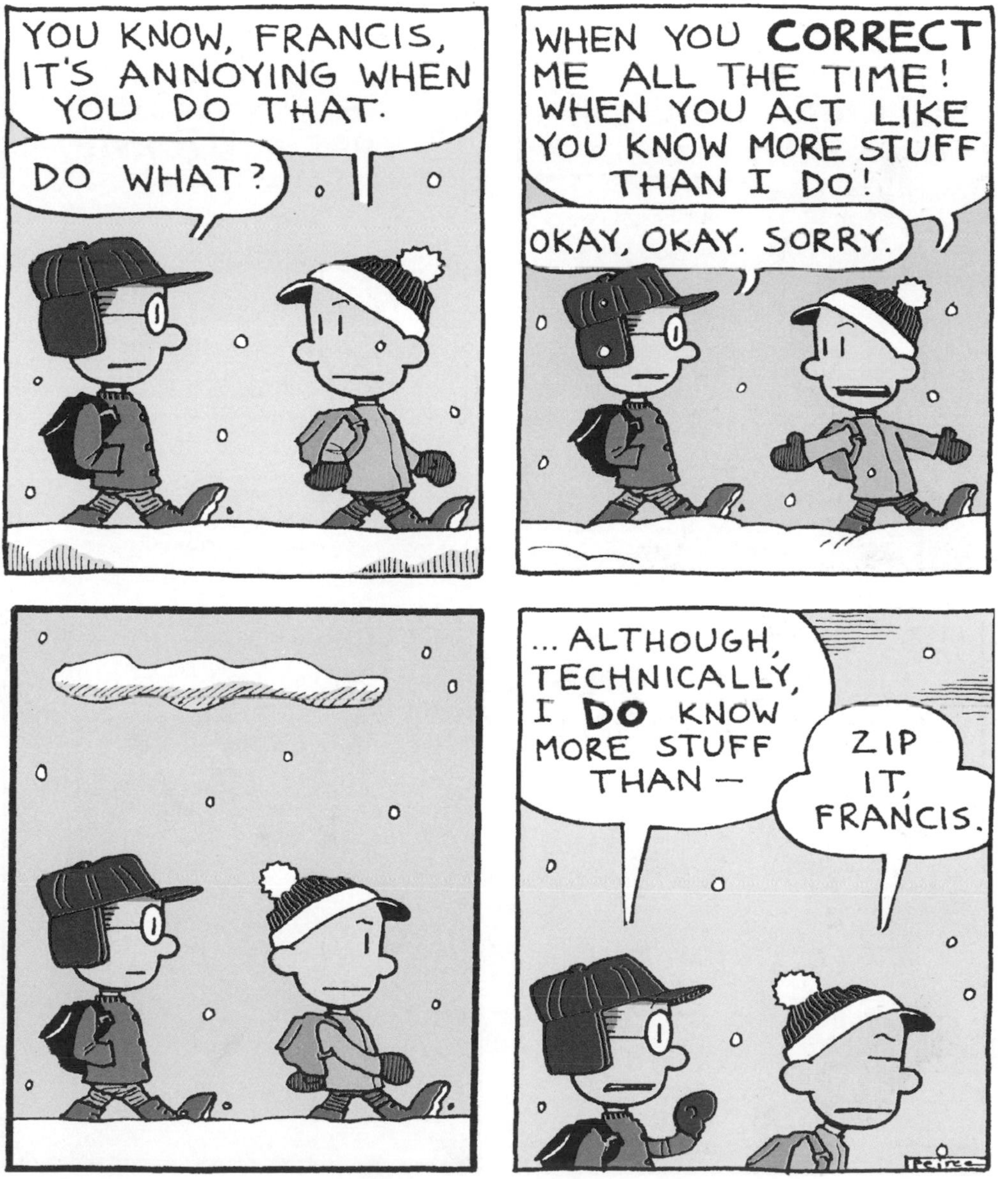
YOU KNOW, FRANCIS, IT'S ANNOYING WHEN YOU DO THAT.
DO WHAT?
WHEN YOU CORRECT ME ALL THE TIME! WHEN YOU ACT LIKE YOU KNOW MORE STUFF THAN I DO!
OKAY, OKAY. SORRY.
...ALTHOUGH, TECHNICALLY, I DO KNOW MORE STUFF THAN—
ZIP IT, FRANCIS.

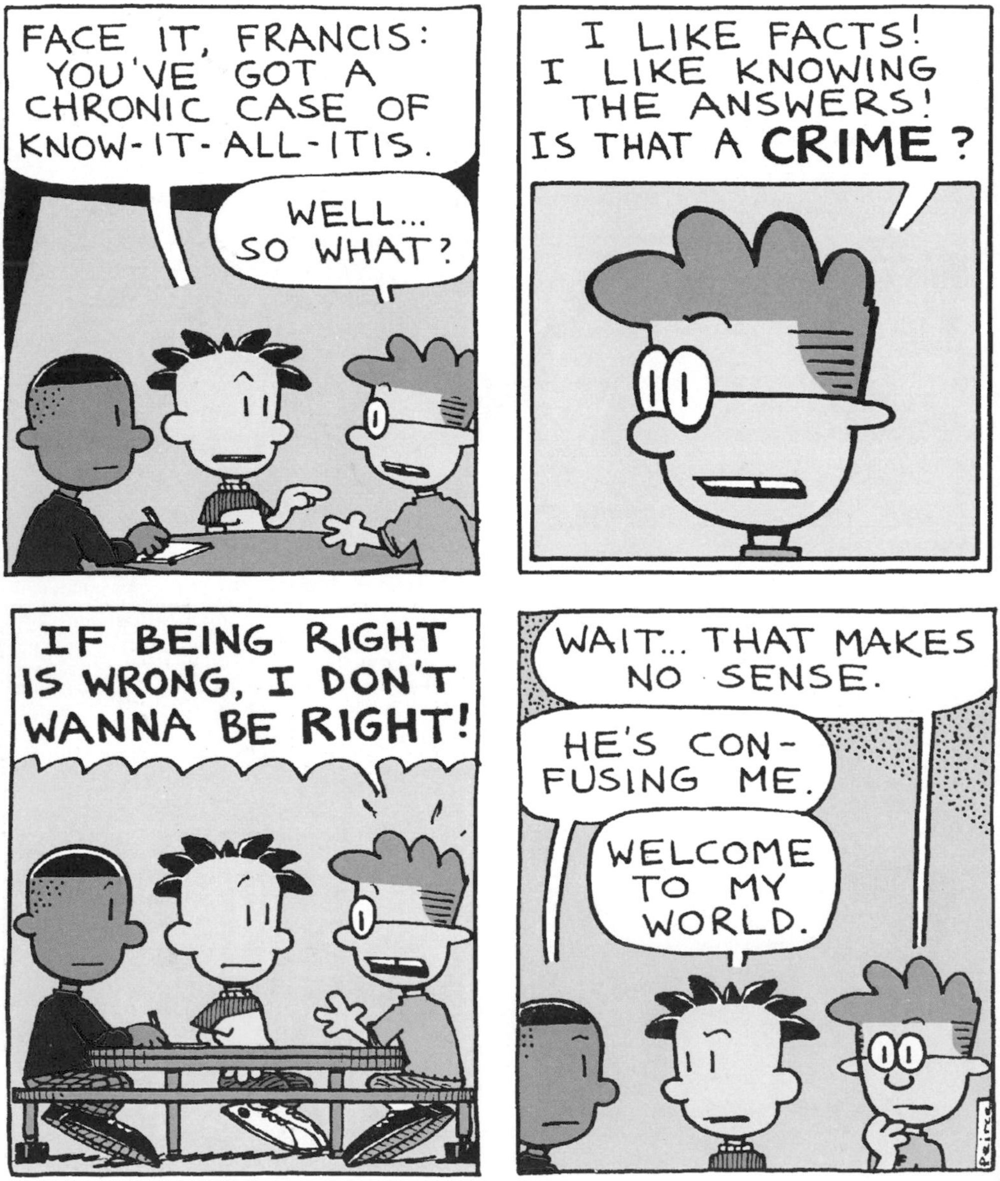
FACE IT, FRANCIS: YOU'VE GOT A CHRONIC CASE OF KNOW-IT-ALL-ITIS.
WELL... SO WHAT?
I LIKE FACTS! I LIKE KNOWING THE ANSWERS! IS THAT A CRIME?
IF BEING RIGHT IS WRONG, I DON'T WANNA BE RIGHT!
WAIT... THAT MAKES NO SENSE.
HE'S CON-FUSING ME.
WELCOME TO MY WORLD.
Peirce

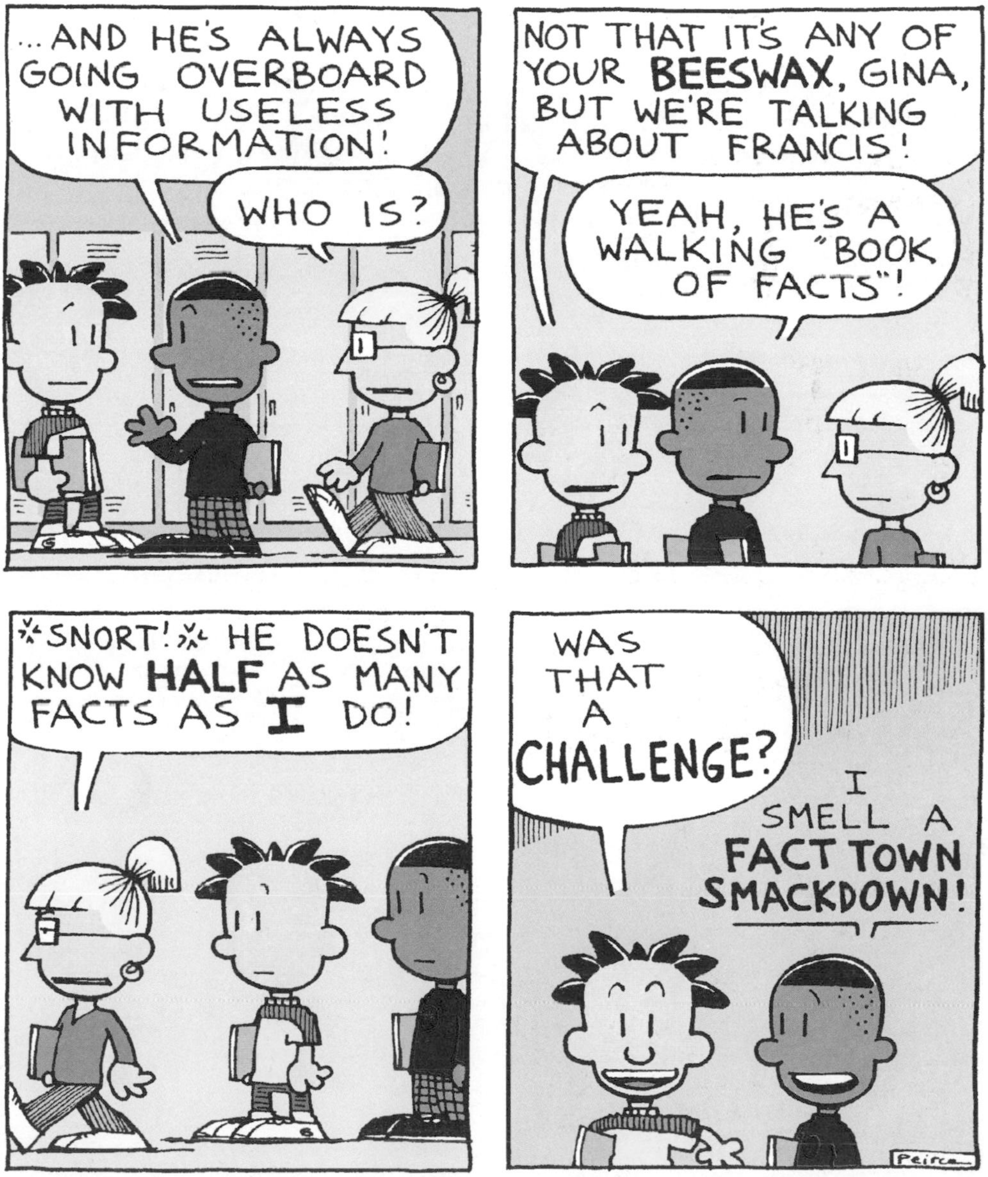
...AND HE'S ALWAYS GOING OVERBOARD WITH USELESS INFORMATION!
WHO IS?
NOT THAT IT'S ANY OF YOUR **BEESWAX**, GINA, BUT WE'RE TALKING ABOUT FRANCIS!
YEAH, HE'S A WALKING "BOOK OF FACTS"!
SNORT! HE DOESN'T KNOW **HALF** AS MANY FACTS AS **I** DO!
WAS THAT A **CHALLENGE?**
I SMELL A **FACT TOWN SMACKDOWN!**
Peirce

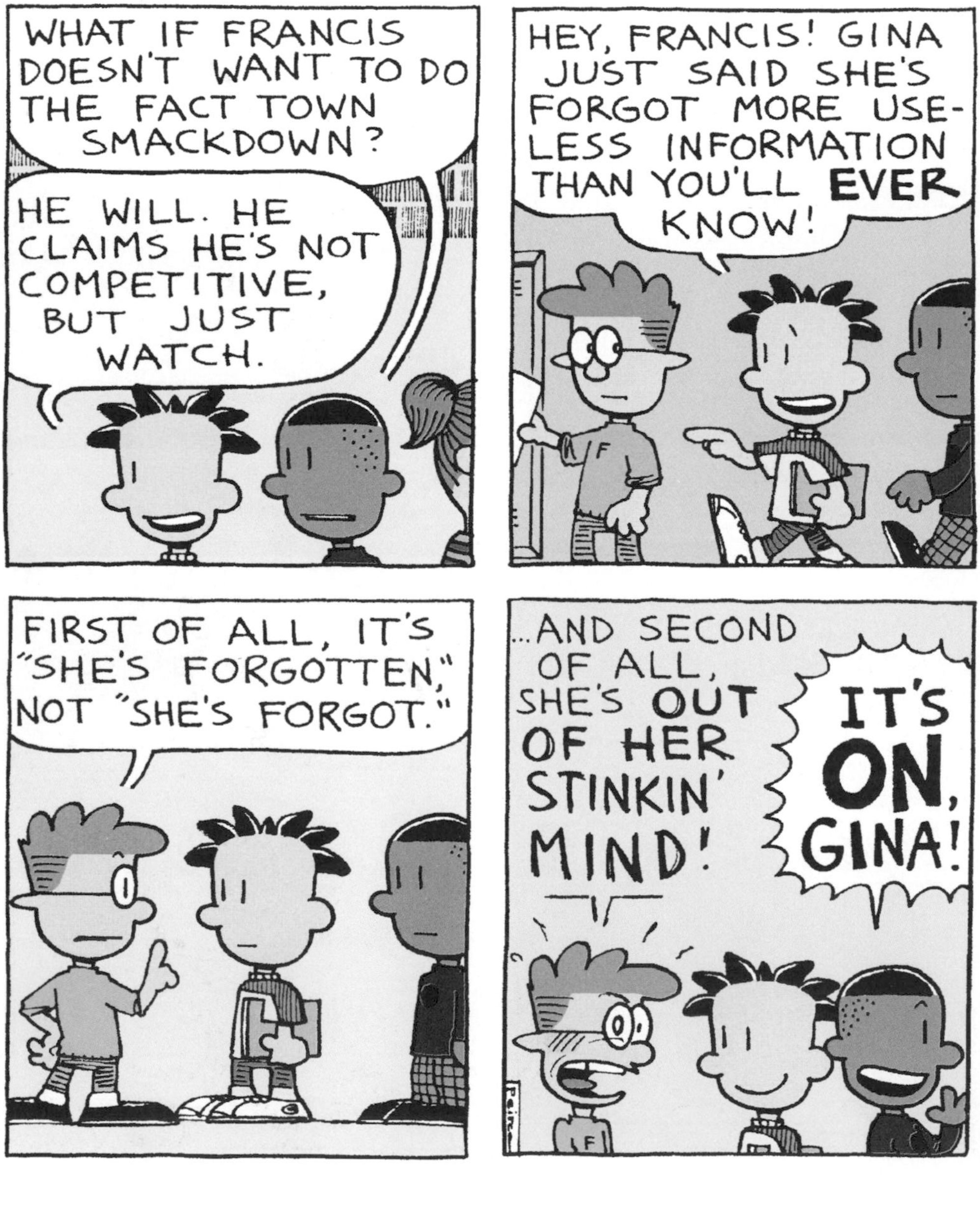
WHAT IF FRANCIS DOESN'T WANT TO DO THE FACT TOWN SMACKDOWN?
HE WILL. HE CLAIMS HE'S NOT COMPETITIVE, BUT JUST WATCH.
HEY, FRANCIS! GINA JUST SAID SHE'S FORGOT MORE USE-LESS INFORMATION THAN YOU'LL EVER KNOW!
FIRST OF ALL, IT'S "SHE'S FORGOTTEN," NOT "SHE'S FORGOT."
...AND SECOND OF ALL, SHE'S OUT OF HER STINKIN' MIND!
IT'S ON, GINA!

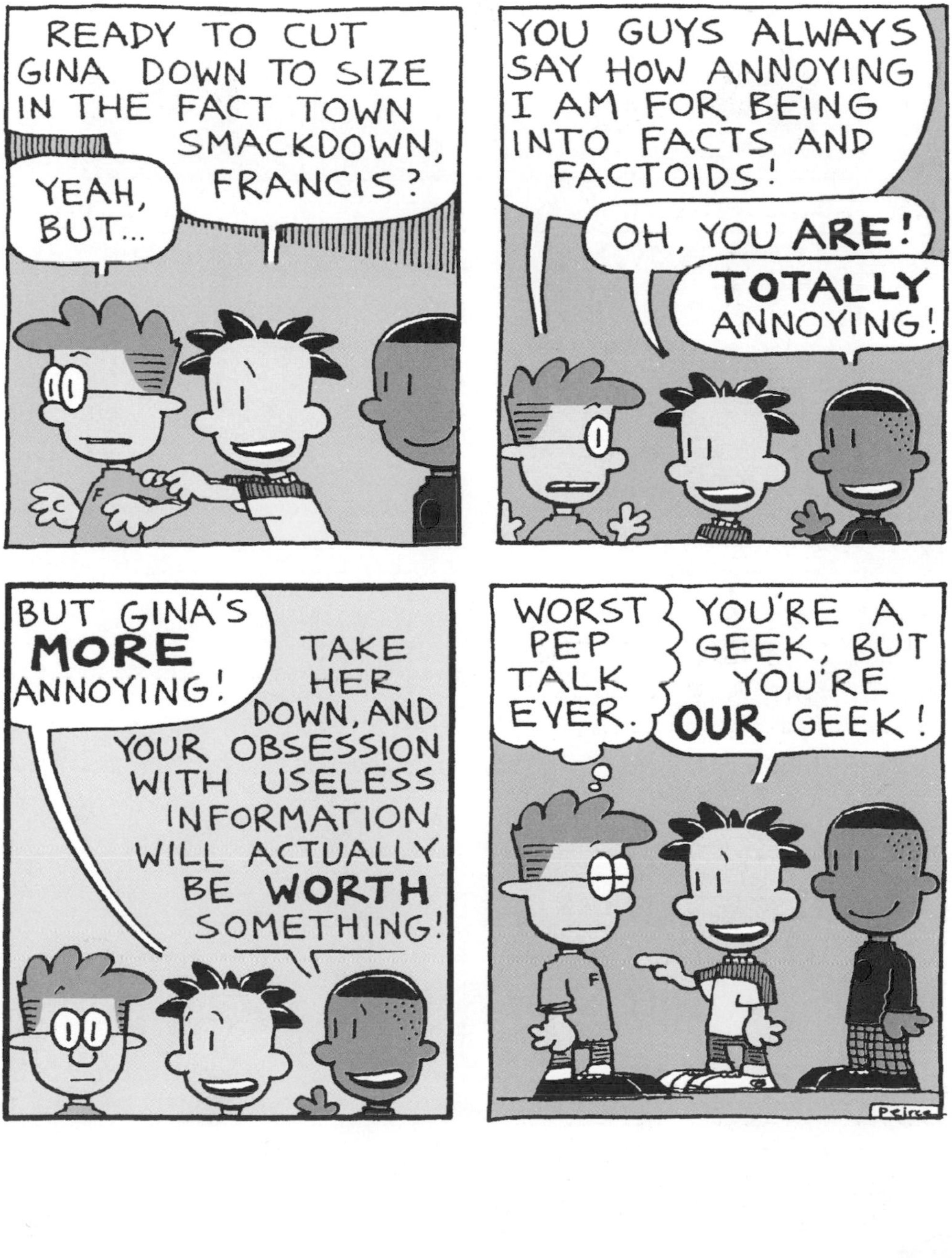
READY TO CUT GINA DOWN TO SIZE IN THE FACT TOWN SMACKDOWN, FRANCIS?
YEAH, BUT...
YOU GUYS ALWAYS SAY HOW ANNOYING I AM FOR BEING INTO FACTS AND FACTOIDS!
OH, YOU **ARE**!
TOTALLY ANNOYING!
BUT GINA'S **MORE** ANNOYING!
TAKE HER DOWN, AND YOUR OBSESSION WITH USELESS INFORMATION WILL ACTUALLY BE **WORTH** SOMETHING!
WORST PEP TALK EVER.
YOU'RE A GEEK, BUT YOU'RE **OUR** GEEK!
Peirce

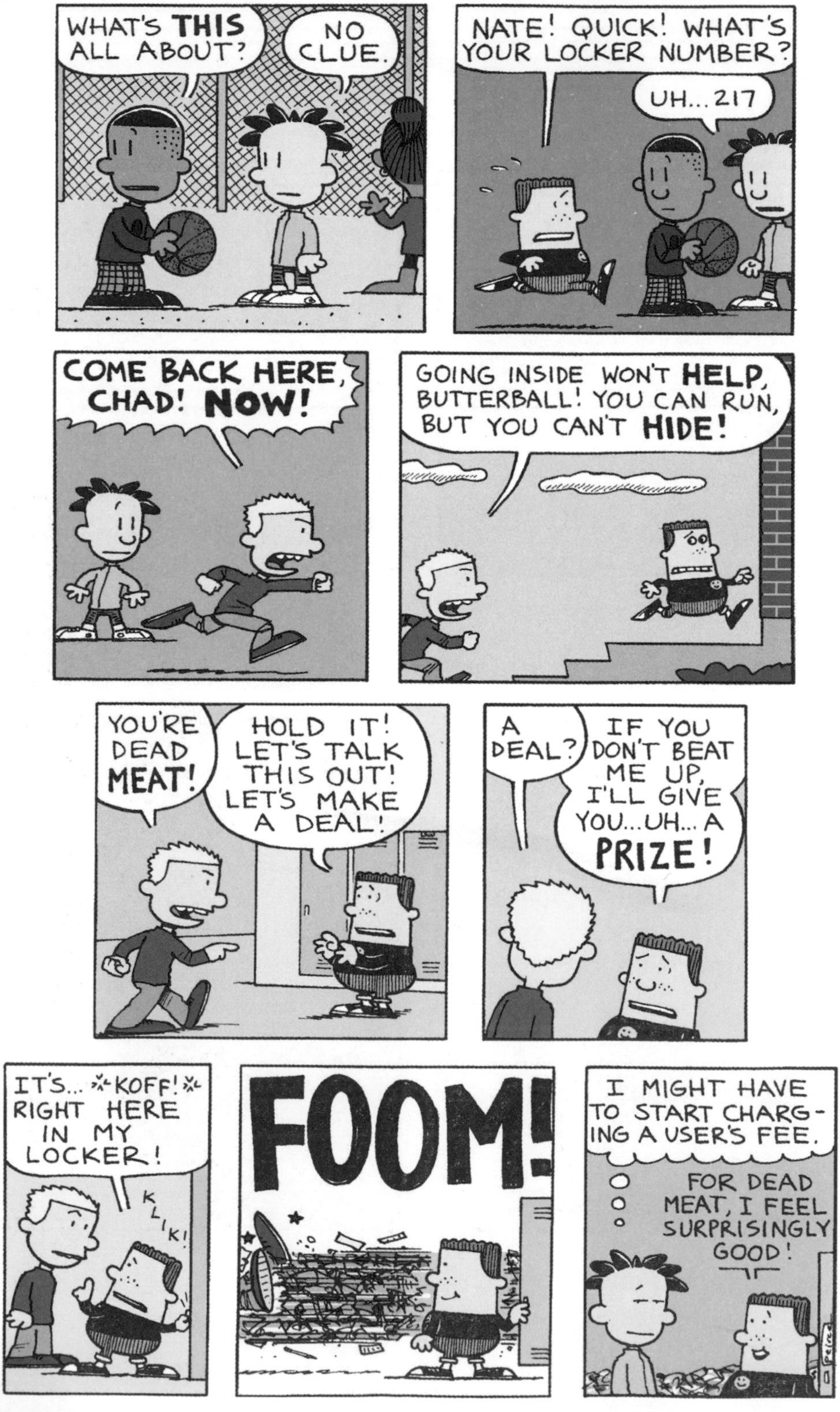
WHAT'S THIS ALL ABOUT?
NO CLUE.
NATE! QUICK! WHAT'S YOUR LOCKER NUMBER?
UH... 217
COME BACK HERE, CHAD! NOW!
GOING INSIDE WON'T HELP, BUTTERBALL! YOU CAN RUN, BUT YOU CAN'T HIDE!
YOU'RE DEAD MEAT!
HOLD IT! LET'S TALK THIS OUT! LET'S MAKE A DEAL!
A DEAL?
IF YOU DON'T BEAT ME UP, I'LL GIVE YOU...UH... A PRIZE!
IT'S... *KOFF!* RIGHT HERE IN MY LOCKER!
KLIK!
FOOM!
I MIGHT HAVE TO START CHARGING A USER'S FEE.
FOR DEAD MEAT, I FEEL SURPRISINGLY GOOD!

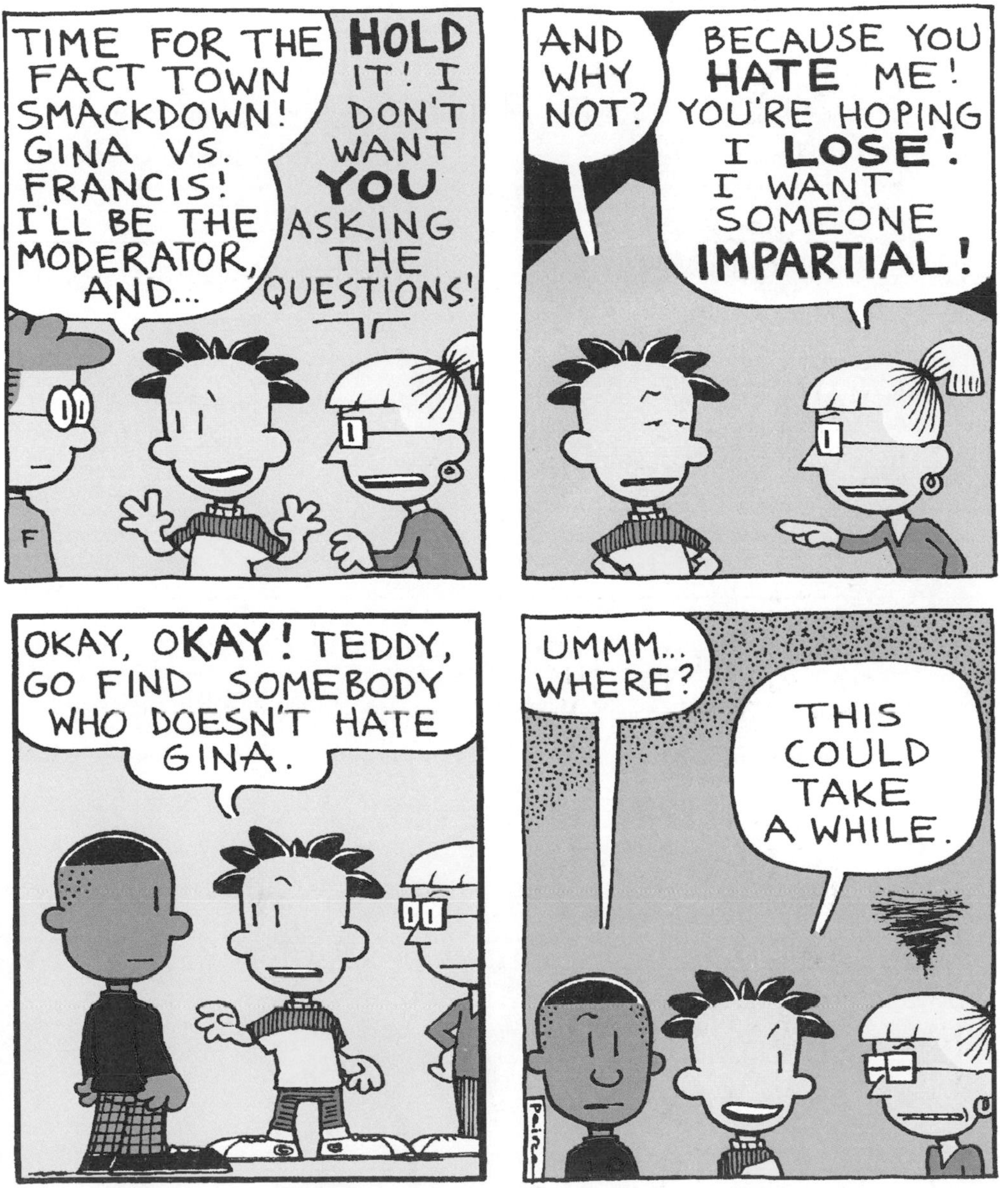
TIME FOR THE FACT TOWN SMACKDOWN! GINA VS. FRANCIS! I'LL BE THE MODERATOR, AND...
HOLD IT! I DON'T WANT YOU ASKING THE QUESTIONS!
F
AND WHY NOT?
BECAUSE YOU HATE ME! YOU'RE HOPING I LOSE! I WANT SOMEONE IMPARTIAL!
OKAY, OKAY! TEDDY, GO FIND SOMEBODY WHO DOESN'T HATE GINA.
UMMM... WHERE?
THIS COULD TAKE A WHILE.
Peirce

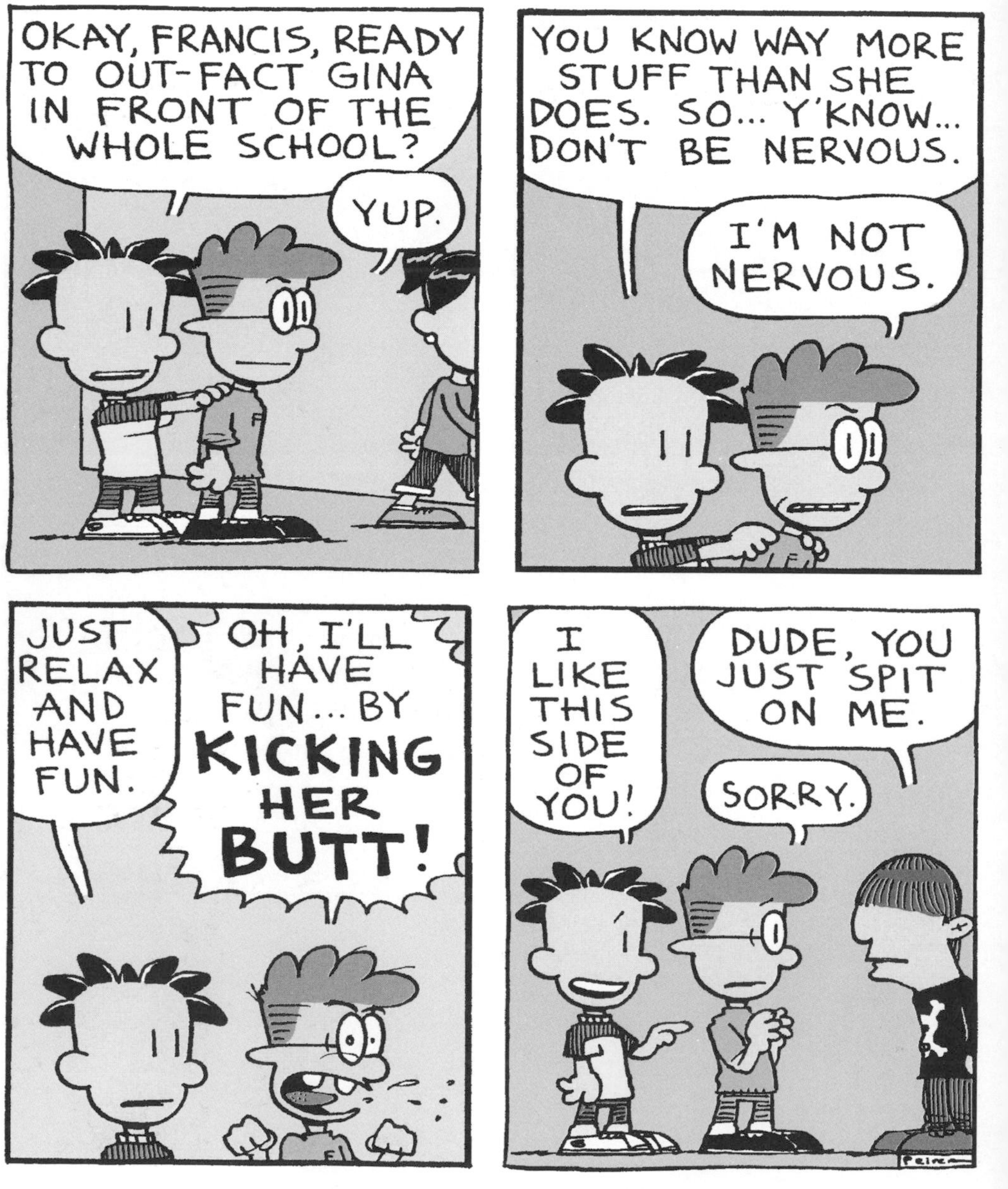
OKAY, FRANCIS, READY TO OUT-FACT GINA IN FRONT OF THE WHOLE SCHOOL?
YUP.
YOU KNOW WAY MORE STUFF THAN SHE DOES. SO... Y'KNOW... DON'T BE NERVOUS.
I'M NOT NERVOUS.
JUST RELAX AND HAVE FUN.
OH, I'LL HAVE FUN... BY KICKING HER BUTT!
I LIKE THIS SIDE OF YOU!
DUDE, YOU JUST SPIT ON ME.
SORRY.

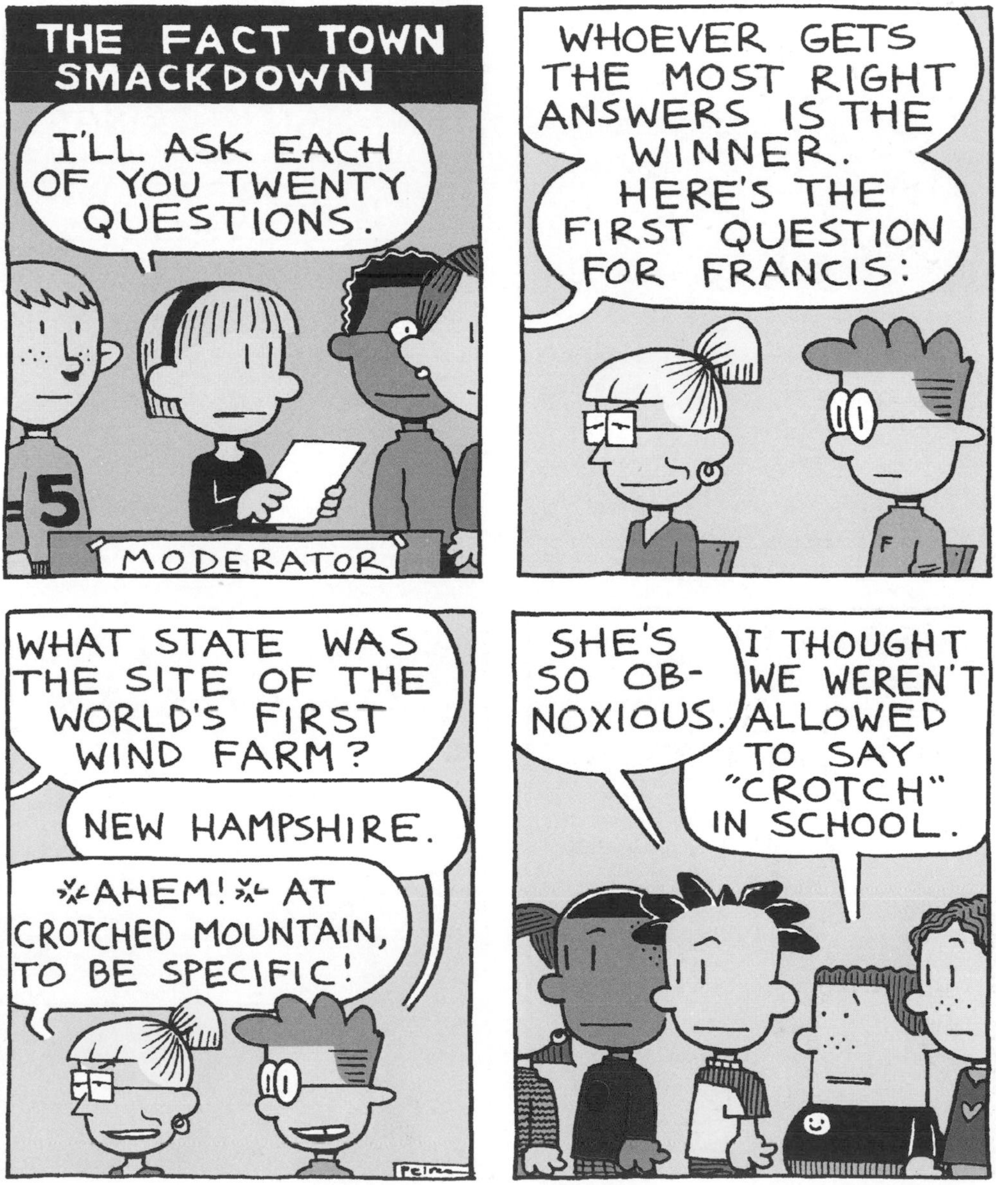
THE FACT TOWN SMACKDOWN
I'LL ASK EACH OF YOU TWENTY QUESTIONS.
5
MODERATOR
WHOEVER GETS THE MOST RIGHT ANSWERS IS THE WINNER. HERE'S THE FIRST QUESTION FOR FRANCIS:
F
WHAT STATE WAS THE SITE OF THE WORLD'S FIRST WIND FARM?
NEW HAMPSHIRE.
AHEM! AT CROTCHED MOUNTAIN, TO BE SPECIFIC!
SHE'S SO OBNOXIOUS.
I THOUGHT WE WEREN'T ALLOWED TO SAY "CROTCH" IN SCHOOL.

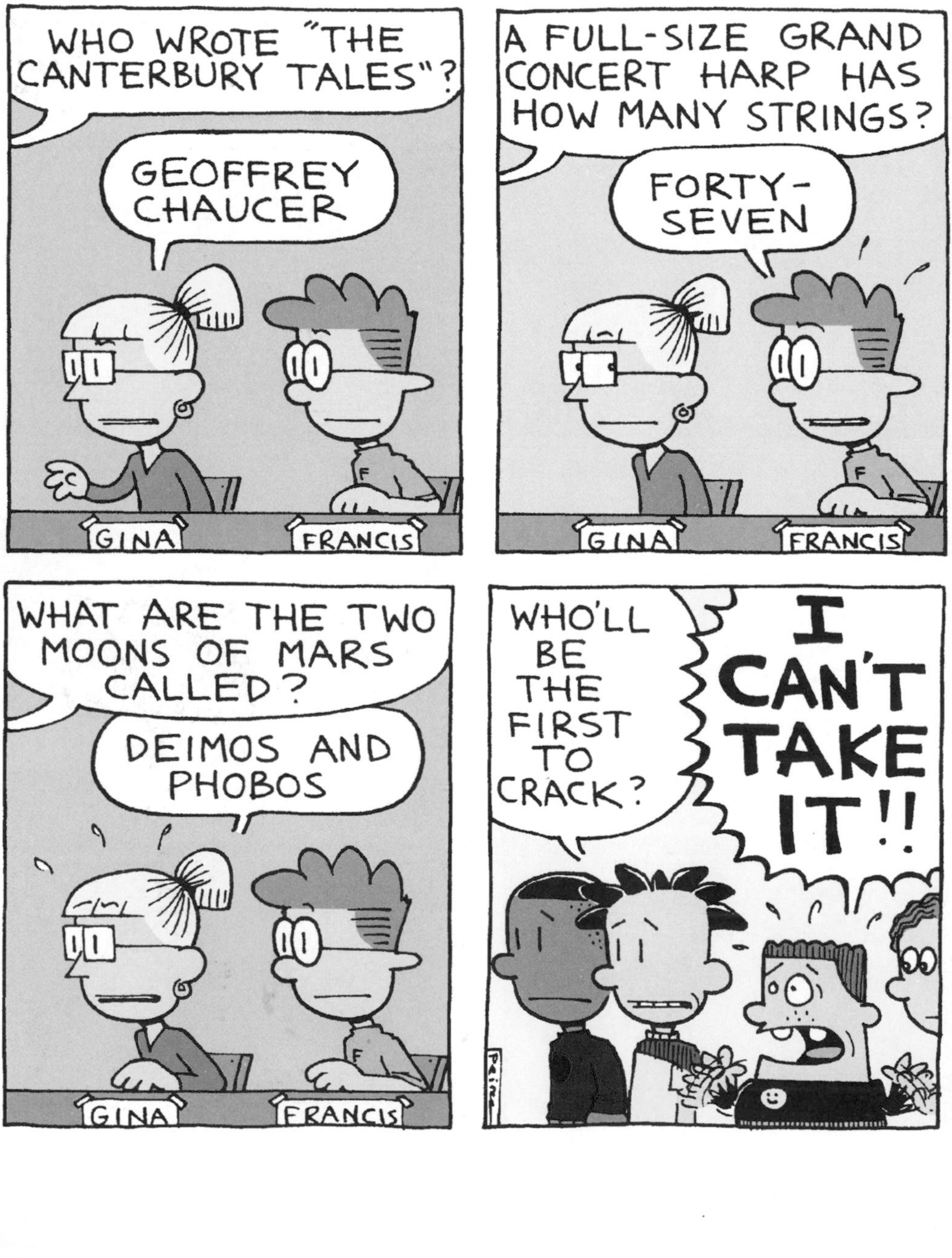
WHO WROTE "THE CANTERBURY TALES"?
GEOFFREY CHAUCER
GINA
FRANCIS
A FULL-SIZE GRAND CONCERT HARP HAS HOW MANY STRINGS?
FORTY-SEVEN
GINA
FRANCIS
WHAT ARE THE TWO MOONS OF MARS CALLED?
DEIMOS AND PHOBOS
GINA
FRANCIS
WHO'LL BE THE FIRST TO CRACK?
I CAN'T TAKE IT!!

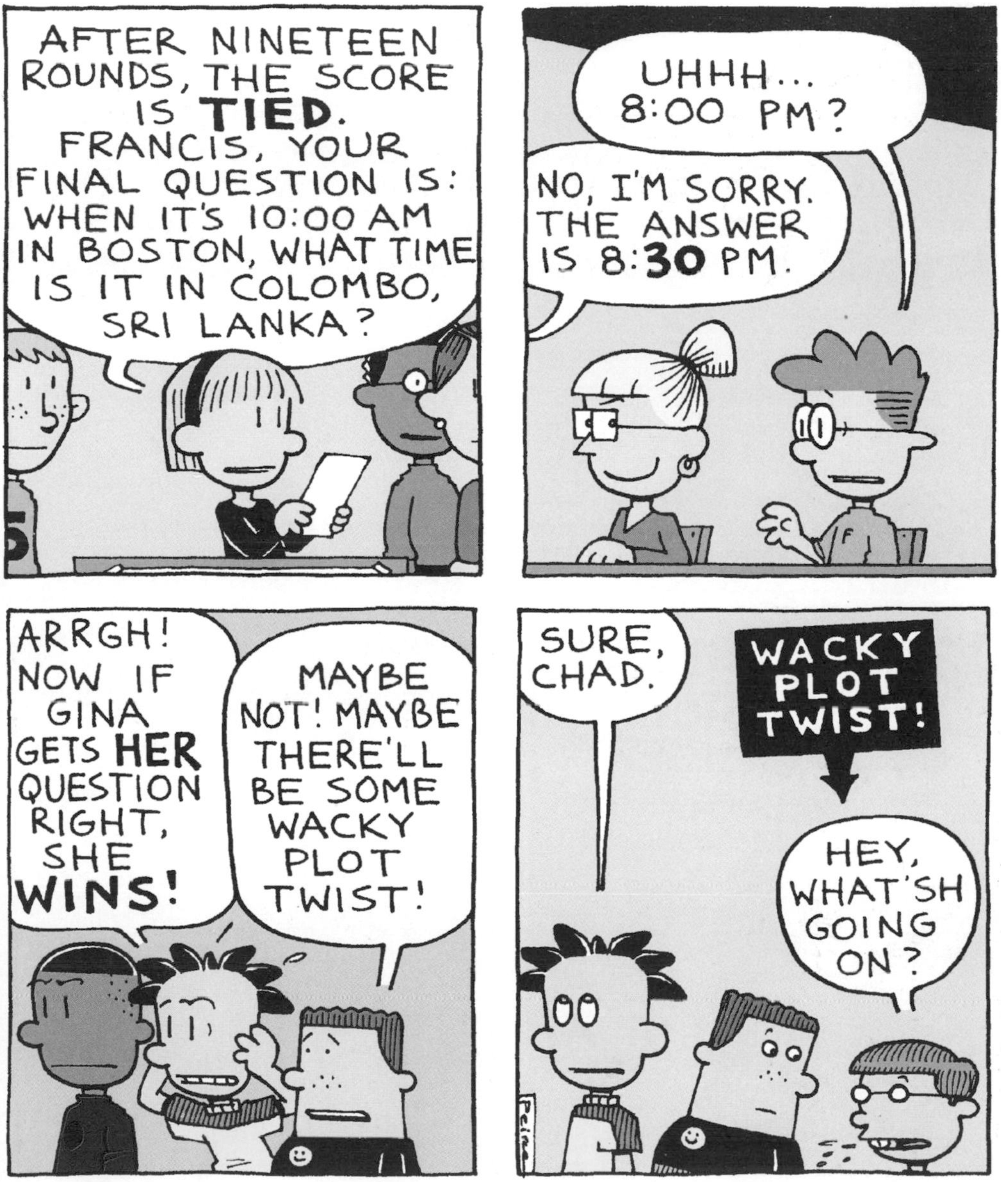
AFTER NINETEEN ROUNDS, THE SCORE IS **TIED**. FRANCIS, YOUR FINAL QUESTION IS: WHEN IT'S 10:00 AM IN BOSTON, WHAT TIME IS IT IN COLOMBO, SRI LANKA?
UHHH... 8:00 PM?
NO, I'M SORRY. THE ANSWER IS 8:**30** PM.
ARRGH! NOW IF GINA GETS **HER** QUESTION RIGHT, SHE **WINS**!
MAYBE NOT! MAYBE THERE'LL BE SOME WACKY PLOT TWIST!
SURE, CHAD.
WACKY PLOT TWIST!
HEY, WHAT'SH GOING ON?

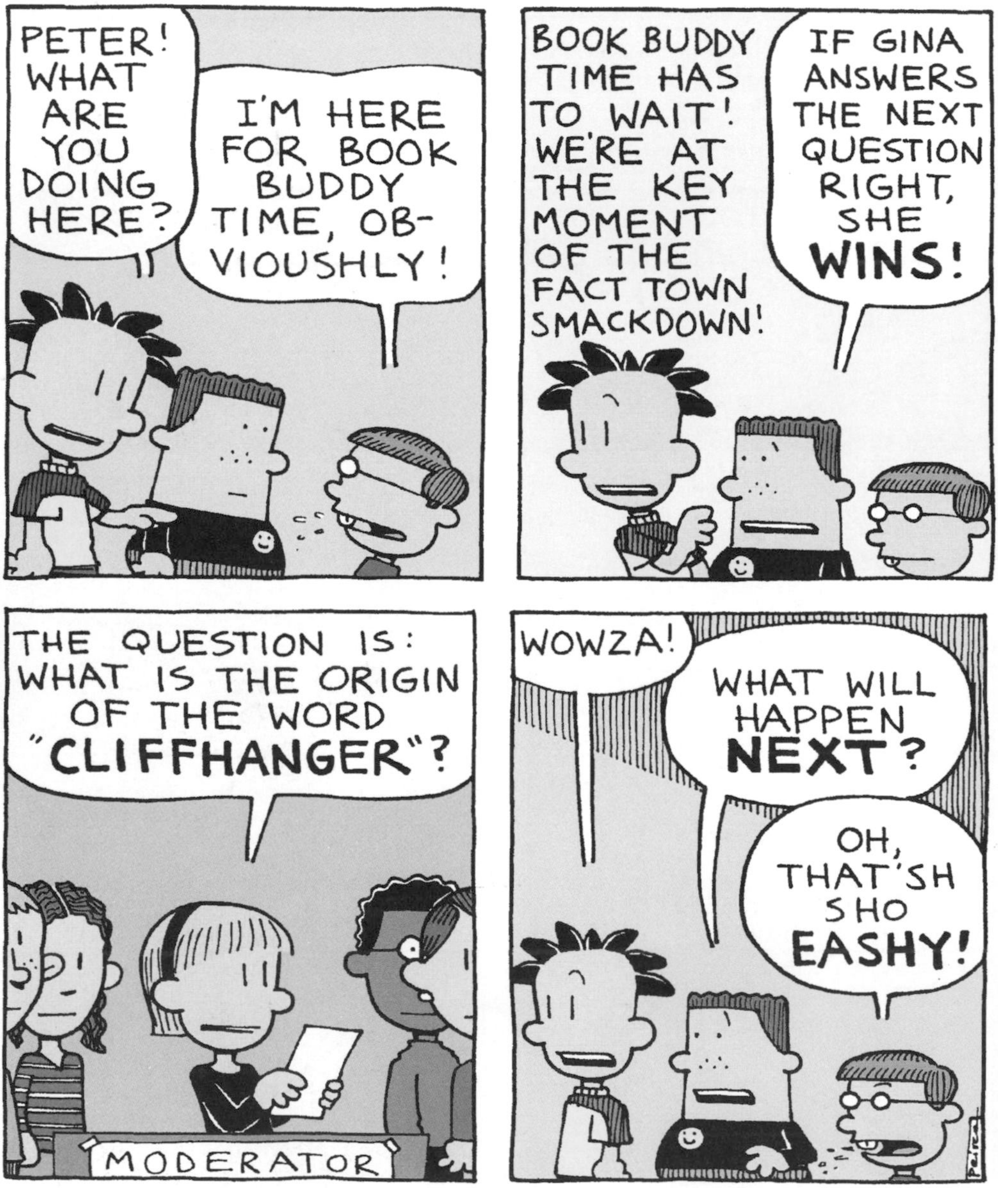
PETER! WHAT ARE YOU DOING HERE?
I'M HERE FOR BOOK BUDDY TIME, OBVIOUSHLY!
BOOK BUDDY TIME HAS TO WAIT! WE'RE AT THE KEY MOMENT OF THE FACT TOWN SMACKDOWN!
IF GINA ANSWERS THE NEXT QUESTION RIGHT, SHE **WINS!**
THE QUESTION IS: WHAT IS THE ORIGIN OF THE WORD "**CLIFFHANGER**"?
MODERATOR
WOWZA!
WHAT WILL HAPPEN **NEXT**?
OH, THAT'SH SHO **EASHY!**

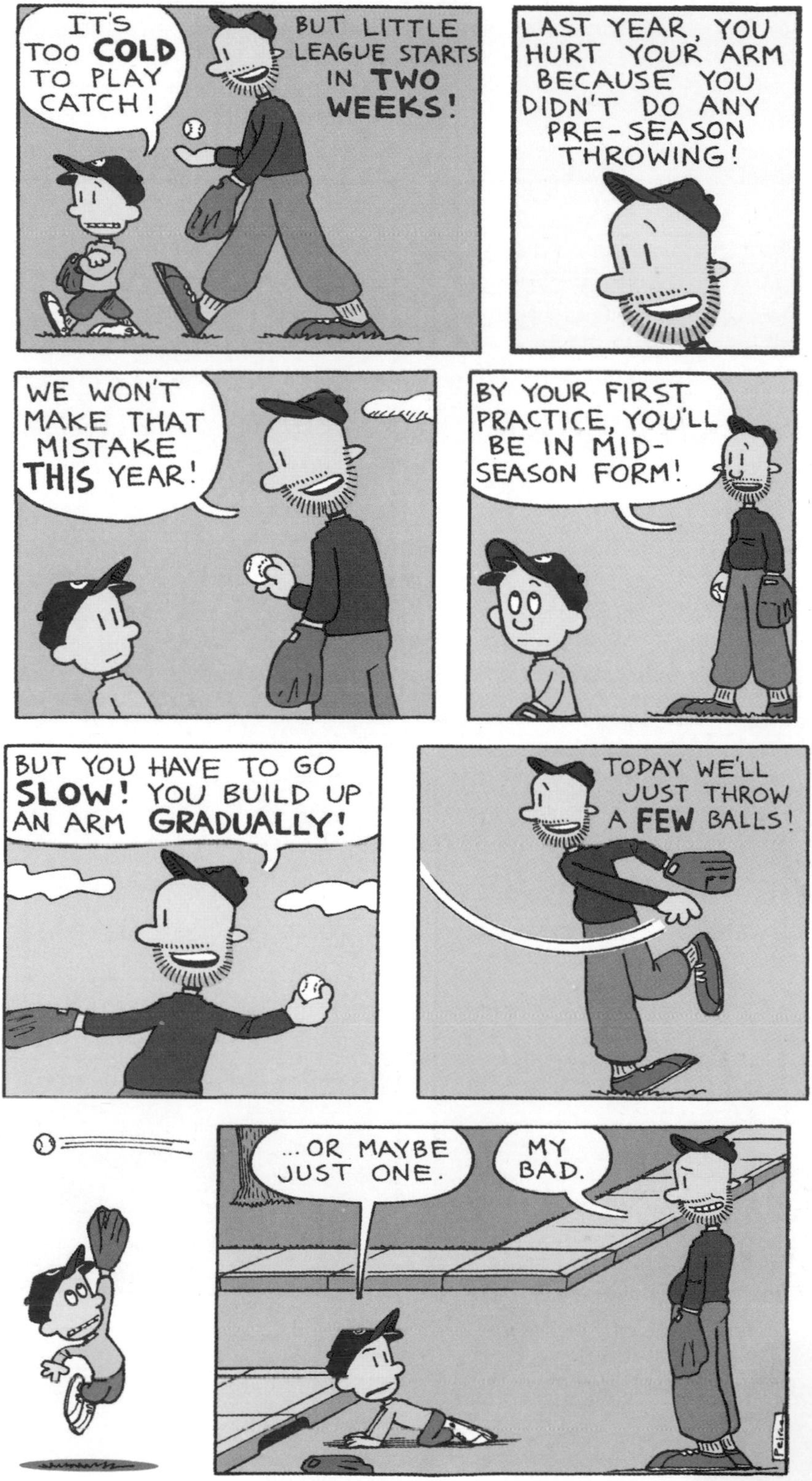
IT'S TOO COLD TO PLAY CATCH!
BUT LITTLE LEAGUE STARTS IN TWO WEEKS!
LAST YEAR, YOU HURT YOUR ARM BECAUSE YOU DIDN'T DO ANY PRE-SEASON THROWING!
WE WON'T MAKE THAT MISTAKE THIS YEAR!
BY YOUR FIRST PRACTICE, YOU'LL BE IN MID-SEASON FORM!
BUT YOU HAVE TO GO SLOW! YOU BUILD UP AN ARM GRADUALLY!
TODAY WE'LL JUST THROW A FEW BALLS!
...OR MAYBE JUST ONE.
MY BAD.
Peirce

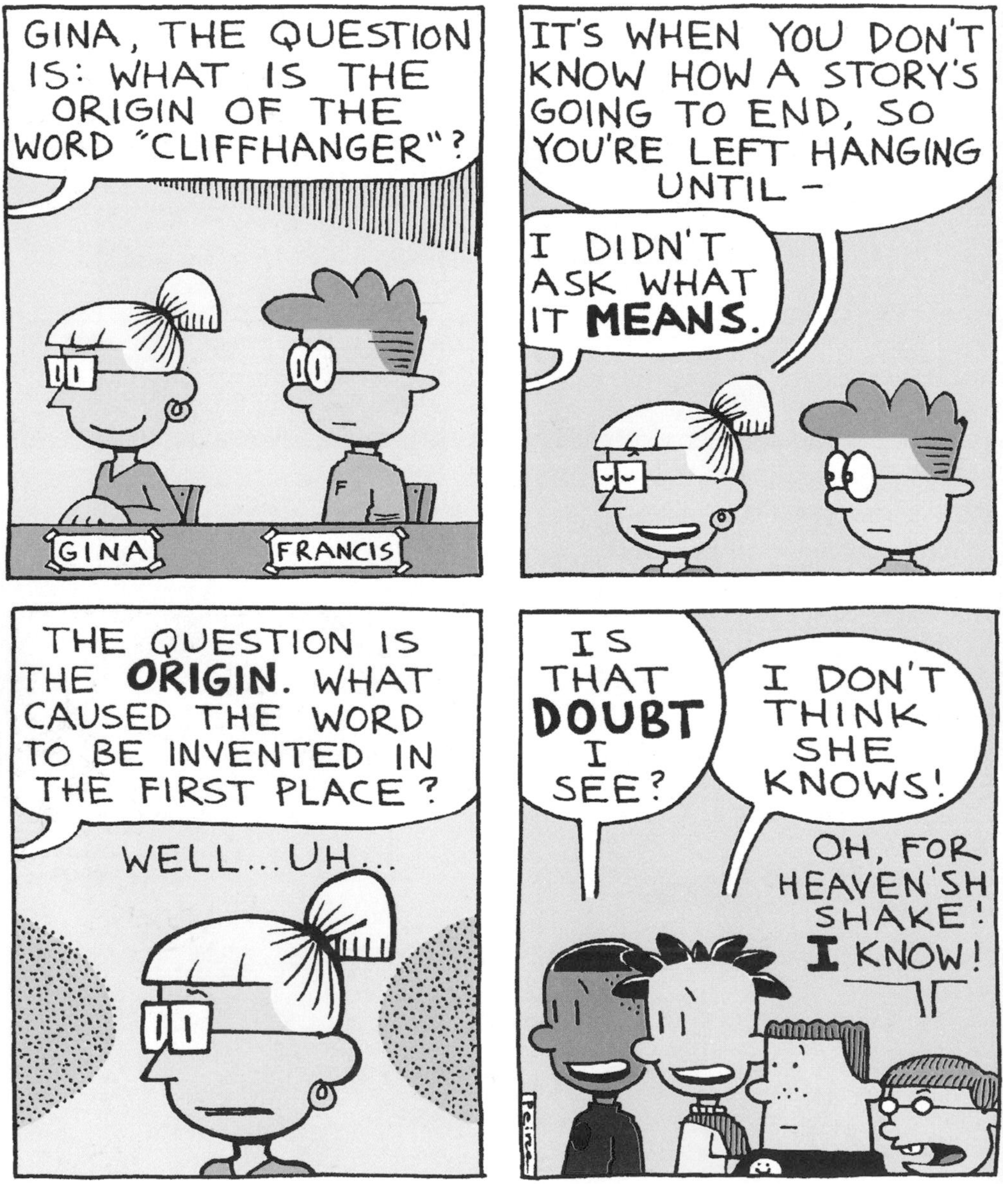

GINA, THE QUESTION IS: WHAT IS THE ORIGIN OF THE WORD "CLIFFHANGER"?
GINA
FRANCIS
IT'S WHEN YOU DON'T KNOW HOW A STORY'S GOING TO END, SO YOU'RE LEFT HANGING UNTIL –
I DIDN'T ASK WHAT IT **MEANS**.
THE QUESTION IS THE **ORIGIN**. WHAT CAUSED THE WORD TO BE INVENTED IN THE FIRST PLACE?
WELL... UH...
IS THAT **DOUBT** I SEE?
I DON'T THINK SHE KNOWS!
OH, FOR HEAVEN'SH SHAKE! **I** KNOW!

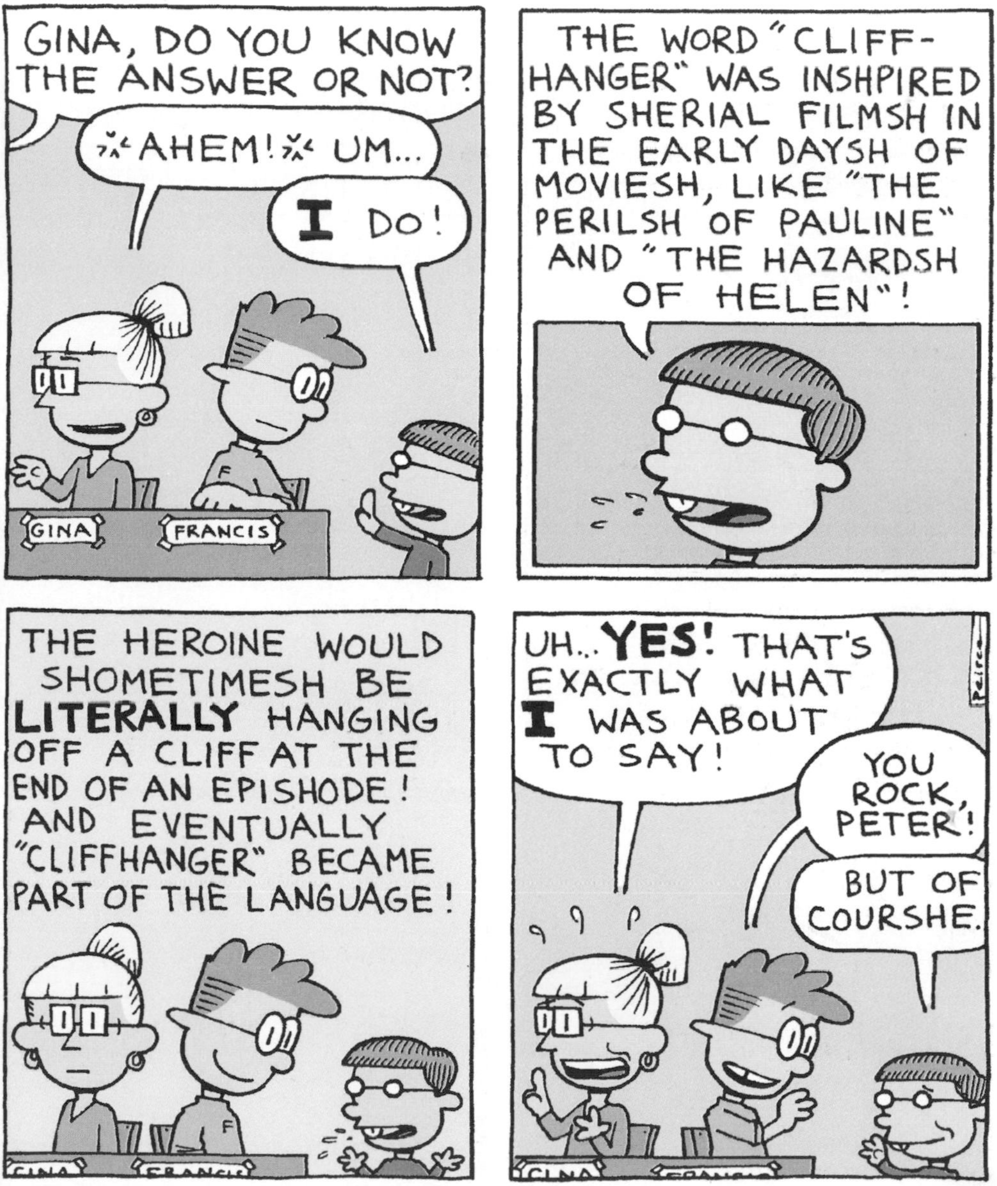
GINA, DO YOU KNOW THE ANSWER OR NOT?
AHEM! UM...
I DO!
GINA
FRANCIS
THE WORD "CLIFF-HANGER" WAS INSHPIRED BY SHERIAL FILMSH IN THE EARLY DAYSH OF MOVIESH, LIKE "THE PERILSH OF PAULINE" AND "THE HAZARDSH OF HELEN"!
THE HEROINE WOULD SHOMETIMESH BE **LITERALLY** HANGING OFF A CLIFF AT THE END OF AN EPISHODE! AND EVENTUALLY "CLIFFHANGER" BECAME PART OF THE LANGUAGE!
UH... **YES**! THAT'S EXACTLY WHAT **I** WAS ABOUT TO SAY!
YOU ROCK, PETER!
BUT OF COURSHE.

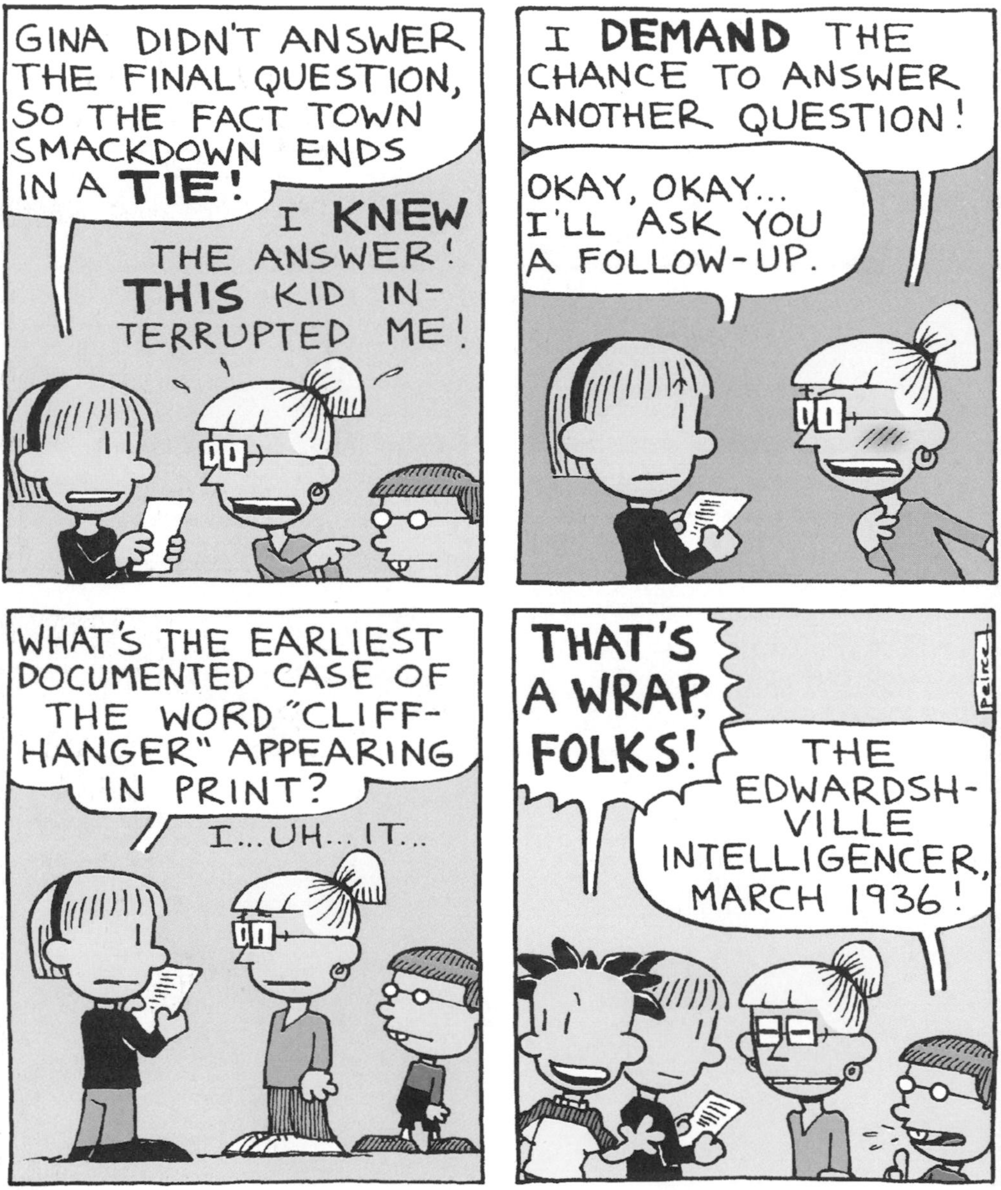
GINA DIDN'T ANSWER THE FINAL QUESTION, SO THE FACT TOWN SMACKDOWN ENDS IN A TIE!
I KNEW THE ANSWER! THIS KID INTERRUPTED ME!
I DEMAND THE CHANCE TO ANSWER ANOTHER QUESTION!
OKAY, OKAY... I'LL ASK YOU A FOLLOW-UP.
WHAT'S THE EARLIEST DOCUMENTED CASE OF THE WORD "CLIFF-HANGER" APPEARING IN PRINT?
I... UH... IT...
THAT'S A WRAP, FOLKS!
THE EDWARDSHVILLE INTELLIGENCER, MARCH 1936!
peirce

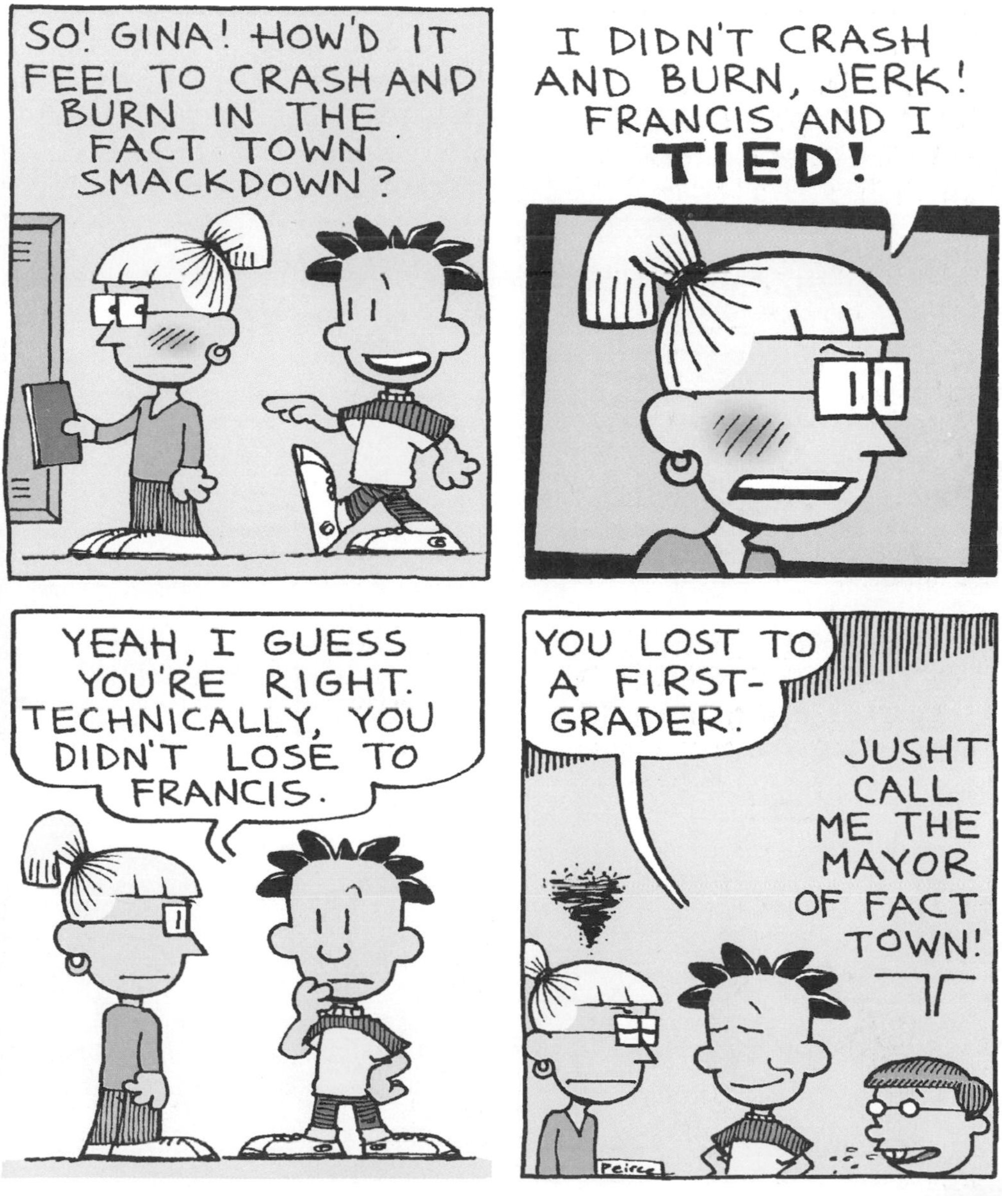
SO! GINA! HOW'D IT FEEL TO CRASH AND BURN IN THE FACT TOWN SMACKDOWN?
I DIDN'T CRASH AND BURN, JERK! FRANCIS AND I TIED!
YEAH, I GUESS YOU'RE RIGHT. TECHNICALLY, YOU DIDN'T LOSE TO FRANCIS.
YOU LOST TO A FIRST-GRADER.
JUSHT CALL ME THE MAYOR OF FACT TOWN!
Peirce

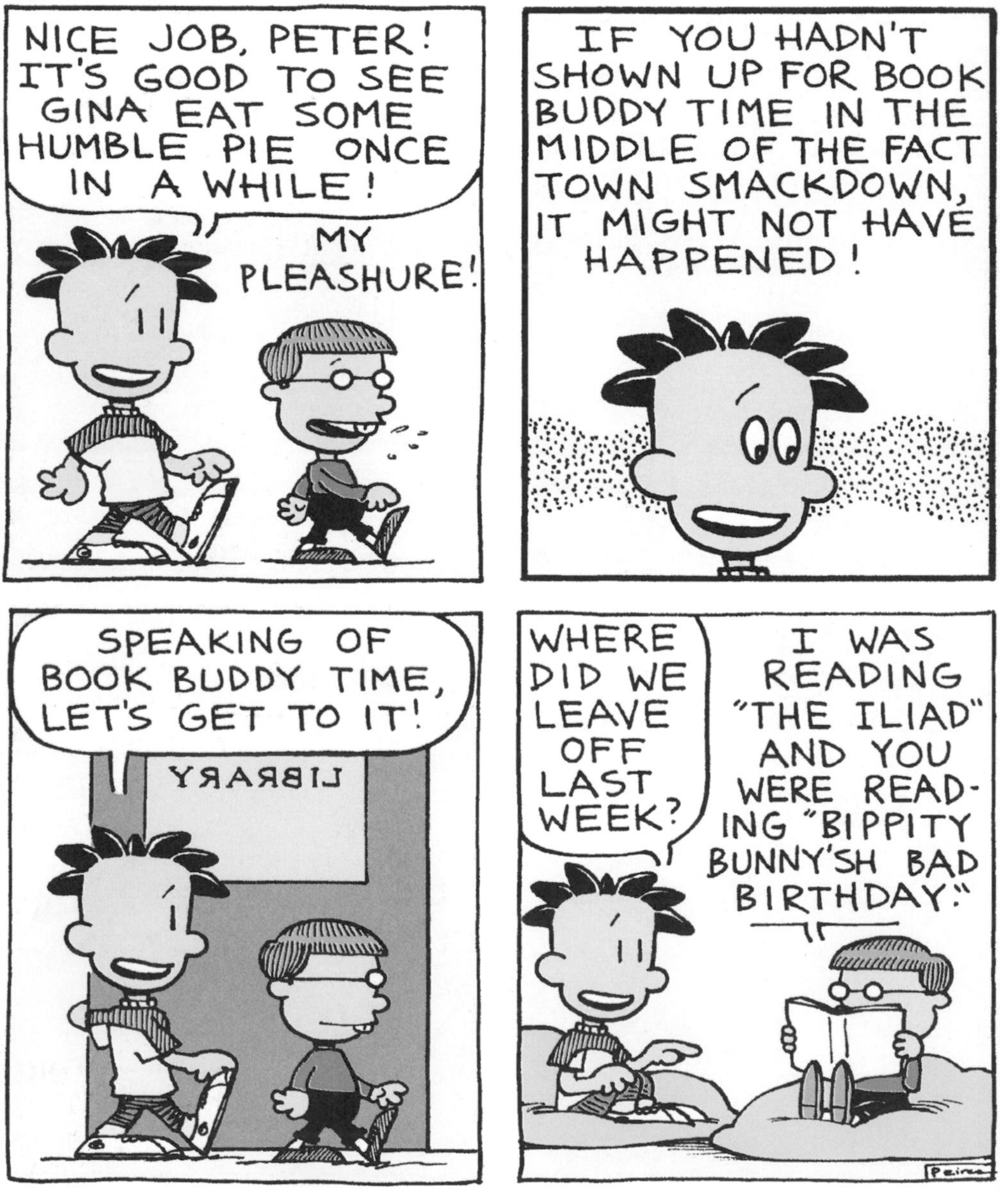
NICE JOB, PETER! IT'S GOOD TO SEE GINA EAT SOME HUMBLE PIE ONCE IN A WHILE!
MY PLEASHURE!
IF YOU HADN'T SHOWN UP FOR BOOK BUDDY TIME IN THE MIDDLE OF THE FACT TOWN SMACKDOWN, IT MIGHT NOT HAVE HAPPENED!
SPEAKING OF BOOK BUDDY TIME, LET'S GET TO IT!
LIBRARY
WHERE DID WE LEAVE OFF LAST WEEK?
I WAS READING "THE ILIAD" AND YOU WERE READING "BIPPITY BUNNY'SH BAD BIRTHDAY."
Peirce

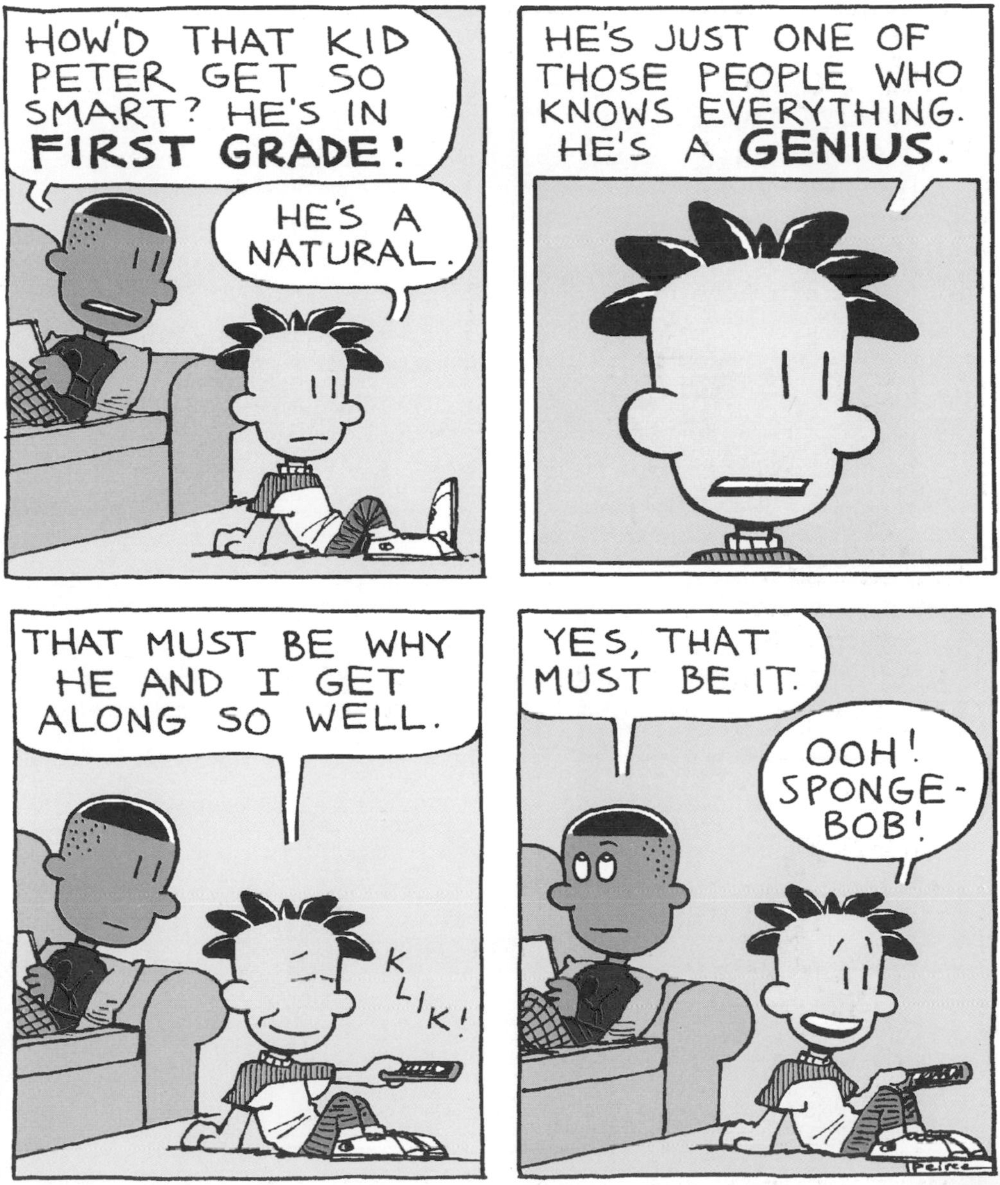
HOW'D THAT KID PETER GET SO SMART? HE'S IN **FIRST GRADE!**
HE'S A NATURAL.
HE'S JUST ONE OF THOSE PEOPLE WHO KNOWS EVERYTHING. HE'S A **GENIUS.**
THAT MUST BE WHY HE AND I GET ALONG SO WELL.
KLIK!
YES, THAT MUST BE IT.
OOH! SPONGE-BOB!
Peirce

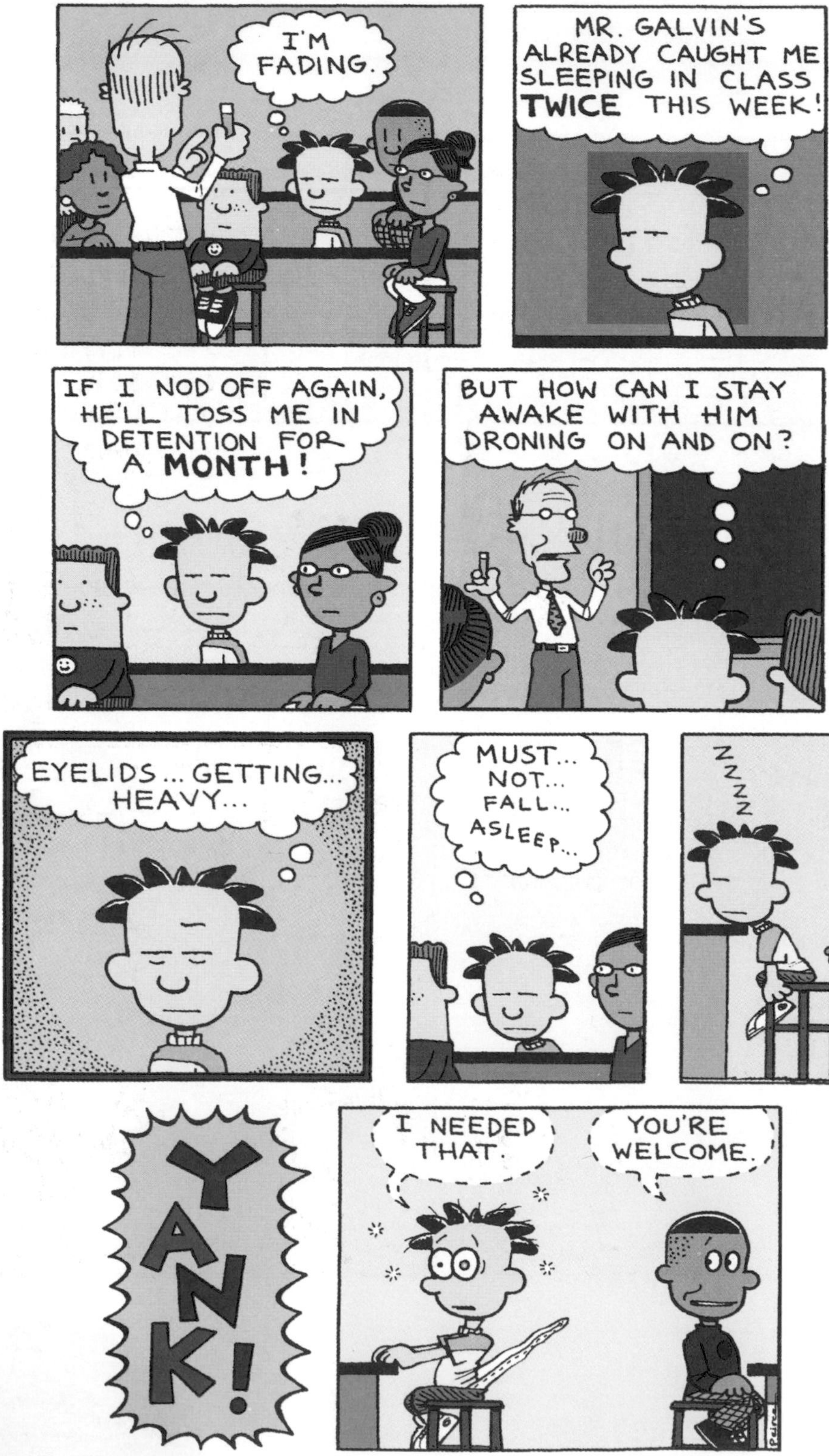
I'M FADING.
MR. GALVIN'S ALREADY CAUGHT ME SLEEPING IN CLASS **TWICE** THIS WEEK!
IF I NOD OFF AGAIN, HE'LL TOSS ME IN DETENTION FOR A **MONTH**!
BUT HOW CAN I STAY AWAKE WITH HIM DRONING ON AND ON?
EYELIDS ... GETTING... HEAVY...
MUST... NOT... FALL... ASLEEP...
Z Z Z Z
YANK!
I NEEDED THAT.
YOU'RE WELCOME.

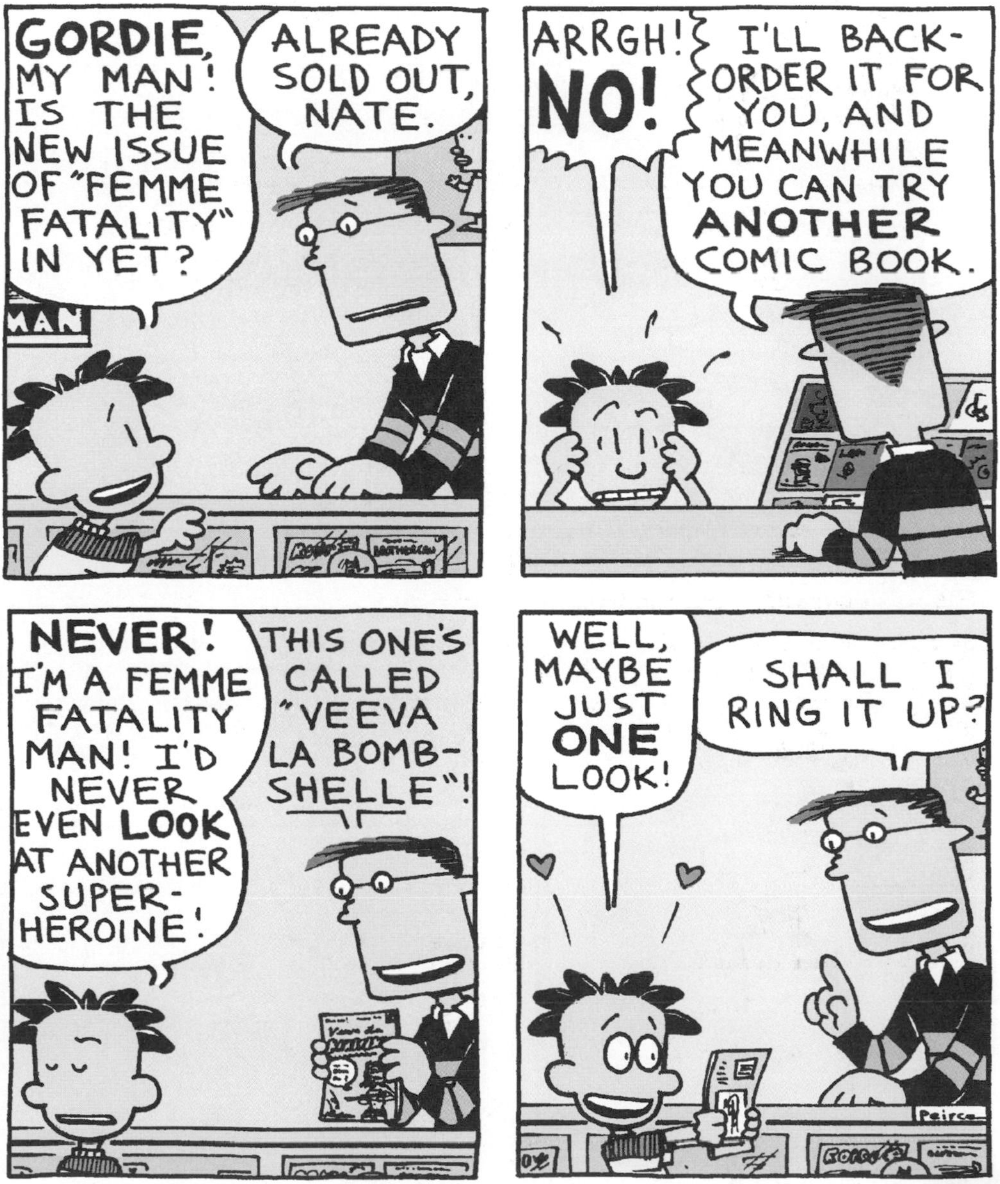
GORDIE, MY MAN! IS THE NEW ISSUE OF "FEMME FATALITY" IN YET?
ALREADY SOLD OUT, NATE.
ARRGH! NO!
I'LL BACK-ORDER IT FOR YOU, AND MEANWHILE YOU CAN TRY ANOTHER COMIC BOOK.
NEVER! I'M A FEMME FATALITY MAN! I'D NEVER EVEN LOOK AT ANOTHER SUPER-HEROINE!
THIS ONE'S CALLED "VEEVA LA BOMB-SHELLE"!
WELL, MAYBE JUST ONE LOOK!
SHALL I RING IT UP?
Peirce

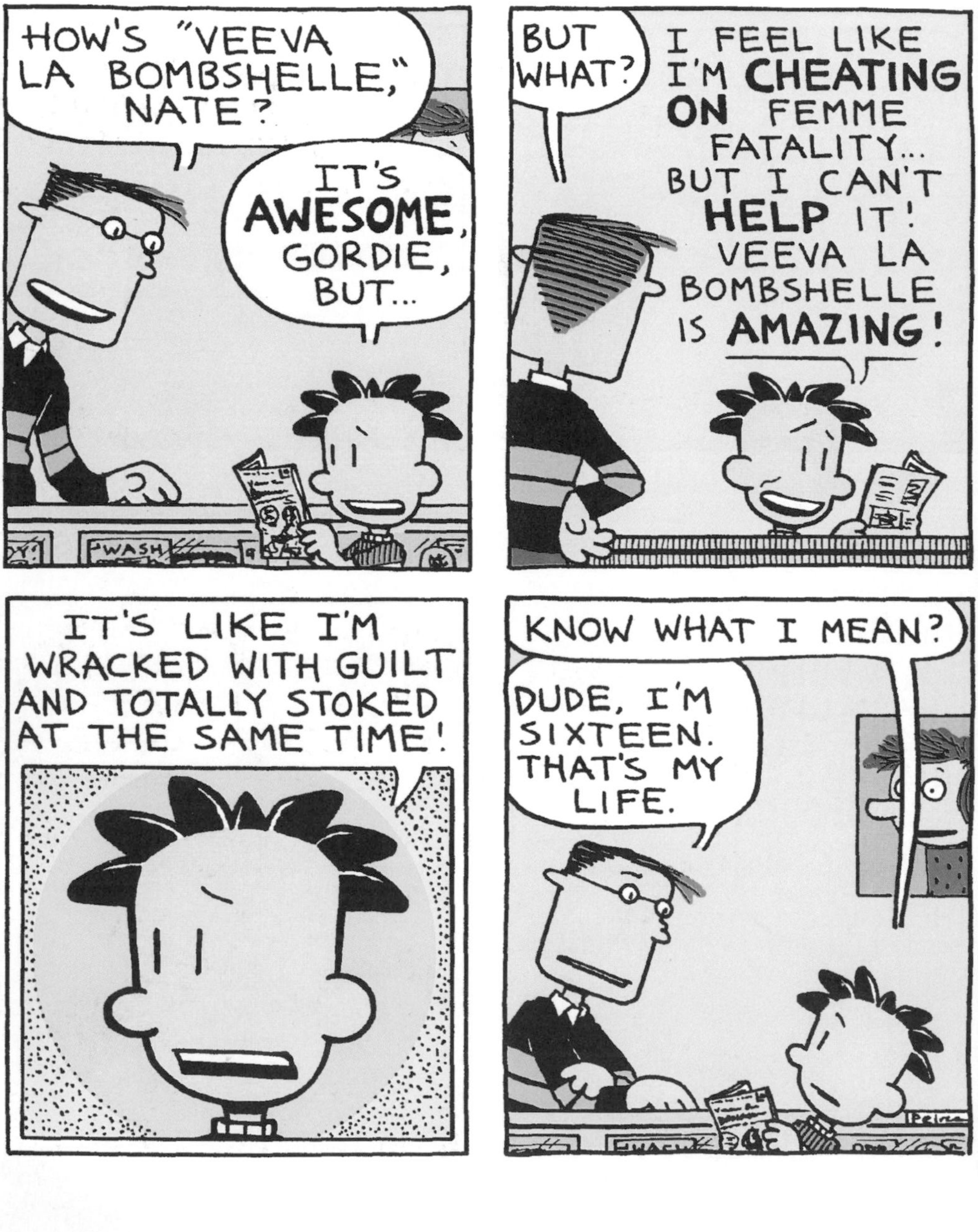
HOW'S "VEEVA LA BOMBSHELLE," NATE?
IT'S **AWESOME**, GORDIE, BUT...
BUT WHAT?
I FEEL LIKE I'M **CHEATING ON** FEMME FATALITY... BUT I CAN'T **HELP** IT! VEEVA LA BOMBSHELLE IS **AMAZING**!
IT'S LIKE I'M WRACKED WITH GUILT AND TOTALLY STOKED AT THE SAME TIME!
KNOW WHAT I MEAN?
DUDE, I'M SIXTEEN. THAT'S MY LIFE.

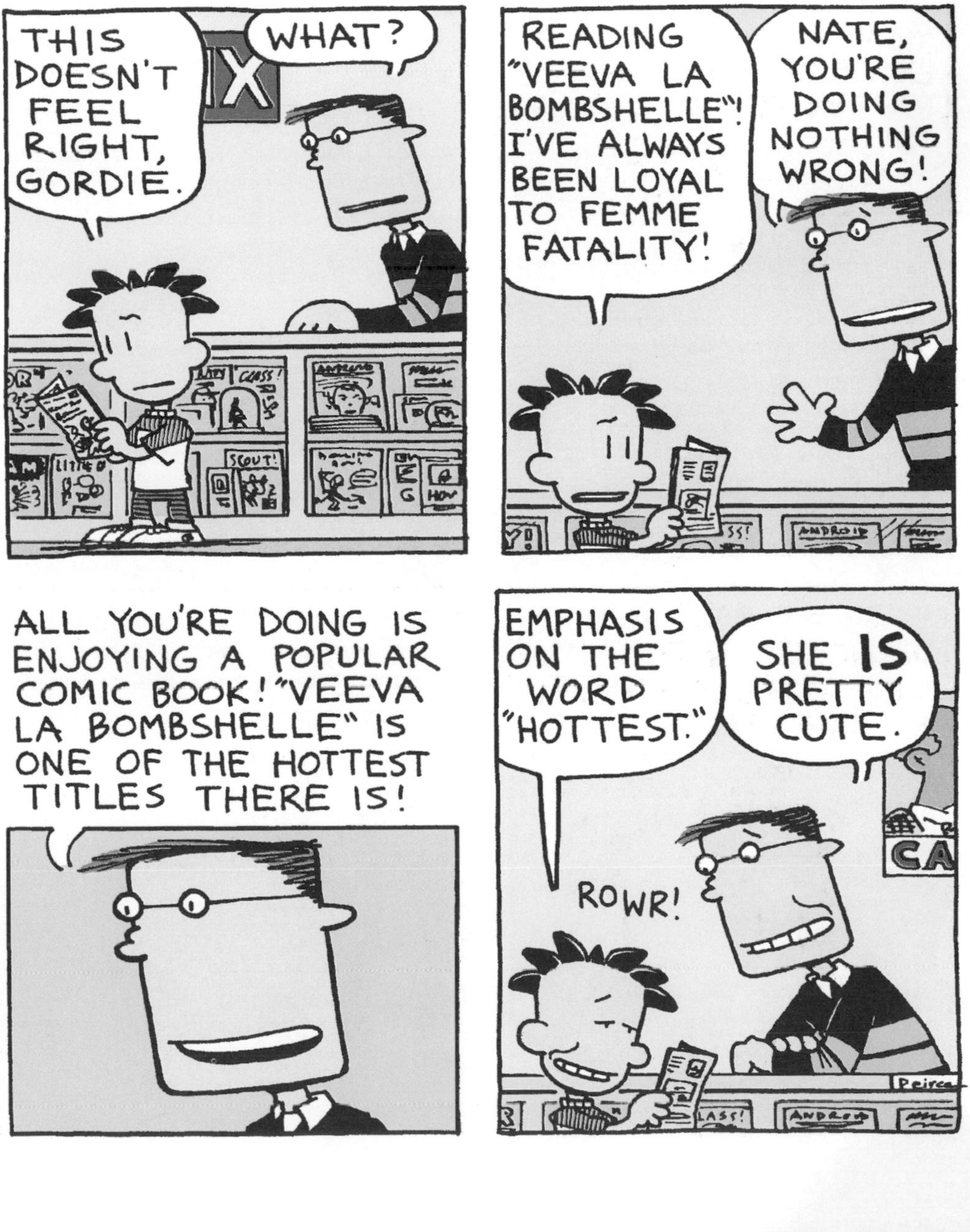
THIS DOESN'T FEEL RIGHT, GORDIE.
WHAT?
IX
READING "VEEVA LA BOMBSHELLE"! I'VE ALWAYS BEEN LOYAL TO FEMME FATALITY!
NATE, YOU'RE DOING NOTHING WRONG!
ALL YOU'RE DOING IS ENJOYING A POPULAR COMIC BOOK! "VEEVA LA BOMBSHELLE" IS ONE OF THE HOTTEST TITLES THERE IS!
EMPHASIS ON THE WORD "HOTTEST."
SHE **IS** PRETTY CUTE.
ROWR!
Peirce

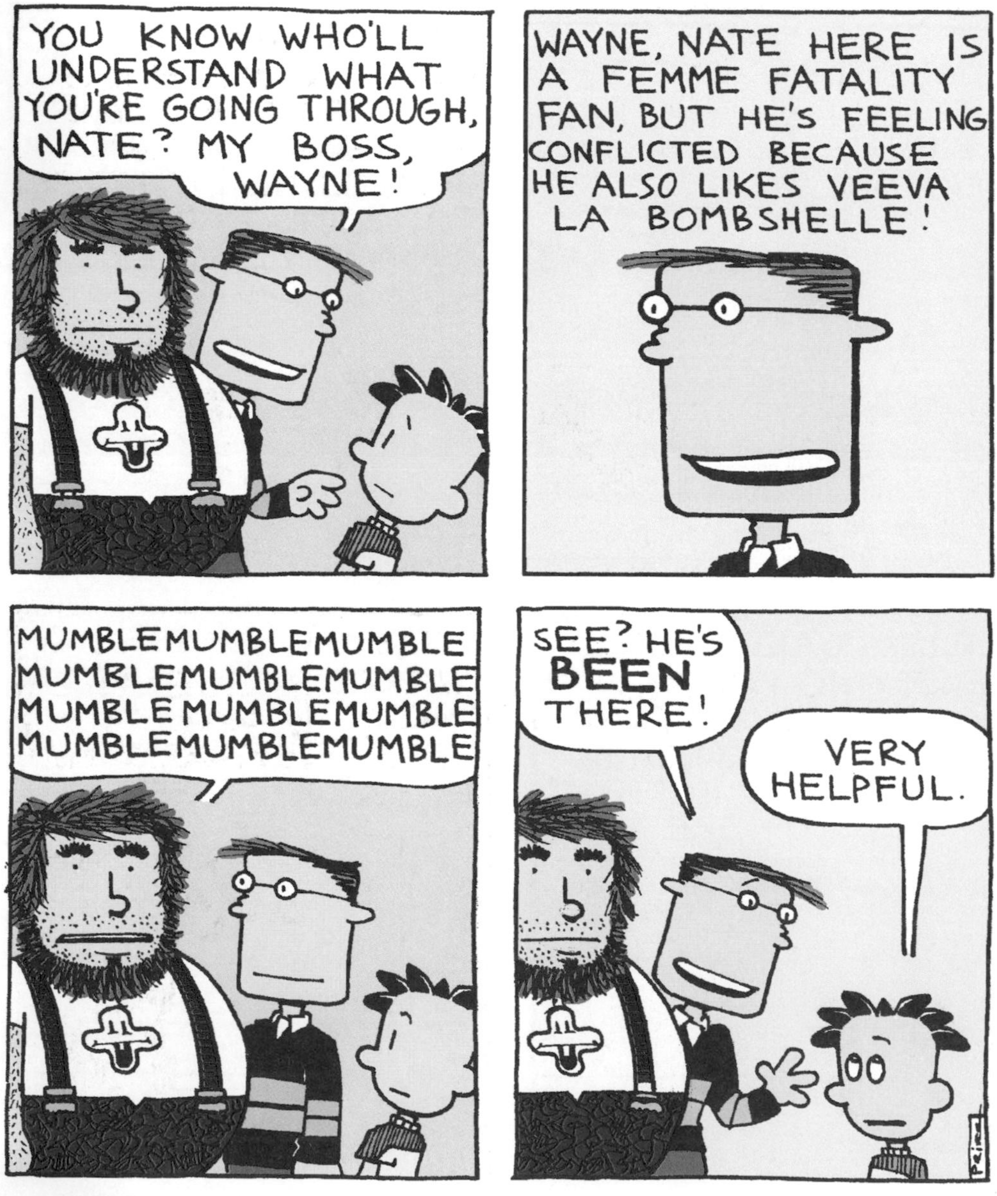
YOU KNOW WHO'LL UNDERSTAND WHAT YOU'RE GOING THROUGH, NATE? MY BOSS, WAYNE!
WAYNE, NATE HERE IS A FEMME FATALITY FAN, BUT HE'S FEELING CONFLICTED BECAUSE HE ALSO LIKES VEEVA LA BOMBSHELLE!
MUMBLEMUMBLEMUMBLE MUMBLEMUMBLEMUMBLE MUMBLE MUMBLEMUMBLE MUMBLEMUMBLEMUMBLE
SEE? HE'S **BEEN** THERE!
VERY HELPFUL.
PEIRCE

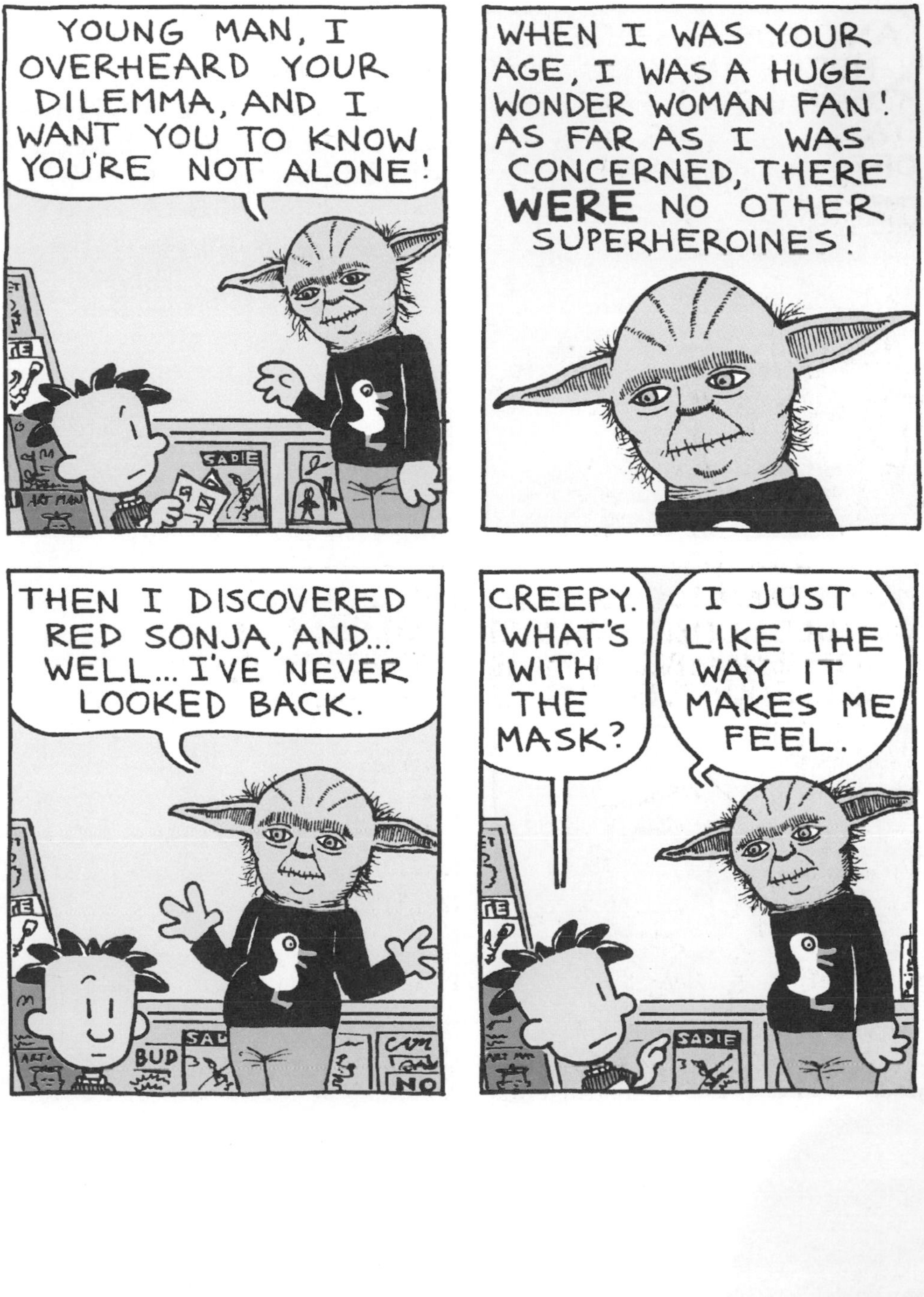
YOUNG MAN, I OVERHEARD YOUR DILEMMA, AND I WANT YOU TO KNOW YOU'RE NOT ALONE!
WHEN I WAS YOUR AGE, I WAS A HUGE WONDER WOMAN FAN! AS FAR AS I WAS CONCERNED, THERE **WERE** NO OTHER SUPERHEROINES!
THEN I DISCOVERED RED SONJA, AND... WELL... I'VE NEVER LOOKED BACK.
CREEPY. WHAT'S WITH THE MASK?
I JUST LIKE THE WAY IT MAKES ME FEEL.

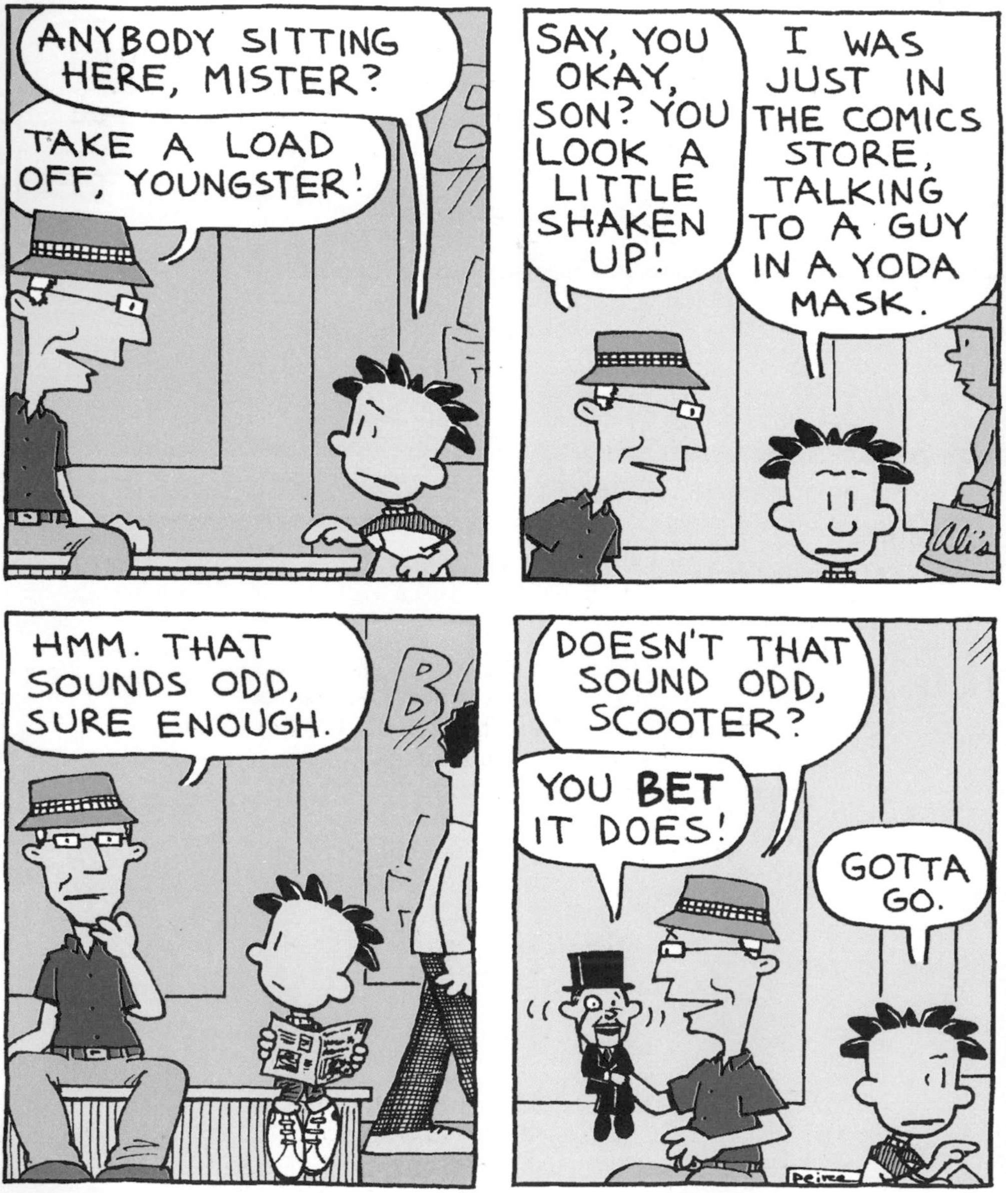
ANYBODY SITTING HERE, MISTER?
TAKE A LOAD OFF, YOUNGSTER!
SAY, YOU OKAY, SON? YOU LOOK A LITTLE SHAKEN UP!
I WAS JUST IN THE COMICS STORE, TALKING TO A GUY IN A YODA MASK.
Ali's
HMM. THAT SOUNDS ODD, SURE ENOUGH.
DOESN'T THAT SOUND ODD, SCOOTER?
YOU **BET** IT DOES!
GOTTA GO.
peirce

Big Nate is distributed internationally by Andrews McMeel Syndication.

Andrews McMeel Publishing
a division of Andrews McMeel Universal
1130 Walnut Street, Kansas City, Missouri 64106

www.andrewsmcmeel.com

18 19 20 21 22 SDB 10 9 8 7 6 5 4 3 2 1

ISBN: 978-1-4494-8991-5

Library of Congress Control Number: 2017947230

Made by:
Shenzhen Donnelley Printing Company Ltd.
Address and location of manufacturer:
No. 47, Wuhe Nan Road, Bantian Ind. Zone,
Shenzhen China, 518129
1st Printing—12/25/17

These strips appeared in newspapers from
October 6, 2013, through March 29, 2014.

Big Nate can be viewed on the Internet at
www.gocomics.com/big_nate

Check out these and other books from Andrews McMeel Publishing

Phoebe and Her Unicorn in
The Magic Storm
Dana Simpson

Rainy Day Unicorn Fun
A Phoebe and Her Unicorn Activity Book
140 Magical Puzzles
Dana Simpson

LASER MOOSE AND RABBIT BOY: DISCO FEVER
DOUG SAVAGE

WALLACE the BRAVE
Will Henry

SUIT YOUR SELFIE
New York Times Bestselling Author
Stephan T. Pastis
A Pearls Before Swine Collection

TYRANNOSAURUS RALPH
NATE EVANS AND VINCE EVANS

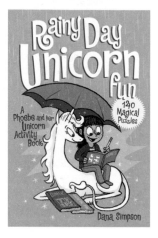

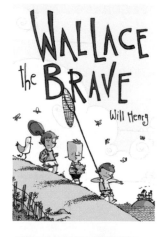